Tuksook's Story: 35,000 BC

Book Four of Winds of Change, a Prehistoric Fiction Series on the Peopling of the Americas

Bonnye Matthews
Award Winning Writer of Prehistoric Fiction

Since 1978

PO Box 221974 Anchorage, Alaska 99522-1974
books@publicationconsultants.com—www.publicationconsultants.com

ISBN 978-1-59433-521-1
eISBN 978-1-59433-522-8
Library of Congress Catalog Card Number: 2014956792

Neanderthal on cover: Author: Neozoom, License: Wikimedia Commons—
Creative Commons Attribution—Share Alike 3.0 Unported

Background on cover: Author: Jens Mayer, License: Shutterstock 873269

Manufactured in the United States of America.

Dedication

for Patricia and Robert

Other Books in the Winds of Change Series:

Acknowledgements

Without the assistance of several people this book, as is true of the others in this series, would not be. These people are first, my brother, Randy Matthews, and then Sally Sutherland, Patricia Gilmore, Robert Arthur, and Pat Meiwes. Each contributed far in excess of what could be expected or hoped for based on family, friendship, or love of reading. I also thank my publisher, Evan Swensen, who had the courage to take on this project.

Finally, I wish to thank Kristine J. Crossen, Ph.D., Chair of Geological Sciences at the University of Alaska, who rescued me. I tried to research various geology publications in order to envision the land in the Cook Inlet area of Alaska in 35,000 BC. I was frustrated for two reasons: (1) I couldn't do the geology research, because the jargon was like a foreign language to me and (2) I was concerned about writing about people in a place where there remains no trace of them today. Kris Crossen using wonderful teaching skills and without the jargon of geology funneled information that I needed down into a vision of the area so I could see it. She mentioned the damage from the Ice Age, helping me understand why, if people were present at that time, there would be no trace of them whatsoever. I could see the land forming and changing, and describe my People alive amidst the vegetation that would become coal deposits—coal deposits that now lie under the salt water of the inlet, singing their siren song to miners. Not only did she provide facts, but also she freed me to write boldly. I am very grateful for her help.

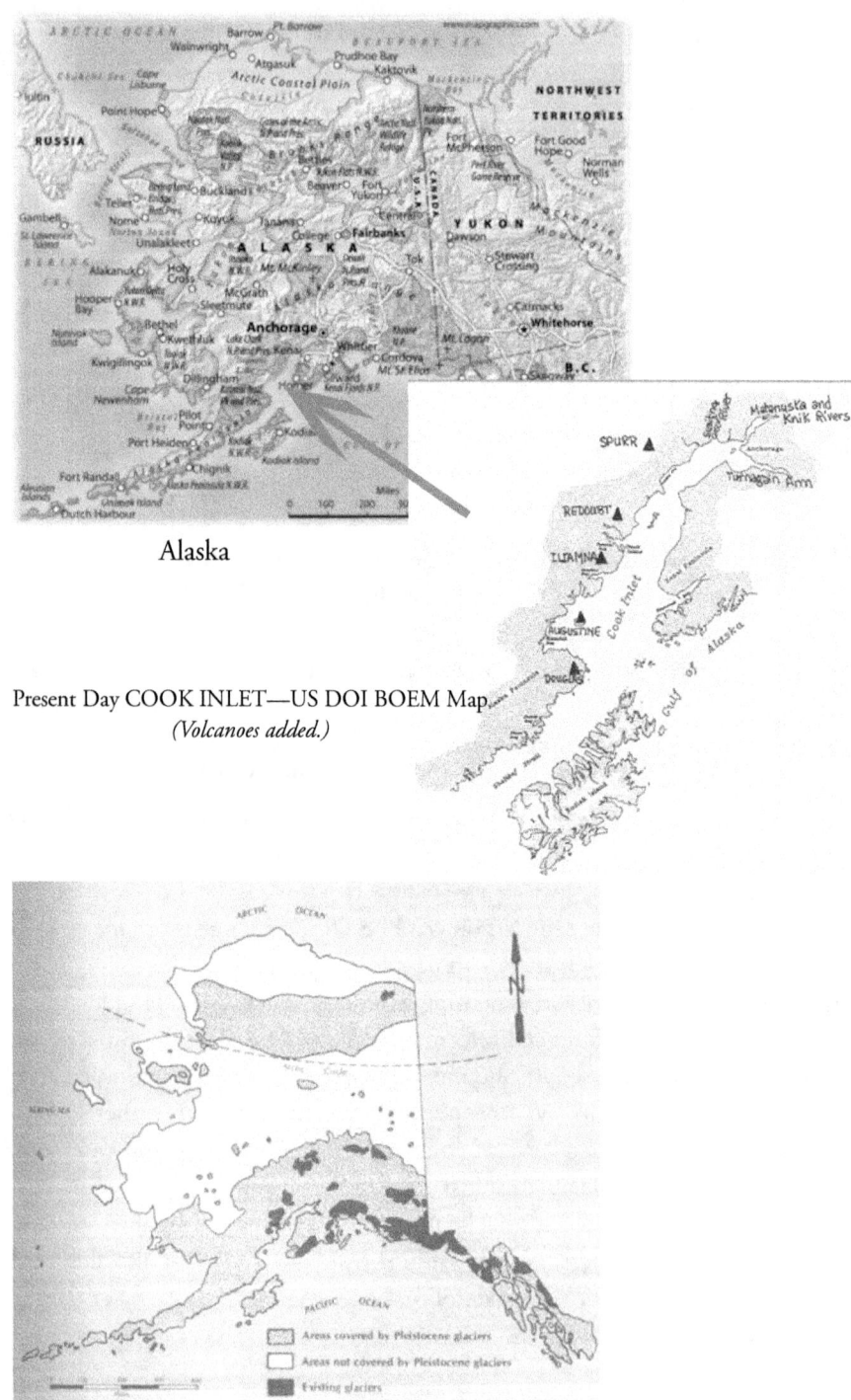

Alaska

Present Day COOK INLET—US DOI BOEM Map.
(Volcanoes added.)

Used with permission from the State of Alaska, Alaska Historical Commission
(from *Alaska's Heritage,* Joan M. Antonson and William S. Hanable, 1986, page 7)

The People

Mongo + Lupo
- Stencellomak + Za
  - Traq + Ulu
    - Lolrin
- Wave + Cadpo
- Tern
- Pod
- Ubassu
- Elfa
- Solong
- Velur
- Upico
- Vole + Mela
- Abet

Taman + Ghopi
- Hamaklob + Amuin
  - Hum
  - Mute
  - Dipcaco
- Rimut + Pito
  - Sutorio
  - Turl
  - Bitro
  - Mo
- Hawk + Meg
  - Guko
- Kiramuat

Kew + Renwen
- Togomoo + Brill
  - Hapunta
  - Noriwhet
  - Oliog
- Pago + Bit-n
- Hai + Monter
  - Meha
- Momeh + Port
  - Oneg
  - Nipe
  - Col
  - Mil
  - Lamo

Ottu + Brudimi
- Loraz + Kouchu
  - Moki + Heek
  - Twim
  - Remui
  - Vel + Gami
  - Enzuvel
- Unmo + Amiz
  - Coo
  - Ragiel
  - Gumui
  - Elfie
  - Kig
  - Wims
- Arvel + Shut
  - Hustep
  - Gilo
  - Ing
  - Guw
  - Pilly

Midgenemo + Item
- Orad
- Lurch
- Tuksook
- Nal
- Ren
- Gel

Chapter One

Tuksook was very angry. The council meeting of the previous evening had left her shocked, numb, and now it had all turned to anger. She felt betrayed. Her father, Midgenemo, the People's Wise One, had sat in judgment on a dispute. It was his duty to so do, but his judgment was wrong in her eyes. It didn't matter whether a person's heritage was the old People, Minguat, Mol, or the People from Big Lake. All were People. It didn't matter whether you were male or female. All were People. Tuksook *knew* the stories. She hadn't told anybody she *knew* them. Doing so would end her opportunity for solitude and stop her childhood. But, she *knew* them. She even knew the significance of each story. Her father had said that the man had authority over his wife. She knew what authority meant, and he misapplied it to lovemaking. He did it in a way that made the stories untrue. The stories made it clear, first, that man was made bigger and stronger than woman to protect her. Second, the stories also made it clear that lovemaking was with mutual consent. Her father's judgment, according to Tuksook, made wives less than People. Rimut wanted to have sex with Pito, his wife, and she had turned her back on him. She said she was in pain. Rimut wanted permission to require lovemaking when she declined. Her father ruled that a wife had no choice. He brushed the issue of pain aside, because Rimut claimed she was whining in an attempt to avoid him. Tuksook was convinced her father and Rimut had no idea what love was. Tuksook concluded that she would never join with a man. If her father, the Wise One, could betray a woman in pain, she wondered, what would someone else do? She hated the ruling, and she had lost all respect for her father. She wondered whether her feeling toward her father qualified as hatred. She knew Wisdom didn't want People hating People.

Moments ago, the Wise One had just told her to fly. He wanted to know into what place the river they were entering would lead. Would it be a good place for the People to live? She had to put aside the anger. This was her responsibility for the People. It was hard to put aside the anger. She went down the steps to her place for solitude. The steps were made of bamboo, the same material as the boat. She went to her place near the water and lay down. Still the anger hinted at return. She had to turn loose of it. She forced herself to relax. It was for the People. Finally, she reached the spirit place where she could fly.

Tuksook *saw* the new land though she appeared asleep. Her name from the old land was the name of an eagle, translating to sees-from-above, a name very strong for a girl of eleven. Her fingers dangled into the salt water. Her spirit was aflight. Tuksook *overflew* the verdant valley into which they were turning. Waterfalls, rivers, creeks, and streams drained into a central river. The valley went far into the land pocked with many lakes and ponds. Other rivers of good size fed the central river. It was like a tree where the central river was the trunk. Yet other rivers branched off from the main one, while yet others branched from the branches. Branching appeared continuous. They would not thirst here, she reasoned. Something heavy hung over the place, not in the present but it was something to come. What she saw was wonderful for the People at this time. What would come was cold and pressing, but not definable and not of this time. She knew it would be well beyond their lifetimes, but how far beyond she did not know. To her the largest rivers lay as a great bird leg with three toes at the north end. The upper bird leg came from the ocean's meeting the river from the north. Three toes split off as the river went far inland. One toe pointed to the north, another to the northeast, and the third to the east. She fixed the vision in memory so she could later draw it, showing how mountains defined the large rivers.

Gumui sat near her assuring that no one entered the part of the boat where Tuksook sought refuge. Elfa started down to check the dogs, but Gumui waved her away before she began the descent to the low level.

The land was so beautiful; it brought tears to Tuksook's eyes. The tears startled Gumui. The green filled her soul with joy. The winds of change had blown. Their land across the sea to the west had become lifeless from a long time worsening drought. This land brought hope for renewal. She *saw* animals in the forests—many of them—and more in the open fields. Some were strange to her. Out of a deep sense of responsibility, she returned to the boat, feeling the tug that indicated her flight reached the conclusion of its purpose. She had wanted to fly further to *see* the massive mountain far to the north. She had a gift, a special skill reserved for a certain person, but that gift came with constraints. She had to be obedient to the constraints. Wisdom made it clear: the flight was for the People's needs, not her curiosity. She was never to use it for personal reasons.

"You're back," Gumui said quietly. The sun glinted in tiny lights from his auburn hair that fell forward as he leaned over her. A leather headband kept it from his face. He watched her deep blue eyes flutter under her brows, pale yellow-white as the grass in their parched land. Her hair of the same color wisped in the slight breeze, tangled. She had the rare, coveted sloped upper head shape, the greatest mark of beauty in women and manliness in men among the People, but the color of her hair was considered the least appealing. He reached for her hand and pulled it from the cold water to her side to let it dry in the sun. Tuksook was just a child, but she fascinated him ever since she began to fly. He felt then a need to protect her. It was an automatic response—not one reasoned in his mind web.

"It's perfect," she murmured, her dark blue eyes shining with new knowledge. A slight smile parted her lips to show two bright white front upper teeth that did not quite touch. She shut her eyes to avoid the glare of the sunshine. She would have much to share when the council met that night. Thoughts of the council made the anger creep back into her belly.

Tuksook lay near the caged dogs. They had learned to remain quiet and still for the long boat sailing after some days of whining and pacing. They had also learned to be careful with food, for it would slip through the bamboo and become unreachable. They enjoyed their freedom once a day when older children let them out so they could clean the cages. For cleaning they lowered birch buckets over the side on strong rope to gather water to pour over the cage floors. It was not a pleasant job, but it had to be done. Dogs were assigned the lower deck only, except for Tictip, the dog favored by the Wise One.

Gumui left Tuksook and climbed over the bamboo log steps to reach the higher level of the boat. "Wise One," he called to a stocky, bald, gray-bearded man of forty years.

Midgenemo, turned and looked at Gumui with an air of expectancy. Instead of speaking, he raised his eyebrows. He was awaiting Tuksook's initial view. Had it been very negative, he'd have considered turning the boat back to sea. He didn't have to tell anyone that. They knew.

"Perfect," was the reply to which Midgenemo and those who heard smiled with enthusiasm and relief. They had found their new home. Almost.

Midgenemo looked up. Quietly, he spoke, "Thank you, Wisdom. This is a place of peace. We will prosper and be grateful here." Midgenemo could hardly wait to put his feet on land. The boat sailing had been very stressful. He rarely slept.

Huaga, a leader of the boatmen, and some of the boatmen had trained the People who would migrate to sail. The training took much time, but the People were passable at sailing. Arriving at the river assured those in the boat that their training had been sufficient. They did not consider themselves boatmen. Midgenemo's overwhelming responsibility was to lead the sailing to their new land.

Rowers muscled the boat mid-river against the current. As they moved up-river, the valley gave them a welcome fragrance of green growing things. Their effort increased significantly on hearing the word from Tuksook. They kept to the middle of the river since they were unaware of its depth.

"Lower depth pole," Togomoo shouted. Depth poles were marked with leather to show the measure of a man height. They were usually four to five man heights. Two men took a bamboo pole and secured it to the holders on the bow of the boat. They lowered it to a man height more than the lowest part of the boat in the water. It would warn them if the river became too shallow for the boat to navigate.

"Look for a place above the lower level of this valley." Midgenemo's voice carried well, even though it wasn't loud. All on the upper level of the boat heard easily. "A level place that has a good view of below," he continued. "A place safe from a surprise water rising and from eyes of strangers. Near running water and forest."

People on the boat listened carefully to the requirements and began to scan the river banks. How they longed to walk on land. Evergreens and hardwoods filled the low-and mid-lands. Tall volcanic peaks stood like watchers. Clearly, there was no drought in this land. They'd never seen a place so inviting. Wildlife noticed them with curiosity not fear. Stencellomak began to sing a rowing song. Rowers and others joined in. Those who rowed put more muscle to it. They were nearing home.

After their evening meal, Midgenemo called out, "Council meeting!" All but the rowers gathered around the central hearth on the upper deck where flat stones surrounded a sand pit. The Wise One took his seat. Everyone looked at Tuksook expectantly.

"Tuksook," the Wise One nodded to her.

Tuksook knelt at the hearth, across from her father, not next to him as usual. He didn't notice. She blew on the ashes to remove them. She spread

14

the sand and remaining ashes for a smooth surface. She drew with a small hardwood twig an amazingly accurate picture of the main rivers in the valley including their relative length and width.

"An eagle seizes the land," she explained. "See how the upper leg of the eagle is the river's exit to the sea. The leg goes over the land and ends with three toes." As she spoke, her graceful hands pointed to the rivers that looked like toes. "White mountains," she said, carefully placing pebbles on the sand to mark snow-covered volcanoes. Mountains of lesser height rose on the sides of the rivers. There were five main sets of mountains. Tuksook sat with her eyes downcast. She didn't dare permit herself to be caught glaring at her father. Pains in her belly from the harbored anger were seizing her again.

The People nodded. They made the vision of the eagle seizing the land a permanent, visual part of their mind webs. They noticed the mountains and fixed their positions in memory. Tuksook had given them a map of their valley even to the relative size of the rivers. They would know where they were as long as they were in the valley.

"Leave the drawing," Midgenemo said. "When you relieve the rowers," he continued as he looked at the men who would be the next rowing relief, "Tuksook will show them the valley. I would like to call this valley Eagle's Grasp. Any objections?"

There was total silence among the People. That meant they all agreed.

"It is aggreed," the Wise One said, using his right fist to strike his open left hand.

The chatter began as the People returned to what they'd been doing. Many comments filled the air—"good omen," "eagles seize what has great value," "good council," "good land," "healthy air," "beautifully green," and so on. Comments floated on the spring air as butterflies, there one moment and gone the next.

Two days later upriver, Amuin, spotted a meadow of great size, barely visible, uphill on the sunrise side of the river as they progressed north. The land was sequestered behind trees. "Look!" she shouted, pointing to the place on the hillside.

Murmuring from the People on the boat clearly supported their agreement. For some it took more time to find the place she saw, but when they saw it, all knew. They had their home. Rowers moved the boat as swiftly as possible toward the place.

The boat finally reached the place closest to the land that they could reach since the depth pole had bent, the boatmen lowered stone anchors, finding that they were in relatively shallow water. Two men, Hamaklob and

Togomoo climbed down the side of the boat and slipped into the clear water. They estimated it was about two man-lengths deep, maybe a little deeper. They bobbed to the surface to alert their boatmen to anchor the boat fully on all sides. The People on the boat appeared calm and quiet, but inside they were very excited. Everyone wanted to reach land to begin their new lives in this inviting place.

Togomoo and Hamaklob swam to the shore with their spears. Quickly they shook off the water and sought the best approach to the upper level. An animal path made a diagonal up the cliff face through trees. Tree tops on either side of the path intertwined above the path. It was not visible to those in the boat. Eagerly they climbed the path looking for tracks to identify what wildlife might use the trail. Those on the boat watched the men. Occasionally, they could see them move through the trees up the path.

Hamaklob reached the flat land, standing at the edge by the trees waiting for Togomoo. He was thirty-five and in his prime. Wet from the swim, his long black hair stuck to his back. His leather headband was soaked and a bit tilted. His wide-open brown eyes surveyed the meadow. Togomoo at age thirty was a time shadow copy of Hamaklob. Togomoo reached the top and noticed the smile on his cousin's face and a hand signal for silence. They gawked. There were four camels browsing. The men didn't know what they were but took them for food animals. Clearly, browsers used the meadow. The space was expansive while well protected by the trees that might have hidden it from them. Evergreens and hardwoods surrounded the flat land. At the far side of the land there was a waterfall about the height of a man. It plunged into a catch pool. They observed that the pool was large enough to store four to six hunts' worth of meat. No caves or large rock shelters appeared to be available. The men wondered how they'd shelter from the cold, but they knew that necessity would be resolved quickly. Hamaklob squatted down. With his strong hands, he dug down into the soil. He raised the soil to his nose and inhaled. "Good," he said quietly, moving his hands toward Togomoo, who also smelled it and smiled. They'd return to the boat quickly to bring the others.

For the People, disembarkation was uncharacteristically loud and disorganized. A new place and new circumstances seemed in part to require patterns different from those to which they were accustomed. Coupled with a delight to be on land again, the People found it hard to contain themselves. They were adjusting but it was awkward. All day the People brought things from the boat to the land above. They had transported much, not knowing what to expect in their new place. Children old enough to help did so with an air of importance, not for themselves but rather for the progress they helped make. Older girls watched over children too young to help. They organized them into skills practice and singing. Some infants or crawlers were simply placed on spread out skins. When they needed feeding, one of the girls took the infant or crawler to its mother.

The release of the dogs brought the People unintended entertainment. They followed the People up the path after a swim from the boat. Each dog stopped at the opening to the meadow, and then they'd take off running all over the wide open space, barking. Old dogs looked like pups. Finally, they'd lie down panting, gazing at their new home. Midgenemo had already chosen the place for the dogs. He beckoned to Elfa to take them to their place to show them their boundaries. He selected the northwest corner of the meadow so the dogs could see the river and warn of anyone below.

Midgenemo and the elders: Ottu, Kew, Taman, and Mongo stood in the central part of the green open area. Ottu was seventy. His thinning white hair blew in the breeze. He walked with difficulty but his deep blue eyes were as sharp as ever. Kew and Taman were brothers, Kew at sixty-seven and Taman at fifty-five. Kew's hair was white while his brother's was just turning to white from black. Mongo, joined with Lupo, Midgenemo's sister, when he was seventeen. He was from the Big Lake area of their old land, northwest of where the People lived. He'd been with the People forty-six years.

The elders were marking the placement for upright bamboo poles to enable them to mark the solstices and equinoxes, when Gumui walked by them with a heavy, leaf-woven box from the boat. He overheard the men mentioning shelter and walked over to them, standing until he was recognized and encouraged to speak.

Gumui lowered his head and slowly raised it, looking into the eyes of the elders as he spoke. "Remember the story about the bent tree house in the time of Ki'ti? I thought of it as I climbed the path and noticed the tree canopy. Would that provide us with good, permanent shelter here?" he asked humbly.

Elders glanced at each other. They visually communicated much without words by using tiny facial muscles: the idea had merit. The Wise One smiled at Gumui. He put his hand on the young man's shoulder. "Find some young men to explore with you. The best area is along the rim of the back forest here," he pointed. "Take your idea and see what you can make of it. You'll need a flat floor surface and trees that will bend. The structure should be more than twice what we need. People will expand in this land, and we'll need to store some things."

Gumui walked off, deeply honored that the elders had given him such an assignment. He enjoyed the slightly damp grass sliding past his ankles as he walked through it. It was like a caress. He tried to remember feeling damp grass in the old land and couldn't. The drought started before he was born. Quickly he carried the box to the area where women were preparing to cook the evening meal. Then, he sought out Tern and Orad. They began to search the rim of the back forest. The elder men turned their thoughts to placement of other common areas in the open space. No one issued orders as to task assignment. The People worked together knowing what had to be done. They were a unit in function.

Some of the women began to prepare the evening meal from the supplies on hand. Earlier in the day men had caught two large sturgeons from lines tied to the back of the boat. They'd never seen such fish. Some older girls had gone to the river to find greens, and others had taken digging tools to hunt for tubers, onions—whatever the land might provide for their evening meal. The girls had been warned not to touch or gather anything that was strange to them. Tuksook went with the girls hunting greens at the water's edge. She was a little young for that group, but she was not very patient with small children. When possible, the People were flexible in task choice, unless some need failed to be met. The older girls fully accepted her. Tuksook normally enjoyed their company.

Ghopi looked up from the hearth construction and asked the women, "Have you seen Sutorlo? How about Lurch and Gilo?"

No reply meant that no one had seen any of them recently. Each would look from time to time to see whether the boys were visible. As yet, there was no need for alarm.

The boys had climbed the hill where the waterfall sent water cascading into a catch pool.

They knelt together solemnly with their fingers in the stream, and Gilo said, "Wisdom, please approve and help with our effort to divert this water. We need it to separate meat storage and bathing into two places."

They dug a trench near the rushing stream. On either side of the trench, they carefully lined the bottom and sides with rocks and moss mixed with mud and twigs, fitted as tightly as possible. The water would fall to hit a flat rock and go into another small stream in its flow to the river. They could use this place for drinking water and bathing. Once the conduit was completed, the boys would open the stream for the diversion. The flat rock below would provide a place to put water holders as they collected it or stand as they bathed. It had already been established that the catch basin at the bottom of the falls would preserve meat from their kills. A drinking water and bathing place needed to be separate from the meat preservation water.

Tuksook wandered away from the older girls, because she was still enraged. She returned to the cooking area with a basket of fern fists, ferns that were in the early stage of development and tightly curled. She had never seen curled fern fists because of the drought, but several stories described them clearly. She sat, cleaned off the brown skin, and took them to the water to wash. They would be a delightful treat for the evening meal. Having done the duty expected of her, she climbed the hill to the east behind the meadow. Near the crest of the hill, she found a rock that jutted from the side of the hill. She climbed it and lay with her belly on the rock. She had to do it in stages, because it was hot from the sun.

As she lowered herself she whispered, "Wisdom, please ease my belly with the warmth of this rock."

She hoped the rock's warmth would calm her belly, but she knew that the bellyache would leave only when she turned loose of the anger. She didn't know how to do that unless her father's judgment changed.

Tuksook could hear someone coming. She didn't turn her head. She just lay there.

"Why are you here, Tuksook?" Gumui asked.

"I warm my belly. Why are you here?"

"Tuksook, you are still a child. You are not permitted to wander off. You could be prey to a bear or whatever lives here."

"I don't care," she replied carelessly.

Gumui grabbed her and turned her over. "What made you say that?"

"I don't know," she lied.

"You lied. You do know," he accused.

She held her words. She'd already said too much.

"You will come back with me, now!" he said firmly. "You will not wander off again. You would do well to remember the stories of Ki'ti." He frowned, threatening.

"You would not beat me." Her belly gripped. She tried to ignore it.

"You're wrong. Do not disobey me, Tuksook. I know you're almost a woman, but right now you are a child. A willful child. The People need you."

"I don't want to be needed! I don't want to be a woman!" Her belly gripped, and she couldn't fail to show the pain she experienced.

Gumui looked at her. Something was troubling her, but he dared not assume what the cause was.

"What's wrong with your belly?" he asked.

19

"Leave me alone," she said and a tear fell from her left eye.

"No," he replied. "Shall I pick you up or are you able to walk back to the meadow?"

She failed to reply.

Gumui began to pick her up.

"No, I'll walk." She was in agony. Why was she not able to have the solitude she craved? She felt the need for solitude as she did the need for food or breathing. It was only in solitude that she could find Wisdom. She walked directly behind Gumui.

Gumui turned and reached for her hand. She withdrew her hands behind her back.

"Why are you fighting me?" he asked as he circled her in his arms and took her wrist forcefully.

"Why are you hurting me?" she asked. Later her wrist would bruise. He did not release her.

"You're being unreasonable. I cannot see you when you are behind me. As a man of the People I tell you, Tuksook, we will go down there. Then you will find a comb and remove the tangles from your hair, before you do anything else. You will not leave the meadow unless another adult of the People tells you to do so. Is that understood? If you do, I vow by Wisdom I will punish you."

Tuksook realized she'd gone too far. Her fury fed her mind web anger food, and she'd been eating lots of it. Her belly rebelled at the anger food, and that made her eat it even more. It made it difficult for her mind web to reason properly, so she failed to see the unhealthy cycle she'd set up in her own body. As an outward show of the tangles within her mind web, she had left tangles in her hair. She did it to keep from being appealing to boys or men. Removing the tangles out of her hair would hurt. Removing the tangles from her mind web would be harder. The People were careful to keep themselves well groomed. Tangles were a sign that something was wrong. Now, she had put herself in a place where Gumui would have to carry through on his vow to Wisdom. Above all, Tuksook respected Wisdom. She would have to remain in the meadow. She had been her own enemy. She was humbled. But, she was still a lesser person to a man as a child and now, almost a woman, she would continue to be treated as a child. It was all so very confusing. She did as she was told while she longed for freedom to slip into a natural, quiet setting for solitude to be with Wisdom.

Loraz, Hamaklob, Stencellomak, Pago, and Wave had spent the afternoon making temporary lean-to shelters at the forest edge. Building clouds caused them to be concerned about rain. The scent of rain was in the air. They began to feel pressure to finish the shelters quickly when Unmo, Anvel, Vole, Momeh, and Hawk arrived to help.

Lupo called the People to the evening meal by hitting rocks together three times and three more times and three more times, just as the shelters were complete. The People gathered at a log where food choices were placed in a line. The eating bowls were in a woven box nearby. Tuksook with combed hair lingered last in line, wondering whether eating was a good thing to do. She took a small piece of sturgeon and a few greens. She went to sit at the far edge in the circle around the cooking hearth. To her dismay, Gumui sat beside her.

"Are you feeling better?" he asked.

She glared at him.

"You must answer, Tuksook. Failing to talk about what troubles you is a serious problem. It leaves others to wonder and often their guesses are wrong. It cuts off those who care about you." His voice was gentle but his eyes were not. He did not like the look in her eyes and met it with strong force from his own eyes.

"I'm fine," she lied again.

"Tuksook, don't you know I can tell you're lying?" he asked caught between anger and amusement. "I asked a simple question, and you've turned it into something offensive. I shouldn't need to remind you, Wisdom hates lies."

"I still hurt in my gut," she admitted.

"What's wrong?" he asked.

"I cannot tell you."

"Come with me and we'll walk down to the trash heap to discard the fish bones," he said.

She did not argue. She feared he might make public what occurred earlier. She did not want to face that until she was ready, and she had been too angered to reason it well in her mind web.

"Is it your father's judgment regarding Rimut and Pito?" he asked boldly.

Tuksook was alarmed. Did her thoughts show so clearly? How had he known?

"Tuksook, I asked you a question."

"I know."

"Don't contrive a lie. Tell me clearly and straight."

"There are some things that are personal."

"When it makes your belly hurt and you eat like a bird, it's not personal anymore. Shall I let your father know that something is troubling you?"

"No, please, Gumui. Please, no."

"So, it is that judgment?"

She nodded.

"That was just a passing failure to reason through his mind web. No man who loves his wife would force her."

She held her words.

"You don't believe me?"

She held her words.

He grasped her shoulders. "Look into my eyes. Tell me what's bothering you about it."

"I need to reason more in my mind web, before I can talk about it."

"Very well, Tuksook. I'll wait until high sun tomorrow for your explanation. Then, we talk. The People do not permit children to keep harmful thoughts in their mind webs. It could cause them to sicken. That, Tuksook, comes from Wisdom. You know it."

And, so it did, she acknowledged. She didn't want to be a child. She didn't want to be a woman. She didn't want to be People. She wanted to run, run to a place where she could be free. What made her happy was learning new things—being with Wisdom, but she couldn't accomplish that by killing herself. Wisdom gave each person something like a spiritual length of narrow animal skin. The lengths varied according to Wisdom's purpose. It was their personal life or time line. They lived as long as the length of their life line. Because it was spiritual and not physical, no one really knew the length of their time line. But Wisdom did. To kill one's self was to steal Wisdom's power over the life line. Stealing from Wisdom was unthinkable. The stories taught the People to be grateful for what length was given them. She knew Gumui would learn what she hid. She wondered whether she could keep him quiet about it. Why, she wondered, was he always there? Why did he care?

Rain began to fall. The People scurried to the lean-tos that had been set up for each major family group. There were ten shelters. Tuksook saw where her father had taken his place and moved to the diagonal spot across from him at the far back. There was a small opening in the side where she could breathe in the fragrance of rain. She covered up with a warm fur. She was cold. She was grateful there would be no council that night.

In her mind web Tuksook prayed, "Wisdom, help to change my father's judgment."

In the middle of the night, Ghopi came to the lean-to calling for Item, Tuksook's mother. Item arose and went to the front of the lean-to.

"What is it, Ghopi?' she asked, wondering why it couldn't wait until morning.

"Pito is losing very much blood. Rimut has been raping her all day long. She is in a bad way."

"Let me follow you," Item said as she picked up a box from the side of the lean-to.

Ghopi led her to the lean-to. They stepped inside to the smell of blood and sounds of sobbing. They discovered that Pito had died. Ghopi and Item were both outraged. They covered her to wait until the next morning for further action. Both glared at Rimut but in the dark the effort was wasted.

Item returned to her lean-to. Midgenemo was sleeping. She kicked him.

"What in the name of Wisdom is the matter with you, Wife?" he asked half awake.

"More important, what's the matter with you!" she returned. "You judged that women had no right to refuse a husband. Pito is dead because you defied the stories and Wisdom."

"Dead? You must be mistaken."

"She's dead and you're responsible. While he should have been working, Rimut raped her repeatedly today because of your ruling. You're partly responsible for her death."

"You're being ridiculous, Item!" he replied harshly. "I ruled properly! If she's dead, it's her own fault. She should have been responsive to her husband." He was awake and quite agitated.

"Old Fool!" Item spat out the words quietly but in great anger. "You are unfit to lead with those thoughts. Our People have never been separated by power over one another. We have lives designed to support one another as two join into one. If a husband rapes his wife, he rapes half of himself. It makes him as a man who had the illness that leaves him with half a working body and the other half seemingly dead. There are times a woman should refuse her husband. You just saw one. It wasn't for lack of loving him, though I don't know what she saw in him. She had a painful sick belly. And he abused her for what reason? I can think of none but to show he's more powerful, as if that could be a reason. You gave him permission to do it. Any man is more powerful than a woman; we're built that way. To take advantage of that to cower a woman is contrary to Wisdom. A man's more powerful for the hunt and to protect the People. He is to cherish his wife and she is to support him and the People. For a man to take any more power than that is a feeble, cowardly, unloving attempt to try to steal power away from Wisdom to use

23

for his own perverse desire. You're the Wise One. You should know that! I am disgusted!" She was yelling. Everyone could hear.

Midgenemo was fully angered. He reached out and slapped her face hard.

"You'll live to regret that," she muttered. She moved near Tuksook. In the far back she slept the rest of the night.

Tuksook had missed nothing. She ached for Pito. Tuksook thought the woman had some kind of sickness and Rimut had literally killed her for her refusal—with the permission of the Wise One. Some Wise One her father turned out to be. Her father, a man she once adored, had proved to be cruel and ignorant of Wisdom. She lay awake all night. She decided her feeling toward her father was hatred. He slapped her mother. She was certain she'd never forgive him.

The next morning little groups of women gathered briefly out of hearing of men. Then, they went about their work as if nothing had happened. Taman, Hamaklob, and Hawk went about digging a grave at the far south end of the meadow. Amuin and Ghopi prepared Pito for burial. Rimut was talking with older girls, looking for another wife. The sun moved higher and higher, though in this part of the world, it did not rise overhead but instead high sun was when the sun reached the south. It seemed to circle just above the horizon except for a brief time at night.

"There you are," Gumui said.

Tuksook jumped. She turned slowly. It was high sun.

"Now, tell me what troubled you yesterday."

"Yesterday you vowed to Wisdom. Do you take your vows seriously?"

"Of course," he said surprised, "what makes you ask?"

"I will share with you only if you vow to repeat nothing that I tell you, no matter how much you may want to repeat it. Do I have your vow?"

"Suppose you need help to sort out your mind web?"

"Then, you may help me." She looked at him with big blue eyes shaded by thick straw colored lashes. Despite the color, he thought he'd never seen her more beautiful.

"Very well," he agreed without reasoning it through his mind web.

"Then vow," she asked.

"I vow to Wisdom never to repeat what Tuksook shares with me now."

"I talk to Wisdom."

"What do you mean, you talk to Wisdom? Do you mean that Wisdom also talks to you?"

"Yes, but differently from how People talk. You wanted me to talk, so are you going to let me talk or keep interrupting?"

"I'm sorry. Please, continue." Gumui was beginning to understand part of why this girl fascinated him. She had a different depth from most People. She carried much inside her that was invisible to the People. He wanted to know more.

Tuksook continued, "I talk to Wisdom. That's why I like solitude. I love Wisdom. My father is our Wise One. He has angered Wisdom by his judgment. He has angered the women here because his judgment led to Pito's death. More women will eventually die if the judgment is not changed. Rimut should be banned from the People. His pride is evil. Even now, he seeks a new wife. Pito isn't yet buried. His children need comfort. He doesn't care. He loves self alone. His parents are comforting his children. The women of the People are outraged. This afternoon late in the day, you will find no woman or children in the meadow." She looked directly and deeply into his eyes. "Remember your vow. Women have had enough. We can live without the men. Women of the People know how to hunt. We will find another place. We will all leave."

Gumui was shocked. He was troubled about the death of Pito, but he never expected women and children to leave the People. Never in all the stories had that happened. And, he was vowed to silence. Still he was transfixed.

"How do you know of this?" he asked.

"Mother asked me to fly this morning. Then, after I found a place, she talked with every woman. Not one disagreed. All are resolved to leave until the judgment changes. Each knows how to leave to find the new place. We go by different ways. Do not ask me where we go or how," she said flatly.

Gumui stood there with his mouth open but with no words to say. He would have been terrified to go against Wisdom, and clearly, if Tuksook had flown, Wisdom was part of this plan. Wisdom controlled the flying. The children, he knew, belonged to women until girls began their flow and boys were of an age and hunter mastery to be called men. The children would obey the women. He knew he was about to see an event that the People had never considered—a unique event that would become a story to be told to future generations.

"But what if you come against a bear," he asked, concerned for the welfare of the women.

"I would rather die from beast attack than the way Pito died. One who claimed to love her betrayed her instead—that is evil. A bear or another beast would have no evil intent."

"By Wisdom, you are brave!" he exclaimed.

"It shows how serious we are." She stood there firm, seemingly fearless. A girl willing to die from a beast instead of from evil. And the women of the People all agreed on the same need. Backed by Wisdom.

"Tuksook, I have looked after you all of your life. I want to go as a hunter to protect you."

"That cannot be, Gumui. Only women and children can go."

He could understand but was greatly afraid for the women and children. All his life he had focused on protecting them. It was the way of the male People. He also knew to look out for men on the hunt.

"Wisdom goes with us, Gumui. There's no need to fear."

"Well, I guess you've finished your mind web reasoning. How's your belly?"

"There's a plan to fix this, so I'm doing well."

He took her hand and examined her wrist, wincing. "I ask for a vow from you," he said quietly. "Will you vow to tell no one you shared this with me?"

"Of course, Gumui. I trust you. You can trust me."

For some reason that he did not understand, her words made him feel wonderful. She trusted him after what had taken place? He would have thought her father's betrayal of women and Rimut's betrayal of his wife would have caused her to trust no man.

There was a call to the grave of Pito. All attended. The Wise One remembered the story perfectly, Tuksook observed. Little by little as the afternoon progressed, Gumui saw women and children wander off. They went in different directions. He kept his word. Somehow, he knew the injustice had to change and this was a plan, one that would capture the attention of the men. The evening meal was just about finished cooking when Shut and Cadpo left the meadow. They were the fastest runners among the women. Each took a different route from the meadow.

The women followed rock paths that led to a central point quite some distance from the meadow. It went uphill nearing the top of a mountain. They kept to the paths careful to leave no trace, if possible, though they knew that eventually the hunters would find them. There was a cave near the mountain top. The face of the mountain was rock. The path up was a good distance beyond the cave. Tuksook saw it on her flight. The women and children climbed up the path carefully. They took the small children into the back of the cave, and had the older ones gather large rocks which they could roll downhill, if needed, when hunters or beasts came. The women no longer viewed the hunters as People. All had been silent when the evil judgment was made. For their silence the women counted the men and themselves as cowards. The women vowed never to be silent in the face of wrong again.

No longer were they going to be cowards. The People were not cowards. Consequently, the adult male People were no longer People in the eyes of the women, because they had made no such vow.

As evening wore on, men began to look to the hearth. At first they didn't realize there were no women or children. They wondered why the food cooked untended.

Suddenly, Kew shouted, "Where are the women and children?"

All the men gathered near the hearth. The smell of the sturgeon from the rock warming area was tempting. Some of them took the food up and placed it on the log, taking a piece to eat as they did. All looked about wondering at the disappearance of the women and children. They were confused.

Midgenemo asked, "Did any of the women tell anyone where they were going?"

There was no answer.

"I suggest we eat, and, if they're not back, we send some men to find them," he said.

"There's something amiss here," Wave said strongly. "As for me, I'd rather go now to find them to be sure they do well. Never have all women and children left at one time!"

"I'll go with you," Unmo added.

"I, too," Togomoo said.

"Then, the three of you go," Midgenemo said as he picked up a bowl. "Our women know how to take care of themselves. Something must have interested them."

"Interested them?" Ottu shouted out acerbically. "What could possibly interest every single woman and child, yet leave all of us excluded?"

Silence felt loud.

Wave, Unmo, and Togomoo looked at each other. Which way would they have gone?

The women had left clear exit paths from the meadow but were very careful after that. There were exit paths going in all directions except towards the water where the men had been disassembling the boat. They also avoided the area east of the meadow where men were building the bent-tree home. Tuksook's flight had helped the women find the rock paths. At the exit paths the three men sometimes found little items, as if intentionally misleading. The men began to follow one path that seemed to have been made by children. It went into the forest and then there was no path. They looked at each other frowning. Mystery was not part of the People. They survived well because of clear communication. At each exit path from the meadow, they found the same thing. The paths were clear at first and then disappeared. The men were confused and hungry. It was becoming too dark to follow a path in the forest. Wave suspected the women had planned this disappearance, but he did not have enough information to feel comfortable voicing his suspicion.

"I suggest we return, eat, sleep, and at first light begin the search. Our women are able to take care of themselves," Wave said with frustration.

Both of the others agreed and they returned. At the council they'd share what they learned.

The council was strange. Midgenemo tried to act as if this event were normal. Not one person agreed. Instead, they began to question him.

"What? Do you question me? I talk to Wisdom!" he said in anger.

"Then, talk to Wisdom and return with an answer for us," Ottu challenged.

Midgenemo stood, miffed, and left the council. He headed to the middle of the meadow and dropped to his knees. He raised his arms, looked towards the sky, and called on Wisdom, and nothing happened. He called and called. Wisdom always replied. He did not understand. He returned to the council.

"I guess Wisdom is asleep," he said unconvincingly.

"By Wisdom's testicles, man!" Ottu said a bit too loud, "You're making that up. It looks to me that Wisdom isn't talking to you! Wisdom never sleeps! You're making things up to suit you. You're putting us in danger!"

Ottu's swearing startled some of the younger men, but the older ones knew he did it when he was totally frustrated. Gumui wondered whether Wisdom actually had testicles.

"This is somehow connected to your idiotic judgment the other night and Pito's death. Is your mind web so tangled and your belly too full of food for you to reason or hear?"

Gumui held his face and body tight to show nothing of his thoughts. He acted as if he were hunting and did not want the prey to spot him. He was grateful for Ottu's insight that Wisdom had deserted their Wise One. He hadn't known that was possible.

"How dare you?" Midgenemo said in an attempt to clear the accusation and return his authority. He was agitated, feeling his heart beat too fast and hard. Pressure in his head was painful. He felt he should defend himself regardless of right—or wrong. He was the Wise One.

"I dare because it's true," Ottu stated flatly. "And you, Rimut, you are worthless. We should ban you. You're unfit to call yourself People."

Murmurings made it clear that others were beginning to share Ottu's thoughts. They began to see.

"So, let us sleep," Ottu said flatly, "and tomorrow we will find our women and children. We will learn whether I am right."

The council normally closed by Midgenemo ended with Ottu's comment. Midgenemo was perplexed. He understood that failure to talk with Wisdom could only mean that Ottu was right. He walked to the center of the meadow and called on Wisdom repeatedly. Wisdom was silent. He knew he was wrong, but pride kept him holding out that there was a chance his judgment had been right. He did remind himself that he hadn't consulted with Wisdom but spoke the judgment assuming he was incapable of error. He was Wise One, after all. Midgenemo for the first time in his life was frightened. He went to his lean-to where Lurch and Orad waited. There was more room in the lean-to, but it was unwelcome.

At first light the rain was falling. That, hunters knew, was not a good sign. More hunters agreed to seek the women and children. When Rimut volunteered, Midgenemo told him he had to remain at the meadow. That angered the man, but he knew some felt he should be banned, so he remained obedient. Loraz, Hamaklob, Stencellomak, and Anvel joined the search.

The men spread out to the south. They followed each exit path, and each one led to nothing. Then they tried the path to the east. The same thing occurred. They tried the paths to the north and one led to a rock path. All men gathered to follow that path. They went without food. They grew hungry by high sun. The path continued. They stopped at a tiny waterfall to drink.

"Do you think we're still on the right path?" Anvel asked.

"If Tuksook flew, this path would make sense. We certainly didn't know it existed. If she flew, she'd know exactly where it went," Loraz said firmly.

"If that's true, then Ottu is probably right," Hamaklob said his thoughts out loud.

"What do we do if we have a Wise One, who's lost his way? He has to judge between two or more who cannot release disagreement. How do we live well, if he's lost his way?" Stencellomak voiced the fear of all of the hunters.

"Wisdom only knows," Unmo said.

"Let's continue while we have daylight," Wave urged.

They walked on for quite some time, until Togomoo who was leading made hand signals to be quiet. His hunter hand signals showed he thought he heard something.

The group remained quiet and Togomoo heard it again. It was in the distance and he had trouble discerning from where. Stencellomak used hand signals to signify that he also heard it. He made the sign of infant, and Togomoo nodded agreement. The others strained to hear, but all seemed silent to them. The noise was far away.

They continued on the stone path. They took more care for silence. The path seemed endless. Togomoo and Stencellomak took the lead, since they had superior hearing. Togomoo stopped. The noise was above them. He looked up at a sheer rock wall. High above them he pointed. There was a cave, he thought, almost at the top of the mountain. The hunters saw it as soon as he pointed. They wondered how they were supposed to reach the cave.

Item leaned over the ledge. The men saw her.

"Go away!" she shouted.

"Please, Item, tell us what made you leave? And what do we have to do to bring you home?" Unmo asked.

"We have no home but this. Once we were People, wonderful People with Wisdom to lead us. Now, Midgenemo would have us led by a man—not Wisdom. We will not stand for that. We are the People. We don't know who you are. We suspect you are cowards, since none of you spoke against the judgment."

"It was his judgment over Rimut and Pito's death?" Unmo asked to make sure he understood.

"Why ask? Cannot you see for yourself?"

Unmo looked up. "We are simply verifying what we suspect. What will it take to bring you home?"

"We will only follow Wisdom, not some man and his unreasoned ideas," she said. Item felt very strange speaking against Midgenemo. She loved him. He had changed somehow toward the end of the boat sailing. She didn't understand it. She continued, "The judgment has to change by vow to Wisdom. Rimut must be banned far away. You will take him by boat to a far place and leave him there. You must vow to Wisdom to kill him, if he returns. For us to view any of you as People, you'll have to vow never to remain silent in the face of wrong."

"Is that your full request?" Unmo asked.

"Unmo," she said leaning over the wall of the cave, "you've known me a long time. That's not a request; it's a demand. Now go, before we start to roll boulders upon you."

The men were shocked, but they turned. The women would roll large rocks down, they knew. Women of the People were careful to say exactly what they meant.

The men arrived back at the meadow just as darkness descended. They took time to eat. The men who remained behind were eager to know what they learned, but custom prevented them from interfering with the hunters' filling their bellies. The dogs walked about on stiff legs in a state of unrest. A man had fed them, not their girl. Something was wrong.

Despite the darkness, council met when the men finished eating and the bowls were cleaned and put in the container.

"Did you find them?" Midgenemo asked.

"Of course," Unmo replied.

"What is the problem with the women?" Midgenemo asked.

"We have a problem—not the women. Ottu was correct. They were outraged at your judgment, which was against Wisdom and them," Unmo said, tired and irritated at Midgenemo.

"So what do they want?"

"They demand, not request, that you overturn your own judgment by a vow to Wisdom, so it aligns with Wisdom, and that you take Rimut by boat to a land far away and leave him there. You must vow you'll kill him, if he manages to return. Finally, to be viewed as People, each man has to vow not to remain silent in the face of wrong." Unmo stared into Midgenemo's eyes.

"Women issuing an ultimatum to me?" Midgenemo was surprised.

"According to them Wisdom has deserted you. They are People and will follow Wisdom, not you. Because your judgment was against the teaching of Wisdom, they no longer consider you People. They no longer consider any of us People, because no one spoke against your judgment. Hasn't it occurred to you yet, that they're right?"

"That's crazy," Rimut spoke up. "I'd die in some wilderness alone."

"Rimut, you made your decisions and acted on them. You have to accept what your decisions return to you. You mean nothing to me after what you did. My wife means everything," Unmo said.

Muttering among the men at the council made it clear that they agreed. Rimut became cold with fear.

"Are you willing to turn your judgment around?" Unmo asked Midgenemo.

"I must reason it through my mind web," he replied.

"Well, you'd better reason fast, or many here and I will desert you for them. I agree with the women completely. I only regret that I said nothing after your judgment. Pito might still be alive."

Again, the murmuring indicated that many of the men agreed.

"I will give you my decision in the morning," Midgenemo said flatly.

Men left the council quietly and went to their lean-tos.

In the morning, the men went to the council area. The sky was gray with clouds. Midgenemo stood before them and said, "I will vow when they return."

"No!" Unmo said. "Either you vow now before Wisdom that you overturn your judgment and return to Wisdom's lead, and you send the boat removing Rimut, or we go nowhere today. Man, your pride is killing you and harming the People."

"I said I would vow when they return." Midgenemo felt like the liquid in a cooking bag when hot rocks were added.

"Who believes that?" Unmo asked.

"I do," Rimut said. Not one other reply came forth.

Midgenemo walked off. The men went to start the morning meal. They would not return to the women that day.

Midgenemo assumed that the women would become hungry and return for food. He had misjudged their resourcefulness. Young boys were learning to hunt and they snared rabbits and small animals. A few women were great hunters. Women had brought cooking pouches and bowls. The exit had been well planned.

Fully seven days passed. Midgenemo realized that the women were unlikely to return. He was losing the following of the men. He feared they were plotting against him and Rimut. Council came together, and it was clear that the men were angered. The gray troubled clouds that had lingered since the women left reflected the mood of the hunters.

"Why do you continue to protect Rimut and your decision made without the guidance of Wisdom?" Ottu asked. "You will bring Wisdom's displeasure on us all. Your pride may cause us all to be killed. You're on the wrong side of Wisdom."

"Wisdom wouldn't do that," Midgenemo replied trying to convince them and himself.

"You've forgotten the stories. You're no leader. Maybe you should be boated off along with Rimut." Ottu was furious. "My wife is old, and this is hard on her. She will continue until she dies there, if you continue this insanity. Before I let that happen, I'll kill you and Rimut myself."

Numbers of other seasoned hunters voiced loud offers to help.

Midgenemo realized he'd alienated the best hunters. Younger ones were confused, but the older hunters were fully able to carry out their threat. He secretly wondered whether his own mind web was failing.

"Call on Wisdom and vow, now," Ottu spat out the words.

Midgenemo realized the time had come. He knelt in the center of the meadow and called on Wisdom before them all. "I vow that the judgment I made in Rimut's favor is overturned now and forever," he shouted. "Wisdom, hear me. I vow that the judgment I made in Rimut's favor is overturned. I will ban Rimut from living here by taking him by boat far away and leaving him there. I vow before you to kill him, if he returns."

Rimut started to run. A bolt of lightning flashed down and felled a tree on Midgenemo's lean-to, crushing it where he slept. Rimut stopped and the hunters caught him and tied his arms and legs so he could not free himself. Another bolt of lightning hit the ground just in front of Midgenemo. He could hear Wisdom say, "Turn away from this vow, and your line of life ends immediately. You will return to me and kill your pride, or I will kill you. You've been given much. You have abused it." The men heard only what sounded like thunder. Midgenemo knew that he had to change immediately, and he returned to Wisdom. Lightning could definitely vanquish pride. He thought others heard Wisdom's words, but it didn't really matter. Wisdom was not constrained by the People. Wisdom would end his life, if he turned back to his evil pride. Of that he had no doubt.

"How many of you are willing to take the boat to ban Rimut?" Midgenemo asked.

Moki, Remui, Pago, Hai, Togomoo, Hamaklob, Hawk, Vole, and Gumui stepped forward.

Midgenemo looked at them. "Gumui, you're too young." He pointed to him to leave the group.

"To make this quicker, I'll also step forward," Vel said.

"I, too," Tern, and Coo added.

"We go now," Moki said. Vel and Hai took the ends of a bamboo pole and carried it to Rimut. They stuck it through his tied arms and legs like an animal carcass they wanted to move. They shouldered the ends of the pole, and started downhill with the man without ever looking back. The other men hurried to the boat. Moki, Vel, Hawk, and Togomoo hastily gathered containers of water and jerky.

The men had stripped most of the upper deck of the boat, thinking they had no need of it. The sail was still functioning but the huts were all gone. It would be a wet ride. They took off, rowing out into the river's central channel. They decided to go to the east on reaching salt water, because that would put ice between Rimut and them. The men were convinced Wisdom was with them. They wanted to leave Rimut and return home as fast as possible.

Midgenemo went to Ottu. "I've been a fool," he admitted.

"Yes, you have," Ottu agreed. "Now's your chance to make amends. Don't fail."

"Well, you heard Wisdom with the flash of lightning," he replied, thinking all heard the thunder in the way he had. "I'll be killed, if I fail to keep my vows. I'm Wisdom's now."

"I will watch," Ottu said. "I will no longer remain silent."

"Will the hunters go now to return the women and children?"

"Ask them," Ottu replied.

"Hunters," Midgenemo called out.

The hunters gathered.

"I have made a fool of myself. I ask the forgiveness of you all. Will those of you, who know where the women and children are, go to them and ask them to return. Their demands have been met."

Loraz and Unmo agreed to go, stating that it was unnecessary for all to go. Before they left, they touched the northernmost pole of their equinox/solstice measuring device. It was a physical manifestation of the spiritual request for help on their quest. Those who remained began to work on the bent-tree home, grateful for the work that provided something constructive and different on which to focus. Gumui loved building it, envisioning the People living there.

Unmo and Loraz arrived at the cave in the afternoon. They hadn't bothered to be quiet on this trek. It went much faster. Unmo called up to the cave, "Item!"

Item leaned over the edge.

"What is it?"

"The Wise One has returned to himself. We stood up to him. He made the vow you demanded and Rimut is on the boat moving to a far distant place. Will you return now?"

Item called back, "Are the days still lengthening?"

Unmo replied, "Yes." He was slightly surprised by her question.

Item said, "Unmo, when the boat returns, only you, Unmo, and Gumui come to let us know. Assure us all is well, and we will return. Be careful to speak truth to us. That is all."

Loraz and Unmo returned to the meadow with heaviness. They had hoped to have the women and children with them. When they returned, the People gathered and they told what the women had said.

"I don't blame them," Ottu said. "What fascinates me is why they chose Gumui."

"I guess they trust him," Midgenemo said.

Gumui stood there while they talked about him. He knew why. Tuksook trusted him. He would keep that secret for a lifetime.

The men worked diligently on the bent-tree structure. It would have been a lot easier to build if they'd had the bamboo poles from the boat they were dismantling. Without them they cut down trees to make the cross members of the bent-tree home for the sides and roof.

Ottu had taken responsibility to feed the dogs. It was rewarding work, he realized, for the dogs looked forward to his appearance. They calmed in his presence. That in turn calmed him. Now that Midgenemo had returned to himself, the dog, Tictip, would come to him and follow him about. Midgenemo appreciated the companionship of the dog, something he hadn't experienced since they arrived at the meadow. Ottu looked on it as a good sign.

Gumui spent time working hard to finish their bent-tree home, but he kept his senses tuned to the water. He was eager for the boat to return so the women and children could come home. He worried about Tuksook.

He needn't have worried. Tuksook was a good hunter. She went out and speared a young giant deer, having no idea what it was. The young boys bled it, removed the skin, which they kept, and cut the meat up for eating. They carried it to the cave and the women cooked some of the meat. The flavor was great. During the time in the cave, women would remove the hair and work the skins. Other women proved that they could also hunt, so the women and children ate well. No other humans were in the area. They were well protected in the cave. They had a nearby waterfall. They had almost achieved their goal. Some women were more than ready to return, but Item made it clear that they had to abide by what she'd said. Return of any one of them would cause their plan to fail, and they were succeeding. The women obeyed her.

Ten days of gray skies and continued lack of women since the boat left had the men irritable.

"What if the boat went down in the sea?" Anvel asked Kew. "Will the women never return?"

"They'll be back," Kew said with confidence.

"I begin to worry since it's been so long. Do you think we should take food to the women and children?"

"Ask Unmo, but I am certain the women have no desire to see any but Unmo and Gumui, since that's what they said. They have been gone long enough that they must be hunting successfully. I don't want rocks thrown downhill at me." Kew turned and walked away. Anvel's question was in every hunter's mind web, but only time would clarify what happened.

Eight days later, the men noticed dogs growling quietly. Kew shouted out, "The boat returns!"

Every hunter raced to the path to the lower river level. Sure enough, the boat was coming upstream. They could just make it out at the bend in the river. The hunters breathed sighs of relief, looking at each other with smiles. The women and children would return!

The men anchored the boat and came ashore.

"I'm starving!" Togomoo shouted, chorused by the rest of the crew.

"Let's find these men something to eat," Ottu boomed out.

With excitement to hear from them, the hunters followed the men from the boat up the path and made a fish meal with greens available. The hunters ate and some stretched out on the ground, happy to be back on land. Finally, when all were finished and the bowls cleaned and put back in the container, the council began.

"We left here and the ocean was fierce and wave tossed. We had to lower the sail for fear it might be broken. Even without the sail we moved very quickly east. We passed the ice and the sea calmed somewhat. Sometimes we rowed until our arms were almost numb when wind calmed. Gigantic chunks of ice floated in the sea. Finally, we saw land that wasn't ice covered," Hamaklob said, stopping to catch his breath.

Togomoo picked up the story, "We kept Rimut tied up and swam with him to shore. On shore we untied his hands. We returned to the boat and came home, not looking back. The winds were calm so we made good progress rowing with great strength to return with speed to our new home."

"We are glad you had a successful sailing," Midgenemo said. "We must all vow now never to remain silent in the face of wrong. Say it with me," he shouted out, and they joined him saying the vow with meaning. Then Midgenemo looked at Unmo. "It's time for you and Gumui to leave."

"What wrong did they do?" Hawk asked, concerned.

"Nothing! They go to tell the women their demands have been met, and they can return," Midgenemo said with a smile. He felt less agitated than he had in a long time.

"Why those two?" Hawk asked.

"The women specified them. Who knows? We just want our People back together."

Hawk looked askance at the man, but asked nothing else. He felt uneasy that the Wise One seemed all too frequently to grasp quick, unreasoned answers.

Unmo and Gumui arrived at the path below the cave. Unmo called up, "Item. I bring information."

Item leaned over the barrier. "What is it?"

"We've come to escort you home. All your demands are met."

"Do you agree, Gumui?" Item asked.

"Yes," he replied.

"We need no escort. You return, and we will come back tomorrow. Do not meet us. Tell the men this—we want to be treated no differently than before the false judgment, and if this occurs again, we will leave permanently."

"I will take your message to them," Unmo said. "We'll see you tomorrow?"

"You will," Item agreed.

The two men left. They were not well pleased to return without the women and children. Gumui suggested that they had a reason for what they did. Unmo grumbled that he'd never understand a woman. The men partly ran back to the meadow.

When they arrived, the council met.

Midgenemo asked, "Where are the women?"

"They wanted no escort. They will arrive tomorrow. Another demand is that we treat them as we did before the bad judgment. They don't want to be met. And, they assure us that if this occurs again, they'll leave permanently."

The men were stunned. Some felt the women's demands were becoming tiresome. Others, who did not want a recurrence, stifled their irritation. The women, they reminded themselves, were entitled to their demands. They showed the men as either poor in judgment or cowardly or both. The men would not forget that soon, knowing the women spoke truth.

Late in the evening the women and children returned quietly to the meadow, bearing heavy burdens. No one spoke of their absence. What startled the men was the amount of meat they brought with them. The meat could feed the People for at least twenty days. The men were acutely aware that the women could survive without them. They had respect for and a slight fear of the women.

Sutorlo and Lurch showed the others where to bring the meat. The two, almost men, saw to the submerging of the meat in the catch pool, choosing heavy rocks to hold the meat below the water.

Item went to Midgenemo and said, "We have returned. Either Eagle's Grasp will become a wonderful home for all the People, or we will depart permanently. I understand that you have returned to your senses."

He stifled a cutting answer and said, "I was wrong to use my own judgment rather than depend on Wisdom. For that I'm well chastened, Item. I have vowed to Wisdom to turn back from my independent ways. I ask you, as my wife, for forgiveness."

"You won't have it immediately, Husband," she replied. "I'll watch to satisfy myself that you have changed. You were ready to make a hurtful reply to my first words to you. I don't trust your change. I also remember you slapped me. Do that again and you will have seen me for the last time."

"Then, I'll have to earn your trust back."

"That you will," she said, turned, and carried a large grass bag of bowls to the container for storage until the next meal.

Gumui found Tuksook. "Did you keep your vow?" he asked. "I kept mine."

"You doubt me?" she asked.

"No, not really. I just wanted to see you and know you're doing well."

"I'm well, thank you. This has been a hard time, but in some ways we enjoyed discovering what we could do as the weaker People. We did very well. Did you see the meat we brought?"

"I saw. The hunters saw also. We are all aware that you women with children are very able to live in this land without us. That's a frightening thought for a man," he admitted.

"Men should be aware of how to treat their wives. Then, there will not be a problem. The stories tell how men should treat women and women should treat men. It's all there. Everyone hears it every year."

"I know, Tuksook."

"Is that Ubassu trying to attract your attention over there?" Tuksook asked.

"She was following me around before you left. She wants me to join with her."

"She what?" Tuksook asked horrified.

"You heard me."

"But there's never been anything between you two."

"I agree and want to keep it that way."

Tuksook felt strange feelings that she did not recognize as jealousy. Somehow Gumui had always been there. He guarded her when she slipped into solitude. She wasn't yet certain she wanted to join with anyone when she became a woman, but if she did, she could think of none other than Gumui. She was a child and he was a man at present, but that would soon change. She would have to reason in her mind web. She craved solitude. Lack of it was killing her, she thought. To talk to Wisdom could clear her mind web to focus on what was important.

"What's the matter?" Gumui asked.

"I need to reason before I can answer," she replied.

"Tuksook, answer me," he demanded. She was a child and he was man, his eyes said.

Tears slipped from her eyes. "Gumui, I don't know whether I'll ever want to join with a man, but if I do, I want it to be you. It frightens me that another girl will appeal to you for a wife. There, are you satisfied? You're pulling out of my depths any sense of privacy I have left."

Gumui had not thought of Tuksook as a wife. He really hadn't thought of anyone as a wife. However, her words had a profound effect on him. They made him feel wanted, needed, and, yes, loved. He felt special. Those were new feelings for him. Without a word, he reached out, hugged her, and lifted her off the ground, as he'd done several times in the past. He held her up by her rib cage. She was of the old People, but her body was thin. He kissed her forehead, as he lowered her to the ground. His thumbs slid over well-formed breast buds. Gumui was jolted, not unlike the feeling when the lightning struck the meadow, but for a different reason.

"My dear, adorable Tuksook. Whatever must I do with you?"

Tuksook shrugged. She didn't know anything had just happened.

Chapter Two

Desperate for solitude, Tuksook walked to the south end of the meadow. She had never felt a close fit with those near her age, but she felt close to Wisdom. She sought Wisdom at every opportunity. Large leafed, tall plants with thick stems and tiny flowers at the top were growing there. She passed between them to hide behind the big leaves. Tuksook looked for snakes or spiders and seeing none, she settled to the ground. The big leafed plants gave her a bit of solitude while she obediently remained in the meadow. Tuksook had been there yesterday, but Togomoo called her to carry some bamboo from the boat to the bent tree house construction, and she had once again missed her opportunity for solitude. Her skin began to tingle and there were red places appearing on her legs and arms. One place on the left side of her face began to tingle where the sun warmed it, but she couldn't see it. Clusters of tiny white flowers formed what looked to be a large, flat flower atop the giant plants. The flowers towered over her. They had a delicate, pleasing fragrance. Tuksook savored the scent. Sun rays warmed her skin as she sat amid the plants. Despite the tingling, she calmed, opening her mind web as usual. Before Tuksook reached that spiritual place where she would be with Wisdom, her arms and legs began to burn. Blisters formed on her skin. It grew worse.

Screaming, she raced from her hiding place to the open meadow to find her mother. She brushed against the plant leaves and thick stems that had formed a rash on her skin from the previous day's exposure. The rash burned. The sun made the burning worse. It had to stop. It affected her ability to use her mind web properly. Her screams rent the calm of their meadow and all turned to see what was the cause of Tuksook's screaming. The girl ran straight into her mother who noticed the rash immediately. Item led her to the bathing area where she helped her out of her tunic and had her stand in the waterfall. She told her to stay in the water while she returned to their lean-to for her herb bundles.

Item knew plants from their old land but had no familiarity with what plant caused the red rash on Tuksook's skin. She'd never seen anything like it. She was certain a plant that grew in the new land, not the old was the cause. She would have to try for a cure instead of knowing instantly what to use. Item chose several previously ground plants, mixing them together to form an analgesic balm. That is what she would have done for painful rashes in the past. She brought skins to hold the balm to the affected areas.

"Be still, my Daughter," Item said, hoping the balm would help. "Does the sun make it worse?"

Quiet now, Tuksook nodded, tears rimming her lower eyelids until they overflowed.

Item applied the balm and covered the rash with the skin strips.

"You'll have to stay out of the sun. The best place for you is the new bent tree house. Rinse your tunic, put it on, and go there. Ask someone where you should stay to be out of the way. Tuksook, what plant did this to you?"

Tuksook described the very tall plant with thick, hairy stems, huge leaves, and tiny white blossoms that made up what looked like a large flat flower.

"I know the one," Item assured her. She left to find Heek and Port both of whom knew plants and their healing properties. The three would examine the plant that caused the red blisters on Tuksook's skin. They would begin to study the plants in the area to expand their understanding of this new place.

Tuksook put her tunic quickly under the waterfall to remove any remaining plant material that might cling to it inside and outside, shook it out, put it on, and left. She followed the shade in the forest to the bent tree house. On his way to replenish his bag of mud, Gumui saw her in the forest and wondered why Tuksook might be outside the meadow.

"Tuksook," he quietly asked her, "why are you outside the meadow?"

"Look at me. I have a terrible rash that the sun makes worse. My mother told me to go to the bent tree house to avoid the sun. I need to do that until this heals."

"That looks awful."

"Didn't you hear me screaming?" she asked.

"I heard something but I was on the inside of the roof putting mud up there, and I wasn't sure what I was hearing. I'm sorry you're hurt. What did it?"

"The tall plant with the big leaves, thick stalks, and tiny white flowers that look like one big flat flower."

He examined the rash on her face closer. "I know the plant. Wow! That looks mean."

"My mother couldn't cover the one on my face. The rest are wrapped."

"Come, Tuksook. I'll lead you to your new bench/sleeping place."

"You built the bench/sleeping places like the ones from Ki'ti's time?" She was enchanted. She loved the Ki'ti stories best of all the stories. Tuksook and others not involved in construction had been told to stay out of the bent tree house because the construction was very busy and people not involved in the work would be in the way. Few knew what the inside looked like. All they knew was the description of the bent tree house in Ki'ti's time from the stories.

"Yes, we did. Yours has a nice caribou skin on it. Come. Let me show you."

Tuksook was astounded that she had a personal place to sit or sleep and that it had a caribou cover on it. She followed Gumui excited to see this new thing. When he reached the part of the structure that contained her place, he stopped. Tuksook's mouth was open but wordless. The bench/sleeping place was a rectangular braced structure made of bamboo about as high off the ground as her knees. Leather straps from the boat were stretched from end to end and then more straps went across, weaving through the first strips, making a strong webbed netting over which to lay the caribou skin. She ran her hand lightly over it to feel its softness. There was a smooth skin and a furred skin from the first wolf she ever killed. Both were folded on her sleeping place for additional covering.

Gumui pointed out that her parents had the big bench/sleeping places with the giant new beaver skin laid across the leather strips. Gumui told her Orad had killed the giant beaver for this purpose. Lurch and Orad prepared the skin so that it was incredibly soft and in perfect condition. Midgenemo and Item didn't know about the gift. It would be a surprise, he explained. Tuksook felt the giant beaver skin. It was softer than anything she'd ever felt. She knew her parents would be very pleased. Then dark thoughts replaced her happiness for them when she thought of her father. There were additional coverings folded there she noticed. Tuksook's place was between Orad's and Lurch's places.

"You'd better sit on your bench now. It's very busy in here," Gumui said. "I must return to my work. See that place up there where the mud hasn't covered the roof yet. I just came down to dig more mud when I saw you in the forest."

"I was told to stay out of the sun, Gumui."

He put his hand on her shoulder. "Little One, I was sure of that as soon as I saw your face. But I will ask what you were doing hiding among the big leafed plants."

"The big leafed plants are in the meadow. I did not go out of the meadow until I had to avoid the sun to reach this place. I just wanted to be with Wisdom. I needed just a little solitude to have that special time. Every time I try, I find it doesn't work." She had twisted her arms and had her fingers interlocked. Clearly, he thought, Tuksook wants to have quiet time with Wisdom—perhaps she even requires it.

"Has it occurred to you that Wisdom may have something to do with that?" he asked without having thought through what he said.

"No. Why would Wisdom block me?" That thought had never entered her mind web.

Gumui was blindsided by her reaction, because he hadn't meant to imply Wisdom's blocking her. It was an interesting idea to him. He gained what he felt was insight. "Tuksook, are you still angry with your father?"

"Well, of course," she replied. "Who wouldn't be? I trusted him and he let all the People down—most of all Pito."

"Tuksook, have you never done anything wrong?"

"Why ask me that? You know I have lied." She hung her head.

"What's to say that Wisdom sees your father's wrong any differently from your lies?"

"My lies never killed anyone!" she said defensively.

"Your father didn't kill anyone either, Tuksook. Rimut did. Midgenemo's a man—not Wisdom."

"He's supposed to *represent* Wisdom."

"Still, he's a man. According to Wisdom's way you must love him, because he is your father. You are supposed to forgive him, if he wrongs you. Forgiving is Wisdom's way. Now, I really must return to my work. Sit on your bench and think about what I've said to you. You can have solitude in here, for People here are too busy to bother you. I will tell you that your father called on Wisdom and Wisdom refused to come while you were gone. Wisdom did not return to him until he changed, vowing to depend on Wisdom, not himself. You may be having a similar experience. It's worth considering. Women and children left us when we did evil against Pito. The women understood Wisdom's ways. Wisdom won't spend time with someone who disregards his ways any more than women will spend time with men who disregard Wisdom's ways. Forgiveness is one of Wisdom's ways. So is truth telling, Tuksook." Gumui turned and went back outside to pick up the bag he had been on his way to refill with mud. He had learned Wisdom's lesson from the women's absence and the fact that Wisdom left the Wise One alone. He had seen the lightning. This should be a simple lesson for Tuksook, he thought. He brought the full bag back inside and climbed the walls crossing to the place where he'd been working and began to apply the mud to the ceiling. That, the men trusted, would prevent stray cinders from settling in the ceiling to start a fire.

As Gumui began to climb the wall, Mongo called to him, "Where's a large hammer stone?"

"Over by the entry to the south part of the building," he shouted back.

Tuksook sat on her bench/sleeping place and stared at the interior of the building. She wanted to learn each tiny detail. The structure was made of two intersecting rectangles, as a flying bird would see it. One long rectangle extended from north to south and the other, equally long, went from east to west. There was a big hearth in the center where the two rectangles of the house met. Above that was a hide-lined hole for the smoke to exit. Tuksook wondered whether the central area would be the council meeting place. There were smaller hearths in the center of each section of the rectangle. Above each hearth, there was an opening in the ceiling. The openings made it easier to see since some light came through. They also let hearth smoke escape.

Mongo and Taman walked rapidly through the west part of the building, seeming not to see her at all. They exited to the meadow.

Tuksook kept hearing noise outside the structure and mumblings. She had no idea what was going on, but she was not free to run about satisfying her curiosity. Instead, she was constrained to stay out of the way of the construction workers and inside sheltered from the sun. Tuksook hurt from the rash, from Gumui's words, and from having to stay in one place, fascinating as it was. She curled up on the caribou hide and pulled the lightweight skin over her. Tuksook watched Gumui mudding the ceiling. Finally, drowsiness overtook her and sleep followed.

Tuksook dreamed. She was flying. She soared, enjoying the sense of the wind under her. Suddenly there was no wind. She tumbled and rolled from the sky. She hit trees on the way to the ground. She fell into a small pond. Tuksook dragged herself from the water and coughed as she walked to the land. She waked up coughing. Construction was going on as if nothing had happened. Nobody noticed her, not even Gumui. Tuksook felt her hair. It was dry. She had dreamed. Nothing more. She thought of the dream. She had been unable to reach Wisdom recently. Her father had the same problem. No one had told her that except Gumui. She wondered whether Gumui had some understanding of Wisdom she lacked. Her belly had no inclination to forgive her father. It rebelled with cramping feelings at the thought. Somehow, Tuksook felt that being Wise One placed him in a different position from the People. He had more responsibility. He talked with Wisdom. Well, so did she. Her father let Pito die. Tuksook could not ignore his complicity in the death of Pito. She pulled the lightweight skin over her head. She was miserable. The skin brushed painfully against the rash on her face, so she removed the covering quickly. Tuksook wondered how Gumui could think Wisdom might see her father's bad judgment equal to her lies and lack of forgiveness. It hurt her for him to think badly of her. It bothered her considerably to wonder whether he might be right.

Wave, Pago, and Hawk had been down by the boat deconstruction where they'd been working for days. They salvaged numbers of logs and tie strips. They planned to make several small bamboo boats to navigate the river. They could fish as well as hunt in this place where food was abundant. By evening they had the first of the boats completed. It was much smaller than the one they dismantled. It fit four hunters—no more. They tied the front and back of the boat to an elevated level much higher than the water level and the center was flat. They had stacked all the oars from the boat along the hillside. Knowing that water could rise without notice, they tied the oars so they could not float away. When they finished the first boat, the men each chose an oar and took the boat for a trial in the river. Other men watched, hopeful the boats would work. In the old land, boat builders had become fewer and fewer, and new ones were hard to find. The best remained in the old land when the People took to the sea for a new place.

The onrushing water kept turning the boat to the side, so the men quickly decided the bottom of the boat needed something to make the boat stay parallel with the riverbanks. What they needed was a keel. The big boat on which they arrived in this land had a keel, but the men were hunters not boat builders, so they had to learn as they went along. As they fought the sideways turns, they soon realized the purpose of the keel. They decided they could construct a downward sloping bottom to the center of the boat. That would become the project for the following day. They reasoned that would keep the boat going in the direction of the river either with or against the current.

"What's that?" Pago asked as they turned for home and could see the pathway from the north where hunters walked carrying burdens.

"It doesn't look like any animal I've ever seen," Hawk said, considering the color of the beast and that it was suspended on a pole by its legs, not quartered like the other animal. "It has the look of a cat."

"The quarters Stencellomak and the others are carrying look like a giant deer," Wave added.

"It seems we have meat, but if that's a cat, it's the biggest one I ever saw. I don't want to eat cat!" Hawk sneered.

"The dogs aren't so hard to please," Pago laughed. "I'm guessing the hunters took it because it threatened them, and the skin looks interesting from here."

"This certainly isn't a land where we should worry about hungering or needing skins," Hawk said.

They moved towards shore and tied up the oars and boat. They had a long heavy rope that was tied to a stout tree at the top of the riverbank. They'd tie the boats to the heavy rope and if water rose very high, the boats would float to whatever height the water rose. The boats would remain above water regardless of weather or rise of the river.

When Pago, Hawk, and Wave had the boat tied up and secured the poles and oars, they climbed the path to the meadow eager to meet the men arriving from the day's hunt. Moki and Remui were entering the meadow with the cat on the pole followed by Stencellomak, Vole, Hai, Tern, Orad, and Taq. They carried quartered meat and a very large skin.

"Whew!" Stencellomak exclaimed to no one in particular, as he lowered his shoulder and let the hindquarter slide to the ground. "I'm not growing any younger and these animals are heavy! Look at the antlers on that head Orad's been carrying." The antlers were enormous and strangely shaped to the hunters' way of seeing deer. "That thing's not going to wander through any forest!" Stencellomak observed. "Those antlers would snag on trees!"

"It was a male giant deer bigger than any of us. It was feeding on water plants at a creek in a big open area high on that hill." Vole pointed to the north. "We killed the giant deer first. After we bled it and began to quarter it, Stencellomak saved my life from the cat," Moki said breathlessly. "The cat never made a sound. Look at those teeth!" The cat had extraordinarily long teeth that extended beyond its jaw; they were serrated on both sides. The fur was gray with black blotches on it, so it blended in the forest making it hard to see. It was very soft.

Lurch, Pod, Ragiel, and Sutorlo had come to help sink the meat quarters in the storage pond, eager to hear about the hunt. They realized the cat hadn't been bled, so they began to untie it.

"Wait on the cat, boys," Stencellomak said. "I have plans for that. I want the skin removed whole including the feet. Can you do that with extreme care?"

The boys looked at him. "The only one of us who's that good is Lurch. He's really good. Want him to skin it?" Ragiel asked.

"Lurch, do a good job with that skin," Stencellomak said firmly but smiling. "And I want the teeth."

"I will do my best work ever," Lurch promised. The boys carried the cat to the far north of the meadow and hung it up between two trees to bleed.

All could hear the rocks banging together announcing the evening meal. Item left the cooking area and went to the bent tree house. "Tuksook," she shouted from the west-facing entryway.

"I am here," came her daughter's voice from some distance.

Item shouted, "Come to eat. You should be fine. The sun is low."

Tuksook stood up and raced to the entryway. She was eager to go outside. Her mother was half way to the eating area. Tuksook thought she looked tired. She left the house and followed her mother. She hadn't been aware she was hungry, but the thought of food made her salivate.

Eilie joined Tuksook on the walk to the place where they filled their bowls with food. "Are you doing better now? I was afraid for you when I heard your screams."

"Staying out of the sun does help. I won't go near those plants again!"

"What does it look like inside the bent tree house?"

"It's just like the house in Ki'ti's time. Everyone has a bench/sleeping place that is their own place. It's larger than you can imagine inside. It's wonderful."

"Do you have to stay there tomorrow?"

"I have to stay there until this rash goes away."

"What do you do in there?"

"There's not enough to do. I'll take some sewing tomorrow. Today I watched the work and slept. At least when I sleep I don't think about the rash."

"I'm so sorry you had such pain. Tomorrow Hustep, Ubassu, Elfa and I will go to the southern meadow to dig up those plants. Your mother calls them mother of red rash. We'll put them on the trash heap to dry out and we'll burn the flowers and roots. It's a plant we want to discourage near our living place."

"I wish I could help."

"It's too dangerous for you to do it. Some of us may have a problem, but so far we don't know about it." We will be careful not to touch it if possible. We gathered lots of old leather pieces to protect our hands from touching the plants."

"Be very careful."

"Our plan is to knock down the mother of red rash, cut off the top and drag if off to the trash heap, and then dig up the root."

"That might work." Tuksook was thoughtful. What the girls were doing was kind, and she didn't want them to experience what she was experiencing. At the food preparation area Tuksook took some boiled greens that she didn't recognize and some fish. She was unsure what the fish was. She also took a small piece of meat that she guessed was the animal she'd taken when they were in the cave. It all tasted good.

Item finished eating and went to Tuksook. "Is the pain better?"

"Yes, Mother. Does the balm need to be changed?"

"I came to tell you to wash it off, and I'll put new balm on the rash. I'd also like to see how the covered areas are healing."

"I'll take your bowl to dump the remains of the bones," Eilie offered.

"Thanks, Eilie,"

Item and Tuksook left, Tuksook heading to the bathing area and Item to the lean-to for the balm she'd made earlier. Tuksook would be glad of freedom of the wraps even if only for a brief time. She didn't like the feeling of being wrapped.

Item arrived with mosses for drying and the balm and new pieces of leather for wrapping. She was tired but felt good. The day had been one of accomplishment and that always raised her spirits. She, Port, and Heek had scoured the area around their home and identified a few plants that were different from what they'd known in the past. They planned to feed the plants to the dogs to see what effect, if any, the plants would have. They would find that nothing in their meadow was poisonous to the dogs. Item was gentler with Tuksook than she had been earlier in the day. The balm seemed to be promoting the healing. Covered areas looked better than the place on her face. Item wrapped the one on her head. Tuksook didn't like the wrapping on her head, but she remained silent about it.

"We need to return to the council fire," Item said quietly.

Tuksook slipped on her tunic and the two headed to the fire.

The council meeting had just begun when they arrived.

Stencellomak was describing the location of their hunt. "When we reached the upper meadow over there, we saw the giant deer eating greens at the creek. It didn't recognize us as a threat at all. There must be no people anywhere near this place. We killed it easily and thanked it for providing us food. We bled it. I stood up to rest my back and noticed slight movement in the grass. I grabbed my spear. That cat was ready to leap on Moki. I caught the cat mid-air with my spear. It leaped right to my spear point."

"I hear you will have Lurch skin it whole. What do you plan to do with the skin?" Moki asked.

"Moki, I want to put the teeth on a cord to wear around my neck. The skin is for our flier. Wisdom used Tuksook to find this place. Tuksook definitely needs a new tunic. This will make a seamless tunic, fitting for our flier. We live in Eagle's Grasp because of her. It is a good place to live. I want the tunic made so it will fit her when she's grown. She's almost grown now. She can wear it when it's finished even if it's a bit too large now. Who will volunteer to make it when the skin is prepared?"

Everyone knew that Bruilimi sewed better than anyone else. She spoke up. "I will make an appropriate tunic as you desire, Stencellomak. I would consider it an honor." Bruilimi really wanted the challenge.

After her treatment earlier in the day from Gumui, Tuksook was not prepared for such kind words from elders. She did realize that the flying was something for which Wisdom, not she, was responsible. Tuksook was shocked that she'd been singled out for the honor. She nodded at Stencellomak and lowered her head as low as it would go. He smiled. She did the same toward Bruilimi. The elder smiled.

"Now that we have mentioned Tuksook, Item has something to share with the council," the Wise One said.

"Earlier today Tuksook had a bright red, painful rash from contact with the large stemmed, big leafed plant we now call mother of red rash. It has tiny flowers that appear to be a single large flat flower. They grow mainly in the south part of the meadow. The balm we used is effective to promote healing and ease the pain. Tomorrow Eilie, Hustep, Ubassu, and Elfa will dig up the plants to remove them from the meadow. Be careful if you brush against one. Apparently they bother some people and not others. Because the sun makes the rash worse, Tuksook is spending her days in the bent tree house at her place. She is not free to wander about until the rash is gone. Tomorrow she will be sewing there.

Mongo said, "Speaking of the bent tree house, how long before we can move in?"

Kew looked at Gumui. "I'm guessing we have about three to four more days' work. Is that right, Gumui?"

Gumui nodded. It felt awkward that just because the bent tree house had been his idea, all the men deferred to him as the authority. Gumui knew that Kew had answers to questions he'd never have reasoned out. Kew knew this was a time of learning for Gumui to become a leader. He was doing very well, Kew thought.

Taman announced, "There will be a time for young boys to learn spear making after the morning meal. Young girls can come, but this is planned for young boys learning hunting skills."

Wave said, "Back in our old country we had many snakes. I have not seen a single snake nor have I smelled one. Have any of you encountered a snake?"

All looked around. There was no response.

"I am beginning to wonder whether snakes live here," Wave said. "I'm happy if they don't."

The People laughed. Nobody really *liked* snakes.

Remui said, "Back to the hunt for a moment. While we were heading up to the high meadow, I saw a bear. It was one of those short faced ones that are tough predators. I do think we should keep alert for those. We have meat here, and that could attract them.

"Well reasoned, Remui," Ottu said. "Somehow, I think I'd take snakes over those bears."

No more contributions were forthcoming, so Midgenemo adjourned the meeting. People went to their lean-tos eager for the bent tree house to be ready.

The next day dawned with a brilliant golden sky. The morning meal brought sounds of happiness through the meadow. People laughed gently and talked of what the day might bring. Young boys were acting more maturely because they were looking forward to their time with Taman. They would be making spears. For most it would be their first spear. It was always a special time when an adult took the time to prepare them for hunting. After a class they were expected to practice the skills learned as part of their routine.

Wims, Unmo's youngest boy at age six, Col, Pago's son at age five, talked with Oneg and Nipe, Pago's twins aged six. Oneg was a girl and Nipe was a boy.

"Aggh! Fish bone!" Oneg exclaimed. "I hate fish bones!"

"Yes, but this new fish they call sturgeon tastes very good." Nipe talked with the white fish meat in his mouth, little bits falling to the ground. "I'm excited about spear making, but I also want so much to learn to row one of the new boats they're making."

"You've been down there?" Wims asked. "My father told me to stay up on this level."

"No, we have to stay here also. There's a tree near the dogs that grows out over the low land. You can climb out on it to see what's happening below." Oneg finished up, putting her bowl to the side.

"You'll have to show me," Wims said enthusiastically.

"When we go to empty the bowls, we can show you on the way back," Nipe said.

In another part of the meadow, Ren, Tuksook's six-year-old sister was trying to obtain permission to go to the hunter's school.

Item was becoming annoyed. "You will tend the infants, Ren, and I don't want to hear any more about it."

"Well, you know Oneg will go."

"Oneg thinks she's a boy," Item said absentmindedly.

"She does not!" Ren defended.

"Ren, this will stop now!" Item had grasped the child by the shoulder and held tight. Ren winced but made no sound.

Finally, Ren gritted between her teeth, "Someday, I'll be a great hunter like Tuksook!"

"That time is not now!" Item said firmly. "Once you learn to love tending children and have expertise in preparing skins and making a good evening meal, then we'll talk about your learning to hunt."

"Well, you love Tuksook better'n me. You always have," Ren whined.

Item slapped the child. Hard.

"Enough! You don't know what you're talking about. I love you. People don't measure love! Wisdom chose Tuksook for a purpose. Wisdom chose your father for a purpose. He chose you for a purpose. You are not ever to compare yourself with others. Each of us has a part in the life of the People. Each of us is equally valuable in doing what we're assigned to do. I have to work with plants to keep our People healthy. Today you'll take good care of children younger than you. In time you'll find what your special contribution to the People is. Your whining is despicable!"

Ren made no sound but tears made lines in the dust on her face. Item had managed to reach her and correct the wrong thinking. At least for this time. Item knew Ren compared herself to her older sister. She also knew that such comparisons were not Wisdom's way and they could foster bad resentments for the future. She noted in her mind web to watch for that behavior in this little one, so it did not become part of her. Item was assured that at least this day Ren would do as she was told. She let go of Ren and wiped the back of her hand across her own forehead to remove the sweat that formed there.

Tuksook had returned to the lean-to for additional sewing tools and heard the exchange. She felt sorry for Ren. She didn't like caring for children, but Ren didn't seem to mind. She'd observed Ren with the little ones realizing she was very good at what she did. The tiny ones loved her. She didn't know what to make of what she heard, so she quietly gathered what she needed and left for the bent tree house.

The women who sewed gave her some pre-cut mittens to sew. They were made from the small beaver pelts, not the giant beaver. She knew how to sew the mittens, loved the feel of beaver, and looked forward to having something to do. She sat on her bench/sleeping place and looked up to see Gumui walking toward her. She sighed.

"Did you think about what I told you yesterday?" he asked.

She folded her arms across her ribs. Then, she replied, "Gumui, why are you acting like my parent?"

He sat on the edge of her bench and looked into her eyes. "There is something you must learn. If you can learn it from me, that's good. If not, you'll have to learn it from a parent."

"What do you mean?" She guessed his meaning, but she felt very defensive.

"Tuksook, you're holding onto anger. That is not Wisdom's way. You must turn loose of the anger and forgive your father. You also must not give yourself permission to lie."

Tuksook looked down at her lap. Did other girls have young men to answer to like this? She wondered. Slowly she raised her head and saw his eyes burning into hers.

"I, I . . . Gumui, I can reason the release of anger to be replaced with forgiveness, but . . . but, I, well, the feelings in my belly stop the reason, as if I walked right into a tree."

Gumui heard her and tried to understand. For him forgiveness was such an easy thing. "And the lying?" he asked.

"I can stop myself from doing that. I've done it to try to make myself appear good in the eyes of others. That's wrong and I can reason it and sort out the feelings Wisdom's way."

"Promise me you'll never lie to me again."

"I promise," she said, thinking she meant it.

"Now, my precious Tuksook, what are you hiding?"

"I hide nothing," she said, thinking she spoke truthfully, forgetting her knowledge of the stories, which she carefully hid.

"You know that if you cannot resolve the anger forgiveness problem, I'll have to turn it over to your father to resolve, don't you?"

Tuksook had been sitting cross-legged on the bench. She jumped into a kneeling position. Gumui watched. He was fascinated and wanted to understand.

"You cannot do that, Gumui. Please, don't do that." Tuksook was leaning against the wall to avoid him.

"Why are you so afraid? You're acting like a little child."

"Don't turn me over to my father," she implored.

"Tuksook, your father is a gentle man. He won't hurt you."

"He'll suck the life out of me." Tuksook was almost growling.

"Okay, Tuksook. I want an explanation. Don't lie. Tell it to me straight, so I'll understand."

"I feel like a trapped animal, Gumui. Do you understand?"

"I don't think I understand. Help me, Wisdom," he said aloud to Wisdom as a prayer. Suddenly, he became calm. She realized Wisdom listened to him. She knew what it was to receive a satisfying answer from Wisdom. She was certain he'd just received one. She became even more agitated.

She crouched closer to the wall.

Gumui stood, reached out and picked her up and sat with her in his lap. He held her tight in his arms, rocking her as he'd rock a small child.

"You are going to tell me now what is at the bottom of all this. Whatever it is, I can help you, Tuksook, but you have to let me help you. Wisdom is with us. Let it out."

"Nooooooo," she said as if in terrible pain.

"Tuksook, I will not leave until you have explained this. If you continue to refuse, I shall take you to your father. He'll pull it out of you. I know you don't want that, so talk to me."

"If I tell you, you'll tell him."

"Is that what worries you?"

"Yes."

"Then, I will not tell him."

"You promise?"

"Yes, Tuksook, I vow unto Wisdom I will not tell him."

"I know the stories," she whispered.

"You what?" Gumui was completely astounded. When he asked what she was hiding, it never occurred to him it could be anything like knowing the stories.

"I know the stories," she whispered again.

Gumui cupped her head in his hands, forgetting the rash on her face. "Why haven't you said so?"

"Because it would end my days to myself. I'd be stuck to my father's side as a spear point is stuck to a spear. And I think I hate him."

Gumui realized he'd uncovered far more than he thought he'd find. And he'd vowed not to tell her father.

"You know that means you're the next Wise One."

"Of course, I know that. For someone who craves solitude, that's like death. I'll be followed all the rest of my life. I'll never have any time alone. My hunting will end. And, now, I don't want to be in my father's presence, because I cannot forgive him. I don't want my life to be spent always available to the People."

He held her tightly. "Tuksook, it doesn't matter what you want. What is—is. You are going to have to make this right."

She buried her head into his chest and wept silently. She knew he was right but wanted to put off the time of doing it.

When she calmed, he picked her up. He stood her on her bench and hugged her. She threw her arms around his neck and returned the hug. Again he could feel the presence of her breast buds against his chest and it swept his thoughts to another place. He knew he loved her. He'd loved her for years, ever since she became the little flier and he chose to look out for her. But he was also becoming attracted to her in a different way. It wasn't time yet—he knew.

Tuksook was devastated. Her secret was out. She knew something would have to happen soon, but she didn't know what or how. She trusted Gumui in a way she trusted no one else. He seemed to understand Wisdom and Wisdom's ways in a manner she wished her father did. She felt warm and safe when he hugged her, as he did now. He held her tight as if to protect her from all the terrible things in life, or so she felt. His scent pleased her. His strength was wonderful. She didn't want him ever to let go. He loosened his hold, kissed her forehead, and hugged her tight once more and then let go.

"We both must spend time reasoning in our mind webs," he said. "This silence about the stories cannot continue. And, Tuksook, you have to turn loose of your anger and forgive your father. He's just a man. Maybe you have to forgive him for being just a man. I don't know. Whatever the case, you have much to reason today while you sew. We will talk later."

"You will keep your vow?"

"Of course," he said slightly irritated that she'd ask. "You had better find some answers."

She felt as if he'd thrown cold water all over her. She sat back on her bench cross-legged and resumed sewing. Tuksook didn't want to think. She began the reasoning process in what seemed like troubled waters, where her anger, lack of forgiveness, and her secret about knowing the stories all glued up the smooth functioning of her mind web. As she did, she couldn't remove the feeling of Gumui's hug from the forefront of her mind web. Then, it occurred to her that she must look really odd with all the coverings on her arms, legs, and head. She wondered why Gumui spent time with her.

Anvel, Wave, Pago, and Hamaklob met Gumui at the central hearth and all went to the southern part of the house.

Tuksook had almost finished one mitten when one of the women began to beat the rocks together to call People to the evening meal. Gumui climbed down from the ceiling and walked over to Tuksook.

"Have you made progress?" he asked.

She showed him the mitten.

"You know that isn't what I meant."

"I know. I just don't want to have to do any of it, so it's very hard. I have reasoned it well. I just still have to match the feelings with the reasoning."

"Sometimes, Tuksook, you have to just go ahead and do something that's hard to do, simply because it's the right thing to do. Then, hopefully, the feeling will follow. If the feelings don't follow, then at least you did what was right."

"What if they don't?" She combed her fingers through the caribou fur. It was pleasing to her touch.

"Tuksook, listen carefully. You must do what's right. It doesn't matter what you want. Wisdom is in control. You have a bit more that complicates things, for Wisdom already uses you. You represent Wisdom, just as you say your father represents Wisdom. Can you condemn him—and, then, do the same thing for which you condemn him? I don't think so. Well, you could, but it would be wrong. Maybe that's part of your anger. You see in him what you see in yourself—and you know it's wrong in both of you. I should remind you that your father has turned from his wrong way. You have not."

"I know what you say is right. I just cannot bring myself to forgive him."

"What do you think you're missing?" He wanted to know what she didn't understand about forgiving.

Tuksook's response reflected a totally different meaning of his question. "I want to explore this land, camp out, hunt, and have solitude with Wisdom to prepare for the time to come. If I admit I know the stories, I'll never be able to do that. I want to know this new land before I am caged."

Gumui and Tuksook were almost to the entryway. Nobody was in the bent tree house. Gumui put his hand on her shoulder. "Let us continue to think on this," he said huskily. "There has to be a solution." They left the bent tree house and headed over to the big log where the evening meal awaited them. Each took a bowl, filled it with a variety of food, sat together in the shade, ate, and didn't speak a single word. When both were finished they walked to the trash heap and emptied their bowls. They returned to the council area hand-in-hand silently.

56

Gumui looked at her as they prepared to separate. "Wisdom has already forgiven Midgenemo. Who do you think you are to withhold forgiveness?" He turned and walked toward his lean-to.

Tuksook froze. So many times Gumui said things that made her think, but it also showed her to be small-hearted towards her father. How could Gumui want to spend time with someone who was ugly, covered with a nasty rash, and was small-hearted? Did he only think of her as a child needing correcting, someone he'd become accustomed to guiding, because he watched over her when she flew? Someone like a dog on a trek? She wanted to cry but didn't dare. He had become special to her. She wanted to be special to him. She went to the lean-to and snuggled under the skin covering.

In the far distance, Tuksook heard what sounded like a big cat fight. There was howling and hissing and growling. It was far in the distance. She wondered how many People heard it. Just as she was about to fall to sleep, she felt a little one crawl next to her, snuggling up with her little back next to her belly. Tuksook put her arm around Ren pulling her close. Ren snuggled closer.

Morning arrived with a heavy rain. Item had gone to the log where covers protected the morning meal. She filled bowls for Tuksook, Nal, Ren, Gel, and herself. To have filled bowls for the men and older boys would have been inappropriate by their custom. They ate happily for food was always good.

"Tuksook, even though it's raining, I think you should go to the bent tree home to continue your sewing. The sun could come out from the clouds."

"I will," Tuksook acknowledged.

"Ren, you are still needed to help with the little ones. Take Gel with you."

"I will," she acknowledged just as Tuksook had.

"Nal, are you going to be with Taman today?" she asked.

"Yes, Mother. We're making tools."

"You'd better hurry. You know he doesn't like People to arrive late."

"I will."

"Do I need new balm?" Tuksook asked.

"Come here by the light and let me take a look at that," Item replied.

Item untied the leather wrapping on Tuksook's upper right leg. That was the worst place she'd been affected. Surprisingly the red was gone and the rash had flattened. It looked very good.

"I think the wrappings can be removed. Put them in that corner," Item pointed to the southwest corner of the lean-to.

Carefully, Tuksook untied the leather strips and folded them so the balm side was inside the skins. She knew Item would wash them for another use. Tuksook enjoyed the freedom from the wrappings. She wiped the excess balm from her skin. Quietly, she gathered her sewing things and returned to the bent tree house.

At the bent tree house Tuksook sat on her bench/sleeping place and felt surrounded with how it would be to live there. She could imagine the rush of the morning meal served where People didn't have to be concerned about weather. She could imagine women having babies there, even herself. She could see the storage place well stocked with food, skins, tools, spears. Tuksook could imagine older women making rope and men reshaping a broken tool. She could imagine the older children teaching songs and dances to the younger ones. She could imagine the cold time stories—even herself telling them at the large hearth. She could hardly wait to move in and watch the expressions on the faces of those who hadn't seen inside yet. After all the years of hearing of the bent tree house in Ki'ti's time, the place was more spectacular than she could have imagined. Little wonder it was in the stories.

Tuksook saw Gumui coming towards her from the far end of the structure. Suddenly her bold thoughts of the future shriveled as she looked at her leg where the rash was healing. She was a mess. She had done her hair and picked her teeth, but she still had ugly hair color and a rash all over. She was just a child after all.

"I see you have your wrappings removed. That's good, Tuksook. How do you feel?"

"Fine. And you?"

"I feel wonderful this morning. I have some thoughts."

Gumui stood before her, his shins almost touching the bamboo of her bench. Tuksook inhaled the scent of him. His reddish chest hair glinted in a few places, catching light from the smoke hole. She thought he was the best looking of all the People. His muscles were so beautifully formed. She wanted to touch him but instead she listened. She hoped it wasn't about forgiveness again. She looked into his face, wondering.

Gumui stood straight and tall. His eyes pierced hers. "After we've moved into this new place and settled in, I would like to spend the number of days as there are fingers on my two hands exploring the area. I will ask the Wise One if he will permit you to accompany me. I could use your flying as a reason for you to go."

It was not at all what Tuksook expected to hear. "Do you think he would let me go?"

"I can't know until I ask. I'd prefer not to guess." He smiled his broad smile showing beautiful white teeth.

"Thank you, Gumui. You'd let me enjoy some solitude on the trek?"

"Of course, and I'd watch over you while you talk with Wisdom. Tuksook, if we explore together, you must tell your father about the stories when you return."

"I'm afraid to think of it, but I vow to Wisdom that I will. Such an exploration is beyond anything I could ever wish to experience."

"I will start talking about it so that he's not surprised when I ask that you accompany me. Tonight at council we'll probably announce the move for tomorrow. I'm excited that the time is just about here. I'm pleased with the work we've put into the structure. It's strong. It should be a good place to live. I expect, though, to find things that need to be adjusted when People start to live here."

To Tuksook, Gumui looked so confident. He was a man, she realized, a young one, but a man. He had great responsibility for the bent tree house, and he'd done well. She'd overheard older men, even elders, speaking of his skill in working with other men, many of whom were older, to assure the place was built well.

"Why are you looking at me like that?" he asked.

"Because I'm so proud of what you've done." For the moment Gumui had become more than a man in her eyes. He was heroic in her eyes as she thought of the bent tree house and his offer to let her accompany him on his adventure.

"I only had the idea. Many have built this place."

"That makes me more proud of you," she said quietly.

"That's nice of you to say. Now, I must start this day's work." He turned and walked off in the direction from which he'd come. She noticed how he moved, strong, purposeful, reasoned. His idea of a ten-day trek thrilled her. Somehow, Midgenemo would have to permit her to go with him. It was the most wonderful adventure she could ever have. She desperately wanted to go. Tuksook settled down to start sewing and had difficulty focusing on the task as excited as she was.

Gumui was half way up a wall by the central hearth when he noticed Midgenemo entering the bent tree house. The man was looking at every detail, clearly delighted.

"There you are," Midgenemo said to Gumui, "This is wonderful."

Tuksook could hear them talking. She froze.

Gumui climbed down and smiled at the man. "I'm very happy with the construction. It's almost finished."

"When you suggested the bent tree house on the meadow, I had no idea you'd make it work so well. The crossed building construction is an excellent idea, and I hear the idea was yours."

Gumui lowered his head. "Thank you, Wise One," he replied.

"Is there anything special I can do for you?" Midgenemo asked.

Gumui didn't know whether to ask about the exploration with Tuksook, but decided that an opportunity like this one would not likely come again. Tuksook held her breath, knowing what he was considering.

"There is one thing I'd like to ask of you. After the People move here and we discover any changes that need to be made and we fix them, I would like to take an exploration of the area for the number of days as there are fingers on my two hands, maybe a little more. I would like to have Tuksook accompany me." The words were spoken. Gumui had asked the question far sooner than he planned. He tried to see what the Wise One might be thinking by examining his face. The Wise One knew how to control his face.

Tuksook barely dared to breathe. She felt as if her world hung on her father's reply. She thought, if you say yes, Father, I shall forgive you immediately. She fully expected him to refuse so she could hate him all the more.

After much time Midgenemo replied, "She attracts you, doesn't she?"

"Yes, she does, but I have put that away for a future time. She is too young yet. But, yes, I find her special and would like to join with her in the future. I would not act on any of that until she becomes woman and makes it clear she wants to pursue that too. Right now I would like to be with her and to have her ability to fly available to me on the exploration. We'd be camping light, and she's a good hunter."

"If at some future time she wants you, you have my approval. You are a fine young man. I will give you permission to take her with you on this adventure. Do not treat her as an adult. She is still clearly a child. Treat her as a child. Do not permit her to wander off. I give you my authority over her while you are gone."

"Thank you, Wise One, I will do what you say." Gumui had to hold himself tightly. He wanted to jump around and shout to free the energy he felt, having received two replies that he never anticipated. He had wanted to give Tuksook time for her solitude with Wisdom, while he studied the land and food animals. He was certain his hope was too big. It wasn't.

"Tuksook," Midgenemo said loud from the central hearth. "I have given Gumui permission to take you with him on his adventure which will come soon. You are to go with him and obey him. You must help him. Is that clear?"

"Very clear, Father," Tuksook acknowledged. "I will obey and cause him no trouble." Silently, she said in her mind web, Wisdom, I forgive my father. Please make the feeling of forgiveness follow my decision to forgive.

"Young man," Midgenemo said, "I will leave you to your work. When will we move here?"

"We plan to announce tonight that tomorrow we move."

"I suppose you are as eager as the rest of us?"

"Yes, Wise One. I want to live here very much."

Midgenemo left the way he entered—from the south-facing entry. He chose not to seek out which place was his. He wanted some surprise remaining for the day of the move. As it was, he was totally unprepared for the luxury of the new home. Everything would have its place. Everyone would have a place. He wondered why they hadn't used this design more often. He smiled when he realized that Gumui cared very deeply for his daughter. They would be well joined. If anyone could encourage Tuksook to become a good woman, he thought Gumui could.

For the time it took Gumui to empty his bag of mud, the two attended to their tasks. When Gumui climbed down the wall, he walked to Tuksook's place.

"I can't believe it was that easy. It's almost as if this trek were meant to be," he said. "Wisdom must want this."

Tuksook looked at him wide-eyed. "I can't believe he said what he did. Gumui, before he gave you permission, I told Wisdom that if my father said I could go with you, I'd forgive him. I had to do that. I have forgiven him. Now, I hope that my feelings will follow, and that I'll stop condemning him every time I look at him."

Gumui smiled. He wanted to hug her, but he remained where he stood. "I'm glad, Tuksook. If you feel yourself about to condemn him, stop yourself immediately and think of other things. You have forgiven him. It's over. I'll be watching. I haven't forgotten you're a child."

"I will," Tuksook replied. There it was again. He was adult; she, child. To her his comment contained a threat. She knew he wasn't happy about her lack of forgiveness. Suddenly it occurred to her that Wisdom might have caused her father to agree, just to test her own resolve to forgive. There was a story that had a similar message. Tuksook couldn't recall it quickly. She knew she was on dangerous ground if she failed to forgive. She wondered whether she'd been wise to ask for permission to accompany Gumui based on forgiving her father, but it was done. She had to live with the consequences of her request. Those thoughts clashed with the joy Tuksook felt that she was free to accompany Gumui, and if they chose to join in the future, Gumui already had permission.

In the meadow Taman's students were free until high sun. Wims ran, calling to Oneg.

"What is it, Wims?" she asked.

"I still haven't seen the tree that overlooks the boats below. Will you show me now?"

"Sure." She smiled at Nipe. "You want to see if Col wants to go too?"

Nipe said, "Yes. Wait here until I return."

Moments later Nipe and Col came running. The four walked off to the northeast part of the meadow and then to the meadow's edge where trees grew and then there was a steep dropoff. With care each crawled out on the tree trunk that grew horizontally from the bank. Showing off, Oneg decided to walk instead of crawl on the tree trunk. She caught her foot in a rough place in the bark, and she let out a piercing scream as she lost her balance and tumbled backwards to the ground below. The boys were terrified. Nipe reached the meadow first and found Pago, his father. His mother, Bit-n came running with strips of leather and some straight pieces of wood as soon as she heard Oneg had fallen.

"I'm too dizzy to stand up," Oneg complained. "My left leg hurts a lot and my left arm." Bit-n realized the girl was in better condition than she expected. The left leg bones in the lower leg were sticking through the skin. That was not a good sign. Bit-n temporarily splinted the leg. Oneg's arm had dislocated, but it wasn't broken. Bit-n pulled the arm back into place while Oneg's screams pierced the quiet. They lifted her to a stretcher and carried her to the shower area. Bit-n was fanatical about washing injured skin thoroughly, and this would be no exception. She washed the wound, realigned the bones, though her daughter screamed loud enough to notify every living creature in Eagle's Grasp of their presence. Suddenly the noise ceased. Oneg had fainted. Bit-n put together everything she could think to use to keep infection away. She sewed the torn flesh back together using hairs from Oneg's head that she rinsed in the waterfall. Then she covered the wound with honey and wrapped the leg carefully—tight enough to hold the bones in place, but loose enough to keep the leg from tingling or becoming numb. The bones had been set the best they possibly could be. It would take time to know how well the injury would heal. Meanwhile, Oneg was immobilized. When she waked up, Bit-n gave her something to drink to ease the pain.

Item called all the People together by beating the rocks together as if she were announcing the evening meal. Once all gathered, she explained that

Oneg had fallen from the tree that overhung the lowland. She told all the young ones that they were not permitted to climb out on the tree. She also told older people that it wasn't a good idea for them either. People chuckled, but all knew she was making a rule for every single one of the People and they'd better do what she told them—stay off the leaning tree. In many ways she was the mother of the People.

Item also told the people they had a complete lack of red sphagnum moss, which would help with Oneg's healing. She asked for a large supply, and reminded the People that the moss needed to be picked clean of objects tangled in it. She said if they couldn't find red, the light colored would be a second best.

Later that evening the last item on the council was from Gumui. The young man had rarely spoken at council and he felt a bit anxious. He wanted to be seen as a man by the People, but he was still young. He cleared his throat and began to speak, "The bent tree house is ready. After the morning meal tomorrow, begin to move your things. Unmo, Pago, Hamaklob, and I will show you where your bench/sleeping places are and where to store tools, spears, food, herbal cures, and so on. We ask you to keep in your mind webs anything that needs to be fixed or changed as you become familiar with your places. Let us know so we can fix problems as soon as they're discovered."

Murmurs went all around reflecting the excitement the People felt. All were eager to move. As the murmuring continued and there was nothing else to add, Midgenemo adjourned the meeting. He glanced at Gumui and Tuksook. How easy it was to see that she was captivated by him. Yes, he thought to himself, she'd be obedient and helpful on the trek. She would want to please the young man. She would want him to have no bad thoughts of her. She was growing up. Not there yet, but growing up.

When morning arrived it was difficult for the People to focus on the morning meal. Everyone was eager to move, but they had to do what was expected first. Little by little, People finished and dumped the remains from their bowls at the trash heap and rinsed the bowls in the wooden container that was filled with water. They turned the bowls upside down on the log and headed to a gathering place near the meadow's edge by the bent tree house. There they stood or sat waiting patiently until they were free to go in.

Finally, Gumui stood before them. He began, "May Wisdom bless and keep this house. Let us dedicate it to peace among us. I have taken a stone at the center. I placed my open hand for peace on the stone. I blew red ochre around my hand to preserve the Spirit of Peace that resides here. Let it be a reminder. This is the west entry. Hamaklob will take Taman's whole family and Mongo's whole family through this part of the house past the central hearth to the south part of the building. That is where their personal bench/sleeping places are. They will go in first. Pago will lead Kew's whole family and Ottu and Bruilimi, along with Loraz's family and Anvel's family to the east part of the building. You'll find extra storage areas in that part of the house near the entry. They will enter second. Then, Unmo will lead his family and Midgenemo's family to the west part of the building. They will go in third. Finally, those of you who store things come to find me once you've seen your bench/sleeping places. We have storage in the south part of the building, the west part, and the whole north part of the building is storage. There is storage above on racks made of the cross pieces overhead. I'll introduce you to the storage areas."

He nodded to Hamaklob. "Taman and Mongo, please lead your families to follow Hamaklob." Quietly the People began to file through the entry into the bent tree house. Those outside could hear comments, "Look at that!" "This is wonderful!" "The central hearth is already lit." "Who'd have ever thought . . . ?"

Gumui nodded to Pago. "Kew's family, Ottu and Bruilimi, and Loraz's family, please follow Pago." In very orderly manner the People followed Pago. Momeh carried Oneg, since her father, Pago, was busy showing People their places. Again, those waiting outside could hear the comments from the People who were seeing the place for the first time.

Gumui nodded to Unmo. "Midgenemo, please lead your family to follow Unmo. Unmo will also lead his family to their bench/sleeping places." Finally, the remaining people could see why the others had been exclaiming. It was truly a sight to see.

Once Item and Midgenemo were shown their bench/sleeping place, they both stared at the covering. Orad and Lurch were grinning. Finally, they told of taking the giant beaver and then working the skins the best they possibly could as a surprise for their parents. Item felt the pelt and it was so soft she was overwhelmed. Midgenemo also felt the prized skin. He was deeply touched that his sons would do that for them. He reached out and hugged both of them. Item did the same.

"I don't know that I've ever been so touched in my life," Midgenemo said trying to control his voice.

"I'm just so proud of you," Item said.

The boys couldn't stop grinning. Tuksook was delighted for her parents. She felt a stab of unforgiveness where her father was concerned, and then quashed the feeling and smiled at both of them.

They had a functioning home in the new land. Though none had ever seen a bent tree house, it somehow felt right, a tie with one of their bigger-than-life ancestors named Ki'ti, built by another bigger-than-life ancestor named Wamumur. What astounded the People was the amazing amount of room the house provided. Between the central hearth and the north part of the house, there was a big log. No one had to ask its purpose. There they'd find the choices for the evening meal laid out there, when they couldn't eat outside.

Gumui stood outside enjoying the warmth of the sun on his skin. He smiled as he heard the sounds of the People happy in their new home. He felt a great sense of relief and contentment. It took a lot longer than he expected for the men and women who had things to store to come back outside. There were already places for storing herbs, stones for making spear points, sticks for spears, skins of a wide variety and left over pieces for many uses, jerky, nets for fishing, cold time clothing, boots, hats, glue pots, ropes, containers. The list seemed endless to him. He knew that Unmo and Item had better understanding of all the details than he did.

Unmo came outside. "They are really happy, Gumui, you did well."

"It wasn't I—it was many of us."

"Young man, you organized it. Without you, we'd still be working on it. You found efficient ways of doing things. We'd all heard the stories, but you seemed to have the plans built into your mind web. I enjoyed working with you. I never came to you and asked what needed to be done and had you give me no answer. You kept track of all that needed doing and the order in which it needed to be done. Again, I say, you did well."

"Thank you, Unmo. It means much to me to hear you say that."

"You've given us a gift. We won't be forgetting it. I like the reminder of peace among us."

More men emerged. Clearly the bent tree house far exceeded everyone's expectations.

They went inside and began to talk about the storage.

As time went on, a piece of mud from the ceiling fell to the floor. Gumui took some leather strips and wove them to the limbs that made the roof. He gathered mud and carried it up there using hand holds, covering the limbs along with the leather strips so it would hold better. In the southern portion of the house, one end of Wave and Cadpo's sleeping place broke apart and that had to be repaired. One of the bins that the People had used on the boat broke. It had been moved to the bent tree house to a storage area designed to hold stones for making tools. One side split, so the bin was attached to another bin and the wall that had split shared the unbroken wall of the attached bin.

Finally, one evening Gumui went to Midgenemo and told him that he planned to leave to explore the next morning. Midgenemo told him to be sure to take plenty of jerky and to make sure that Tuksook carried her share. Item overheard and asked what they were discussing.

Midgenemo told Item he'd given permission for Gumui to take Tuksook on his exploration of the Eagle's Grasp area, so if he needed someone to fly, she'd be there. He explained that he waited to fix whatever might need fixing on the bent tree house, but he was ready to explore the area. Item was dumbfounded that he'd given permission for Tuksook to accompany a young man alone on such a trek. She thought the idea of his need for her to fly was preposterous, but kept silent about it.

"Listen, Item," Midgenemo tried to explain. "Gumui eventually wants to join with Tuksook, if and when she's ready. He's as aware as you and I that the time is not yet. He's a young man who's responsible and wise beyond his years. I think this trek would be good for both of them."

For some reason that Item could not understand, the idea seemed somehow acceptable. She too liked Gumui. She decided not to try to change Midgenemo's mind web. Instead, she found a bag into which she'd put herbs for taking care of minor problems they might encounter. She'd go over the contents with Tuksook.

After the evening meal and the council, the People settled down to sleep. Tuksook was so excited that she could hardly slow her mind web to allow for sleep. She looked across the part of the bent tree house where her sleeping place was and saw that Gumui was moving about trying to find a comfortable spot. So, he also was excited about the adventure, she thought. She forced herself to calm as if she were going to talk with Wisdom, and she fell asleep.

Chapter Three

Gumui had been awake for a brief time. He touched Tuksook on the shoulder. She opened her eyes and excitement flooded her. She stood quickly, eager to start the journey. When she returned from her run to the privy, she saw that Gumui had put on his backpack and was ready to help her put on hers. She folded the covering on her sleeping place. She turned to see Gumui attaching a water bladder to her backpack just as he had to his own. He helped her shrug on her backpack. He picked up the spears he'd set aside before going to sleep. He handed her two of them. While the People slept, the two walked quietly from the bent tree house. They crossed to the center of the meadow where a central bamboo pole stuck up from the ground. Tuksook walked directly to the pole and touched it flat-handed with her fingers pointing upward, leaving her hand to rest there. The pole was significant. To her it symbolized Wisdom's way of being prepared. There were a few other poles in the meadow. They all related to the central pole.

Tuksook whispered, "Spirit of the Rising and Setting Sun. Remain in the laws of Wisdom that guide you while we are gone from our People." It was a prayer, not an order.

The People loved the new land, but they had to make one strange adjustment. It had to do with light. The sun's position in the south indicated high sun. Sun in the northeast indicated daybreak. Sun in the northwest indicated the setting sun. At night it was possible to see to work. The sun would dip below the horizon, but there was still residual light in the sky by which to see. The People had to force themselves to sleep in light, so that they obtained adequate rest. When they arrived in the new land, the elders placed bamboo poles in the ground to mark the sunrise and sunset in relation to geologic features such as a mountaintop or a valley at the top of a mountain. Before a man became a hunter, he was obligated to learn how to set up and use poles for markers. They checked the markers daily as long as the sky wasn't too cloudy. They needed to know what the new land would tell them about life there. They wanted to fix the equinoxes and solstices for an index to seasons, so they had an estimate of how they related to the cold time. They lived in the present but always prepared for the cold time. The People realized that the sun's duration in the sky was lengthening. They agreed they should have time to gather food to last through the cold time. Women began the call to the evening meal when the sun was in the west. That provided time for eating and cleaning up, time for council, and time to prepare children for sleep. Then, the adults would sleep. Some had to pull skins over their heads to keep out light in order to sleep in what they considered light of day. They hoped it would be easier in the bent tree house than the lean-tos. The first few days in the bent tree house were encouraging.

The two left the central pole and headed toward the north, past the dogs, to the stone path that led east into mountains. They crossed to another path that led north. Tuksook did not know the way Gumui planned to go. She was filled with joy just to be accompanying him. As they left, questions began to come to her. Where was he going? When could she have some quiet time with Wisdom? How far would they travel that day? There was a morning quiet as the sun shone on clouds that looked like gold. There was also a bright pink to the sky. It was so lovely that it did not invite her to speak. She simply enjoyed the beauty of the morning and knew that one way or another, her questions of the day would find answers.

Some ancient force carved the path they followed. Land above the path appeared to have broken off a little more than the width of a man's shoulders from the land on which they walked. Gumui learned of the path from the hunters who recently brought the cat skin. It was a good path, because it was a level rock ledge on which there was no soil to encourage plant growth. The two walked in shadow once they reached the rock ledge, because the mountaintops blocked the sun. They could see the river to their left. As Tuksook saw it from this perspective, she remembered the flight. She could see where they were in relation to the whole.

Tuksook kept watching Gumui in front of her. He'd wrapped his soft aurochs skin around his shoulders after he'd put on his backpack. It served as his sleeping skin and as a wrap to ward off the cold. It was pinned in the front with a piece of fowl leg bone rounded at the ends. Tuksook's skins were rolled and tied atop her backpack. She wore a cloak for warmth made of the pelts of many rabbits. Women wove the pelts together from strips. The women didn't want to put much stress on rabbit pelts because they were weak skins. The way they wove the skins gave them flexibility. The effect of the woven pelts made the cloak attractive, warm, and soft. Her cloak had a hood. Rabbit cloaks provided good warmth, but they didn't last long. Her cloak was white and gray. The pelts came from the old land. Like her tunic, someone had used the cloak before Tuksook wore it. Because of the fragility of the cloak pelts, her cloak in back went over the backpack, not under it.

As high sun neared, the path led out onto a lovely meadow. There were camels grazing at the far east end and bison with young browsing or resting toward the southern part of the meadow. Gumui used hand signals to tell her to follow him and remain quiet. They went to a place where they could see the whole meadow, but they were partly hidden among young birch trees that grew close together with some interspersed spruce. Gumui signaled her to help him remove the aurochs skin. He laid it out on the ground, helped her remove her backpack, and motioned for her to sit on the skin. He removed his backpack and sat near her. Gumui watched the wildlife intently. He wanted to study the animals to know their ways. He let her know they'd be there for quite some time. If she remained where she sat, she would have plenty of solitude.

Tuksook had never been so close to anyone when she met with Wisdom. For a time she simply sat there watching the animals and watching Gumui watch the animals. It occurred to her that his study was for hunter knowledge of the ways of camels and bison in this place.

Slowly she began to turn loose of the world in which she lived to drift to the world of the spirit, a timeless, formless place that Wisdom created for her benefit—a place where she could meet Wisdom apart from her tangible world. It was a place where Wisdom took on a form that Tuksook would recognize and understand. She knew it represented Wisdom—it was not Wisdom. At last, she was there in a room-like cave with brilliant white walls. She'd been there on other occasions. Wisdom rested on a large carved stone with a wall behind for leaning back a small amount. Wisdom's feet were on the ground. The ground was like a dark, clear blue stone. It had the appearance of great depth. Two white steps bordered the sides of Wisdom's resting place. She climbed the steps, walking in the spirit to Wisdom. Wisdom's hair was white and there was much of it. In some ways it struck Tuksook as bright white light directed outward in many directions. Wisdom wore a long, white leather tunic. Tuksook would not ask from what animal it was made. She'd never seen an animal that could produce such a large pelt. At the top of the two stone steps, she threw her arms around Wisdom's bent knee, where she rested her head. She felt welcome, for she knew she was. Wisdom's large hand rested upon her head lightly.

"May I speak?" Tuksook asked.

"Of course," Wisdom replied in a deep voice that seemed born of the sea.

"Wisdom, I know recently I disappointed you."

"You displeased me."

"I have forgiven my father. I will not lie again."

"You forgave your father for gain. You will lie again."

"Does that mean I failed to forgive him?" Tuksook purposely ignored the second part.

"It means you forgave him in words and perhaps in deed—but not in spirit."

"There are so many levels!" Tuksook complained.

"Tuksook, there are as many levels as there are. That is my way. I establish the levels. You have to stop your self-centeredness. Complaining of levels is self-centeredness. You will be Wise One—not Wisdom. You can replace a Wise One, but you cannot replace me. Already you cannot recall the stories fast enough. You must practice daily. Your People depend on this. When the present adventure for you ends, you will tell your father about knowing the stories. You will tell him that you visit me. You will admit truthfully that you withheld the knowledge to prolong your childhood. If he punishes you for hiding the information, you will accept it without a word. You will begin to practice the stories daily. That is my way."

"I understand," Tuksook replied slightly trembling. She adored Wisdom yet was fully imbued with fear of this being. Still she wondered whether she might find a way to prolong her childhood.

She shielded her eyes from Wisdom's face from which colors of red, orange, yellow, and white streamed out, colors through which she could see, but brilliant enough to exceed the comfort of her eyes. They emerged as if from an enraged hearth fire. Wisdom's dark eyes flashed occasional glints of light blue, as if the light emanated from flame.

In a very deep voice with no compassion, Wisdom said, "Your thoughts are unacceptable. How would you feel to return to your new bent tree house to find every one of the People dead?" A smaller-than-life visual occurred on the floor near Wisdom's feet. It showed Tuksook exploring along the river bank, skipping a stone on the water's surface, while in the meadow above the People were dying off one by one. In the visual, she climbed to the meadow to discover she was alone. She knew the visual wasn't real, but it was as if she could watch herself there, viewing it from above. The images were completely life-like, not misty at all.

Tuksook slid out from beneath Wisdom's hand and looked directly upon the face that was at first compassionate and now seemingly brutal with intensified flame-like colors emanating from it. She was shocked. She knew great anger existed in Wisdom, but she'd never seen this much of it. She knew Wisdom had destroyed people in other places. There were some things Wisdom would not accept. Tuksook didn't know what they were, simply that there were some. Had this been a place like her world, Tuksook was certain a big wind would have blown her off her feet.

"Why respond to me in such a way, Tuksook? All I have done is to show you to yourself. Truth. You continue to want to prolong your childhood? You do so and your People could perish. Learn, Tuksook. Stop putting yourself first in your mind web and belly."

"I'm sorry, Wisdom," Tuksook said sincerely.

"I don't care to hear about your sorrow. Your sorrow can be compared to your having a belly ache. You focus completely on self. I want to know that you have fully understood and your self-centeredness is dead. You belong to me. It is not the other way around. Your People depend on you now and in the future. Your life is lived for them—not yourself. You must learn to give strength to many. Prepare yourself at this time, so you will be ready. You are no longer a child."

In her instinctive way she blurted out, "My father thinks I am."

Wisdom picked her up with a finger and a thumb, as if she were an undesirable bug. She dangled over his chest. "Tuksook. Do not speak again unless I give you permission. You fail to listen. Now, LISTEN." Wisdom put her back down in the same place where she'd been standing.

Tuksook lowered her head as low as she could, stretching her neck, she knelt beside Wisdom on the second step, scarcely breathing.

"You resent your father's authority. I tell you, I am the one with authority over you. I give him permission to have authority over you even as he has given Gumui permission to have authority over you. You are too blind and ignorant to realize that you need People to have authority over you, because of your childish self-centeredness. I didn't choose to use you because you're smart or clever. I chose to use you because I chose you. You did nothing to earn it or deserve it. Is that clear?"

Tuksook nodded.

"I did not choose you because you are special and, you are not special because I chose you. Is that clear?"

Tuksook nodded.

Wisdom said, "You think Ki'ti was special because she became Wise One?"

Tuksook started to reply, but she remembered not to speak, looked up at Wisdom, and nodded affirmatively. She felt pressed to the earth, as if a mammoth foot stood atop her back, so she unfolded herself from kneeling on the second step to lying on her belly on the step.

"Ki'ti was not useful to me until she lost most of her self-centered pride. She and you are not more special than others. That is not my way. She was far easier to reach than you, but she was not easy. That is a condemnation of your way and hers. I could choose a rock to deliver the information to the People. I could choose a bison or a cloud. In this case, I chose you. Ki'ti would be heartbroken to know of your self-centeredness. She is, after all, your ancestor."

Tuksook was ripped apart. She hurt too greatly to cry. She felt as if all that lay within her had been vomited to the earth. She wondered whether this is how it felt to die.

"No," Wisdom said flatly.

Tuksook crept quietly to the ground where she continued to lie flat upon her belly. She felt completely empty and did not understand the "No." She looked at the dark blue ground which seemed to move below the surface in a spiral.

"No, this is not what it is to die. Death is nothing but a new beginning in the spirit world and is nothing to fear. What faces you now—that is something to fear. What if by your flippant responses, I chose to let you and Gumui return to a place where all the People had perished?"

She looked at Wisdom. The terror on Tuksook's face spoke much.

"Your People depend on you NOW," Wisdom thundered. "What happens many years from now depends on what you do this day."

Tuksook trembled uncontrollably. She coughed quietly. The spiral below her seemed to gain width and depth. The speed of its rotation slightly increased.

"Their survival depends on you from now until the day you die. Do you finally understand what this means?"

She raised her head, nodded, and looked directly into Wisdom's eyes.

"I will speak to them through you. They must respect you to respect me. You lost respect for your father. All have forgiven him and freed their mind webs of his error except you. Why? Because you have more awareness of the responsibility that lies on the shoulders of the Wise One. It is no light responsibility I have given you. I don't have to ask your permission to give it to you. You have to receive it. Tuksook, you must become a person the People can trust to do what's right—now and always. The People must know that you represent me. You cannot do that, if you put yourself first even for a moment. You just saw what happened when your father made a judgment that came from him, not me. Fail to prepare and that's what will become of you. The time for you to prepare is now. You have put it off too long. Your father is fully able to prepare you. I have spoken."

Tuksook lay on the ground face down. She was fully broken.

After long silence, Wisdom said, "Tuksook stand."

Slowly, she stood. She was near Wisdom's feet, standing on the blue ground.

"On this trek, Gumui will learn much for the hunters. You will learn much of what I expect from you. You may speak."

"I love you, Wisdom," Tuksook admitted sincerely.

"I know," came the reply, as if from the voice of great waters. Wisdom's face was calm, filled with compassion. "I love you, Tuksook."

Tuksook nodded and lowered her head. Slowly she returned to the meadow. Tuksook was no longer seated. She lay on her back. She wondered how she changed position. She moved slightly to find Gumui's hand on her belly, pressing down, cautioning her. Tuksook opened her eyes and saw a bison just outside the line of trees where they protected themselves from the animals. She lay perfectly still. Her mind web remained filled with the visit to Wisdom, but Tuksook was acutely aware that she must not move in this present, tangible world. Her solitude with Wisdom was not what she'd been anticipating. She would have to reason.

Tuksook looked at the hairs near the browsing bison's nose. She looked at its head. She wanted to laugh at the thought of Wisdom using a bison to tell the People what they needed to know. After the stress of the meeting Tuksook wanted to laugh and laugh. But that bison was no bison to talk to the people! To avoid an explosion of laughter, she fought hard and finally succeeded in moving the thoughts of a talking bison to some more distant place in her mind web.

Eventually the bison turned and moved away. Gumui whispered that they would leave. He shook out, folded, and rolled the aurochs skin they'd sat on, and he tied it to his backpack. Tuksook laid her cloak over the top of her backpack. They continued north.

While Gumui was delighted to have had the opportunity to observe the camels and bison, Tuksook was overwhelmed with the experience she'd had. Finally, she'd had her time with Wisdom and it had completely turned her life around. For the rest of her life, Tuksook would never forget the life-changing moment when Wisdom showed her what it would be to return to the People to find all had perished while she played. The effect of that simple, visually charged moment would forever caution Tuksook to stay in Wisdom's way. She knew Wisdom's way wasn't like her statement that if her father let her take the trek, she'd forgive him. Wisdom wasn't warning her to do specific things or else there would be severe consequences. Wisdom was stating the obvious. Tuksook had to prepare herself to deliver to the People what Wisdom wanted them to know. Wisdom would assure the life of the People through her. Tuksook would be like a bird bone flute through which Wisdom would blow the music. She was the instrument; Wisdom, the musician. It was an overall way of being, a massive change required of her, not a specific either/or choice. The message wasn't at all lost on Tuksook. She had to leave her childhood immediately to become the bird bone flute. The change had occurred. All that was needed was the right habits to form.

They were cresting the top of a bald hill and in the far distance, Tuksook could see many huge mountains, but one stood out far larger than all the rest. She touched Gumui's shoulder. He stopped.

"Look!" she exclaimed. "That's the great mountain I told you I saw when I flew." She paused and continued, "Spirit of the Great Mountain, I greet you!"

Gumui looked where she pointed and gazed at the great mountain. It seemed to sit atop other mountains. The size of it was staggering. He'd never seen a mountain like that. Of all the beautiful white covered peaks near their home, this dwarfed them all. He shrugged off his backpack and helped her remove hers. He sat on a rock nearby to spend more time looking out over the land.

Tuksook was hungry. She felt around in the backpack and came out with four pieces of jerky. She handed two to Gumui and hungrily bit into one of hers.

"This must be what it is like to fly," Gumui mused.

"This is how it is to see from where I fly," she clarified.

"Do you feel air rushing below you?" he asked while his eyes were fixed on the huge mountain.

"Gumui, it's the world of the spirit, and in that world I have only the sense of air moving below me, not the feel of it. It's not as you might imagine. It's not the way a bird flies, for birds must do things to remain aloft. For me there is nothing to do to remain aloft. Wisdom creates the flight in my mind web. Wisdom assures that I see what I am supposed to see. Imagine you're in a dream. You can compare it to that. In this world you can touch things. In that one, it's not the same. Your senses are dream-like, slightly deadened, while your spirit's part of the mind web functions in a more perceptive way. In a dream you have a sense of touching things, but it's only a sense of it. It's not real. Sometimes I want to go beyond Wisdom's limits. I don't know whether it's possible. It displeases Wisdom, so I don't try. While being in the spirit's not real in our world, in some ways it's more real than real."

The last comment caused a change in the features of Gumui's face. He knew the words meant something to her, but his mind web could not reason them. He looked directly at her face as if to find an answer there. Gumui wondered at the change. She looked somehow different, but he was unable to detect specifically what the difference was.

"Do you ever have difficulty knowing which world you're in?" he asked.

"When I was very young, yes, I did. Now, there's no question in my mind web where I am."

While they rested, a noise in the sky attracted their attention. A number of trumpeter swans flew over them heading for the valley below. The long-necked white birds seemed to chatter to each other as they flew. Gumui and Tuksook smiled at each other. The bird flight was a beautiful and interesting sight. Gumui and Tuksook drank some water and continued on. They followed a wide animal trail up the west side of a mountain, across the top, and down the shaded east side. When the two reached the lower third of the mountain, a lovely waterfall shattered the quiet of the place with noisy splashing. It was a welcome sight. There was a catch pool at the bottom. Gumui and Tuksook had trekked for quite a long time.

Both looked at each other with grins. They were hot and tired. They removed their backpacks, took off their clothing, and ran for the waterfall, adding their squeals as they ran into the icy water. They enjoyed the water and splashed each other, laughing as they did so. Finally, they stepped out of the water, much colder than they expected. Tuksook pulled her hair over her head and twisted it into a long rope to squeeze the water out. Then she shook it out. They dried off on a soft piece of leather. Tuksook quickly put her tunic on. It was longer than usual, mid-calf length. Her tunic had a split on the side that enabled her to take long strides. It was formless, brown from the hide's having been smoked. Before the tunic was hers, it was worn by someone else. For the trek, Gumui had worn his red belt. A triangular piece of brown leather extending down from the belt covered his male parts. From the end of the triangle, a thong passed to the back of the belt to tie there. His clothing was minimal when the weather was warm. Gumui opened his backpack and took out his short tunic. He put it on quickly.

The two young People followed the water to a large lake at the base of the valley. Gumui took his favorite spear and left to hunt food for the evening. Tuksook began to build a lean-to after gathering wood and starting a fire. Gumui was surprised that there was not an abundance of animals in this place. He was eager for real food—not more jerky. Gumui ran across the meadow at one place in the valley and was distracted by a small noise. To his disbelief, he saw movement and realized he'd found a very new camel. Gumui stepped over to the place where the animal was resting and saw it had a broken leg. He killed the animal swiftly and pulled it over his shoulders to carry it back to their camp site.

"That was very fast," Tuksook exclaimed.

"The little one had a broken leg. I'm going to take it down there," he pointed to a place where land jutted into the creek. "I'll bleed it there, skin it, and be back soon. It looks as if you have things prepared well here. Call out if you need me."

"That was good hunting, Gumui," she said as he left.

Tuksook began to look about to see whether she could find any suitable greens. She was limited to some plantain and new fireweed leaves, but they'd go well with the meat. She carried them and her bowl to the lake and washed the plants. They could drain in her bowl. She didn't open Gumui's backpack. There was so little that the People had that was specifically theirs. A person's backpack was his alone, a treasured private thing.

As soon as Gumui could butcher a piece of the meat, he ran to Tuksook with a roast. He laid it on the rock by the hearth. "Here's a knife you can use. You might want to cut the meat into pieces that will cook faster," he told her. Then Gumui was gone to finish the butchering.

Tuksook took a piece of bark from a birch tree and laid the roast on it. She used the knife to cut the meat into bite-sized pieces that would cook easily on sticks held over the fire. She found a couple of good sticks, two for each of them. They could cook their meat at the fire. She thought he'd brought a lot of meat for two people, as she skewered the meat on the sticks readied for Gumui's return. Some meat remained on the bark.

Gumui returned after washing. He pulled his bowl from his backpack and Tuksook divided the greens between them. Each held the sticks over the fire, eager for food. Light was fading rapidly from the valley when they began to cook the meat. The hearth fire cast dancing light upon them.

"How was your time with Wisdom?" Gumui asked. He still felt it had made a visible change in Tuksook, but he could not reason what the change was.

"It was not what I expected," she replied. Silence followed.

Gumui wasn't clear whether she didn't want to continue, so he asked, "What happened?"

Tuksook had become accustomed to a feeling of obligation when it came to answering his questions. Without considering whether she wanted to share, she began, "Wisdom was displeased with me for putting off telling my father about knowing the stories. I saw his anger. Wisdom showed me how failing to do what is expected of me could cause the People to die. It was as vivid as a shining sunrise. I saw it as if all the People and I were tiny, and I could see it occurring before my eyes. I saw myself playing and the People dying. Seeing it broke me, Gumui. Wisdom changed me in the blink of an eye. It was painful. I understand the need, but it hurts even now. It hurts because I chased after my own wants and displeased Wisdom."

Gumui was dumbfounded. In moments Wisdom accomplished what he'd tried with no success to do. He was grateful. Finally, he thought he understood the change in her. She reflected the absence of childhood or her childish ways. Her petulance was replaced by genuine concern for the People. Suddenly he realized he was about to overcook his meat.

"We probably need to put the meat in our bowls," he said. He pulled his off, dropping it into his bowl where it imparted flavor to the greens, and he added more meat to the cooking stick from the pile on the birch bark. Tuksook did the same.

They began to eat while holding a stick over the fire.

After sating his hunger, Gumui asked, "What does Wisdom look like?"

Tuksook continued chewing her meat. Finally, she swallowed. "Wisdom is spirit. For our meetings Wisdom prepared a place that's not real, but it makes sense to me. Wisdom has a cave with white walls. There is a stone chair for him. Beside the chair are two steps, each tall, that I can climb to reach his right knee. I climb those steps to embrace the knee, and I usually put my head upon it. Wisdom's knee is what I can reach. Wisdom touches my head. He has white hair, as if the hair were light shining brightly. Remember this is all spirit, so it's like a dream. Wisdom has a long, white tunic. I cannot imagine what animal it comes from because it's huge. It may just be a visual thing, made for my eyes to see, not real. Wisdom's feet rest on the ground. From the ground to his knee is taller than I am. The ground is like a dark blue, clear rock that you can see into. It appears solid. I walk on it. Inside the blue rock you can see spiraling swirls. I don't know if water is under the rock. But it's all created, so it may have meaning that I don't understand. Wisdom's face can be filled with compassion one moment and brutally afire the next. There is always reason behind everything Wisdom does." Tuksook became quiet. She took another piece of meat.

"Aren't you afraid there? You speak of brutality."

"Afraid?" she replied with food in her mouth. She swallowed the meat. "I fear Wisdom, but I'm not afraid of him. Wisdom will not cause me physical pain, I don't think. Wisdom shows me Truth. To have to face my own self, that is very painful to my mind web and my belly. I'd like to be better than I am, and nothing escapes Wisdom. Brutal? I feel it's brutal, Gumui. That may not make it brutal. It's very harsh, but certainly deserved. It may be that brutal is the wrong word. What Wisdom does is right. Wisdom works to correct wrong behavior in ways that are unforgettable."

"I think I'd be terrified," he admitted.

"I've been doing this since I was a very young child. I love Wisdom. Wisdom wants what's best for the People. Wisdom has a way and wants the People to follow that way." She thought for a moment and then said, "Wisdom is Truth." She became silent and suddenly let out a sob from the bottom of her belly. "I feel so inadequate, Gumui."

He was right beside her immediately. He hugged her to him. She was, he reasoned, just a child. Maybe too much was facing her, but then he realized Wisdom was in the lead. He would defer to the judgment of Wisdom always. He did feel deeply for Tuksook. She was finding her path into Wisdom's way. That had to be a frightful experience, he considered.

"Why do you feel inadequate, Little One?" he asked while hugging her tightly to him.

"I feel unworthy, dirty, evil, mean-spirited, and self-centered." Tears fell unchecked from her eyes.

"Tuksook, that I can understand. Little One, you are human. You are comparing yourself not even with another human, which is not Wisdom's way, but you are comparing yourself with Wisdom. That is folly!" He held her tight. "Tuksook, you love Wisdom. Trust that you'll learn and change with Wisdom's guidance on this trek. Relax. Wisdom knows you're young and human. What's the worst thing that could happen in your time with Wisdom?"

She looked deeply into his eyes. Her seriousness was tangible. "To be barred from Wisdom's presence," she whispered. "Wisdom is more important to me that breathing or eating."

He held her gently in his arms. They looked up at the starry sky. After much time, Tuksook relaxed. "Thank you, Gumui. There was just so much pressure today. You are kind to me."

"Tuksook, I love you. I'm here for you on this learning adventure and as long as we live."

After a long time of quiet, Tuksook said, "I did find out something interesting today. Ki'ti is one of my ancestors."

"That's interesting information. She was an amazing woman."

"Not according to Wisdom. She was almost as hard to deal with as I am."

"Wisdom told you that?"

"Yes. Wisdom told me that. Wisdom also said that to tell the People what they need to know—Wisdom could've used a rock or a cloud or a bison instead of me. When I waked up there was a bison eating right by me. Even though I didn't want to make any noise, part of me wanted to laugh and laugh and laugh. I had to work hard to move the idea to the back of my mind web, as close as that bison was. Why would I want to laugh when there was a wild bison beside me? It certainly wasn't the bison that would tell the People what Wisdom wanted them to know!" At that, the laugh that had been stifled burst out from her, starting with a little giggle and growing to laughter she couldn't control. It was contagious and Gumui joined her. She laughed until her back hurt.

When the laughter subsided, Gumui said, "I think we both needed that."

"I know I did," she replied.

She stood up and took both bowls to the lake. She rinsed them well and shook them. She returned and placed the bowls on the rock near the hearth. She took her sleeping skin from her backpack and began to lay it out. Gumui walked over to her.

"Wait," he said.

She stood there with her sleeping skins in her hands. He took his large aurochs skin and laid it on the ground fully extended. He pulled out another skin from inside his backpack. He took her skins and placed them on the aurochs skin. He unrolled his beside hers.

"Tuksook, I am here. I will not desert you. When things become overwhelming, turn to me. I am not Wisdom, but I love you and I'm here to stand beside you. You do not have to go through this alone. You can share with me. What you're doing with Wisdom is going to benefit the People. It will benefit me—and you. The least I can do is to stand by you. Just don't close me off, Little One. Share with me. Will you promise?"

She looked up at him. They were standing facing one another. "I will promise, Gumui. You are a good man." He hugged her to him gently. She ripped his belly. She was undergoing great change. It was for good. It was huge change for someone her age. She seemed strong but weak all at the same time. He adored her.

"Come, Tuksook. Let's sleep."

She walked over to the aurochs skin. She stepped on it hoping not to dirty it. She knelt under the shelter of the lean-to and crawled over to her place. She slipped under the coverings he had laid out. Gumui joined her after banking the fire. He faced her and encircled her with his arm. She felt safe and warm. She fell asleep quickly. So did Gumui.

They awakened to a bright cloudless sky overhead, birds announcing the day, and a rustling sound near the place where Gumui butchered the camel. Gumui was wary and quickly picked up a spear. The rustling sound concerned him. He looked carefully at the area but didn't see anything. He realized he'd have to walk nearer to find the source of the noise. Gumui took the animal path on the other side of the lake. He didn't have to go far. A bear had found the quartered camel remains even though Gumui had carefully sunk them in the water. He returned to Tuksook and the two of them quickly gathered their things and left the area crossing the hill to the north. They began a long trek down a valley between two long mountains that lay north to south.

For days they followed the valley until it opened onto a river and a wooded land beyond, different from the ones they'd traveled. They crossed the river. Spruce, hemlock, alder, willow, and cottonwoods filled the forest. A quiet spread through the area as if the forest itself ate sound. It carried a sense of age that drew respect. Some of the ancient forest grew trees upright from horizontally fallen trees, using the dead trees as soil. Moss and lichen grew in abundance everywhere. There was a visual softness to the place that belied the predatory habitat that it was. The area was different from all that surrounded it. It seemed as if every space in the forest supported life. Gumui and Tuksook were spellbound. They retraced their steps to emerge from the special place before speaking.

"What is that place?" Tuksook asked.

"I've never seen anything like it. It's old! Did you see how thick some of those trees are and how tall?"

"I tried to grasp it all with my eyes, Gumui. I just couldn't see it all at one time." Tuksook looked beside her to see a wild rose climbing a tree trunk in the bright sun. Three brilliant pink roses bloomed. She saw a log and took one of her leather sleep coverings and laid it on the top. The two sat on the skin-covered log looking at the special forest across from them.

"There is a place just inside the forest where a lean-to would be well placed. I'll hunt while you set up. Tuksook?"

"Yes?"

"Do not visit Wisdom while I'm gone."

"I will obey," she replied.

"I do not understand this place. We need to know what predators are here before we can be comfortable. It's too quiet. Predators would not give themselves away from noise. You will obey?"

"I already told you I would obey!" She was irritated.

Gumui was having to grow accustomed to the change in her. She was no longer doing childish things, but his trust did not come easily.

"I will do this as quickly as possible."

"I wish you good hunting, Gumui. Stay safe."

"Thank you."

"I thank you," she replied.

Tuksook lifted her backpack to carry it into the edge of the ancient forest. Then, she went back to pick up Gumui's. It was heavy but she was strong. She busied herself preparing a lean-to for the night. Then she gathered rocks and made the hearth. Tuksook had some difficulty there. In this special forest things were damp. Outside the forest, deadfall logs had dried out. She had to go outside the forest to gather useful wood for the fire.

She took a spear with her. Carefully, as she'd been taught, she used her nose before her eyes. Tuksook smelled nothing that alerted her to animals. She looked carefully in the open area. There was nothing she could see. She listened carefully. She walked to the forest they'd come through. She managed to find fallen limbs, and she began to gather them. Tuksook smiled as she returned to the lean-to. Tuksook thought she must look like a caribou with all the limbs and branches she carried. She laid them beside the hearth and returned to the forest across the river. She gathered as many as she had on the first trek. The amount satisfied her as adequate.

Tuksook spent some time breaking the branches to hearth-sized lengths. Some were too difficult to break, so she apologized to a tree into which she whacked the long branches, easily breaking the wood into several pieces. Carefully she stacked them near the hearth.

She started a fire, because it was becoming dark. She knew how Gumui would arrange the bedding in the lean-to, but she still would not touch his things. She dragged a log over to the west edge of the lean-to so they could sit there to watch the fire. The way Tuksook set the log would provide good predator protection from the front. Three large trees grew into each other just behind the lean-to, providing protection from the rear.

It was dark when Gumui returned. He carried a goose.

"I tried to pull all the feathers off," he exclaimed as he arrived back at the campsite. "I gutted it and left its head for another to eat. I think we can cut it into smaller pieces so we can eat before morning," he laughed. It was very late.

Tuksook was quick about taking a knife, removing the legs, cutting slits into the legs, and spearing them. She put the legs on long sticks to roast over the fire, and she took other sticks and speared smaller pieces bite-sized to feed them quicker. She put them on food spear holders to cook over the fire. Tuksook had found some greens earlier, and they were ready for him to pull out his bowl so they could be divided. Gumui took the meat that wasn't cooking down to the river where he submerged the pieces and covered them with heavy rocks. He washed himself and returned.

"Tuksook, you know where my bowl is. You are free to open my backpack any time and take out what is necessary. Stop acting as if you are not allowed to open it."

"I will," she replied. She went to his backpack and pulled out his bowl. She divided the greens and went to check the small pieces that were cooking. She turned the meat and sat on the log. She thought how much she loved this adventure. She also wanted to return to Wisdom.

"Gumui, can we remain here tomorrow? I'd like some time with Wisdom."

"Of course," he replied. "I'd like to see more of this forest. I'd like to know what lives here and why this place of all the places we've been is so different. We will go out before high sun and then again later. Will your time with Wisdom fit between the two treks?"

"That should be good," she replied. It seemed to Tuksook that Gumui was always a little ahead in planning. She wasn't surprised, but she wondered whether he'd ever say that he hadn't thought that far ahead. Gumui spread the aurochs skin out under the lean-to roof. He gathered her covers and his and arranged them just as he had been doing each night.

Tuksook stood up to check on the small pieces of goose. They appeared to be fully cooked, so she handed Gumui a bowl and she took hers. They slipped the meat from the sticks and dropped them into their bowls. The two returned to the log and began to eat. The goose was a little tough, but the flavor was good. They ate hungrily. When they finished they walked to the river and rinsed out the bowls. Gumui and Tuksook stood side-by-side looking at the starry night.

"I think I've never been so happy in all my life," Tuksook said.

"I, too," he replied.

"Gumui, when we return and I am learning to be a Wise One, will you occasionally take me on a trek like this?"

Gumui was troubled. He was unsure how to answer. "You will be under the total power of the Wise One, Tuksook. If he will give me permission, of course, I'd be glad to do it. But he may see that as too much danger for you and the People. We must do as he says. I can consider this: when we join, we could leave for a special place, and I could have some hunters provide a discreet surround."

"When we join, I would love to return to this place, Gumui. This place is like none other!"

"This is a long distance from home," he said.

"Is there a limit to distance?" she asked.

"Ah, Tuksook, you ask questions for which I have no answers to give. I think coming here is too far."

Gumui was thinking thoughts prematurely again, and he had to stop his desire. He so he turned Tuksook towards him, bent over and caught her so that her hips were placed on his shoulder, and he secured her legs with his free arm.

"What are you doing, Gumui!" she shouted. "Put me down!" She pounded on his back with her fists.

She struggled, but he was too strong. He trotted back to the camp with her on his shoulder. When they returned he put the bowls on a rock by the fire and slid her off his shoulder onto the aurochs skin.

"I think it's time we slept," he said.

"Why did you do that?" she asked disconcerted.

"Because I wanted to stop *your* questions and *my* thoughts of joining," he admitted.

"Why?" she probed.

"Tuksook, I want you, but you're not woman yet. It is tempting out here with no one around to seize the moment and approach you, as if you were woman. I will not do that! So I have a fight with myself."

"I wanted to ask you to kiss me."

"Don't, Tuksook. It's not time yet. Don't tempt me to do what is wrong."

"Lots of young people fake join, Gumui. You know that!"

"That's not right for me, Tuksook. You're not woman, Little One. I will be joined with you with words, BEFORE, we join physically. And you will fake join with no one. Is that clear? Fake joining steals approval authority from Wisdom."

"I understand, Gumui."

"Do not tempt me. It's hard enough without that. If you tempt me, I will punish you."

The specter of her father raised up in Tuksook's mind web. He had given Gumui permission, even more had insisted, that he treat her as a child. She had fallen from their seeming to be equals on this trek to his being adult, her being child again. It caused her much discomfort. She tried to keep it in the perspective of "what is—is" but it was hard. She adored Gumui. She wanted to be as close as she could. She realized she had to be very careful. Unfortunately, she was not aware of what women did that tempted a man. That training was to occur when she became woman. Some girls seemed to know before that, but Item had not yet prepared her.

"Gumui," she said somewhat timidly, "I may not know all I need to know to do what you ask."

"Then, if I warn you to stop doing something, heed my words."

"Thank you, Gumui."

"I'm going to make water. I will return. It's time for sleep."

Tuksook went to the lean-to and slipped beneath the coverings. She was tired. She thought of herself on Gumui's shoulder and for some reason it caused her to laugh. I must have looked like a giant deer quarter, she thought.

After some time, Gumui slipped in beside her, put his arm around her, and drew her back toward his belly, the way they'd slept the whole trek. She wondered how that wasn't tempting, but she gave up those thoughts with the reasoning that she was not man.

In the morning they ate the goose legs after Tuksook heated them over the fire.

"That's really hot!" Gumui said surprised.

She nodded, realizing she'd probably overcooked them. She'd been up for a long time.

They sat on the log eating the goose legs. Despite the toughness, the meat tasted good. They watched as a small brown bird with a reddish chest and short tail stared at them from a branch of the tree across from them. It remained there briefly as if examining them, and then it flew away. Gumui laughed lightly.

"Why do you laugh?" Tuksook asked.

"I guess it didn't care for the looks of us," he said smiling.

Tuksook smiled with him. She gathered the bones and placed them in her bowl. She took both bowls to the river to dump the bones there and to rinse out the bowls. She returned to the camp. Realizing she was a little chilly, she put on her cloak. She noticed Gumui had put on his tunic.

"I'd like to warm a little before we leave," he said. "Tuksook, I don't want to frighten you. Did I frighten you last night?"

"You didn't frighten me. I am ignorant when it comes to women and men. I don't want to tempt you without awareness. But you have said you'd tell me to stop, so I'm not concerned. It does, however, make me feel uncomfortable to have to realize you are adult, and I'm a child. On this trek I've let myself feel like a hunter, as if we are equal. It shatters me like a broken bone when I realize that you are adult and I am just a child. I reason that I fight against what is, and that's futile, but that is how it is."

Gumui sat there on the log and chuckled.

Tuksook stepped over to him and bent down to look in his face. "It's NOT funny," she said with all her strength.

He laughed harder. "To recognize you do something futile, and to continue to do it as if you might stumble over a different result—that's funny! You're too smart for that."

For some reason even he couldn't understand, he continued to laugh. The laughter enraged her. She made fists and hit him about the shoulders. At one point she hit his ear and he stopped laughing, grabbing her, pinning her to the ground on her back, straddling her, and holding her wrists to the ground on either side of her head.

"Don't ever hit me again," he said firmly. "You may sometimes go to the spiritual world, but you live in the real world. In this world you ARE a child. Whether you like it or not, you are a child. You have no authority to hit me. If you doubt that, ask Wisdom." He pulled her up to her feet roughly in front of him.

Tears ran shamelessly down her face. She was emptied. He had the same effect on her that Wisdom had recently.

"You are right, Gumui. I will not hit you again. Will you forgive me?"

"I'll forgive you, but do not repeat that. You realize that you just proved my statement to be true. Tuksook, you are in many ways mature for your age. In other ways you're very immature. Some of what you do is acceptable; some is not. You are a great hunter for a girl and your age. As long as you live, you'll never be as good as a moderately good hunter. That's just how life is. It's because you're female. You cannot gain the strength. It's not your purpose in life. Out here, I trust that you have the hunting skills you have. If I broke a leg, you'd do a fair job of feeding us. But you could not bring me back to our home. If you broke a leg, I could feed us and carry you back home. For you to keep pretending that you're an adult when you're not is absurd. I cannot conceive why you'd want to pretend that. Worse, to compare yourself as you have to a male hunter is absurd. It makes no sense. That's why I laugh. Who do you think you are?"

"I want to be the best I can be."

"Then, stop trying to be better than everyone else. It isn't going to happen in this life or any other."

"What?"

"You cannot be the best Wise One, wife, hunter, fisher, healer, shelter builder, and so on. Wisdom's way is not to compare yourself with others. You compare yourself with adults when you're a child. You compare your hunting skills with hunters' skills. You even compared yourself with Wisdom! All of that is self-centered. You step outside Wisdom's way repeatedly. It's tiresome."

Tuksook finally understood. She was going against what Wisdom taught her just days ago. Tuksook, knelt on the ground and wept. She knew her error. He was right. She wondered what was the matter with her.

Gumui went to her and raised her up. He sat on the log with her beside him. He put his arm around her and let her weep. She had much to change. Wisdom had made a huge difference in her, but there was still much to change. He decided that they'd forgo the morning trek and Tuksook would have her time with Wisdom. He noticed the cloak was carrying twigs and a lot of dirt.

After she calmed, he said, "Your cloak is dirty, full of twigs and leaves of evergreens. You need to tend to it."

She looked at him in disbelief, but she took off the cloak and examined it. True, it was dirtied and carrying all manner of forest floor bits. She looked at him accusingly, since he had pinned her to the ground, but said nothing, recognizing that she had gone against Wisdom's way. She carefully shook the cloak and hung it on a stub from a broken branch on a nearby tree. She picked bits of dirt and vegetation from the cloak, then went to the other side of it, and found a few more things to pick from the rabbit skins. She left the cloak hanging on the stump.

Gumui put his hand on her shoulder and said, "I'm sorry I laughed at you. It was my turn to be childish. Will you forgive me?"

She looked into his eyes and sighed. "Of course," she replied.

"Tuksook, go into the lean-to. If you're chilly the coverings are still laid out on the aurochs skin. Take your time for Wisdom now. I will guard from here." She was a little surprised by the change, but glad.

Tuksook lowered her head and went to the lean-to. She crawled into it and carried her coverings to the far back where she lay down. She covered herself with the furry covering and pulled the hairless skin over her head. Slowly she felt herself drift to Wisdom. She wondered what this time would reveal.

Tuksook entered the room. She began to walk to the steps when Wisdom said, "Stand before me, Tuksook."

Tuksook walked to the blue ground in front of Wisdom's feet. She stood there silent, waiting.

"Tuksook, if you have someone to teach to turn loose of self-centeredness, how do you do it?"

Tuksook looked at Wisdom confused. She had no idea. Finally, she replied, "I do not know."

"The fact is that you don't know anything about teaching, isn't that right?"

"That is true."

"You don't know because you avoided having anything to do with those younger than you. You hated caring for the babies, as you thought of it."

"That's true."

"So you are sorely deficient in teaching ability."

"I am," Tuksook admitted.

"Observe," Wisdom said and suddenly from above pieces of rose plants, flowers, leaves, stems, thorns, roots, dirt, and all came showering down upon her. It made a dirty pile around her so that she could not have walked from it without stepping on thorns. There were bits of the plant and dirt adorning her hair, tunic, and skin.

Tuksook didn't move.

"What is the significance of that?" Wisdom asked.

"You know that I don't know," Tuksook replied dismayed.

"When you have to teach, you have to learn how to learn."

Tuksook lowered her head. The pile of rose plants and dirt around her was clearly something from which she was supposed to learn. Instead it just looked to her like a mess that needed to be cleaned up. Her mind web drifted.

"Tuksook, focus," Wisdom said sharply.

Tuksook looked at Wisdom's face.

"I have just showered you with blessings."

"What?" Tuksook was certain she hadn't heard what Wisdom said.

"I have just showered you with blessings."

Tuksook looked about her. She had a thorny piece of stem sticking to her tunic on the shoulder. She picked it off. She looked questioningly at Wisdom.

"I don't understand."

"I know," Wisdom replied. "You don't understand because you reason too shallowly."

"What?" Tuksook asked.

"Consider the rose plant, dirt and all as a blessing from me. Consider the flower, it has a delightful fragrance and lovely bright color. It's a blessing. Consider the thorny stem and leaves with the thorns on the underleaf. That's a blessing. Consider the roots and the dirt. They are blessings also. But in your shallow way of thinking the thorns are curses. Am I right?"

"Of course, you're right. Who'd see a thorn as a blessing?"

"Someone who could learn from the lesson of the thorn, Tuksook."

"Oh," Tuksook barely breathed out.

"Tuksook, I have been and will continue showering you with blessings. Every single thing that happens to you is a blessing from me to you. It is your destiny to reason how the things you would have seen as curses are blessings. Do you understand?"

"I do understand, Wisdom. Some of the things that have seemed harsh to me will be hard to see as blessings."

"Regardless of how hard it may seem, I tell you now that I shower you with blessings. You are to reason each of the thorns and dirt carefully. Do not consider them curses for they are not. Be grateful for all that occurs. You are not allowed to despair or feel sorry for yourself or your People. You are to stand up to every event and thank me. I expect it. Do it even if you fail to feel it. If for no other reason, do it from respect. But know that there is a blessing there. If you need help to see the blessing after you have sincerely sought with all your might, ask me. Otherwise, accept what I have said, for I speak truth. To be an effective leader in this time, you must be positive. I am there with you through every event. Know that."

"I acknowledge, Wisdom. I understand what you've said. I hope I can learn this well, for it seems filled with places where I may fall."

"You will fall sometimes. You will pick yourself up and start again. One other reason I meet you today. I want your promise."

"All right."

"When you become woman, Gumui will ask to join with you. Regardless of how you feel you are to answer him affirmatively immediately when he asks. If at that time you both are arguing about something, put it aside. I demand this of you and I want your promise now."

Tuksook looked at Wisdom.

"Why are you hesitating?"

"You know."

"Say it," Wisdom demanded.

"I thought I might not want to join with anyone."

"And why might you say that?"

"Because of the way my father treated Pito, women are viewed as children."

"You've blown that way out of reason. Item solved that problem."

"But it rests under the surface."

"Tuksook, I don't give you permission to follow this way of thinking. You need Gumui now and for the rest of your life. He has learned how to live with you. I want your promise, NOW!"

Tuksook felt utterly trapped. She looked at the pile of rose plants around her. Blessings? she wondered. She knew Wisdom was waiting for a reply. She just found it so hard. Finally, in a very tiny voice, she replied, "I promise."

"I can't hear you," Wisdom thundered.

"I promise," Tuksook said clearly.

"That's better."

"What did you learn from your father's error?" Wisdom asked.

"I learned not to fail to ask you what the People need to hear."

"Then, all was not lost. You were blessed by his error. Is that correct?"

Tuksook felt trapped again. She replied, "Yes."

"A thorn, Tuksook. A thorn. A blessing in the shape of a thorn."

"I understand, Wisdom," Tuksook said, and she did.

"I have seen some progress with your work on losing self-centeredness. It's hard for you, sometimes, but with Gumui, you have help. He understands. He delights in the progress you've made. Continue. Add to that the recognition that all that happens to you is a blessing from me. All."

"I understand," she said.

"And when you are woman and Gumui asks you to join, you will agree immediately and the two of you will join quickly. You have no alternative in this."

"I understand, Wisdom."

"Do you have any questions?"

"Yes. When we join, I want so much to return to this wonderful forest. Will I be able to do that?"

"What did Gumui tell you?"

"He thinks it's too far."

"It is too far. The answer is no, Tuksook. You have a one-time visit to this forest. Now, start working to see that as a blessing. Now!"

"Very well, Wisdom." Tuksook was compliant. She had expected the reply, since the place was far indeed.

"Tuksook, enjoy your time at this forest, for you will not return."

The finality of it stabbed her, but she vowed to herself to savor every part of this special place to put it into her mind web for memory forever. Tuksook looked down and the pile of rose pieces and dirt was gone. She looked at Wisdom surprised.

"That should not surprise you."

"Truly, it should not," Tuksook smiled.

"I am pleased with your progress." Wisdom reached down, picked Tuksook up, and laid her across a strong beating heart. Wisdom's soft hand covered her.

"I love you, Wisdom," she said, arms outstretched as if to hug Wisdom.

"I love you, Tuksook."

Wisdom put her back on the blue ground, and Tuksook slowly began the transition from Wisdom's world of the spirit to her world of reality. Gumui saw her moving as if to return. He wondered how it went.

She lay there under the coverings. She removed the skin from her face. She hadn't moved from the position she took before she left for the spirit world. She looked at Gumui. He patted the log beside him telling her to sit with him there. She didn't want to stand up to walk over there, but she did.

"Was that better?" he asked.

"Wisdom is happier with me," she replied.

"Anything new?"

"I stood there and Wisdom dumped roses, thorny stems and leaves, roots and dirt all over me. That was for me to learn that Wisdom always showers me with roses which means blessings. Sometimes I might mistake a blessing for a curse, like the thorns. I am not allowed to do that. I am definitely not allowed to do that. If I cannot figure out how something that seems awful is a blessing I'm supposed to ask."

"That makes good sense," Gumui said.

"Wisdom also told me that when I become woman and you ask for me to join with you, I have to reply affirmatively and we have to join quickly."

"Wonderful!" he said with enthusiasm. Gumui hugged her quickly.

"Wisdom said you are good for me for the rest of my life."

Gumui smiled, trying not to gloat. He was touched that he'd received a compliment from Wisdom.

"Wisdom told me that this is the only time I can come to this forest. Gumui, that hurts. Can we stay here a few extra nights? I want to keep all this in my mind web forever. I've never been happier in my whole life than right here with you."

"You've shed a lot of tears to be so happy."

"Please, just take my words as true. They are."

Gumui put his arm around her and kissed her lightly on her forehead. "We'll see what the days bring, Tuksook. We know little about this place. I think we remain at the campsite this day. We will go up the trail tomorrow early. I want you well rested for that trek. You look tired. There is darkness under your eyes.

Tuksook began to protest, but she gave up and relaxed. "I'm glad, Gumui. My belly hurts, so I hope rest will make it better."

"Do you want to lie down?" he asked.

"No," she replied, though she really did.

Gumui looked at her carefully. "Well, I think it would be a good idea for a while at least. You lie down and I'll gather some wood for the hearth."

Tuksook realized he was telling her what to do, so she did it obediently. He was relieved that she put up no fight. He was tired of that.

Tuksook slept briefly, and when she waked up she was in more belly pain.

She stood up and felt damp. She raced to the privy only to see blood on her leg. She was confused and, then, suddenly, she realized what was happening. She was woman in the middle of nowhere with Gumui. She went to the campsite and began to gather moss as close to dry as she could find. She went through her backpack and made the best belting she could to carry the moss. She went to the river and bathed, put on the moss belt, and washed off the spots on her tunic and put it on. The pain in her belly was a cramping pain and it was very uncomfortable. She hoped that wouldn't occur each moon. She sat on the edge of the aurochs skin with her feet pulled up and her knees held tight to her belly. She had piled up moss at the back of the lean-to. She had accomplished nothing else.

Gumui returned with what was his second load of wood. He looked at her and suddenly it hit him what was wrong with Tuksook's belly. "You are woman?" he whispered.

She nodded as if it were something to be ashamed of.

"What's wrong, Little One?" he asked, concerned.

"This is a terrible time for this," she said holding her belly.

"It is cramping?" he asked.

"Yes. How'd you know?"

"When we become men we are taught some things about women. This is a wonderful thing, Tuksook. So now I'll ask. You'll join with me?"

"Yes," she replied and pressed the cramp in her belly. "This hurts," she said.

"Think of it as a thorn," he said with a grin, "and a blessing. Be grateful to Wisdom."

"I wish I hadn't promised not to hit you again. Why don't you go gather some wood or something?"

"We have plenty of wood, Little One. This is a wonderful day!" Gumui was delighted and it showed. Tuksook had agreed to join as she'd promised

Wisdom she would. It brought joy to him to think that they would join when they returned home.

On the third day of her flow, it ceased. Tuksook was delighted. She and Gumui had made one trek to the high open land in the middle of the damp forest. The silence was unnerving. They observed giant deer females and their young. They browsed. A cat entered the area and tried to take a newly born giant deer. While they watched, the female giant deer raised up, and with her two front legs, she pounded the cat to death. Gumui and Tuksook were astonished at the precision and swiftness of it all.

That evening Gumui was preparing for them to leave the next morning. Tuksook sat on the log and asked him to come to her to sit a moment. He sat beside her. A large silver fish with dark pink skin was opened, skewered, and cooking by the hearth.

"Gumui, I do not want to bring on your displeasure. We have permission to join. I am woman. I know that I will never return here, and yet this is the one place I wanted to have my first nights with you. Can we not have a few nights here to join? You may see it as wrong, but I don't. In the eyes of my father and Wisdom, it cannot be wrong."

Gumui considered it. Midgenemo had given his permission for them to join. Wisdom had made Tuksook promise to agree to his question and she had. Wisdom had stressed a quick joining. Since the waterfall, Gumui had not seen Tuksook undressed. He went to her and pulled her tunic over her head. He removed his belt. He lifted her in his arms and carried her to the river. At the river they stood in the water. Stars were rising in the sky.

Following the words of the joining ceremony, Gumui said, "I offer myself to you as husband for as long as my life extends."

Tuksook looked straight into his eyes and replied, "I offer myself to you as wife for as long as my life extends."

"I say to Wisdom and to People everywhere, Gumui and Tuksook are one." Gumui said the words strong and loud so they echoed through the side valley of the eastward pointing toe of the Eagle's Grasp of their homeland.

They touched carefully. They bathed. They returned to the campsite, chilly but highly excited, and stretched out on the aurochs skin. They lost themselves in each other while the fish overcooked and fell from the skewers.

In the morning when Tuksook awakened, she knelt by the hearth. She said quietly, "Wisdom, thank you for the blessing of making me woman here. You gave me a large blessing through what I saw as a thorn. You let me have my wish that Gumui and I could have our first nights here, even though I can never return to this special forest. You made it possible. You are vast, Wisdom.

Your understanding and power is incomprehensible to me. You are kind. Your love is boundless. Thank you for the thorn. If you could see fit to make the cramping I feel less painful in the future, I'd appreciate that a lot." Gumui hadn't moved but he was awake. He listened to her prayer. He realized she was learning. It was painful, but she was learning the tough lessons Wisdom had to teach her. He was grateful that he was part of it. His gratitude to Wisdom went up silently.

For three days they remained at the campsite, coming to know each other differently. Finally, they knew they had to return home.

Chapter Four

"Tie a slip loop in that rope and hand it to me when I'm in the water," Togomoo said as he lowered himself over the side of the boat, entering the water quietly. He hadn't mentioned his plan.

Hai tied a small loop in the rope and then threaded the rope back through the small loop. He carefully leaned out over the boat and handed the slip loop to Togomoo. He watched carefully as Togomoo swam to the sea floor in the clear water. The boat was in the sea just offshore west of the mouth of the river. He realized what Togomoo planned as soon as he saw him approaching the sea creature from behind.

"I think he's going to make a slip loop around a sea creature's tail!" Hai announced to Hawk and Vole. He leaned back over the boat's edge. "Oh, there seems to be a problem!" he exclaimed.

Togomoo's head popped up in the water. "Hawk, help me. I'm trying to put the slip loop over the animal's flukes. They're just too wide apart for me to do it alone without alerting the animal."

Hawk eased himself over the side of the boat. He had a good idea what Togomoo had in mind and was excited to be part of the capture. He took his part of the slip loop and swam deep down with Togomoo to the sea creature that was grazing on large vertically growing strips of seaweed known as kelp. Carefully they stretched out the slip loop to encircle the flukes. At a nod from Togomoo, they slipped the loop over the tail and Togomoo pulled the loop tighter by swimming with it. Hawk immediately helped him. The sea creature reacted, but it was slow and lacked any knowledge of what to do, let alone show any instinctive fight.

The sea creature was huge and shaped a bit like a giant seal with an upper lip that looked like a very short elephant trunk at one end and whale flukes at the other. The animal was dark, almost black and stood out visually in the water. Apparently, its primary food was seaweed, based on the unnaturally large accumulation of pieces of kelp that high tide left on the shore. Togomoo had noticed that where a pile of kelp lay on the shore, these sea creatures were likely feeding offshore. From their very limited experience with it, the animal was slow to move and showed no fear of them.

As soon as Vole saw the creature was secured, he hooked the part of the rope that was attached to the animal to the tie down inside the boat, using only a part of the entire rope, so the unused part of the rope was neatly coiled on the bottom of the boat. As long as the loop to the sea creature's tail held, the animal was secured. If it swam hard or fought to escape, it would take the boat with it. He wondered why Togomoo decided to capture this animal. It could be dangerous. Pulling it ashore would be very difficult.

Togomoo and Hawk swam as fast as possible to the boat, urging Hai and Vole to row even before they climbed aboard. They reached the boat very cold. Both grabbed an oar and began vigorously rowing to help warm up.

After warming up a little, Togomoo said, "That thing has to be six man-lengths long!"

"Agreed," Hawk said, his teeth still chattering and his body shivering.

Togomoo shouted out, "That's a tough hide! Did you feel it?"

"Enough to know it'll be hard to butcher."

Hai and Vole listened to every word. They both felt honored to be part of this boat travel to capture the strange beast.

The sea creature was not pleased to be pulled backwards through the water. Others of its kind heard its plaintive cries, but they did not try to help. Nothing prepared them for the taking of one of their members. In time the animal would quiet. The men rowed up the river wondering at this new food source, hoping that for the effort the animal would feed them well and have a good taste. It added a distinct heaviness to their rowing.

Two days later Vole called out, "We're home!" Though the riverbank looked little different from when they landed there to begin life in the new land, it stood out to these hunters as if it were brightly marked.

People began to leave the meadow and file down the path to see what the men had brought from the sea. There was obviously nothing in the boat. A few hunters noticed the rope hanging off the back of the boat. The rope wasn't moving. Those who noticed the rope wondered why it was in the water.

Hawk handed the coiled rope that was inside the boat to Unmo and Kew. "Please tie this up to a strong tree," he said.

The older men carried the rope to a hefty evergreen and tied the rope, looping it twice around the girth of the tree. They tied it in knots that would be difficult later to untie.

Unmo, ever curious, waded out into the water and then swam to see what was attached to the end of the rope. When he surfaced, he shouted, "What is *that?*"

Togomoo laughed. "That's a sea creature that should provide a lot of food and they are easy to capture. They don't see us as predators, and they don't fight. We're going to need to have as many men and strong boys as possible to haul it to land." Togomoo dived down with his knife to kill the animal. Since he was underwater, he thanked the animal in his mind web for giving its life so that the People could live. He found killing it difficult, not because the animal fought, but because the hide was as tough as hard wood and as thick as cottonwood bark. He had to slice open its neck where the flesh was softer.

Sutorlo ran fast up to the meadow to call for help. Men and boys came quickly in response. Even Ottu, who found the path up and down difficult, followed the ones who hurried. He was as curious as they were. By the time Ottu reached the anchored boat, the sounds of "Pull . . . Pull . . . Pull . . ." had become a cadence like a heartbeat as more and more joined to pull.

Women and girls who were not tending to things they couldn't stop gathered at the top of the meadow to see what the men and boys were pulling up. Item couldn't resist, so she walked down the path to see what this creature was. She expected another huge, ugly sturgeon until she saw the dark outline in the water of something with little shape. She wondered whether it was a whale.

When the animal was beached, the men tried to lift it as high as they possibly could, pulling the rope over a tree limb, hoping to bleed it that way. It was too heavy. All were amazed at the look of the animal.

They began to butcher the creature. Cutting into the hide was almost impossible. It took a very long time to make one cut from the neck to the tail. The skin would be slit and then cut back at the fat, rolling the skin to reach the meat. They didn't try to quarter it.

Fortunately, Taman and Mongo's meat smoking house and the outside sun drying poles were completed and Taman started a fire to ready the smoker for some of the new meat. He used alder wood for the savor. As men below cut meat from the beast, they sent it to the women and older boys in the meadow to prepare it for smoking or drying. Togomoo asked that roasts be cooked for that evening's meal, so they'd know how the meat tasted. Some of the boys carried fat up to the meadow for the women to render into oil. There was a lot of external fat, though the meat was relatively lean. Other boys transported meat. The People worked rapidly and in harmony as a single being in the task of making the catch useful to them in the future. They tried to use every part of it, since that was Wisdom's way, but they couldn't find any use for the skin, so for now it would be hauled to the center of the river and allowed to rush away with the waters. They deemed everything else useful—even the beast's white bristles, that were in the place of teeth, made it into the sewing kits of some of the women. They would eventually find a use for the skin.

Renwen stopped working at the spit, wiping the sweat from her brow. She looked over the busy meadow and thought of the hive of bees that used to live near their home in the old land. The People were busy like the bees, she thought. Sometimes Renwen still felt pangs of homesickness, but this new land was life giving, she reasoned, while the old land had become life taking. Most of the People she loved were in this new land, though she still mourned for the loss of a few friends and her sister who remained behind. At sixty-eight, Renwen felt old. Her body wasn't as flexible as it used to be; her reasoning wasn't as sharp; her vision and hearing weren't as clear; and some of her teeth had worn down to nubs, while others had been pulled out. Renwen was in no real pain. Still, she was in love with her husband, Kew, had a wonderful family, and fully appreciated each new day of life. She smiled to see the People so purposed.

Kew had called Taq, Momeh, Remui, and Coo to cut up the meat for drying. He'd shown them how to do it. This was the perfect time for them to show what they'd learned. Eilie, Ing, Mela, and Elfa were called to cut small rope, thread it through the slit the hunters made in one end of the strips, and tie the strips to the bamboo poles to dry. They cut the meat on rocks at the catch pool, so they were careful to wash the meat to remove grit and any dirt in the waterfall before hanging it.

Vole ran up the path with two small roasts and went straight to Renwen. "There's more coming," he said as he turned and ran back down the hill.

Renwen speared the roasts and put them on the spit. To her, the meat looked more like meat from a land animal than something from the sea. She was eager to know how it tasted.

Item went to the spit to examine the meat. She looked at Renwen. "That doesn't look like fish at all!"

"I'm eager to know how it'll taste," Renwen said. "And I agree. What kind of meat is this?"

"Strangest looking fish I ever saw!" Item replied.

"I don't think it's fish," Renwen muttered.

As the noon turned to evening, the roasts were causing anyone in the meadow who could smell them to salivate. Renwen had cut off a sliver and tasted it as soon as the outside of the roast had cooked. She could hardly wait to eat. Finally, Renwen hit the rocks together, calling all to the evening meal. By then all the work was finished and the People had showered. They were eager to taste the new meat. There were many greens and some tubers to eat along with the meat. For any who didn't like the new meat, there was some leftover sturgeon and camel. Renwen expected the leftovers would remain leftovers.

As soon as the People began to taste the new meat, there were exclamations. "This is better'n aurochs!" "I could eat much of this!" "Good meat!" "I want more!"

Because of the comparison to aurochs, the sea creature acquired the name of sea aurochs. At council, the People agreed that the amount of meat from the sea aurochs well compensated for the four-day-four-man boat travel. Hunters who also swam well and liked boats were eager to try to capture another. With a number of travels to the sea, the People could be well prepared to endure the cold time in this place using the meat they could dry or smoke. Meat for which they genuinely hungered.

In another part of the Eagle's Grasp, Tuksook and Gumui prepared to stop for the night. Gumui set up the lean-to and Tuksook started a hearth fire. He took the remaining meat from the last camel, cut it into bite-sized pieces, and skewered them on sticks they could each hold over the fire.

Gumui brought a skin and put it on the ground near the fire. They sat and began to cook the meat. The sky overhead was filled with stars and clear of clouds. Silently each pondered the fact that their exploration was concluding. The abandon with which they'd been themselves and not part of the group would end.

"Gumui, I've had more delight on this trek than at any time in my life."

"I, too, Tuksook. It's been wonderful to learn this land and to learn you."

They laughed. They had definitely learned each other.

"Gumui, I'd like to spend some time with Wisdom before we return. Will you watch over me in the morning?"

"Of course," he replied.

"The moon is trying to peek out from that mountainside," she said quietly. She was pointing. An owl flew across the sky.

"Big owl," Gumui observed. "By the time we eat, the moon should be partly out."

"I love this new land," she said, "almost as much as I love you."

"I feel the same. I'm so glad we migrated. And you can thank your father for that. He saw that it was important for us to move. Imagine how it would be if we were still in the parched old land. Our children will have a wonderful place compared to the old land."

"Our children. You don't think I'm already pregnant, do you?" she asked.

"There's no way to know except let time pass. Would that make you happy?"

"Any time I can have your child, I'll be happy."

Gumui smiled. He'd never felt as she caused him to feel. She had grown so much on this trek, he thought. Of course, he reasoned, he had also grown.

Tuksook leaned against a tree, picking her teeth with a twig. My father was responsible for our migration, she mused. I wonder whether Wisdom told him we had to move. Is that how Wisdom has us assure the People's safety? She realized her father didn't credit Wisdom with the idea of the migration. She was curious how Wisdom used Wise Ones in ways other than just telling the stories.

Gumui smoothed out the aurochs skin under the shelter of the lean-to and gathered their covering for the night. He slid the backpacks under the protection of the lean-to. There was no expectation of rain, just dewfall.

Just as Tuksook was about to drift off to sleep, Gumui said, "There's a question I have that I am thinking you can answer?"

Fully awake and a little irritated, Tuksook murmured, "What's that?"

"It's probably too ridiculous to ask. I feel crazy even mentioning it."

"Don't tell me you kept me from sliding to sleep with a question you want me to answer but won't ask." She propped herself up on a stiff arm.

"Well, you'll think I've lost the way in my mind web."

"Just ask the question, so we can have some sleep!"

"I'll ask it this way—Is Wisdom male or female?"

"What?" Tuksook began to giggle. "You're right! That's a crazy question. What made you ask that?"

"While you and the women and children were gone, Ottu became so angered at your father, he swore by Wisdom's testicles."

"Ottu did what?" she asked, dealing with an idea far beyond her sphere of imagination.

"He swore by Wisdom's testicles."

From somewhere deep inside, Tuksook began to giggle and then laugh and laugh. The incongruity of Ottu making such a statement, the idea itself, and Gumui's question were more than she could contain, so out it came in laughter. Gumui wasn't laughing, which made her laugh harder.

"When he swore, I couldn't help but wonder," he said over her laughter, "whether Wisdom had testicles."

At that Tuksook laughed harder. She rolled up into a sphere shape, trying to keep the muscles in her back from reacting to the laughter by tightening.

"Well, are you going to answer me?"

Among her peals of laughter, she said, "Well, Wisdom has no breasts like women." And then she laughed all the harder, thinking of Wisdom in the room wearing that beautiful, long white leather tunic with breasts. She, too, wondered whether Wisdom had testicles as Ottu suggested in his swearing. "But then," she laughed, "I've never noticed male parts either. The representation of himself that he shows me is clothed in a long leather tunic, Gumui." Her laughter began to calm.

When her laughter subsided, she said, "Gumui, Wisdom is spirit. I don't think spirits join. I don't know whether Wisdom is male or female or has characteristics of both or neither. Wisdom is Wisdom. And, I'm not going to ask Wisdom that question. I will tell you that I think of Wisdom as male, but that is the thinking of a person who, days ago, was a child. When the People refer to Wisdom, they refer to him, as if he were male. But we have to remember he's spirit."

Gumui thought over her words. "So maybe Wisdom shows a male form to People to communicate to them in ways they can understand?"

"That's what I think; but I doubt there's a single human who knows. Now, I'm wide awake, so I suppose you'll have to lull me to sleep, my husband," she said smiling.

The night was short.

When the sun rose, they were in shadow but the increased light overhead waked them. They ate and then Tuksook went to the far end of the lean-to to cover herself so that she could have some time with Wisdom.

Tuksook drifted to that spirit place where she could meet with Wisdom. She arrived at the white cave room and started to climb the two steps.

"Stand before me, Tuksook," Wisdom said.

She walked on the blue cave ground and positioned herself out from Wisdom's feet, centered between them. She stood there with her hands at her sides looking on the face that Wisdom showed her.

"I approve your answer about whether I am male or female. For you to know better than to ask is wise. It is another thing when someone opens your mind web to strange imaginings, that you not pursue them. Imagining me with breasts or testicles is unworthy use of your time."

"I understand," Tuksook said thoroughly shamed. "Will you forgive me?"

"Yes."

Tuksook lowered her head.

"Tuksook, today we talk about what changes you must make now. You are returning home to submit your learning to become Wise One to your father. That's where we start. Let me show you how your lack of respect is outside my way. I chose you and I chose your father as Wise One. You're not there yet. He is. Did he deserve to have me choose him?"

"No, I have learned that."

"You are correct. I chose him because I did. That's all you need know. Now, the very fact that I chose him should have led you to respect him, simply because I chose him. Remember I do not choose those who deserve to be chosen. If I did, I would find no one deserving. I have to work through People. You must respect him from this moment forward, because I tell you you must."

"I understand," Tuksook replied.

"You must learn the stories well enough that they come to you immediately when there is a similar situation. You must learn them to work through events for which the stories have no parallel but show how the People stood up to earth's severe changes. In your life you will be seen as a leader. You must be prepared to lead. Do you understand?"

"In part, Wisdom."

"Tuksook, you are learning."

Tuksook lowered her head.

"You must continue to lose your self-centeredness and grow your humility. Never forget the source of your knowledge and wisdom."

"I understand."

"There will be times when others are so impressed with you that they will praise you. Recognize that praise is not yours alone."

"Wisdom, I do understand."

"I expect you to demonstrate respect for your father, so that others recognize that you respect your father. I do not mean to overdo it. I mean the normal respect you had for him before he erred."

"I understand."

"I want you to interact from time to time with the little children. They are no less important to the People than those your age or older. They need to come to know you, not be dismissed. Learn to teach them things by doing it so they can watch. Encourage them to puzzle out answers to hard questions"

"I understand."

"Do you have questions?"

"I have one. It has troubled me. When we migrated, it was at my father's command. Did you tell him we needed to migrate, or was it his decision alone?"

"I told him."

"That leads to my next question. Since the idea was yours, why didn't he tell the People that? I am trying to learn when it is expected that we credit you as the source of ideas or commands."

"Credit me when credit is due. Credit a person when credit is due the person. Never take credit for another's idea or work. Now, in the case of your father. He is a man. He doesn't always do what he should any more than you do. Do not condemn him for his failures. Live with them. If they are too much for me to accept, I will deal with him. It is not your place to do that. Does that answer your question?"

"It does. I understand, Wisdom."

"Tuksook, let this truth fill every part of you: You are not better than your father in the past, in the present, or in the future. Knowing that will make it easier for you to deal with the truth of your past lack of forgiveness and problems that may soon arise. You are not better than your father. Neither are you worse."

"My pride rebels, Wisdom, but I know that your words are truth. Help me keep your words foremost in my mind web. I will strive to stop my bad habit of making comparisons of myself to others."

"Including me!"

"Yes, Wisdom, especially you." Tuksook lowered her head.

"Tuksook, we shall not always meet like this. Sometimes I shall speak to you when there is an immediate need. You know my voice. If you hear it, stop what you do and give heed."

"I understand and will obey, Wisdom."

"Tuksook, do not listen to any other spirit voice but mine."

"I will listen to your spirit voice only."

"Come."

Tuksook climbed the steps and hugged Wisdom's knee, laying her head upon it. Wisdom's soft hand enfolded her. Slowly she returned to the physical world.

"You're back," Gumui said with enthusiasm. "We have a little to do before we can finish our trek."

"I'm hungry," Tuksook said quietly.

"We still have a fire. I'll cook the remaining pieces of the giant deer meat."

"Wonderful," she said quietly placing her arm around a tree trunk and gazing at the valley.

"Did it go well?" he asked.

"Yes, Gumui. It went very well. Wisdom doesn't want me to talk with any other spirit. He warned me to treat my father with respect. Wisdom chose my father and me. Wisdom reminded me that my father and I are no better or worse than the other. We didn't deserve to be chosen. Wisdom said that my father was chosen to lead. I should respect his leading because, if it went too far, Wisdom would step in. It appears from what you've said that Wisdom did step in to make my father change while we were gone."

"That did happen. We saw a lightning bolt hit a tree, felling it right where your father slept in the lean-to. Fortunately, he was in the meadow. We also saw a lightning bolt hit the ground close to your father. He heard Wisdom speak through it, but the rest of us just heard crackling and the roar of thunder."

Tuksook heard him but replied, "That smells so good! I hoped we had some left."

"It will be ready soon. Come, sit."

She went to the log where he'd put the skin that he'd already packed. He handed her a skewer and took one for himself. The meat tasted good.

Gumui finished first and extinguished the fire. He packed up the skins and skewers and they began the trek to home.

Sutorlo, Lurch, and Gilo had been busy since the morning meal felling and limbing trees. They carried the trunks over by the area where the dogs stayed. The boys had learned some construction techniques by observing their bent tree house. They decided to keep the dogs safe in the cold time, they should build a sturdy shelter for them. Gilo set up the back of the structure against the hill behind the dogs. Sutorlo and Lurch buried two stout evergreen tree trunks upright in the ground opposite the hill. They tied a crosspiece to the standing trunks at the top. The three boys took the logs placing the heavier end atop the hill and the lighter end atop the crosspiece. The structure was wobbly.

"I think we need two more standing logs each between a standing log and the hill," Gilo said.

They worked hard and soon had two more logs buried. They tied a log from front to back to the new side logs. The structure had definitely gained stability. The boys soon had all their logs lined up and ready for covering.

"Now I know what we needed that sea aurochs skin for!" Lurch laughed. It would be perfect to lay over these logs to hold the rocks and dirt we could put on top. "Let me ask when the men will go again." He left at a run.

He came back to share that a boat left to bring back another sea aurochs that morning. The boys decided to work on the sides, hoping for the skin. They'd ask at council that night if they could have the sea aurochs skin for the dog lodging.

Elfa walked over to see what the boys were doing. "That is thoughtful of you," she commented. As she continued, she scratched behind the ears of first one dog and then another. "We depend on them to carry many of our things when we hunt, to alert us to what they know sooner than we know it, and to protect us when animals are near that could harm us. It makes good sense to be sure to take good care of them."

Gilo approached her. "We're going to ask tonight whether we can have the sea aurochs skin they'll bring back. That would be great to cover the logs with. Then we'll pile dirt and rocks on top of that. We'll be working on the sides to protect them from the wind. Part of the front and the river sides will remain open so they can alert us to anything on the river."

"From your description, I can almost see it. On behalf of the dogs, I thank you," she smiled and walked off towards the food preparation place.

"She's nice," Lurch said. "I think she likes you, Gilo."

"She likes everybody," Gilo said.

"Have either of you thought who'd you'd eventually like to have for a wife?" Sutorlo asked.

"I haven't," Gilo said.

"Me either," Lurch replied. "Have you?"

"No. It's just that we've been here for a while now. Before our sea sailing, we weren't allowed to have new joinings and nobody could be with child and make the sea crossing. I would think there would be a lot of People who want to join now.

"I'm sure there are," Lurch said, "My brother, Orad, seems to find Hustep attractive, but then who wouldn't?"

"Do you think they'll join?" Sutorlo asked.

"Who can say?" Lurch laughed. "I thought Coo would join with Enzuvel, but Enzuvel seems to find Tern attractive. And then, there's Remui. He's old!"

"I think he was in love with Meg, but when Hawk's first wife died, Hawk joined with Meg right away. Maybe Remui still loves her."

"That would be awkward," Lurch said.

Ren led Guko, Velur, Bitro, Col, and Twim to the south part of the meadow. She had tied a sphere to a string and hung it from a long horizontal tree branch that pointed to the north. Ren had taken two slingshots and the youngsters had gathered pebbles on the way. They took turns trying to hit the leather sphere while it simply hung still from the tree branch. In time all the youngsters were doing well, so Ren took a fallen tree branch and set the sphere to moving. The youngsters aimed at something moving. It was a lot harder. Their effort was taken seriously, but when they missed, they'd issue pretend groans and when they were successful, they'd shout for joy. For most of the day, the youngsters did not tire of the practice. They became better and better.

As the sun made it to the west and beyond, Wave shouted out, "I think Gumui and Tuksook are nearing."

People gathered to see the two walking the edge of the mountainside, on the path that seemed made for the purpose. They appeared to have acquired skins and looked a little top heavy. Orad and Coo ran to meet them to help them carry some of the load.

When they reached the meadow, they faced the People, all of them, eager to hear anything about their trek.

Midgenemo shouted out, "Quiet! They will unpack, eat, and then at council they can share." The crowd began to disperse. Midgenemo followed Gumui and Tuksook to the bent tree house. Orad and Coo ran with the skins they carried and laid them by the bent tree house in a lean-to built for new skins.

"Father, may I speak quickly to you now?" Tuksook asked.

"Speak," he replied.

"There are two main things I wish to say quickly. The first is that while I was gone, I became woman. You had already given Gumui permission to join. We are joined. The second is harder. I have done a very selfish thing. I admit to you that I know the stories and have known them for a long time. I did not let anyone know, because I wanted to enjoy the times I could find solitude to talk with Wisdom, and I wanted to be a child. Yes, I talk with Wisdom even as you do. I know that you need to know these things straight away. Father, I am sorry for hiding my knowledge of the stories. I ask your forgiveness."

The Wise One stood there staring at her with his left hand on his hip. Gumui stood there almost failing to breathe. Tuksook wondered what would happen.

"I thought so," the Wise One finally said, exhaling as if he'd stored his breath for a long time. "You always had that air about you, and you flew.

Yes, Tuksook, I forgive you. You both know that I could beat you for this, Tuksook. I could order Gumui to do it, since he's your husband. But, you both have probably suffered enough already just from thoughts of what would happen when you informed me. Tomorrow, Tuksook, you will spend the day reciting stories to me. We will do this, as you well know, day after day, until I am convinced that you know the stories, the habit has formed, and that you will practice daily for the rest of your life. How long have you and Wisdom talked?"

"For years and years, father."

"I see," Midgenemo said, pausing. Then, he continued, "I'm glad you joined. Gumui, make certain she no longer falls into the self-centeredness that has consumed her until now."

"Yes, Wise One," Gumui said quietly. He agreed with Midgenemo. He didn't like that part of Tuksook either.

Renwen hit the rocks together, calling all to the evening meal.

"Let's eat. You have something special to try," Midgenemo said.

"What is that?" Tuksook asked.

"You'll see," he said smiling. The relief he felt knowing that there was a Wise One to train was filling his soul. He had been worried for a long time, needlessly. He loved his strong-willed, self-centered daughter. To see her well joined made him very happy. To know she would be the next Wise One filled him with great joy.

The evening meal was laid out on the log outside because the weather was so beautiful. The People loved to eat in the open. When Tuksook and Gumui reached the log and began to put food in their bowls, Gumui asked what the dark meat was.

"It's a sea aurochs," Togomoo explained. "It's a huge sea creature we captured just outside the river in the sea. The sea aurochs eats seaweed. They're easy to capture. They haven't learned to fight. We called it a sea aurochs because it tastes better than aurochs. Try it. Take plenty!"

Because they were hungry after the trek, they both took plenty. They laid the meat on their greens, knowing the meat would flavor the greens. They walked to a partially shady spot and sat to enjoy their food.

"This is wonderful!" Gumui exclaimed. "Togomoo," he shouted, "You're right. This is the best meat I ever ate!"

Togomoo nodded and smiled.

The People finished and those who ate any fish walked to the trash heap to empty their bowls of the small bones. Little by little they gathered on the flat stones in the meadow for council. Some families brought skins for wives and children to sit on.

Midgenemo began, "As you all know, Gumui and Tuksook have returned. We'll wait for Gumui's finding about Eagle Grasp until he's ready to share. First, know that Tuksook is woman and the two joined while on their trek. I had already given permission but had no idea it would be so soon. It is good. There are some who would speak. Gilo," the Wise One nodded at Gilo.

Gilo cleared his throat. "Today we began the shelter for the animals who serve us so well. We began the frame for the roof, and realized that we have a use for the skin of the sea aurochs. It would work well to lay one or more across the roof to keep rain, snow, dirt, and rocks from falling through the logs. We ask for the next two sea aurochs skins for the roof of the building we make. Until the hunters return, we can continue to build the sides of the dog house."

There was silence.

"If anyone sees reason to deny this request, speak," the Wise One said. Time passed.

"You may have as many skins as the dog's house needs and the hunters provide," the Wise One ruled. The young boys were delighted.

The Wise One said, "Stencellomak and Bruilimi," and nodded at them.

Stencellomak shifted and said, "A while ago I speared a big cat with long teeth. I wear the teeth on this leather strip around my neck. I asked Lurch to skin the cat and prepare the skin, and Bruilimi volunteered to make a fitting tunic from it for Tuksook, our flier and next Wise One. The cat skin is finished. Tuksook, please put on the cat skin as a gift from all of us to you."

Tuksook blushed. She was touched and realized she'd done nothing to deserve the skin. Bruilimi helped her slide it on quickly. "I accept the skin with deep gratitude. I credit Wisdom, not myself, for making it possible for me to accept it as your flier and next Wise One. It is Wisdom who made those decisions. I did nothing to deserve it."

Midgenemo looked at Tuksook as if he'd never seen her. Where and when did she make such a change? She must have spent much time with Wisdom, he mused.

Bruilimi helped her with the neck of the new tunic. The leather draw needed to gather the neck skin equally to look right. The new tunic was shorter in front than the old one. The back hit her mid-calf and the front ended at her knees. The tunic wasn't a real tunic of the style they'd always worn. This one was first of all made from a single skin that had not been split open. Second, the upper foreleg skin of the animal had been left in place but split on the inner leg to make a sleeve-like arm covering hanging from the neck of the tunic. The forelegs hit the top of her forearms at the bend of her arm. The neck had been cut to conform to a human neck and a narrowly cut cat skin strip had been threaded through cuts to pull the neck together where it tied in front. It had a soft, feminine look. Bruilimi had constructed very simply a work of art. The skin was so soft Tuksook kept looking to be sure it was there. It was a little large for her, but she had not finished growing. She could wear it well just as it was.

What Tuksook could not see was that the color of the skin and the color of her hair made an incredible complementarity, transforming her into an exotic looking young woman. Gumui looked at her with his mouth open. He loved her but now saw her transformed into something amazing to look upon. Tuksook was unaware of the transformation, assuming the murmurs from the People were approval of Bruilimi's work on the tunic.

Tuksook went to Stencellomak and hugged him. Then, she went to Bruilimi and hugged her. She smiled at both of them. "Thank you so very, very much," she said. It was the first new clothing Tuksook had ever worn. She knelt next to Gumui.

The Wise One looked at Gumui.

"I would like to have until tomorrow's council to start to share my findings. It may take several nights to provide a complete description. I need to spend some time reasoning it through my mind web."

"Very well, I for one am eager for tomorrow night's council," he said.

The People nodded and made affirmative statements.

"Ottu, Mongo, are the days still lengthening?"

"Yes, they are," Ottu replied.

"Is there anything else for this council?"

"Yes," Item replied.

Midgenemo nodded.

"We need many beaver pelts. The cold time will be colder here. We need to make protection from the cold now."

Many hunters nodded to Item. That let her know she'd have the skins, more than needed, soon.

"Is there anything else for this council?" Midgenemo asked.

Silence.

"Council has ended," the Wise One boomed out.

The People began to head toward the bent tree house. Gumui stopped Tuksook. He held her by her elbow and kissed her. She responded. He felt her in the new tunic. It was so much lighter and more flexible than the heavier leather tunic she'd worn. He knew every curve and could feel them through this skin. He drew her towards him and hugged her almost too tightly. They walked hand-in-hand to the bent tree house, where this time they'd be sharing his bench/sleeping place. Gumui hung his tunic on the peg by his sleeping place and Tuksook's by hers.

"I have some bench/sleeping place expanding to tend to tomorrow," he whispered.

"Is that really necessary?" she asked.

"Yes!" he whispered.

Under their sleeping skins, Item whispered to Midgenemo, "Old Man, in letting her go with Gumui, you proved to be Wise One. When you did it, I thought you'd lost the way in your mind web."

Midgenemo laughed loud enough to be heard throughout the house. Then he whispered back, "I sought Wisdom's counsel for that one."

A few days later, the dogs' barking awakened the People. Hunters ran out from the bent tree house to find that the sea aurochs hunting boat was in sight of home. People raced wildly all over the meadow preparing for the new meat. They had experience with sea aurochs now. The drying and smoking racks were ready. Everyone was prepared. Lurch, Gilo, and Sutorlo were delighted to be able to have a sea aurochs skin for the roof of the dog house. Women quickly laid out the morning meal of food that could be carried by hand.

Tuksook and Gumui were slower to respond than some of the People. They had no specified function in the sea aurochs arrival, so they dressed, took some smoked aurochs sticks, and walked down to the boat. Apparently, the men had brought back two of the beasts. Gumui waded out into the water to see for himself what the creatures looked like. He was dumbfounded. Item's description of a full grass berry bag with flukes was very good, he considered. Tuksook wanted to protect her new tunic, so she didn't go out in the water. She walked back up the path and looked into the water from above. She could see two large dark blobs in the water. Suddenly she remembered that she was supposed to be reciting stories to her father, and she began to seek him. She found him inside the house, apparently looking for something.

"Oh, you're here. Good. I was looking for a furred skin to sit on while we go through the stories."

"Do you plan to do that inside the house or outside?" she asked.

"I'm a little stiff, so I thought the sun would be good. I know a good place."

"I'll wait for you outside, then," Tuksook replied.

"You'd better find something soft to sit on to protect your new tunic," he said. "We'll be sitting on a rock."

Tuksook went to her old sleeping place and picked up the furred sleeping skin. Midgenemo came out and the two walked up the hill to the rock where once she had warmed her belly. They found comfortable places to sit, laid out their soft skins, and sat.

Midgenemo wasted no time. "Tell the story of Maknu-na and Rimlad."

Tuksook began, "Notempa was the greatest of the great ones that Wisdom called on the land. He had long white hair and a fierce face. Clouds would gather at his head and be slowed up there making ovals in the sky. People loved to look at Notempa. The People had been visited by two Others who called themselves traders. They brought exquisitely beautiful purple, shiny shells from the salty water. The shells were large and made wonderful dippers or food holders. They had an edge with holes so that the dippers could be tied for travel. Some of the People wanted dippers, but the traders told them they had to trade something for the dippers. Some of the People thought they should just be given the dippers for their hospitality. The People knew that hospitality was required by Wisdom. Strangers were to be taken in and cared for well, so not to anger Wisdom. Strangers didn't have to recompense for hospitality. While the disputes over the trading occurred, Notempa fumed. Smoke arose from his head, and the smoke smelled like bad bird eggs. Many times Notempa fumed, smoke rising from his head, letting the People know that they were supposed to remember Wisdom's way of hospitality."

"While the People argued with the Others, Maknu-na and Rimlad went hunting. They didn't like the excessive squabbling over the dippers. They ranged far to the north, farther than they normally went. They could see Notempa in the great distance. One day they saw that the smoke had become a great column. It rose high into the clouds. Notempa shook the land and made a great noise that they could hear even where they were. They could see the cloud still rising. Parts of the cloud column had started to look like a tree falling back to earth from the sky. Other clouds were racing down the face of Notempa and coming right at them. The falling smoke cloud came toward Maknu-na and Rimlad at great speed. They were terrified. They could feel the warmth of the cloud coming at them. They could hear it. They grabbed reeds and jumped into a pond to try to save themselves from the wrath of Notempa. They submerged themselves in the pond and only the reeds kept them breathing, which was not very easy. Both expected to die."

"After a long time, the air seemed to clear and they raised themselves from the pond. The whole landscape was the same color. An ugly gray. It was hot and smelled awful. They looked at Notempa. Notempa had been so angry that he had blown his own head off. No more white hair, just an empty place cut off at the neck."

"Rimlad and Maknu-na looked at each other. They knew that their group of People was gone. They could not have survived the horrible downrushing hot cloud they'd seen. While still in great fear, they realized Wisdom had spared *them* specifically. And they wondered why. They walked as far north as they could to avoid the terrible fury of Notempa. The air hurt their breathing passages. The caustic gray gritty material burned their feet and legs and arms. They desperately pushed on. When one would tire, the other would urge him on. They feared Notempa, and they didn't want to die. They found animals covered in the gray material, dead, and they ate raw meat from those animals."

"On the third day, they found a group of the People living beyond the dead land. They were taken in and well cared for. The People at first had thought the travelers were ghosts of the dead because they were pale colored from head to toe, until they washed up and were given clean clothing and food and what they wanted most, water. They had bad coughs which finally went away. The People gave them good sleeping skins and let them sleep. Maknu-na and Rimlad were treated differently from the way their People had treated the traders of the Others. They were ashamed when they thought of their People and the travelers with the dippers."

"They were asked to live with these People who took them in and accepted the generous invitation. The air didn't clear from the explosion for a long time. There were many years of very cold weather. The People had to make clothing for cold weather. Sometimes people would have a toe or finger turn black and fall off when it was very cold. If it became too bad, they would die. One man cut off his black finger and took a white hot stick from the fire and touched the sore place with it. His hand healed very well."

"For years along with the cold weather they also had beautiful sunsets. The colors of brilliant orange and red and purple and yellow were like none they'd ever seen. However, the cold didn't last forever and the sunsets were only there briefly. They learned of Wisdom's wrath when People failed to offer hospitality to travelers. First, Wisdom made Notempa become very hot and explosive and then he would cause the world to turn icy cold. Never again would the People fail to offer hospitality freely to those who were traveling by. After a long time passed, People said that Notempa's head was growing back. Wisdom would not forget the People. And Maknu-na and Rimlad realized they'd been spared so their story would become a story for the People, a story that would remind them of Wisdom's way of hospitality. That was all a very long time ago."

"You did that well, Tuksook. Now, tell the story of creation."

"In the beginning, Wisdom made the world. He made it by speaking. His words created. He spoke the water and the land into existence, the night and day, the plants that grow in the dirt, and the animals that live on the dirt, and those that live in the water and in the air. Then he went to the navel of the earth. There he found good red soil and started to form it into a shape with his hands. He made it to look a little like himself. Then he inhaled the good air and breathed it into the mouth of the man he created. The man came to life. Then he took some clay left from the man and he made woman. He inhaled and breathed life into her. Wisdom created a feast. He killed an aurochs, skinned it, made clothing for the man and woman from the aurochs, and then roasted the aurochs for the feast. The man and the woman watched carefully and quietly to see how he killed the aurochs, how he skinned it, how he made clothing from its skin, and how he roasted it. They paid good attention and they were able to survive by doing what they had seen done."

"The People were special and Wisdom announced that the man was to treat the land and the water and the animals and the woman the way he wanted to be treated—good. And the same was true of the woman. And it went well for a long time. But Wisdom hadn't made the People of stone. He had made them of dirt, knowing that they shouldn't have lives that would go on too long, for they might become prideful and forget Wisdom. That is good, because People should not be without Wisdom. They would die."

"That is why the People return to Wisdom when they die. They are placed in the earth and Wisdom knows. When Wisdom hears of a death of the People, Wisdom waits until the grave is filled back. He waits until it is dark. Then he causes the earth to pull on the spirit of the dead to draw that person's spirit back through the dirt of the earth. Wisdom draws that spirit to the navel from which all People came, the navel of the earth where the red clay for making the first man was. The spirits of the dead depart for the navel of Wisdom. That is where they reside for all time. All People's bodies return to the dirt. But their spirit, that essence of the person made by the One Who Made Us, is pulled back to Wisdom in the place where first man was made, and Wisdom keeps all those he chooses with him there. Safe and loved. There they live forever. There is a cycle Wisdom made, a cycle from the navel to the navel. He keeps the spirits of those whom he chooses and he destroys those whom he hates. Wisdom hates those who hate him, those who ignore him, those who would be hurtful to him or the land or water or to those living things Wisdom made including People."

"You have done well Tuksook."

"Thank you, Father. I have a question."

"Speak."

"How does Wisdom tell you things that you have to tell the People? How did you know we had to migrate?"

Midgenemo moved around a little to be more comfortable. He said, "You have to listen. Often, Wisdom's voice is very quiet. You talk to Wisdom so you know his voice. On the subject of migration, I was walking alongside a creek bed that was almost dry. It had been a wide river. I heard the voice of Wisdom say, 'It is time to migrate east. Take the People and go.'"

"Did you just tell everyone then that they had to move?"

"At council that night, I said, 'It is time to migrate east. We must do this now.'"

"And they just followed, even though you didn't mention that Wisdom told you to migrate?"

"After the People follow you for a long time, they just know that what you say comes from Wisdom."

"How do they know that?"

"Well, where else would they think it came from?"

"If someone didn't want to move, they might think it came from you, not Wisdom."

"The People are smarter than that. Oh, I begin to see where your questions arise. You're thinking about Pito. I was wrong on that, Tuksook. Rimut told me his story so often, I believed Pito was just a whiner. I didn't know she was ill. I erred by listening to Rimut instead of asking Wisdom's counsel. I almost lost Wisdom's willingness to talk to me over that. I was just wrong, Tuksook. The People are much more aware now that I can err. It may be that your question is a good one. I should, perhaps, begin to state flatly when something I say came from Wisdom. I will reason that through my mind web. Now, Tuksook, let's hear the story about Moraka-na and Pekutla-na."

Tuksook stretched out on her soft caribou skin on the rock. She lay facing up to the sky. She began, "Long ago far south from here, Moraka-na and Pekutla-na were planning to cut down a tree to place over a river so they could reach the other side by walking over a tree trunk."

"Father, far south of us is ocean. Shouldn't that story start with "Long ago in the south in our old land . . .?"

Midgenemo thought. "Tuksook," he said after a while, "Through all time we have sworn not to change the words of the stories, so they remain as true as the day they were created. Part of becoming Wise One is vowing never to change the words of the stories. I have reasoned this way. Restart the story and this time, add to the beginning, "This is a story from our old land."

"Thank you, Father."

"Start again."

"This is a story from our old land. Long ago far south from here, Moraka-na and Pekutla-na were planning to cut down a tree to place over a river so they could reach the other side by walking over a tree trunk. A large tree grew by the riverbank and they chose that one. They had their hand axes and knew it would take much effort to cut that one down. Other People came to help chop. They used a variety of tools to cut down the tree."

"They had learned how to chop the tree down to make it fall in the direction they wanted. They made the wedge and continued on making it larger, for the tree was very thick. If they were successful, the tree would fall across the river from bank to bank. For days the People worked to chop the tree down. From time to time, men would put their hands high on the tree and push in the desired direction of the fall. It continued to hold."

"Moraka-na waked up one morning and said that he thought the tree would fall that day. He urged all those who watched the chopping to stay out of the way. He even said they should stay far enough away that, if it fell in a different direction, they should be safe."

The People trusted the hunters that were chopping away at the tree, making the wedge larger and larger. Suddenly, the tree made an explosive sound and fell away from the river opposite to where they expected it to fall. It twisted on its fall and frightened the People terribly. A man named Amatlen-na was trapped under the tree where he died. The tree was so thick the man was never seen again. The People could not understand what happened."

"Finally two men from the Mol came by and they showed the People what happened that awful day. The men showed the People that they had chopped down a left-handed tree. If you put your hand on a tree, with your thumbs up, the bark makes little lines that go either like the fingers on a right hand or the fingers on a left hand. Left-handed trees don't fall like right-handed trees—they are unpredictable. They went to the river and showed the People how the bark went to the left up the tree, not to the right."

"The People decided to test the Mol's tree knowledge. They found another large tree downstream from the left-handed tree that fell the wrong way. This was a right-handed tree. They spent days cutting down the large right-handed tree. Again, the People came to help the cutters and to watch. All were careful to stay out of the way of the fall, whichever way it might fall. This time when one of the People pushed the trunk of the large tree, it fell exactly the way it was supposed to fall—from one side of the river to the other."

"From that time, when People plan to cut down a tree, they will check to be sure that they are cutting down a right-handed tree."

"Tuksook, there has been no hesitation. You know the stories. Your telling has been error free."

"Thank you, Father."

"We will stop now and return at high sun."

She reached out a hand to help him stand on his feet.

In the meadow below, Gumui walked over to the place where Lurch, Gilo, and Sutorlo were building the dog house. They hadn't constructed the walls like the bent tree house. Instead they had cut blocks of turf from the lower area near the river and stacked the blocks atop one another. Grass would grow out from the sides. The walls were far thicker, and, Gumui considered, the dogs were probably going to be a lot warmer and their house possibly more stable than the bent tree house. He would talk to some of the men about doing the same on the outside of the bent tree house. There was enough time before the cold time, and they all thought they were farther north than where they used to live, so they could expect it to be much colder. Gumui also thought it could turn cold sooner in this land.

Gumui saw Tuksook coming down the hill with the Wise One. He ran to greet her, hugging her around the waist and swinging her in a great circle.

Tuksook was startled. "Gumui," she said, laughing. "What has become of you?"

"Tuksook!" he replied.

"She did well, Gumui. She knows the stories," Midgenemo interjected.

"Good for you," he said with a grin to Tuksook. "I thought she would, Wise One," he said to Midgenemo.

"Come with us," Tuksook invited. "We're going for some water."

The three of them went to the food preparation place.

Later, Gumui thought about the night's council. He'd already spent a few nights talking of the habits of the animals he observed. This night Gumui planned to share the wet forest. He knew that the strangeness of the place would cause a few hunters to find reason to go there. It was something to see. He would also talk about what he saw at the dog's house that he'd like to add to the bent tree house to make it warmer and stronger.

The Wise One and Tuksook returned to their rock and the storytelling began. The People were busily preparing the products given by the sea aurochs. Earlier, Hamaklob and Togomoo had dispatched the animals after thanking them for giving their lives for the People. The meadow was alive with meat preservation activity.

Lupo began to hit the rocks together and the People put down their tasks. They washed quickly at the waterfall for bathing and hurried to the food preparation place. The savor of the sea aurochs was drawing them to hunger that just moments ago they didn't have.

The older People were always served first, so others waited patiently, bowls in hand.

"Did the rest of the storytelling go as well as this morning?" Gumui asked Tuksook.

"I am so ashamed. I made an error in a story. I left out a word. That'll never happen in that story again, I assure you."

"Don't be so hard on yourself, Tuksook. That's what this practice is designed to do."

"I know, but it's embarrassing."

"You're not perfect, remember?"

"Oh, I remember, and if I didn't, this will definitely bring it to the front of my mind web!"

"Here we are! Oh, that smells so good!" Gumui said with feeling.

They took their bowls and went to the meadow's edge where they liked to eat with their backs against certain trees. They didn't talk.

The council that night was filled with many things. When it came to Gumui, the Wise One said, "Now, Gumui, you said last night you'd tell us about the wet forest. Please."

Gumui smiled. He was more comfortable now talking in council. "Tuksook and I traveled far. Near the toe of the eagle in our valley, the toe that points east, at the far east part, there is a wet forest. I call it that, because we have no name for such a place. After the drought we've seen, this place is beyond imagining. Trees grow monstrous. When a tree dies, it lays itself down and other trees grow from its trunk, as if the tree were dirt. Moss covers everything. It's a pale green. Inside the wet forest the moss stays wet all the time. Just outside the wet forest, the same moss is dry. You just step from a dry area to the wet one, and everything changes."

"Tuksook and I hiked into the wet forest. It is a little fearsome, because the wetness deadens sound. A woolly rhino could creep up on someone easily and never give itself away." Gumui looked up. "I haven't seen a woolly rhino in this land." He paused. "In the wet forest, you don't hear little things scurrying about. It's as if all sound is sucked out of there."

"At the top of the wet forest in one of the meadows there, we saw the huge deer with the strange antlers. A cat was going to attack a newly born giant deer. The mother raised up on her hind legs and beat the cat to death with her front legs. She was so tough defending her young one! It all took place in silence. She must've broken every bone in that cat's body and she did it so quickly. Once the cat was dead, everything returned to normal, as if nothing had happened. For me it was quite some time before my heart beat normally."

"I've asked Tuksook to draw the location of the wet forest. Let me smooth out the sand here," he said. They had a pile of sand that eventually would move to the house where the council would take place inside when the weather was cold. It hadn't been completed.

Tuksook drew the same picture of her flight. She marked the part of the eagle's toe where any hunter could find the wet forest.

"I have an additional thing to add at council tonight," Gumui said.

The Wise One nodded at him.

"I went to observe the construction of the lodging for the dogs. It greatly impressed me. I am persuaded that the dog's house will be warmer and stronger than ours because of the blocks of dirt, roots, and plants the young men have harvested. There is plenty of time, so I would like to add those blocks to the outside of the bent tree house. Because they harvested the blocks from the lower level of this valley, taking the blocks would not affect the meadow. I am concerned that we live farther north than in our old land and that the cold time can be colder here and come sooner. Those are the reasons I urge you to approve my request and help in more construction."

There were murmurs all around, but they sounded positive. The Wise One let the comments continue until they died down.

"Are there any negatives?" the Wise One asked.

Silence.

"Then any willing to work on this project, meet Gumui after the morning meal."

"Is there anything else the council needs to consider?"

Sutorlo nodded.

The Wise One nodded at Sutorlo.

"We would like to thank the hunters for the skins for the dogs' house. The two are exactly what we needed."

"You're welcome to them," Hamaklob said.

"Is there anything else for the council?" the Wise One asked.

Silence.

"The council ends," the Wise One said.

Chapter Five

The cold times arrived: the People watched the leaves on the hardwoods yellow and fall; the days shortened; lower mountains near the white-topped ones received snow, which melted until now, when the icy crystals just continued to increase; and the temperature was significantly colder. The north part of the house was very well provisioned with much dried meat from fish, sea aurochs, giant deer, camels, horses, and dehydrated vegetables and berries. Elders estimated that their food supply would keep them fed until the summer solstice, so they were overly prepared. The People could have added many horses, but they deemed horse meat sticky and preferred other meats over it, though they added it to the food for dogs. The bent tree house was sided with blocks of turf, following the construction plan of the dog's house, and despite the cold outside, it was very warm inside. The People had even sewn the skins of sea aurochs together and over covered some of the roof of the bent tree house with the skin as added protection.

Hapunta, Togomoo and Brill's first child, a ten-year-old daughter, had been feeling unwell all day. She staggered from her bench/sleeping place to make a run to the privy. She coughed, sitting back on her sleeping place. She wouldn't be running anywhere, she realized. Togomoo instantly stood up. The cough did not sound right. He went to Hapunta and felt her arms and forehead. She was burning hot. Brill arrived at the side of the sleeping place.

"She's very hot," Togomoo told Brill.

"Let me find Item," Brill said and left quickly.

"Father, I need to go out."

"First, let's see what Item has to say." He gently caressed her sweaty forehead, pushing the wet hair that covered her face towards the back of her head. She was limp in his arms while he sat on her sleeping place holding her.

"Let me see her," Item said. "She is hot." Item made the comment matter of factly, but she was concerned. Hapunta was very hot. Item put her head ear side down on Hapunta's chest. "Brill, ask Heek to make some willow tea."

"She wants to go to the privy, Item. Is that okay?"

"Carry her there," Item replied. "Her lungs are filled with mucous, so doing much walking is not a good idea. Has she been like this long?"

"She wasn't hot until tonight."

"I think to be safe, she should take one of the sleeping places in the north part of the house. There are two sleeping places there. Just in case she has an illness that can make others sick, it's best to keep her at a distance. One of you two should stay with her, not both of you. Hapunta will need to drink much water while she has this illness. During the day, not at night, put some red sphagnum on her chest and let it remain there as long as it has warmth. Do it two or three times a day."

Item left and walked over to the west side of the house to Tuksook and Gumui's bench/sleeping place.

"Tuksook, Gumui," she said, interrupting a conversation between them. Both looked up at Item.

"Hapunta is very ill. Because you, Tuksook, are learning to become Wise One and you're young, I want you to stay away from Hapunta and Brill. If Brill asks you for something, come find me. Gumui, you are also young and I want you to avoid Hapunta and Brill also. If there is a way this illness can spread, we cannot have Tuksook acquire it nor you, because you look after her. Do you both understand?"

"Yes, Mother, I will obey," Tuksook replied.

"I also understand and will obey," Gumui replied. "Is there anything we can do to help?" he asked.

Brill returned to Togomoo and Hapunta. "Heek will be happy to make the tea," she reported. "I'll stay with Hapunta in the north part of the bent tree house."

"Right now, I'm going to take Hapunta to the privy. Would you wrap that skin around her, Brill?" Togomoo asked. He stood up so Brill could cover the girl. Then he headed to the east entryway. When he stepped outside, he came to a complete stop, almost dropping Hapunta.

Hapunta looked up. "Is the earth on fire, Father?" she asked.

Togomoo whistled his "Come—now!" hunter whistle. Hunters from the house jumped up and raced to the east entrance of the house. When they reached outside, they were shocked. The entire sky was new blood red.

Midgenemo whistled a call to come to all the rest of the People. The house emptied fast. Once outside, there was dead silence. They stood there, never having seen anything like it. They feared, not in the way a hunter might fear. This fear was more of a spiritual nature. Red sky was outside their knowledge. It conjured up thoughts of evil and bad omens. The sky seemed to move as flames—but not flames. There were no words for what they witnessed. Some of the People wondered whether someone had broken from Wisdom's way and brought evil on them all.

Tuksook thought she heard something. She stepped away from the group moving to the north to try to hear better.

"Tuksook," the quiet voice said.

"Wisdom?"

"Yes. The red sky is a normal part of this land. There are other times the lights in the sky will be white, green, or blue. There is no cause for concern or fear."

"Thank you, Wisdom," she said softly.

"Keep my way, Tuksook."

"I will, Wisdom," Tuksook whispered.

Togomoo quietly walked to the privy carrying Hapunta. Poor child, he thought. Her hair was soaked and now this red sky. What was it a sign of? He wondered. Was something awful about to happen, or was this a normal part of the place to which they'd moved? The girl made water, and then she stood there, coughing up lots of mucous. Togomoo carefully covered it with dirt from the fill back hill they'd made at the edge of the ditch. The back fill was frozen, so he had to fill it in hunks. He left her standing on the ground for a moment while he wrapped the skin around her better. Then, he scooped her up and headed back to the People. The sky continued to be red.

When he returned, Brill met him and held out her arms. "Let me take her in and put her on the new sleeping place."

"She coughed up much mucous," Togomoo said.

"I'll share that with Item," she told him.

Brill took Hapunta into the house. She'd already transferred the sleeping skins and the bench/sleeping place cover from Hapunta's sleeping place to the one in the north part of the house. She laid Hapunta on it and noticed that the tea Heek had made was ready. Heek had gone outside and come back in to be sure the tea was ready as soon as possible.

"Thank you, Heek. I appreciate your kindness," Brill said.

"You are more than welcome. I wish Hapunta well. Here are several pouches that contain measured amounts of willow for the tea. If you need, return the pouches for more. I hope this helps."

Brill nodded, thanked Heek, and took the tea to Hapunta.

"I want you to drink all of this," she told her daughter.

Hapunta looked at her. She really didn't want anything, but she knew as all the children of the People knew, when a parent, adult, or elder told you to do something, you had to comply. She sat up and dangled her feet off the sleeping place. She took the small steaming bowl and began to sip the tea. It wasn't a taste she'd choose, but it wasn't bad. She'd had it long ago.

Brill was patient. She sat on the edge of the sleeping place and watched Hapunta finish the willow tea. Then, she had her lie down and Brill carefully covered her. "I'm going back outside. I will return soon. Sleep, my daughter," she said, pulling a furred skin around her own shoulders.

Back outside, the night sky was still flaming red. Whatever the red was, she could see stars through it. It was very late. The color seemed to be decreasing in intensity. As the People watched, a very strange thing happened. The color faded and the red left the sky. The night sky looked like any other night sky they'd seen since arriving at Eagle's Grasp. The People returned to their sleeping places wondering at the red sky.

Brill checked on Hapunta and found the girl sleeping. Togomoo brought Brill some skins for her sleeping place in the north part of the house. He regretted that she would not be sharing his sleeping place as usual, but understood the need for one of them to be available to Hapunta.

After some time, Brill found Hapunta definitely had cooled down. Brill slipped into the extra sleeping place and made herself comfortable. She fell to sleep right away. When Hapunta stirred, Brill jumped up and went to touch her daughter. She was hot again. Brill went to the food preparation place in the house, with tongs picked up a hot rock near the expiring fire, and dropped the rock in the boiling bag. The water began to boil. She took the little leather bag of willow that Heek had prepared for a single dose and put it in the small bowl. She added the hot water to the herbs. She stirred it. Carefully, she carried the small bowl to Hapunta.

Hapunta drank it, knowing the effect it had. Soon she felt better and went back to sleep, but the cough was still there—maybe not so bad as earlier. Brill was disturbed. Nobody else had anything like this lung sickness. Brill knew there were many lung sicknesses, but you'd never know what the illness was until it had progressed for several days.

While she was up, Brill went to the east entrance and stepped outside. Momeh, her nephew, was at the entrance outside.

"I didn't expect to see you here," Brill whispered.

"I didn't expect to see you here either, Aunt. I am on watch tonight. Since we had the red sky, I wanted to see whether it returned. It has not returned all night."

"It was strange, but it didn't seem to do any damage."

"I agree," Momeh replied. "This is an unusual land. Have you ever heard of a red sky?"

"Never," she whispered.

"If it were up to me, we wouldn't have any more of them. It makes me feel as if strange spirits take huge steps among us."

"If that bothers you, talk to the Wise One in the morning. I'm going to try to sleep before Hapunta wakes up again." Brill left and went to her new sleeping place. She didn't want to have her mind web troubled with red sky and spirits. She had enough to occupy her mind web with Hapunta.

In the morning the People were subdued, wondering about the red sky and whether it might be an evil omen. The People took the morning meal quietly. After he finished eating, Midgenemo touched Tuksook on the shoulder and said, "Come outside with me so I may talk to you."

Tuksook wasn't finished eating, but she put her bowl beside Gumui, leaving him with a knowing look, and followed her father. She turned back for a moment to grab a hairless sleeping skin to put around her shoulders.

"What is it, Father?" she asked.

"You talked with Wisdom?"

"Of course."

"I haven't talked to Wisdom yet. What is the importance of the red sky?"

"Wisdom said it is a natural occurrence. We may see lights of blue, white, and green. It is nothing to fear."

"Do you wish to share that with the People? They are troubled."

"Father, I think you should tell them that Wisdom says they are natural in this place and there's nothing to fear." Midgenemo was glad she didn't choose to be the one to deliver the message. He didn't want the People to know that she had spoken to Wisdom about it while he hadn't. He didn't think to ask whether she or Wisdom initiated the interaction.

"I will. Come inside and let's calm their fears."

Tuksook followed him into the house. She had gone out barefooted. She needed to remind herself to put boots on her feet. It was too cold for uncovered feet. Tuksook returned to Gumui and he handed her bowl to her. She resumed eating, as if there had been no interruption.

"People," Midgenemo called out. Slowly all the People gathered at the central hearth.

Once the People assembled, he said, "Wisdom has spoken. The red sky is a part of this land. There will also be sky lights of white, blue, and green. There is nothing to fear. Do not trouble yourselves over last night's red sky."

Most of the People visibly relaxed, because clearly the Wise One was not concerned any longer. A few, who had lost their complete trust in the Wise One, wondered whether he had made that up to keep them from feeling too anxious. Each decided individually that time would make it clear.

Brill went to check on Hapunta. The girl was in a heavy sweat again. "How do you feel?" she asked.

"I feel bad. My legs, arms, and even my fingers ache. I think I would like some more willow tea."

Brill felt her. She was very hot. She patted Hapunta's shoulder, picked up her small bowl, and went to make more tea.

When the tea water was boiling, Brill added it to the small bowl, stirred the mixture, and carried it to Hapunta who had fallen back to sleep. She shook her to waken her. "You need to sit up and drink this. Then you may sleep again."

The girl pushed herself to a sitting position, leaning against the tree that was part of the bent tree house. She ached terribly but knew she would feel better after she drank the tea. It was hard for her to remain awake, so she drank the tea as fast as possible, sipping carefully to avoid burning herself. Brill warmed some red sphagnum and laid it across Hapunta's chest. The girl seemed to enjoy the warmth.

A few of the hunters dressed warmly and went outside to check to be sure that the red sky had done no damage. By the dog house, Stencellomak laughed with Loraz, "The Wise One may be right. I see no damage anywhere except my fingers and they're becoming terribly cold." He was trying to withdraw his hands further inside the fur he had wrapped around himself.

"Yes. I'm having the same problem. I should have put on hand coverings," Loraz complained.

"We're a funny looking People. At least we can cover our heads with the skins. Remember the time we put caribou skins over us to try to fool the caribou into thinking we were one of them? We were funny looking then! If it's this cold now, can you imagine the shortest day of the year?" Stencellomak said as he stepped over to check with the central sun tracking pole.

"That's going to be very cold. Makes me shiver to think of it. I wonder how much snow we'll have," Loraz said.

"I'm thinking much more than we had in our old land. The days are still becoming shorter—that's no surprise," Stencellomak said, his breath white, lingering in the air.

"Probably we'll have more snow than we did back home. It was so dry back there. I don't know what snow would've come from. When we were young, we had some snow but lately with years of no snow at all, some of the young People will see snow for the first time this year. The women are making beaver head and hand coverings for us. These boots are wonderful! They're making something else, but I'm not sure what it is."

"Let's hurry back. I need to thaw," Stencellomak said.

They were the last of the hunters to survey for damage. They gathered in the south part of the bent tree house and assured each other that there was no damage. Each went to his own part of the house and put away the skins they'd used for protection against the cold.

Toward high sun, though nobody checked to be sure it was high sun, Item hit rocks together. All the people gathered at the central hearth, sitting in their assigned areas.

Item remained standing. "I have called you here to let you know, first, that Hapunta is very ill. She lies in the north part of the house. Avoid her. Second, I have a surprise. The women have finished the cold time protection for the hunters and Elfa. Elfa is included because she feeds the dogs. They are still working on protection for others, but the hunters' cold time protection is complete. Try on the hat, mittens, pants, and jacket now so that we know they fit."

Each hunter's wife carried a fur jacket, fur pants, mittens, and a hat that covered the head and had a short capelet that went from the hat out over the shoulders. For hunters who were not joined, their mothers handed them their protection. The hunters would be warm indeed. Those hunters who had just gone outside realized immediately the value of what they'd just been given. As expected, there was no one whose protection failed to fit well. Elfa's cold time protection fit well. Hers was made from giant beaver.

"Women," Kew said as he turned around and around. "This will keep us very warm, but it doesn't make moving around very easy!" He was trying to be entertaining by exaggerating limited movement, and the young men and children laughed more than the women and girls, who had worked hard on the cold time protection.

Item was still standing. She said, "We would like all of you to go outside and stay a while and then report back as to how warm the protection is. Don't forget your boots. You, too, Elfa."

The men who had started to remove the garments put them back on. They dutifully filed outside dressed for protection against the cold. Elfa followed.

"Where was this earlier when we were out checking for damage and our fingers were freezing?" Stencellomak said dramatically to Unmo and Hawk who walked nearby. What they discovered quickly is that the protection was too warm to wear tied closed. They needed to untie the garments because they had begun to sweat. They carried the mittens, because they were too warm with all the other protection. They realized that they would have protection that could adapt to the cold temperature. They did not remain outside long. They'd report back to the women, and the women would work diligently to finish the protection for the rest of the People.

Once inside, Unmo said, "I think we need to find a way to take off the mittens and secure them so we can use our hands, but have the mittens quickly available once we've done what we need to do with our bared hands."

The women chatted about various ways to solve the removal of mittens. Hunters carefully removed the cold time protection and folded them exactly as they had been folded. Women would take lengths of leather. They'd sew the center of the long piece of leather to the center back neck of the jacket. They'd run the leather through the arms of the jackets and tie the mitten through a slit to the piece of leather. Then, when the hunter wanted to remove his mitten, it would dangle near the sleeve, ready for him to put it back on.

Item met Brill in the north part of the house. "How's she doing?" she asked.

"Not well," Brill replied downcast.

Item placed her hand on the girl's head.

Hapunta opened her eyes. She struggled, but asked, "Item, am I dying?" Then she began to cough hard.

Item was visibly startled at the question. She patted Hapunta on the shoulder. "I see no signs of that, Hapunta. There's no need for worry now. Just make full effort to improve."

"Brill, she needs to cough that mucous out of her lungs. Have her drink much water all day. Also, when you finish using the warm red sphagnum on her chest, have her bend at the waist dropping the upper part of her body over the sleeping place, so the mucous will flow downward towards the ground. Have her do that until she coughs up as much mucous as possible. Give her a bowl to catch the mucous. Don't use that bowl for any other purpose. Run water over the bowl to clean it at the privy. Don't put it in the communal rinsing bin. When she recovers, discard it in the fire."

"I will do that. How often during the day should she hang like that?"

"I'd say four or five times a day. Treating it first with the red moss should help it to flow. It's important to keep that mucous from drowning her."

At that thought, Brill determined to have Hapunta hang over the sleeping place at least five times that day. The very idea that Hapunta could drown while in the bent tree house was more than Brill could accept. If she had anything to do with it, her beloved daughter would become well.

Near the south entryway Mongo and Taman had gathered to make stone spear heads. They loved the cold time when they were free to make and repair tools all day. Young boys were fascinated and would sit nearby to watch and learn from these elders. Mongo hummed while he worked, barely aware that he did.

Women all over the bent tree house were busy making cold time protection for the rest of the People while Ing and Turl were fixing the mittens to leather strips attached to the jackets. Small groups sat together and chatted as they worked. Renwen and Kouchu, the wife of Loraz, were beginning preparation for the evening meal. Kouchu had, at Item's request, checked to be sure every bowl was very clean. Item did not want Hapunta's illness to spread. Item was certain that some illnesses could spread, especially when accompanied by excessive body heat. She didn't know how the illness spread. She simply strove for cleanliness, avoiding the ill person, and keeping eating and drinking containers separated from People who were not ill.

Tuksook was reciting stories to the Wise One. Story after story transported her to different times and places, all telling them things they needed to know to survive.

Gumui and Orad had put on their cold time protection, taken a spear, and gone outside. As soon as they went out, snow began to fall. The flakes were enormous, looking like down feathers from geese or eagles. They were transfixed from the sight of it.

"I never become too old to react to the allure of snow. It stops me and holds my attention with its beauty," Gumui said.

"It is beautiful. These flakes are huge!"

"Orad, it's sticking to the ground. Do you think it'll melt before warm weather returns?"

"That, as you well know is a wait-and-see, my friend."

"Already the back fill for the privy is frozen. We've never had to back fill with chunks."

"You would think of something like that!" Orad said teasingly taunting. "From the allure of snow to back filling with chunks!"

"Let's go up the hill to see what we see from there."

Orad and Gumui ascended the hill and realized that even with the bulky cold time protection, they were still able to climb up easily. They could function well, just slower.

"Look!" Orad shouted.

From the north a giant deer was entering the meadow. The giant deer presented quite a vision of the species. His antlers were massive, his coat prime, his health appeared to be perfect. The animal stood inside the meadow, having left the few trees that grew in that space. He surveyed the meadow.

Gumui said, "I think he must come this way on his migration. Look how he views the meadow, as if he owns it. It's like he's noticing something's different. Maybe he wonders about the changes."

"I'd like to know how he manages to carry those heavy antlers on his head. You felt how heavy the antlers were that the hunters brought when they first took a giant deer here. These look even larger."

"Well," Gumui replied, "I'm just glad we don't have to carry antlers to show the girls how handsome we are!"

Orad laughed, imagining. Then he said, "Wisdom, protect this one. Give him a long life, with all the food he needs to remain healthy, and may he father many."

The giant deer looked right at Orad and Gumui. It walked proudly down the meadow. The dogs made small sounds, but did not bark.

"Do you think he knows what I just said?" Orad asked, startled.

"Who can tell?" Gumui replied with a grin.

Gumui and Orad walked over to look at the giant deer tracks in the snow. They stored the shape, size, and distance apart of the tracks in their mind webs for future use.

"Ready to go back?" Gumui asked.

"Yes, but it's going to be a long cold time in the bent tree house. It's a good size, but it's confining. I feel it already."

"I know what you mean," Gumui replied. "With our cold time protection we should be able to go out to walk the meadow, if for no other reason than to be outside the house and move around."

Snow fell to a depth of a man's forefinger. Then the sky cleared and there was sun. The sun looked weak, but it was there.

Inside the north part of the house, Hapunta's body heat had become very high and stayed there regardless of the willow tea. She wandered in her mind web or slept the sleep from which one could not be wakened. Item told Brill she must cool her down. She suggested they put her on a skin on the ground and cover her with snow. Togomoo went outside and gathered a large bowl of snow. It took several gatherings to have enough to cover her. She shivered, but her mind web was far from them. Finally, her shivering became harder, and the body heat returned to normal. Brill picked her up and laid her back on the sleeping place, covering her carefully with the skins. Hapunta did not waken. Brill noticed that Hapunta was becoming very thin.

Four days passed. Early in the morning before the People were awake, Brill went to check on Hapunta. She found the lifeless body of her daughter staring out wall eyed through clouded eyes. It ripped her belly from end to end. She closed the girl's eyes and propped a skin under her chin until she could find a chin strap to hold her jaw in place. Brill wept soundlessly while sitting beside her daughter's body. She would miss this special little one. Brill wasn't terribly surprised. In the last day or two, Hapunta seemed already to have left. She stood up and walked quietly to Togomoo. She touched him, waking him. She shook her head negatively and he stood up and followed her. He saw his daughter's body and it tore his belly. Hapunta had been so special. He sat with Brill and both wept silently.

As People awakened, more and more came to see what had happened. Hamaklob, Stencellomak, Wave, and Loraz dressed in their cold time protection before the morning meal, gathered tools, and headed to the part of the meadow on the south side where the People had planned to have a spot for burials. They moved the snow away and began to dig only to find the ground was frozen. The men, undaunted, gathered some wood and bones and built a fire on the frozen meadow land. They let the fire thaw the land. Once thawed they dug as deep as possible. They set another fire on the frozen ground and began again. It took a long time to dig the hole because of the need to thaw the ground. Once they had the hole the depth of a man's waist from the bottom of the hole, they decided that was deep enough. They returned inside.

Because not all the cold time protection was ready, the Wise One called all together at the central hearth for the grave side tradition. One by one People told what they chose of their memories of Hapunta. Finally, the circle of People had completed a round, and the Wise One told the creation story. At that point, Togomoo carried the skin wrapped body of Hapunta. Brill accompanied him. They were joined by Hamaklob, Stencellomak, Wave, and Loraz. Togomoo laid his first child's wrapped body in the hole in the ground, refusing permission for his mind web to think on the coldness of it all. There were no flowers, so Brill took some red ochre powder and sprinkled it over the wrapped body of her daughter. They covered her body with the skins she'd soaked with her sweat. Then, Togomoo and Brill returned to the bent tree house. The men began to fill back the grave. Already the ground they'd dug up was refreezing. It was a rather lumpy back fill. They stomped the ground after filling the hole, hoping to mash the lumps into a more cohesive cover. Then, they brushed the snow back over the grave. The men returned to the bent tree house.

Turl and Solong wept for their friend. The three of them had done so much together. It would feel very empty without Hapunta.

Item went to the wood lean-to at the side of the house. She chose a piece of wood about as long as her forearm. It had no bark. She took a food preparation place knife designed for cutting small pieces of food. She made a notch in the wood. She took the wood to her sleeping place and put it in her sewing basket under the sleeping place. She would count the days to twenty since the death of Hapunta. If no one else had become sick like Hapunta in twenty days, they were probably safe from the illness.

It was evening. Twenty days had passed. Item opened her sewing basket. She pulled out the wood piece she'd been notching. She cut the twentieth cut into the wood. Fortunately, no one else had hot body heat like Hapunta had. The twenty days should make it clear that the danger of becoming ill like Hapunta had passed. She would share the information at council and put the stick in the central hearth to burn. She felt showered in relief. Item had no understanding of what caused Hapunta's death. She knew she knew a lot, but she felt there was much she didn't know too. At such times she felt helpless.

Tuksook wanted to visit Wisdom again. She knew that she could lie down on their sleeping place, but she feared interruption. She wanted to go outside. She wanted to go to the rock up the hill. Gumui was walking towards her.

"Tuksook!" he greeted her with enthusiasm.

"My husband," she greeted him.

"I have come to know you well, I think," he said with a smile. "I am thinking you might like to spend time with Wisdom outside. We both have cold time protective clothing. What do you think?"

"You have stolen the thoughts and words from my mind web," she said.

The two pulled their cold time protection from the pegs where they hung on the wall by their bench/sleeping place. They dressed carefully. They wanted the clothing to last for a very long time. Gumui was impressed each time he put the jacket on. What impressed him was the way the women had attached the mittens. He thought the idea solved the problem exceptionally well. It seemed simple, and so often, he reasoned, simple solutions were incredibly bright.

The two left by the west entryway. They stood in the meadow briefly adjusting from the dark of the bent tree house to the stark white snowy meadow. The sun was out and the large flakes on the meadow reflected back a variety of sparkling colors. Tuksook breathed in deeply. Her outgoing breath was white, making clouds in the clean, cold, and invigorating air. The two headed toward the path up the hill to the rock.

Once there, they realized that snow melt during sunny times had caused ice to form on the path to the rock. The footing was slippery at best.

"Tuksook," Wisdom's small voice came seemingly from the air.

"Yes, Wisdom?" Tuksook replied aloud while Gumui looked at Tuksook and turned, looking for something that would represent Wisdom. He hadn't heard any voice.

"Do not climb the hill. To climb the hill invites broken bones. Ice is under the snow. Follow my way, Tuksook." Wisdom's voice drifted away on the air.

"We can't go up there," Tuksook said. "I think I just had my meeting with Wisdom."

"How? I didn't hear or see anything. I realize you two met, but it's something I don't understand."

"It was the spiritual voice of Wisdom that he told me he'd begin to use to talk to me. I could hear his voice clearly. It was the second time I've heard his voice this way."

"I believe you, but I have to leave it at belief. It's not something I can reason. I could hear or see nothing. We certainly won't climb to the rock, Tuksook. Should you tell the People that they should avoid the hill?"

"I'll tell Father. He can decide whether to deliver the message or have me do it. As long as the message is out there, all's well."

Back in the house, Ottu and Kew were chatting in the north part of the house near the dry fish and meat place for the dogs' food.

Ottu said, "Well, Hapunta became ill at the same time as the red sky. I just think that somehow the red sky kept her from becoming well. I think it was an evil sign."

"How can that be when Wisdom told the Wise One that the red sky is part of this land and that other lights of different colors are also something we'll see here?"

"Suppose he made it up?"

"Ottu, I don't believe that. He vowed to stay in Wisdom's way. You saw that tree felled by lightning on his sleeping place in the lean-to. You saw the lightning strike right beside him, where he heard Wisdom tell him never to leave his way again. You can't fake that. It happened in front of all of us."

"I suppose, but I just find it so hard to trust him after the crisis he created with Rimut and Pito. He's an opportunistic man quite pride filled, I think."

"Well, Wisdom chose him, and that's sufficient for me."

"Kew," Ottu continued confidentially, "just wait until we have another red sky and let's see if something evil happens."

"I will wait and watch with you," Kew replied humoring the old man rather than really concerned that another red sky would bring death.

Tuksook and Gumui hung their cold time protection clothing on the pegs by their bench/sleeping place. Tuksook went to find her father.

"Father," she said, "I have something to share."

"Come, sit. We should be about the stories. Speak."

"Wisdom cautioned me while Gumui and I were about to climb the hill to the rock. He said that ice lies under the snow on the hill and it's a place for broken bones."

"Do you wish to share that tonight?"

"Father, I think you should tell the People that Wisdom cautions against climbing the hill behind us, because the ice under the snow could cause People to fall and break bones."

"Are you sure you would have me tell this?"

"Yes, Father. I think it is right that you tell it."

"Very well. I'll do it." Midgenemo was struck that twice his daughter had him deliver information, information that she could have delivered to grow her credibility with the People. He knew it wasn't an issue of shyness. He began to wonder whether she might be leading him, but he quickly dismissed the thought as being beyond her years and capability. It was his responsibility to lead her, not the other way around. No, he reasoned, she could not be leading him. At council he'd deliver Wisdom's message.

Many days had passed. The land grew snowier and colder. Hunters cleared away snow for paths to the sun trackers and the privy. They cleared away snow to the path that led to the lower level, careful to keep just enough snow so that they could walk with a grip of snow instead of sliding on ice. From time to time the hunters would climb to the top of the bent tree house to be sure that the snow didn't appear too deep. They were unsure what they sought, having to learn during this first cold time. Days were still shortening, they discovered, checking the sun trackers at each opportunity of clear sky.

At the morning meal, Taman announced, "Today, any boys or girls ages five to ten who want to test for animal tracking, join me at the south entryway after we eat."

Excitement rippled through the young children at the invitation. If they passed, they'd be called trackers. It was one of the first steps in becoming a hunter. Girls were as welcome as boys.

"You must let me go, Mother," Ren insisted.

Tuksook was behind Ren, and Tuksook smiled an encouragement to her mother to let Ren attend. Item didn't miss Tuksook's smiling plea for her sister.

"Very well," Item replied. Item actually spoke to Tuksook but Ren was unaware.

Ren was dumbfounded. There was no protestation. Her mother had just approved her request. Ren was thrilled. She'd learned the tracks from Lurch. She was certain she'd be successful. Her small round face was glowing. She ate too fast.

Once the confusion of the young ones dressing for the cold and assembling in the South part of the house occurred, Taman designated the hunter that would accompany each young one. Taman began the pairing: "When your names are called, leave by the south entryway. Be careful not to step on animal tracks. Nal, go with Remui. Ren, go with Hawk." The four left quietly. Only the hunters carried spears.

"Kig, go with Orad. Wims—where's Wims?—oh, there you are. Wims go with Vole." They left quietly.

"Guw, go with Lurch. Velur, go with Pago. Olog, go with Momeh. Nipe, go with Moki." They left.

"Col, go with Taq. Jum, go with Togomoo." They left.

"Bitro, go with Stencellomak. Guko, go with Vel."

"Finally, Solong, you go with me." Solong and Taman left the house quietly.

In the east part of the house, Oneg finally let go of the sob she'd been holding in. She wept. She was planning to be a great hunter like her grandfather, Kew. Here was her first trial and she missed it because she still had to wear the splint on her leg. Her belly was ripped apart at not being able to participate.

Bit-n went to her, carrying an extra skin and red sphagnum moss. "I know you had your plans to shine in your tracking skill, my daughter. This is not your time. You must remember always to take care not to injure yourself. Keep your risks very low. Have you learned that?" Bit-n laid out the skin and Oneg swung her leg across it. She watched as Bit-n unwrapped the leg while the splints remained on. The leg was healing without infection, for which Bit-n was well pleased.

Oneg controlled her sobbing and looked with large eyes at her mother. "I was without a mind web, Mother. I have learned that lesson the hardest way possible."

"Well," Bit-n reasoned, "Maybe not the hardest way. I think death would be the hardest way." Bit-n washed the leg with white moss and took the very warm red moss and laid it on top of the leg over the place, where she'd sewed the skin together with Oneg's hair.

Oneg was silent briefly. She looked deeply into her mother's eyes when Bit-n looked up. "Do you think that you can learn when you can no longer apply the lesson? If I learned and then died, how can I say I learned— because I'm dead?"

"Good question, Oneg. I'll have to reason on that. I will provide you a lesson today in something the others don't know. Be quiet until I return."

Bit-n went to her bench/sleeping place and slid out a woven box from beneath the bench. She gently picked up a wrapped cylinder from the box and slid the box back under the bench. She carried the leather wrapped cylinder to Oneg.

"You must handle this with the greatest care," she told the unhappy girl.

Oneg watched, fascinated as her mother carefully and slowly unwrapped the cylinder.

"This is a flute made for me when I was your age. I played it a lot. When I began to have children the flute fell into disuse, for I had other things to do. I still have too many very young ones that take my time. You can learn to play this while you have a broken leg. Perhaps, you can learn to make pleasing sounds to make the People happy in the house, especially while the cold is on the land."

Oneg never had known her mother played the flute. She looked at the fragile looking bird bone her mother held tenderly in her hands. Oneg's mind web was entranced by the uniqueness of the experience. She focused on nothing but her mother's teaching, gently and simply, while the children outside did what she had not been able to do. She found herself desperate to learn to play the flute. Bit-n had never seen Oneg so interested in anything. It was a special time for them.

As Oneg played the three melodies, Bit-n removed the cooled red sphagnum from her leg and took the materials she used to treat Oneg's leg to dry so they could be disposed of. She smiled to think how well the leg was healing.

By the time the children began to return to the bent tree house, Oneg had learned three melodies and was beginning to experiment with the sounds produced by each covered hole by one or more fingers. Each sound was firmly set in her mind web. She had learned to count as she played, so that the melody fit properly with a rhythm. It was an entirely new world and Oneg wanted to absorb it all well.

A few children saw what she had and asked to try it. She told them the flute was special to her mother and she did not have permission to share it. It gave her something to do while she couldn't use her leg. That satisfied the children.

Ren went to her and asked, "What is that?"

"Hi, Ren. It's my mother's flute. She is teaching me to play it, to give me something to do, since I can't go outside to test for tracker. How'd you do?"

"I passed the test, Oneg. I am so excited. I passed it."

"I'm happy for you, Ren. I know you really wanted to pass it. That's great!"

"Oneg, will you play for me?"

"I'll be happy to. Listen to this one." Oneg played the first melody her mother taught her. It was simple to play, but even in its simplicity, it took the mind web and carried it to restful, calm places.

Ren's eyes widened as she listened. "That's beautiful, Oneg. Can I come back and sit here and listen to you play it?"

"With your mother's permission," Oneg told her, secretly hoping Item would give her permission, because she was often lonely. Others were always busy doing things she couldn't do.

Item gave permission to Ren to visit with Oneg. Ren was captivated by the melodies.

At council that night, the children who passed the tracker test were recognized. Taman said, "First, let us thank those hunters who conducted the testing."

The People nodded towards hunters they knew participated. Many actually said aloud, "Thank you."

Taman continued, "Our new trackers are: Nal, Ren, Kig, Guw, Bitro, Solong. For those of you who tried, good effort on the part of all! The biggest difficulty lay in separating the camel, horse, and sheep tracks. Some had trouble with the hare and squirrel. For those of you who didn't pass this time, continue your effort. There will be another test. Be ready. Remember next time the tracks may be different. Also, remember that it is the droppings, sometimes, that are the clue when you have difficulty with the tracks. It is also wise to follow the tracks back and forward, for that may provide more information. Again, good effort all."

A few days later, Ottu reported at the morning meal that the shortest day had finally passed. The People were looking forward to days lengthening. By evening, and for the third time that day, the Wise One experienced pain in his chest. The last episode left him breathless and sweating. Finally, at his wits end, he told Item.

"Why didn't you say something earlier?" she asked, already knowing the answer.

He just looked at her as she put her head, ear side down, on his chest. She drew back and looked at him accusingly. "You've been having this problem for a long time," she said.

"Yes," he replied.

"You know that your heart is beating irregularly?"

"Well, no, I didn't know that," he told her. "Am I dying?" he asked.

"I don't think it's come to that," she said lightly, though she really had no idea. "I do want you to take some tea that I'll fix for you. Stay there," she told him.

He was resting on his bench and had no energy to apply to moving anywhere.

Item took some white bark from the spruce tree from one of her leather pouches. She poured hot water over it and carried it to Midgenemo. "Now, drink this," she said. "I have one other thing to bring you, so drink that down."

Item took some wild geranium root, thinking of the lovely blue flowers that the plant showed when it bloomed. She cut off some and poured hot water over it. She carried it to Midgenemo. She put the bowl on the ground and took the small bowl he'd just emptied. She put her head, ear side down, on his chest. The heart still had the same irregular heartbeat.

She handed him the second small bowl. "Drink all of this," she said.

"I will," he replied, taking the bowl from her.

He drank all of it. There was nothing in the bowl to make him drowsy, but he suddenly felt very sleepy.

"Pull yourself all the way on our sleeping place, and sleep a bit. It will make the things I gave you to drink work better," she said. She knew she'd made that up, but she wanted him to think positively and knew he was quick to fear death from small things. This was no small thing—she knew. She was afraid for him, and she couldn't let him see that.

Flute music began to play in the east part of the house. Bit-n was on her way to treat Oneg's leg. She smiled. Her daughter was doing well.

She took the warmed moss and skin and went to Oneg. Oneg immediately put the flute down.

"Mother," she asked, "What did you reason?"

Bit-n wondered what she had missed. She looked at Oneg with a blank face.

"Mother, you said you'd reason to decide whether you could say someone learned something, if, just after they saw what they needed to see, they died."

"Oh, that. I did spend a little time reasoning it. I can see why you say what you say. Let me suggest you ask Tuksook," Bit-n said as a way to defer to those who might have a better answer.

"I'll do that, Mother. Thank you. Oh, that is very warm!" she said surprised.

Bit-n put a small skin over the moss to hold the heat longer.

"I'll let Tuksook know you have a question for her," Bit-n said.

"Thank you, Mother," Oneg replied.

Bit-n left her, heading to the west side of the house where she could see Tuksook.

Tuksook stood up as Bit-n approached. It was the polite thing to do when an older person approached.

"Don't stand up," Bit-n protested.

"Are you looking for me?" Tuksook asked.

"Yes, Tuksook. Yesterday Oneg and I were talking and I asked her whether she'd learned not to take risks like the one that caused her fall. She was upset that she missed the tracker testing. She said it was the hardest learning. I said I thought that the hardest learning resulted in death. Then, Oneg asked whether you could consider learning something, if death followed, and you couldn't apply the learning. She's young for questions like this. I told her I'd ask you to answer the question."

Tuksook looked at Bit-n. "That is a question beyond her years, but one that she's had plenty of time to reason. I tend to agree with her, Bit-n. We're certainly taught to learn and apply, until those words are paired in our mind webs. We're even taught that if you haven't applied it, you haven't learned it. I'll be glad to talk to her about this. I have heard her play your flute. It's lovely. I hope she really likes it, because it gave me great pleasure yesterday."

"Please, Tuksook, when you talk to her, let her know that."

"I will," Tuksook smiled broadly at Bit-n.

Tuksook stood up and headed to the east part of the house. Wisdom had made it clear to her that she needed to talk to the younger people. This was a start. Slow start, but a start.

She looked at Oneg, Ren's favorite friend. The little girl had red curly hair and blue eyes. She looked very worn out with the splint and having to be immobilized. "Oneg, I have heard the flute music and it is very lovely. It made me so happy yesterday. I hope you'll play more today."

"I'll do it, Tuksook. I have so much to learn, but it is wonderful to have something to do that takes my mind web off my leg. I like playing it."

"Good. Everyone should be happy to hear that. Bit-n said you have a question about whether, if one dies just after learning, it could be said they have learned. You have been taught just as I have been taught that you don't learn anything unless you apply it. Learn and apply; learn and apply. We're taught to put that in our mind webs early in life. I think your question was well reasoned, Oneg, and I'd tend to agree with your thought. So, yes, maybe one of the hardest ways to learn is through pain. There is another way that may be tougher. What would you think of having to learn a lesson because something you did hurt someone else."

"If I hurt someone else, it would be worse than hurting me. If I'd had to learn not to risk myself in a dangerous situation, because doing that hurt someone else—that would be harder than if I hurt myself. That way two People are hurt instead of one: the one who was hurt and me, because I'd hurt for hurting someone else."

"How about if you hurt ten People, because you needed to learn something."

"I see what you mean, Tuksook. You've made me think hard. Hurting many People would be very painful. I'd hurt for each one and for myself."

"Well, Oneg," Tuksook said putting her hand gently on Oneg's shoulder, "It's fortunate that you didn't die. Now, please put your effort into learning to play that flute as you put effort into learning well to become a hunter. Then, I'll be so proud of you. Playing the flute well can give something to this house that comes from nowhere right now. Instead of hurting anyone else, it's like a gift to everyone."

Oneg was so touched that she reached out and hugged Tuksook. Tuksook was startled but returned the hug.

"I promise, Tuksook."

"Good."

Tuksook headed back to her place in the west part of the house. Gumui had just come in from outside and hung up his cold time protection clothing.

"You have been visiting Oneg?" he asked a little surprised.

"Yes. She had a question she'd asked Bit-n, and Bit-n referred the question to me."

"What could a six-year-old ask Bit-n that she'd need to refer to you?" Gumui chuckled.

"She asked if you learned something and then died, whether you'd really learned it, since there was no opportunity to apply it."

"She asked what? That kid has a mind web that works like yours!"

"Yes, I guess you could say that. She does reason things out, and, when she cannot find an answer, she asks." Tuksook sat on the edge of the bench.

Gumui sat beside her and put his arm around her.

"So?"

Tuksook laughed. "So, I reminded her that we're taught very young here to learn and apply, learn and apply. I agreed with her reasoning that if you learn something and then die, you'd probably not call it learning, since there's no way to apply it."

"I love you," Gumui said with a hug.

"I love you, too. I'm so happy the days are growing in length."

"I am, too. I love this house, but I like to be outside more often than is comfortable now."

"At least the sun doesn't leave us completely. Do you think there are places where the sun disappears?"

"In our old land, some traveling hunters talked about a far north land where there is no sun for part of the year."

"I hope the sun never leaves us completely."

"I agree. It's very cold outside with the little sun we have. The wind makes it a lot colder."

"What wind?"

"Oh, we've had a breeze out there blowing in from the north. It's convenient we're in this meadow in the trees. It keeps a lot of the wind away from us."

Item went over to Midgenemo and though he still slept, she put her head, ear down, on his chest to see how his heart sounded. There was no change. The knowledge troubled her a lot, but there was no one with whom she could share her concern. She fixed another tea, mixing the white inner bark of the spruce with the wild geranium root. She took it to him and wakened him.

"I really went to sleep in the day?" he said surprised.

"Yes, you did. You must be tired." She handed him the tea.

"This tastes different," he remarked.

"That's because I put two things together. It's fine this way."

"Oh, I'm not worried about that. Thank you, Item. You are a good woman."

"Thank you," she said. "Tell me, when did you first notice that you didn't feel right?"

"I think it was back in our old land, before I learned from Wisdom that we had to migrate. I had some awful pain. But, then, it went away and I didn't think about it much after that."

"So, it's been going on for quite some time."

"Yes. But that's encouraging to me."

"Why's that?" Item asked.

"Because I can keep on going. If I were in a serious condition, I'd be unable to attend to my duties."

"I see," Item replied. She could follow his reasoning, but it was faulty. She wasn't sure she wanted to talk to him about that yet.

Tuksook couldn't help but see her parents from where she and Gumui had their bench/sleeping place. She had seen her father have some problem that looked like pain. Her mother had given him some kind of tea twice now. She wondered whether her father was ill.

Item left Midgenemo and walked to where Gumui and Tuksook sat together. "Tuksook," her mother said, "Your father is not feeling well. You will have to take his role at council tonight."

"Tonight?"

"Are you hearing well?" Item asked her.

"Yes, Mother. I just don't know whether I'm ready."

"If you're not ready, you'd better talk to Wisdom fast, because you have a responsibility at council tonight and you have to do it."

"Very well, Mother. I'll do my best. What's wrong with Father?"

"I'm not sure. He's been having chest pain. This is different from what Hapunta had. He has no lung congestion. I'm just giving him some teas trying to help and watching to see what develops."

"Don't let him worry about tonight. I'll tend to the council."

Item returned to Midgenemo.

"You're unsettled about tonight, aren't you?" Gumui asked her.

"Well, wouldn't you be?"

"I guess I was the first time I talked about the bent tree house until I started and then I realized I had something to share, and I forgot about myself."

"Maybe that'll work for me."

"It's not like you don't know how it works."

"You're right, Gumui."

The people ate the evening meal and by council most people in the house had noticed that the Wise One was lying down. Item brushed it over by saying he was being cautious because he had some pain in his chest. The council would take place and Tuksook would lead. That drew some interesting facial responses, but no words were spoken.

Clean up finished and council was called by Item. All gathered at the central hearth. Since Midgenemo and Item's bench/sleeping place was the most central in the house of all those in the west part, he could oversee Tuksook and hear everything that took place.

Tuksook began. "This evening, the Wise One is taking care of his health and I will serve in his place. We have happiness to share. Orad and Hustep have decided to join, and they have the approval of the Wise One. We no longer have a first nights place, so they have the shielded area in the north part of the house. Orad and Hustep," she called them forward.

"Orad," Tuksook said.

Orad took both of Hustep's hands and said, "I offer myself to you as husband for as long as my life extends."

"Hustep," Tuksook said.

Hustep said, "I offer myself to you as wife for as long as my life extends."

Tuksook said, "I say to Wisdom and to People everywhere, Orad and Hustep are one."

There were murmurs all around. As the two gathered their things, they accepted congratulations and left for the shielded area in the north part of the house.

"Is there any other information for the council this night?" Tuksook asked. Silence.

"Then we will have a story now."

Tuksook began, "This is a very, very old story. It is the story of Kukuk-na and Timkut-na. Timkut-na and Kukuk-na were hunters. They had trekked far looking for meat to feed the People. It was a time of drought and meat was not easy to find."

"Tumkut-na and Kukuk-na went to places where they had known deer to gather. There were none. They went to places where trees grew in groves providing shade from the sun for animals. There were no animals there. The men went to the highlands where they used to find grazers. There were none. They went to the lowlands and found nothing. Hunger was everywhere, but the two of them were determined that they would not let their People starve—not if they could help it."

"Kukuk-na and Timkut-na were exhausted. They looked for a place to sleep. Wisdom was sucking color from the land fast. Below them was a grove of trees and they stumbled towards it. Timkut-na was the first to arrive. He noticed a spring that had not dried up. He kneeled and began to drink, for his thirst was great. Suddenly he felt a hit on his hand. A serpent had been harboring in the grass beside him, and it bit his hand. He noticed it was a cobra. He cursed himself for being so careless. Kukuk-na arrived. He saw what had happened, and Timkut-na showed him the direction the cobra had gone. Kukuk-na found the snake and killed it. He looked for others and found none. There was no cure for the bite. Either Timkut-na would live or die."

"Kukuk-na tried to make a lean-to from what was available. He helped Timkut-na put out his sleeping skins and lie down. He made a fire and handed Timkut-na a piece of jerky, but the hunter declined. He wasn't hungry. Kukuk-na ate it. Timkut-na's hand was beginning to hurt severely. He became nauseated and vomited, but there was nothing in his stomach to eliminate but a little water. His eyelids were drooping and his hand and arm were swelling. Timkut-na was in obvious pain. Kukuk-na was agonizing over his friend. He kept the fire going and watched over Timkut-na carefully, while his friend slept fitfully. When Wisdom restored color to the land, Kukuk-na saw that Timkut-na was struggling to breathe. He saw him breathe his last."

"Kukuk-na took the digging tool Timkut-na carried in his backpack and dug the best he could to bury Kukuk-na. When he had him in the hole and covered by dirt, he still needed to find more dirt to cover his friend. He did not want any animals to dig the man up. Slowly he brought more dirt and covered the body. Then he found rocks and covered the mound. In the distance he heard what sounded like voices. He thought it was just his being alone that he was hearing things that weren't there."

"Kukuk-na sat by the lean-to and wept. He wept because his People hungered. He wept because there were no animals to feed his People. He wept because he and Timkut-na were starving. He wept because Kukuk-na died. He wept because he was alone."

"The voices came closer. Kukuk-na didn't notice. It was two hunters from his People. They had found meat. They came to call the hunters home."

"This story is the reason we always check thoroughly for snakes and spiders when we look at a place to camp or live. Even if you are terribly tired, you must look to be certain that the place you are planning to stay is free of harmful living things. Timkut-na died because his thirst was more important than his safety."

Tuksook looked at the People gathered there. Oddly, she had felt comfortable at the meeting. It was not as frightening an experience as she thought it might be. In truth, Tuksook admitted, it was enjoyable.

There was silence.

"Any additions to the council this night?" she asked.

Silence.

"Then, the council ends now for this night." She knew the Wise One said something but she had forgotten how he disbanded the council. Her words worked, for People were heading to their sleeping places."

"Well done," Ottu told her.

"Good, Tuksook," Unmo said touching her shoulder.

Item walked over and close to her ear said, "Your father is proud of you."

"Thank him for me, please," she replied.

Gumui handed Tuksook her jacket. He led her to the entryway in the west part of the house. Outside the wind was picking up, and in the sky there were green bands of color. They moved seemingly faster than the red ones, but then the red sky lights they saw had covered the whole sky. These were strips of green color. Gumui poked his head into the entryway and whistled the general "Come." He put his arms around Tuksook and they watched the sky light bands. As with the red ones, you could see stars through the bands of color. Some bands were straight overhead and some were in the distance. It was amazing to behold the display. It seemed that some of the sky lights were tinged with blue, others with white, but they found themselves uncertain. Just watching it was enough.

People used the east, south, and west entryways to go out to see the sky lights. There was a fascination with them that drew People to them. For some reason the green was not as frightening as the red sky had been. This by comparison seemed friendly. Midgenemo came out in his jacket and hat. He wore his boots. His mittens were on his hands. Item had clearly been involved in his pursuit of the sky lights. He stayed long enough to enjoy a good viewing of them and then he returned to his sleeping place.

Gumui looked at the roof of the bent tree house. The wind seemed to blow harder now. He and Tuksook returned inside. Both were filled with the beauty of the sky lights.

As the night wore on, the wind blew stronger and stronger. For some of the late night, the wind howled. No one went outside while it howled. Few adults slept well. Some didn't sleep at all. Occasionally, the People could hear a limb from one of the bent trees being tossed in the wind. Twice it sounded as if a limb from the top of the bent tree house broke and at other times it sounded as if a tree blew over, its thump on hitting the ground reverberated throughout the house.

When morning arrived, a few hunters, including Gumui dressed warmly and went to search for damage, if there was any. Clearly, from the inside of the house, there was no damage. Outside, it did seem that some of the tree tops needed to be tied down again with additional leather strips. But that was true of only two places. It was something they could finish in a day. There was some sea aurochs skin available, and Gumui and Togomoo decided to cover the two places that needed the additional tie downs with the sea aurochs' skin. When warm weather returned they'd cover their roof with it. The hunters went inside to report their findings on damage. What damage there was from the wind was slight. Gumui was greatly relieved they had put the turf blocks against the side of the bent tree house.

"Now, see, I told you so," Ottu said to Hawk. "The Wise One becomes sick and the sky lights come all in the same day. I tell you it isn't coincidence."

Hawk was convinced that the sky lights and the Wise One's illness had nothing to do with one another, but he said, "Yes, elder, we'll just have to wait to see what develops."

Tuksook went to find Item.

"Mother, how is Father doing. He's not on his bench."

"He's much better today," she said smiling a real smile. Midgenemo's heart seemed better to her and he definitely felt better.

"I am so glad."

"He was so very proud of you last night. So was I. You have done well."

Tuksook blushed. "Thank you," she said lowering her head.

Chapter Six

Tuksook knelt just outside the west entryway to the house while most of the People were still sleeping. Her shins touched the cold ground, something she didn't notice. She sat on the heels of her boots. Her hands, covered in mittens lay on her upper legs. She talked with Wisdom. She had thought long and hard about the change in the way she saw her father.

"When I was young, I saw my father as larger than a normal man, Wisdom. He was my idea of the best. He could do no wrong. Father knew everything. He was strong. I thought he was like you. Then, he made a single, huge judgment error. My image of my father shattered into what felt like uncountable pieces that no one could hope to put back together. My belly lodged feelings that traveled fast from love to hate. It was all based on one single judgment error. I expected perfection from him. What does that tell me about my love and hate? Are they parts of the same thing? I based my love on my imaginings, not reality. What an ugly, poorly reasoning mind web! My father was the same man. Did I see him as something he wasn't? I have to admit, I did. Then, when he erred, did I make more of that than was warranted? I did. Was my love so shallow that it couldn't survive a single judgment error? Yes. I think I resented his shattering the perfect image I had set up in my imagination, as if that were unforgiveable. I certainly carried an unrelenting unforgiving spirit, which is contrary to your way."

"Is that part of why I fought against becoming Wise One? Is it that I thought I had to be bigger than life? Tuksook, having to be perfect. I wanted to remain a child, because children were expected to err? Did I see becoming adult as Wise One too great a challenge for me? Did I assume, and probably rightly so, that I would fail, even as my father failed. Oh, Wisdom, I begin to see, and what I see is not a good sight!"

"Your eyes open a bit. Tuksook, you are one of the People—no more, no less," the small, quiet voice of Wisdom said.

"I understand," Tuksook replied. Then, she continued, "I look at my father now and worry. He seems to have overcome whatever made him ill recently, but I still worry that what caused the illness is only hidden. I fear it will come again. Wisdom I love my father. I don't love him as someone who's perfect or hate him as someone who's outrageously horrid—I love him as he is, as one of the People who has a large responsibility and can make mistakes. I don't want him to die soon."

"His illness will come again, but his line of life is not at the end yet. He will remain Wise One for a while. You are not ready to take on the full responsibility of Wise One. You must take some time to continue to examine your reason and what's expected of People in life. You need stability. How can you go from thinking your father is perfect one moment to virtually murdering his character the next?"

"Murder!"

"Why does that term bother you?"

"Wisdom, murder is a horrible thing to do."

"Anything that is not my way is a horrible thing to do, Tuksook. Do you think murder is worse than lying?"

"Yes, of course."

"You are wrong, Tuksook. Lying involves murder. Lies attempt to murder the one who lies, the one lied about, and me. The liar tries to change himself into what he is not—he murders who he really is, usually to make himself look better than he is. The liar tries to change the one lied about into what he is not, usually to make the other person look worse than he really is. That's a type of murder, Tuksook. It's all outside of my way. Going outside my way leaves scars that take long to be forgotten, if they ever are."

Tuksook was startled by the revelation of the equality of wrongdoing regardless of the specifics. It required her to look again at the way she saw things. Gumui had been right all that time ago when he wondered whether her sitting in judgment on her father wasn't equal to what her father had done. Gumui had been right! "Oh, Wisdom, I have to become Wise One and Gumui is so much more mature in understanding than I am."

"That's why he's your husband, Tuksook. Remember and never forget, I chose you—not because you're perfect—I chose you because I chose you, wrongdoing and all. The People can see that I choose People who are not perfect for Wise Ones, and that gives them hope. They should see you grow in my way as time passes. That gives more hope. Tuksook, there has never been a perfect person of the People; there is not one now; there will be none in the future."

"Do you think many of the People understand that?"

"Far more than you credit, Tuksook. Certainly, not all. You discredit many of your People in an unthinking, uncaring way. It is your self-centeredness and pride that keep you from clear vision. You continue to think that you're better than many of the People. That is unacceptable. It's the error your father made."

Tuksook let the pent up tears fall. As cold as it was outside, she had to wipe her face to keep ice from forming on her skin. Instead, it formed on the beaver fur of her mittens.

"You have made progress today, Tuksook. You must continue to examine your thoughts, whether they are in my way or whether you're off on some of your thinking, which has an immaturity of its own."

"I will obey, Wisdom," she said.

"It is only in looking straight at what you've done that you can grow in the future as a plant that stands straight up, reaching for the sun. Or, you may be one that grows bent over and confined to the shade for life. That is a choice you make in life."

"Wisdom, help me reach for the sun." Tuksook's face, full of hope, looked into the sky above her.

"Your request is asked naïvely. To start what you ask, you begin with patience. Patience is gained only through very troubled times."

"What?"

"You know to be careful what you choose to request of me. Tuksook, you are not ready to ask my help to reach for the sun. You ask for trials that are sometimes overwhelming. Future Wise One, grow your understanding first. Slow your reactions and increase your reason. Let my spirit breathe through you the fresh air of life, instead of relying on the limited breath of your own spirit. To do that you must know the stories, apply them to all things to which they relate, and listen to me. Also, you have a wonderful teacher for what I want you to learn, for he has learned it well. That person is Gumui. Now, watch."

Having no visual reference for Wisdom, Tuksook did not know where to look. Across the river, the closest of the year-round white covered mountains made a rumbling sound and a column of what looked like smoke rose from its top. She heard it and felt the tremors with her whole body. The wind was blowing toward the meadow. Tuksook realized that the volcano was erupting and the material it was spitting out was headed for them. She whistled the hunter's "Come—now!" alert, and hunters came out of the house quickly. Tuksook pointed to the erupting volcano.

Gumui came out and gave her a hand to rise up. They watched the long, slender cloud sweeping towards them and it was visibly dropping materials on the meadow as it approached. Gumui pulled her to return to the bent tree house, but she resisted.

"I really want to see what it's spitting out," she said. "I am concerned for our house and the meadow."

"Very well," he replied. "I'll be right back. I need my full cold time protection to be out here." He ran back inside to put on his pants, hat, and mittens, returning as soon as he was more warmly dressed.

Tuksook realized that Wisdom either caused the eruption or knew it would take place when it did. Her first thought is that Wisdom caused it. She reasoned that it probably didn't matter, but in her mind web, Wisdom certainly had the power to cause an eruption.

Little bits of fine ash began to fall along with particles the size of her little fingernail. The ash and particles began to pile up on the ground like the snow did, but to the hunters it was not as welcome as snow. It was like small gritty pebbles—pebbles that could burn the skin from what heat remained or burn not from heat but rather something inside the pebbles that irritated skin. Finally, hunters decided that the People should go inside until the ash fell no longer. Tuksook had no alternative.

Inside the house, those who had been involved with construction realized that the ash was coming into the house through the smoke holes. Heat rising from the hearth fires was keeping some of it out, but there was an entryway for the ash through the smoke holes that could not be denied. Gumui and the others talked at length of ways to prevent ash from entering the house, knowing from the stories that ash is not something People should breathe.

The People ate the morning meal. They were interested to see what the volcano would bring but were not overly alarmed. Tuksook was curious, because Wisdom had told her to watch. She would diligently give her attention to anything related to the volcano's eruption.

Gumui brought his bowl and sat beside Tuksook. "You were out with Wisdom?"

"Yes. It was good," she replied.

"Did anyone know where you were?" he asked, concerned.

"Lurch went out when I did. Then, he returned."

"Tuksook, it concerns me when you go out alone. That is not the way. You are supposed to be protected at all times. When you wish to go out to be with Wisdom or for any other reason, tell me. Wake me if I sleep. Promise me."

"I promise, Gumui. I'm sorry I gave you reason for concern."

"You must reason before you act, Tuksook," he said sternly.

"I promised, Gumui. I will not forget."

"Good," he said not certain he was relieved. "We are going to try to find a way to prevent ash in the future from entering the house when it falls."

"Like making a hat for the smoke holes?" she asked.

"Yes, but the smoke still has to be able to go out."

"I see."

From the east part of the house a sweet melody on the flute began. This one was different. Tuksook wondered whether Oneg had created it or whether it was a new one Bit-n had taught her. The tune was pleasant and calming in the busy house. It was longer than the others she played.

The dogs began to growl a low growl that they used to alert the People without making too much noise. That created concern. Hawk and Momeh decided to find out what was causing the disturbance. They put on their cold time protection quickly, took a couple of spears each, and left by the west entryway. The ash was falling more to the north, so they were able to travel across the meadow without being covered in ash. It was about half a man's finger deep on the snow on the meadow. The dogs were bristled and focused on something on the river level. They went to the dogs and quieted them. They looked in the direction the dogs looked. To their amazement, there was a man in a boat on the river.

They watched carefully. Surely, the man would have heard the dogs.

"That can't be Rimut, can it?" Momeh asked.

"I don't think so. The man isn't dressed for the weather very well."

"It looks like he's seen our boats," Momeh observed.

"He's coming here. I'll keep watch. Will you go back and call for five hunters?" Hawk asked.

"Of course," Momeh agreed and left at as much a run as he could on ash on snow over ice.

He returned with spear-carrying hunters before the man made it to their boats. They all watched below as the man climbed out of his boat and tied his boat to a small tree. He looked about and in a brief time realized where the path upward was. He began to go up the path. He noticed a group of hunters at the top, but he continued to climb. When he reached the top, he was winded. The hunters began to question him. The man's name was

Wikroak. At first they thought they could not communicate at all. Little by little, they realized that there were many commonalities of language. The hunters escorted him to the bent tree house where they sat at the council area. The People, busy at their tasks, became very quiet so all could hear.

Wikroak coughed off and on. He had breathed the ash, because he had no choice. What the hunters discovered is that Wikroak had become lost from his people in the fury of a storm. There had been others in the boat. Two were lost overboard in the storm. One became very ill and died. Wikroak lived far to the north, but he was unsure how to find his way home. He lived where the salt water froze. He lived where the sun failed to appear at the coldest time of the year. He lived in the land of great white bears. The People didn't realize salt water could freeze. They were astounded at the idea of a white bear. Wikroak was about twenty-five. He had a wife and four children. He desperately wanted to return home.

"Why did you come up our river?" Ottu asked him.

"My land is far to the north. The sea is violent right now. I hoped to find a river that would take me as far north as possible, so I could avoid the violence of the stormy sea. This river seems to narrow down too fast to take me all the way to my far north land. It seems I have to face the violence of the sea if I am to return to my land."

"You are welcome to stay with us until the violence of the sea lets up," Midgenemo offered.

"You are very kind. I have to admit that my people would not be so quick to offer permission to a stranger to stay among them."

"We are taught that sharing our abundance with travelers is something that Wisdom requires," Kew said.

"What's wisdom have to do with it?" Wikroak asked, confused.

"Wisdom is God," Kew explained and expanded, "Wisdom is the Creator. Wisdom made all things including us. Your eyes show you all that is here. Who made it? Who is the one who created it all? That is Wisdom."

Wikroak laughed heartily. "To my people, being wise means having wisdom, something you create by reasoning. Being wise means one is cleverly perceptive, especially when it comes to survival. Yet, you believe wisdom is a god? We don't believe gods made us. We believe we are alive today as men. We make us when there is a new birth. When we die we may return as seals, walrus, whales, ravens, persons, or something else. All life is cyclic."

"Well," Midgenemo asked, "Who decides what way you return?" Midgenemo wondered how they thought the first man and woman, the earth, the stars, the sun and moon came to be. He decided not to keep probing into what he perceived to be nonsense. Die and return to life as a seal? Ridiculous! The man was free, however, to reason in the way he chose.

"I think it has something to do with what's available and whether one lived well," he replied.

Wikroak kept looking around as if he expected aggression. Hunters noticed he seemed disturbed, but could see no reason for it.

Midgenemo asked, "Wikroak, you seem ill at ease here. Are we doing something to cause you discomfort?"

"I see your hunters with spears. I wonder when you will use them against me."

The People were dumbfounded. Quickly the hunters stored their spears.

"We wouldn't do that," Togomoo tried to assure the man. "That is not Wisdom's way."

"Back to Wisdom," Wikroak said quietly, "What is Wisdom's way?"

"With strangers, it is required that we treat them as well as we treat ourselves. It is required that we provide food and lodging for the duration of the stranger's stay. If the stranger is ill, we are required to try to heal him," Togomoo said.

"Our people are very different. Our people would likely be plotting your death in this length of time. They certainly wouldn't be inviting you to sleep in their lodging."

"Did your people have a bad time with strangers?" Mongo asked.

"Well, we didn't dream up being wary. Of course we have reason for wariness. We've had numbers of hunting parties find their way to us. They have stolen things from us. They have been rude. Some fought with us to try to take away our land. We have good reason to be wary."

"Well, you're our first stranger, Wikroak. Have no fear of us. We largely outnumber you, but we are a peaceful people willing to share what we have with you. You may stay as long as you desire and share our food and lodging," Midgenemo offered again.

"If that is true, I would like to remain so I can gain some fat and let the storms abate somewhat. Right now, I don't think I could make it home. I am too tired and too weak."

"Then, stay with us and relax with us. Fill your eating bowl as often as you like. When you are ready to leave, we will provide you with plenty of jerky to feed you on your way," Ottu said.

"There is a bench/sleeping place in the north part of this house," Midgenemo said, pointing to the one Bit-n had used while Hapunta was ill.

"We will supply some sleeping skins. While you are here, that will be your place. No one else will touch anything in your place."

Wikroak suspended his urge to flee and decided to stay with these people. Trying to flee at this time would result in certain death, of that he was sure.

"I am desperately tired," the man said. "May I have permission to lie upon that sleeping place to sleep now?"

"Certainly," Midgenemo told him.

Wikroak followed Midgenemo to the bench/sleeping place. He was amazed at the bent tree house and the bench/sleeping place. Both were things he'd never seen. He dragged himself to the place, pulled off his jacket and boots, and sat on the bench.

"There are pegs where you can hang your jacket and anything else you want to hang," Midgenemo pointed out. The man stood to hang his jacket.

Those who could see the stranger were appalled at his thinness. Surely, they reasoned, he had been attempting to return home for a long time without much to eat. Sympathy flowed in the bent tree house. Wikroak laid himself on the sleeping place, finding it to be very comfortable. Item brought two sleeping skins. Wikroak reached for them, but Midgenemo took them from Item and said, "Be still, Wikroak, I'll cover you." He did.

Quickly the man drifted into deep sleep. He was too tired to fear. He couldn't remember the last time he slept without fear.

Hunters went quickly down the hill to examine the boat the man was using. It was entirely different from anything they'd ever seen. The boat was made of pieces of wood for a frame, covered by a thick, soft skin over the sides of the boat. It reminded them of the way a person was made with a skeleton over which skin was stretched. There was a place for a sail, they thought, but the mast was broken and no sail lay in the boat. They wondered what the boat's skin covering was. There was only one oar in the boat, and it appeared to be broken. The People did not touch the boat except to feel the skin once, but confined their examination to the use of their eyes. They knew not to take unoffered freedom to examine with their hands things others might not want touched.

After examining how the boat was made, hunters who had worked on the bent tree house and others who were interested gathered in the west part of the house to discuss how to cover the smoke holes. They would make flaps to swing open with a propped pole from within. The pole could be lowered to close the smoke hole to whatever angle they decided. That way they would keep out ash and let out smoke. It was simple enough and the men began to work on it quickly.

Wikroak slept in the bent tree house for three days. When he awakened, he was disoriented, seemingly having forgotten where he was. Little by little the memories returned and he sat up.

Midgenemo went to Wikroak and asked, "Are you better?"

"I am well rested. Thank you for your kindness. I appreciate it. I was so tired when I arrived. I hope I was not rude." The man coughed roughly.

"You were not rude at all. Come, I'll show you to the privy and to the food preparation place where you can take something to eat." The two went outside by the west entryway.

For many days the man lived in their midst, sharing their way of life and telling about his.

Wikroak told the People, "I was the youngest of all the men and had the least experience. I would have thought before our sea travel that if anyone died, I would be the first, because of my age and lack of experience."

"That's not Wisdom's way," Hawk spoke up.

"How's that?" the man asked.

"When you are born, Wisdom gives you a life line. The length of that line determines how long a life you have. Clearly, yours was longer than the lines of the others on your boat."

"We don't have Wisdom to give us life lines," he said.

"You don't have to know Wisdom for Wisdom to give you a life line. Every person born has a life line."

The confidence with which Hawk spoke caused Wikroak to question the assurance he held that Wisdom had nothing to do with him. "You sound convinced that Wisdom gave me a life line, even though I don't know your god."

Hawk smiled indulgently. "Wisdom made all life. Every living thing has a life line. Wisdom doesn't depend on your knowing him to be real. He made all. He is real, even if none of us acknowledges it. We depend on Wisdom, not the other way around."

The stranger was silenced for a while. These people used their thoughts in a way that differed from the way he used his. It didn't mean they couldn't communicate, it just meant that the basis on which their thoughts stood was very different. They had to recognize that difference each time there was a perspective disconnect between them.

"Let me reason this well. According to what you believe, this god gave me a life line when I was born? He also gave one to the other people in the boat? They died because their life line ran out, not from the storm? This god, Wisdom, somehow knows me, even though I don't know him?"

Midgenemo said, "You understand very well, Wikroak."

"But why would Wisdom care about someone who doesn't know him?"

Midgenemo said, "Because he made you. When you make a tool with your hands, is that tool not more important or seen differently from the tools made by others?"

Wikroak looked straight into Midgenemo's eyes. Wikroak was an expert at carving ivory fishing hooks. He understood Midgenemo's comparison of his making a tool to Wisdom's making people.

"I understand that. My people believe that when my wife and I come together, we make a baby. Wisdom isn't doing that. We are."

"You and your wife could come together all day, every day, but if that seed you plant in her isn't given life by Wisdom, it doesn't live. That's how dead babies come—Wisdom hasn't given them the spark to start life." Kew tried to help the man to understand the simple fact of Wisdom's role in life. It seemed so clear and easy to him.

Wikroak began another coughing spell. "That ash is tough on lungs," he said.

"I'm just glad it's over," Taman said. "While you slept we made covers to try to keep future ash from entering the smoke holes."

"We don't have volcanoes like you do. I'm glad."

"Is it much colder where you live?" Mongo asked.

"It is probably very much colder, but as you've discovered here, once you're dressed for the cold weather, you don't notice it."

The hunters who had gathered to talk quietly laughed a knowing laugh of agreement. The man's words were so true.

"Do you men have any ivory?" Wikroak asked.

"What's ivory?" several asked at the same time.

"It's the long tooth from the mastodon or mammoth."

"They live here? We haven't seen any since our arrival," Hawk said.

"Have you gathered no bones that might be ivory?"

"We've gathered many bones. You are free to look whenever you like. I can show you where we keep them," Hawk offered.

"That would be good. If I can find any ivory or good bone, I can carve some fish hooks for you before I return to my home. Then, I will make some replacement oars."

"Did you have a sail?" Unmo asked.

"I lost it in the storm when the men fell overboard. The mast broke in half. The sail was in the way, so I had to toss it overboard."

"What do you use to make your sail?" Unmo asked wondering whether it might be helpful for them to know what was used in this land.

"Oiled caribou skins. I realize now that I should have folded it and tried to keep it."

"Young man, you have had quite a journey."

"I have, and it's not finished yet."

"Come," Hawk offered, "Would you like to see the bone pile?"

"I would like to see it very much," he replied. "I need to be able to carve."

The man went to dress for going outside. His clothing was terribly battered by the storm experiences. He dressed and readied himself.

Hawk gave a look at him and called to Item. Item came to them wondering why Hawk had called her.

"Item, Wikroak's cold time protection is in bad condition. Can you women fix it for him?"

"Wikroak, when you return from your time outside, I will have a tunic for you on the hook by your bench/sleeping place. Put the tunic on and bring me all of your cold time protection. We will see what we can do to help you."

By this time, Wikroak had learned that it was appropriate to lower his head, so he lowered his head to Item. She smiled.

The two men went to the bone pile. They had to brush off snow and ice. They moved bones around. There were many, some very large. Some looked like bones but were hard as stone and looked like stone.

"Hawk," Wikroak called out, "This is what I seek. This should be enough right here." He carried a piece of bone that he called ivory in his right arm. It was about the length of his forearm, tubular in shape, heavy.

They returned to the bent tree house and Wikroak found the tunic on the peg by his bench/sleeping place just as Item said it would be. He found these People interesting. What happened to him in this place would never happen to anyone in his home. By now they'd have killed a stranger and taken the body to the sea to drop it to the sea floor. He learned that what he saw of the People is what the People were. There was no pretense, no sense of cleverness, no deception. Wikroak admitted to himself that, if he had no wife or children, he'd have been happy to remain with these People to share their peaceful, interdependent difference. Where his people were tough in one way; these People were tough in a different way. He preferred this way but lived the other. The People worked together, he reasoned, as a flight of birds in migration. They would twist and turn and each knew when to do what to keep from causing another to fall from the sky. Only in the rarest of cases did anyone tell another what to do. They just knew, even the children. Wikroak felt certain that if he told others at his home of these People, his people would laugh and accuse him of lying.

"Let us walk outside before the evening meal," Tuksook said to Gumui.

"Let's do it. Dress warmly."

The two put on their cold time protection and walked to the west entryway. Snow still covered the ground. Where they'd had to dig it out to reach certain places in the meadow, it was easy to walk. Otherwise the snow lay mid-thigh to Gumui. They walked to the dog's house, to the central pole where they measured the location of the sun, and to the path to the river level. The sun was shining, about to descend. It made sparkles on the snow, a sight that delighted Tuksook.

"Obviously, I didn't become pregnant when we were in the wet forest," Tuksook said.

"True," Gumui replied. "Does that sadden you?"

"No," she said with a smile, "I have to trust that when it's time, Wisdom will spark a life in my belly and we will have a little one. Right now, it seems, I have much to learn. I just keep my mind web on what I need to learn. It's interesting and it makes me think so many things I'd never think on my own. I am happy, Gumui."

"I am happy also. We have a good, warm bent tree home. The volcano has decided to calm down, and we have the house fixed so that any eruption in the future should bring very little ashfall into the house. We have plenty of food to eat, even if we couldn't go out to hunt at all. By the way, Midgenemo told me that my days as a hunter of large beasts is over. My primary hunter responsibility is protecting you."

"Oh, Gumui, I'm so sorry."

"No reason to worry, Tuksook. I suspected as much when I knew I wanted to join with you. I realized it would probably result in a choice between you and hunting. I will admit that I am glad I became a hunter first, so I'll always be considered a hunter, even if the big beasts are something I can no longer hunt. I've done a large amount of large animal hunting. I have the memories. It's a challenge, but I'd never choose you second. Always—Tuksook first."

She walked close to him and took his arm. She adored him.

"I'm glad we don't live like the stranger," Tuksook said.

"I, too. It must be unsettling and troublesome to live suspicious of strangers, always wondering whether someone wants to take your things or kill you. That is no way to live."

"I love your cold time protection, Gumui. The beaver is so shiny and it looks good on you."

"Well, Tuksook, I love the giant beaver on you. The lightness of the pelts make you look like a furry little animal that I'd like to grab with my arms and hug tight." He acted on his words.

"Gumui!" she protested.

They played in the snow, rolling in it and laughing, forgetting the ash.

"Ah, I have come across two beavers, romping in the snow. I think I must spear them," Unmo said gleefully, spear raised.

Gumui and Tuksook stood up laughing.

"What fun that must have been. You make me remember my young days," Unmo said.

"Life is good, Unmo," Gumui said.

"What better to do on a day such as this?" Tuksook said smiling.

"What better to do, indeed," Unmo replied. "Except, hope that days become longer soon. I'm wanting to have the freedom to move with ease."

"I agree with that," Gumui said.

Someone began to hit the rocks together calling for attendance at the evening meal. The three walked to the bent tree house together.

While she was taking off her cold time protection, Tuksook noticed the stranger was sitting on the edge of Oneg's bench. She finally noticed he had the flute in his hand. She wondered what the stranger was doing with the flute.

Gumui put his arm around Tuksook and they went to take a bowl for the evening meal. Tuksook could see that Oneg was wrapping the flute and putting it away. Bit-n approached Oneg with a bowl.

Time passed and the meadow ice rotted and melted away. Where it might have been swampy, the drainage of the meadow was wonderful. The People could walk on it without becoming mired in mud. The ground thawed. Hunters went out on a few searches and returned with a camel on one hunt and a bison on another. The People and the stranger feasted.

Finally, the stranger said at council one night that in a few days he would have to begin the search for his home. He planned to follow the river to the sea, go west until the land let him turn north into another sea. Then, it would be a long travel home following the shore. That is what his memory held for him. The women had made him a sail from giant deer hide which they oiled with sea aurochs oil. Wikroak said it was thicker than the caribou hide, but should be fine. The hunters would help him repair the mast.

The following day, after the evening meal, Wikroak addressed the council. He was not accustomed to speaking at meetings of his people, but he had learned much during his stay with the People.

"First, I want to thank all of you. Second, I want to thank Wisdom. I don't know Wisdom, but I know that if it weren't for Wisdom, I wouldn't have been welcomed and treated so well. I might be among the dead now. But such is not how it is. I have some things to share. First, in this bag there are fishing hooks. In my land, I make these and many people want them. I made these from your ivory for your fishing boat travels. Just add some fish or meat to the hooks and you should be able to catch fish. He passed the bag first to Midgenemo. Midgenemo examined the fish hook that he lifted from the bag first. He was surprised. He knew Wikroak had made fish hooks, but these were things of beauty. He handled it. It was so smooth. In the bag there were many others. He reached in and pulled out several. Each differed, but each was a work of art. Each had a smoothness that made him want to let it linger in his hand.

"These are beautiful," Midgenemo said, "They should call many fish. Let us hope we don't lose them to a fish that wants to wear one in its mouth forever." People laughed. Midgenemo passed the bag to Ottu.

"My next gift is to those hunters who paddle boats. I had to make oars. You have so much wood available that I decided to make some of the oars in the style of my people to leave with you."

He went to his bench and pulled the oars from beneath the bench. He pulled out four of them, leaving two behind. The poles were long and had paddles on each end instead of being just one paddle on one end of the oar. He had colored them in blacks, reds, and whites. The People were unsure how he made the colors. The oars were works of art.

"Finally, one thing while I was here made my belly soft and warm. Instead of food, it was the tunes Oneg played from the flute. When I saw the flute, I saw how fragile it is. I tried to make some more from bird bones. These are a little less fragile. Oneg has tried them all to be sure the sound is right. Bit-n's flute has a high pitched sound. The ones I made are deeper. The holes, we found, have to be spaced very carefully to make the sound right. I leave all but one with you. The one I carry with me will be for whoever of my people will try to learn to play it. If none try, then I shall. I have learned the basics from Oneg and Bit-n."

"I ask that you not change your ways but remain in Wisdom's way forever. You have taught me so much. I would like for the rest of my life to remember you as you are. It will give me warmth of the sun when the sun hides from us in dark cold time. Wisdom, if you're real and can hear me, know that your People are wonderful, and I cherish the memories forever. Keep them in your way."

The Wise One asked whether there were anything else for the council. Since there was nothing else—what could anyone say after what the stranger said—the council ended.

The next day the People had the morning meal and then they helped the stranger pack up his boat to leave. The People knew he liked sea aurochs and since they didn't have sea aurochs where he lived, they gave him much of it to feed him on his way. The man had fattened and was relatively strong again. Days of being at sea would return him to full strength quickly.

"Wikroak," Midgenemo said to the man who was no longer a stranger, "Travel carefully. If a storm comes up, beach and wait it out. It's best to arrive there alive than not to arrive at all." The Wise One embraced him. "Wisdom, stay with him," Midgenemo asked.

Then all the People said, "Wisdom, stay with him." The act was unplanned. There was joy in the communal prayer.

Togomoo braved the icy water to push Wikroak's boat out into the river, and soon the boat was in the current of the river heading for the sea.

"He'll make it home," Tuksook whispered to Gumui.

"That does not surprise me," he whispered back. "I wonder what he'll tell his people of us."

"I think, Gumui, very little. He will want to protect us."

They returned to the bent tree house to see Oneg outside in the meadow walking without the splint. It was clear that she had not used that leg for a long time. She was frustrated.

"What's wrong with my leg?" she cried out to Bit-n.

"You haven't been able to use it for a long time, so the leg has to start with just a little use today and a little more tomorrow and a little more the day after that. You cannot push to be normal the first day or you could re-injure yourself," her mother tried to explain. "At least you are starting the last part of a return to normal."

"I will return back to normal?"

"Oneg, I cannot promise that. The break in your leg was a very bad break. Just take your time with this. Try to be patient. Don't re-injure your leg. Let it take time to grow strong again. Let's go to the shower. I hear the water is running."

"Oh, Mother, Ren had a shower and about froze. She said she was shivering all over. She did say she felt cleaner than she'd felt all during the cold time, but freezing like that—it's pretty tough to wash clean."

"Come on, Oneg. Where is my tough girl's spirit? Let's go make ourselves clean."

Oneg rolled her eyes at her mother. Bit-n walked quickly into the house returning with some skins for drying. She and Oneg headed to the shower.

Hunters gathered in groups planning hunts, or in the case of Togomoo, Hawk, Vole, and Taq boat travel to capture a sea aurochs or two was in their mind webs. The new oars Wikroak made would have a trial. They were eager to eat meat that hadn't been dried, and they wanted the skins to cover the full house roof.

A crashing noise came through the wooded area to the south of the meadow. Then, the distinct sounding of the mammoth warned all People to beware. Hunters raced to their spears most of which were still in the house. They came back out at a run, just as the beast was breaking into the meadow. Oneg and Bit-n had just begun to shower. They didn't hear the beast because they were talking loud over the waterfall. Bit-n turned and saw the animal. She pulled Oneg closer to the rock wall. She handed the girl a skin to use to dry off. Oneg pulled her hair over her head, twisting it to drain the water out. She wiped herself with the towel. She made small movement as she pulled her tunic over her head. Bit-n was doing the same thing. Both were quiet. They stayed against the rock wall, heading south to the east entryway to the bent tree house. Oneg followed Bit-n.

The mammoth stopped in the center of the meadow. It seemed confused by the People and by the things in the meadow. It went to the center pole for tracking the sun. It wrapped its trunk around the center pole and raised it up from the ground. It laid the pole on the ground.

Dogs were growling their warning growl. They were trained not to bark, except on command. There was no command. The dogs were not tied, but they were taught to remain in their area, the dog house and a perimeter around it of about two man heights, and they used the sloping hillside for their privy. It was a large area. The dogs bristled, watching the mammoth. The great beast noticed them. It had a wariness of these animals. Wolves? The mammoth was shy of them, keeping itself as far to the east as possible.

Not having the ability to reason what to do easily, the mammoth followed its instinct, leaving for its traditional route to the summer feeding ground. It headed to the north and then curved to the east to follow the rock path for a brief way before turning north again. It bellowed from time to time, easing some of the stress built up from confronting the changes in the meadow.

The elders gathered to discuss the event. They wondered why there was only one mammoth since those beasts lived in groups, not alone. They wondered why it chose the center pole to pull from the ground.

Ottu said, "I have seen a large rock that we could have the young people bring here. It could serve as our center pole."

"Where is it?" Mongo asked.

"It's through the wooded area south of here. There's a path I took when I saw it—I think that's the trail the mammoth used!"

"Is it far?" Kew asked, thinking if Ottu had found it, it couldn't be but so far.

"No. Would you like me to show you?" Ottu offered.

"I'd like that very much," Kew replied with a questioning glance at Mongo.

"Let's take our spears," Mongo reminded.

All the men took their spears and headed to the south part of the meadow. Ottu came along, white hair and beard flying in the breeze. He looked delighted to be about showing the rock to the others.

They found the path, and the mammoth had definitely used it. They kept following it for a while and suddenly they came to another meadow.

"It seemed to me when I first saw this place, others must've lived here just like we do now. I think this stone may have been their center stone. Come over here."

The others followed, fascinated that Ottu had found this place and remained silent about it.

"See how, if you stand here, the mountain tops line up on the horizon? You can see how they could have followed the line of the sun from rising to setting."

"Why have you not mentioned this until now?" Kew asked.

"I didn't see any need to mention it," Ottu replied.

"There's a hearth over there and some flat stones for a council like we have. There were not many at the council if all had a stone to mark their place to sit. Someone made tools over here. Look at the chipped pieces of stone."

Kew and Mongo exchanged glances.

"The place is very old," Ottu continued. "Maybe it was just a place hunters stayed to hunt or fish. It's not possible to find any remains of what they lived in. I'm guessing a lean-to."

"Well," Kew said, "That would mean it was a temporary place. Maybe the whole group of them came here in the summer and left for somewhere else in the cold time."

"I brought you here for this rock. I think our young men could bring this to our meadow where we could use it for our center pole. No mammoth could pick it up and move it."

"Let's go back to see whether we can find enough young men interested in the effort. It is a beautiful rock," Mongo said. "It would be interesting to have it in our meadow."

Kew looked at Ottu. "I can't believe you found this and didn't tell anyone."

"I told you when it was time for it to be told."

Kew chewed on that idea as they returned to their meadow.

Back at the meadow, Mongo did a whistle that called hunters to assemble. It was not an urgent call, but it did have an expectation that hunters would gather soon. Hunters began to arrive, interested to find why the assembly was called.

When all the men gathered, Ottu said, "The mammoth pulled up the center pole. That reminded me of a place where I'd seen some large rocks. There's a perfect rock to replace our center pole—one that a mammoth cannot destroy. It would mean some strong hunters would need to move it here. Are any of you interested?" he asked.

Hamaklob said, "Elder, I think it would be best if you show it to us. Then, we could make a decision based on how well we thought we could move it and how."

"Very well," Ottu said. "Follow me." He led them back down the path through the forest to the once occupied meadow to the south. The men were amazed to find an ancient living place that until now apparently only Ottu knew existed.

Hamaklob, Togomoo, Hawk, Stencellomak, and Wave were determined to find a way to bring the stone to the meadow. The People were capable of anything—the younger men were convinced. It was just a matter of solving the problem, and that would enable them to move the rock.

While the younger men pondered the options, the elders returned to the home meadow, went into the bent tree house, and enjoyed tea, not saying a word but remembering their middle years, when they were given hard problems to solve and mostly they found solutions to the problems. In the comfort of the bent tree house with their tea, the men looked at each other, eyes twinkling, imagining the younger men problem solving.

From her bench Oneg played the new flute Wikroak made her. She had several but the fullness and depth of the sound of this one delighted her most. She played tunes that no one had heard. They were tunes of long ago and far away. It caught the mind web and brought it close to something in the long past without making the connection clear. The tunes she played seemed to capture and hold everyone who heard it in timeless sound communication. Oneg had touched the spirit of music, and it was infusing her with special talent and connection to the ancient. It was as if in her confinement, she ventured back in time to make music with those from another time. She couldn't see the ancients or hear them exactly, but they seemed part of her and she felt part of them. It was something very special. This experience enabled her to become a unique contributor to the People, and it kept her from feeling so alone while her leg improved.

Bit-n and other women circled near the hearth, sewing or making narrow rope. There were some of the People who needed new tunics. The men had asked for narrow rope. They were in no need of the thicker rope, which normally they made. When Oneg began to play the flute, the women became silent. The music made the hairs on the backs of their necks stand on end. It was haunting. It seemed to speak without words, speaking through feeling and time.

Tuksook listened and went to the girl. She sat on Oneg's bench, listening to the tune and watching the girl. When Oneg finished playing and laid the flute beside her, she looked into Tuksook's eyes.

"You have been with the ancients?" Tuksook asked.

"Is that who they are?" Oneg asked. "I can't see them or hear them, but I can play music with them. It's their music, but they seem to become part of me and I am part of them when we play the music."

"Oneg, listen to me very carefully. You are touching something that can be very wonderful and very frightening. Do not try to talk to the ancients. I don't see a problem with learning the music from them. But don't talk to them. If they try to talk to you, call the Wise One or me immediately. The tunes they teach you are lovely and will be special for the People, but Wisdom has told us we are forbidden to talk to anyone who has died. Do you understand what I tell you?"

"Are you saying it's okay for me to learn the tunes, but I am not to talk with them at all?"

"That's exactly right."

"Well, Tuksook, I cannot understand them. Their words make no sense to me."

"Good. Put the tunes in your mind web, because if ever these People are able to talk to you, you will need to leave them forever. That's where the Wise One or I can help you. Do you understand?"

"I do, Tuksook. You care about me, don't you?"

Tuksook put her arm around Oneg. "Very much, Oneg," she said. "I want to protect you from harm."

"I have heard your words, and I have them in my mind web. I will not forget."

"Good. Did you see the mammoth?"

"I did. Mother and I were showering when it came through. We had just finished and were drying the water off. We fled down behind the bent tree house to come in for safety. It was huge!"

"It was. I had no idea they were that big. Were you playing a flute Wikroak made?"

"Yes. This one has a deep sound that I love. It's wonderful to have different flutes. Each has a voice just as People have different voices. With the ones he gave me, I returned Mother's flute to her, so I wouldn't break it. She can play it when Mil and Lamo grow older. Then, Mother and I can play together."

"What a wonderful idea," Tuksook said encouraging the idea.

Back in the meadow where the large rock was, the men had decided how to move the rock. They tied it with ropes and forced it on its side where they had laid short pieces of cut tree trunks. The tree trunks would serve to roll the rock. When the rock rolled over the last log, it could be carried to the front so the rollers worked all the way to ease the passage of the rock. Older boys would keep the logs moving by running them from the back to the front. Hunters would pull on the ropes. Some would push from the sides of the rock. To their delight, when they tried their solution, it worked. The rock moved. Not fast, but it made progress. They would have a replacement for the center pole that day, a replacement that would stand long after they were gone. The men started a rowing song and enjoyed the hard work after having been in the house for so long.

When the men had the rock near their meadow, the elders could hear the rowing song. They knew that the hunters had succeeded. They put on their jackets and went outside. They would direct the placement of the stone. They smiled knowing smiles. It was a good day.

"You did well," Ottu said to Hamaklob.

"It was a dirty work," Hamaklob admitted. "We're going to need to shower. There was mammoth excrement on the path and the rollers transferred it to the rock and all over us. Nevertheless, we have a stone. Where do you want it?"

Ottu walked to the exact place where the pole used to be. "Right here," he said. "Once you place it here, there may be a need to adjust it, so wait when it's first raised to be sure it's positioned right. We'll examine the placement when it's up."

"Whatever you say," Hamaklob replied. All the hunters were beaming. They had solved a hard problem. They would have a special stone in their meadow. They all felt the joy of achievement.

With much effort, the men stood the stone where Ottu had shown them. Ottu walked to the south part of the stone and sighted along the top.

"It needs to move just a bit to the west," he said.

The men shouldered the stone, but had no success. Finally, using a hardwood tree trunk for leverage, they lifted one side and twisted it and then lifted the other side setting it down just a little to the west.

"How's that?" Togomoo asked.

Ottu stood south of the stone. He sighted again. He smiled.

"Perfect," he said.

Wave and Momeh had gone to the bent tree house and called for some large water holders. They asked for someone clean to carry them to the shower to fill them. The rock needed to be washed off.

Item, with the pretense of forbearance for the men used a hand signal to call Heek and Amuin to fill two large containers with water to shower off the rock. "Be careful, she cautioned. Who knows what's on the rock." The women laughed, and took the challenge. Item was glad it turned out as it did. She wouldn't have wanted the men to contaminate the containers with whatever was on the rock. Women would be careful.

As it was, it took the women four fills each of water to clean the rock. It smelled awful.

Days later Togomoo, Hawk, Vole, and Taq gathered the things they'd need for five days. They took them to one of the boats and prepared to pursue another sea aurochs or two, if possible. They had plenty of rope. They had the four oars that Wikroak made. This would be the first use of the new oars. Just to be certain about what they were doing, they carried four of their old oars in the floor of the boat. If the ones Wikroak made didn't work for them or for their boat, they wanted to have available what they needed. Oars were special and all unused oars were tied to the boat.

The river's current was very fast. The runoff from the mountains as the snow melted swelled the river to its fullest and created a swift current. They made it to the sea in a single day, not two. They began to row to the west, looking for piles of seaweed on the shore. They had to row for half a day to find what they sought. There was the evidence of sea aurochs eating their favorite food.

Togomoo and Hawk prepared to enter the water. They found the wind cold when they removed their jackets and tunics. Hawk put his hand in the water.

"We're going to have to do this very quickly," Hawk said to Togomoo.

"Cold?" Togomoo asked.

"Makes the shower at home feel warm!"

"If either of us becomes too cold, we have to return back to the boat," Togomoo said firmly. "Sea aurochs is good, but our lives are worth far more."

"Agreed," Hawk said.

Hawk prepared the slip loop and handed it to Togomoo after he was in the water. The cold of the water took Togomoo's breath. Quickly, he dived and Hawk was right behind him. They managed to secure the loop around the first sea aurochs' tail and then swam to the surface fast, freezing.

Vole had watched from above and had the rope tied to the boat. The freezing swimmers climbed into the boat and told the others to row while they dressed.

Teeth chattering, Togomoo said, "One sea aurochs this time is enough."

Vole asked, "Would you like Taq and me to swim down to tie one?"

"I think Hawk will agree with me that we hung right on the edge of danger to ourselves. We've done this before, so we knew fast exactly what to do. You need to wait until the water warms before you try it the first time. When the water warms, it's still cold! Let's go home," Togomoo said.

"I agree with Togomoo," Hawk said starting to row.

"I like these oars that Wikroak made. They make it easier for us to row faster than the other ones," Taq said.

"I do too." Vole said.

The men rowed with great force, but it took them almost three days to reach home. They arrived just as the sun was rising. The reason was the force of the current in the river. It was taking the snowmelt from the mountains and there was a lot of it. The sea aurochs capture effort seemed to require four days regardless of season.

They returned home and the hunters and older boys came to meet them. They knew their roles from the last year. The sea aurochs was set to roasting as soon as the first roasts were delivered to the meadow. The strips for drying and smoking were being done quickly. Before the evening meal, everything was done that needed to be done. Elfa fed the dogs some of the fat with their dried fish.

By the time everyone had filled their bowls and seated themselves for the evening meal, there was a jolt. Earthquakes were not new. The People had experienced earthquakes for thousands of years. This one was a large hit followed by a roll. The People continued to eat. Then another earthquake hit. It was a little larger. The People continued to eat. After they had put their bowls away, another hit, but it was smaller. There were no more that evening.

When they went in the house, Gumui looked carefully to determine whether the quakes had left any damage to the bent tree house. Only here and there a little mud had fallen from the ceiling. He was delighted to see that the home was holding up well. He knew, if they had a big shaker that lasted any significant time, it could tear at the roof, possibly destroy it. With this earthquake, however, all was well.

Council that night was called off. There was nothing to report and the People were fatigued after the effort to process the sea aurochs.

Tuksook snuggled close to Gumui under their blankets. She thought of the shower of roses. She was blessed. She had begun at night before she slept to think of the blessings Wisdom had showered upon her that day. Tuksook smiled a faint smile. She had grown so much in this new land. Wisdom had been there leading her to right thinking time after time. She felt it was a blessing that now she knew she loved her father as she should have at the beginning. He was a man with a burdensome responsibility. He made errors just as others. He learned from his wrong doing and turned away from the wrong thinking or behavior and went on. He was truly a Wise One. Tuksook realized it came from Wisdom. Where once she had fought the very idea of becoming Wise One, she had learned that a chance to be with Wisdom outweighed anything else she could hope to do with her life. She was learning at an incredible rate about Wisdom, about how to be with other People, about staying in Wisdom's way. She savored the memory of her playing while the People died. She would guard against that all her life. Tuksook finally understood it and was glad to have the reminder.

She thought back to her time with Oneg. The little girl had had a tough time with her broken leg. Suddenly, Tuksook realized that she was seeing Oneg growing towards the sun. This little girl had learned to play the flute like no one Tuksook had ever heard, because she'd been immobilized by the broken leg. Tuksook understood instantly what Wisdom had meant. Tuksook definitely didn't want a broken leg to teach her patience so she could grow to the sun. She was overwhelmed with how beautiful it was to hear Oneg's flute playing, but the immobilization, that was long term and very frustrating. No, she didn't want to learn patience. She was grateful to Wisdom that her request was denied. Wisdom truly looked after his People. She had lots of time in her life to learn. She wiggled herself against Gumui as if she could become any closer. She shut her eyes and drifted to sleep.

All the People except the night watch, Loraz, were sleeping. Midgenemo rose up without waking Item and put his boots on. Around his shoulders, he wrapped a skin that hung on a peg near their bench/sleeping place. He walked quietly outside. The night was cold, but not freezing. He whistled a very light whistle and from the dog house a large black dog came toward him at a trot.

"Tictip, my dog friend," Midgenemo greeted the dog.

Tictip came to him and sat in front of him, looking at Midgenemo's face as if to identify the purpose of the call.

Midgenemo walked to the log where they laid the food choices when the People ate outside. He sat on the log and the dog sat next to his leg facing the same direction Midgenemo faced, toward the bent tree house. A few bats flew overhead. Early in the year for bats, he thought.

Without much forethought, Midgenemo reached down and scratched behind Tictip's left ear. The dog looked at him adoringly. Overhead a single light streaked across the sky. They had learned from the stories in Manak-na and Ki'ti's time that the source of the lights were little pocked rocks that fell from the sky to earth. When they hit the earth they were very hot. To the Wise Man, that did not eliminate the lovely effect in the night sky they made.

While continuing to pet the dog's head, Midgenemo spoke aloud but very quietly, "Wisdom, it has been long since we talked. I have missed our times together. I have been so ashamed. I had become prideful and outside your way. It rips my belly every time I think of it. I know I asked you to forgive me. I know you forgave me. Somehow, I find it impossible to forgive myself."

"Midgenemo," came the very unique voice that the man knew so well, "For you to fail to forgive yourself when I have is conceit. Do you think yourself a better judge than I?"

"No, Wisdom, I question myself in all things now." His words were true. Midgenemo stroked the dog. The dog turned his head and gazed at Midgenemo. Then, the dog looked off to the side, the north side of Midgenemo, the seeming source of the very quiet voice of Wisdom.

"Turn from what is past, Midgenemo. Move forward avoiding the errors of the past, but moving forward without the weight of carrying what I've already forgiven. You carry a burden that is not necessary and it clouds your judgment for the present. It burdens your feelings with weight from which you have been freed."

"I understand, Wisdom."

"I will tell you what I have told Tuksook. There has never been a person of the People who was perfect. There is none at this time. There never will be one. You are no better or worse than any of the People."

Midgenemo looked up. His hand rested still on Tictip's back. He carried a burden that there was no need from Wisdom's view for him to carry. It was a burden from which he was freed—but he continued to carry it. He understood! The weight he carried since the lightning struck was one he could turn loose. It was that simple. The heavy weight of worry seemed as dew on the meadow in summer to evaporate in the warmth that came from the love Midgenemo felt from Wisdom.

Tictip could feel the emotion in Midgenemo. He did not stand up, but he turned his head to look at Midgenemo's face. The dog easily detected the great feeling that filled the man. The dog turned back to the invisible source of the voice.

"You fear that you are nearing the end of your life line," Wisdom stated, not asking a question.

"Yes," Midgenemo replied.

"You have two cold times still in your line," Wisdom said. "You should live fully and freely. Always remember to consult with me, but live, Midgenemo. While you live, help your daughter to eliminate the same weight of concern she carries. You need not know what the concern is, but only that she has it and you're freed of yours. She should be free of her burden as well."

"Wisdom, sometimes I am overwhelmed at the love you have for me. I think of me on this land. To you I could be only less than a grain of sand. Yet, you know me. You know when I hurt. You relieve pain that I experience from needlessly carrying a burden. My heart is grateful Wisdom. When I heard Wikroak speak to you, it made me realize that some people live their lives without ever hearing of you. How can people live without you?"

"It is enough to know that some people do, Midgenemo."

"My belly fills to overflowing with love and gratitude to you Wisdom. Please never leave us."

"I do not leave my people. I never have; I do not do it now; I will not do it in the future."

"When I think of all the People who make the stories we tell, and I think of all the People who are to come, it is overwhelming that you are constant with all of us. And all of us stumble and think more of ourselves than we should. But you remain constant, guiding. We are truly blessed in you Wisdom. What is reassuring is that other people can see that we are blessed in you. It shows to people who never heard of you."

"Remain in my way, Midgenemo."

"I will to my utmost ability," the Wise One replied.

Tictip seemed to realize the source of the voice had left. He whined almost inaudibly.

"It's good, Tictip," Midgenemo calmed the dog. "I just had a wonderful time with Wisdom and he healed my fatigue from carrying a burden I didn't need to carry." Midgenemo spoke to the dog, certain that the dog had no idea what he was saying, but he wanted to make the words come out. There was too much joy to contain within his body, so it had to come out in words.

Midgenemo picked up a stick that was near the hearth. Rising to his feet, he threw the stick some distance to the west. The dog ran after the stick and brought it to him. Midgenemo threw it three times and the dog retrieved the stick each time.

"Good dog, Tictip," Midgenemo said. "You haven't forgotten."

Midgenemo walked with the dog back to the dog house. He gave the dog the hand sign to stay at the place. Midgenemo patted the dog's head, turned, and began to walk back to the bent tree house. He was happy in a way he hadn't felt in years. He felt lighter somehow. He felt connected to all that was around him. Midgenemo felt truly loved by Wisdom.

He entered the bent tree house quietly, though Loraz heard him and checked to see who was walking through the house. Midgenemo waved to the night watch. He continued on to his sleeping place. He removed the skin cover he'd used and hung it back on the peg. He removed his boots. With utmost care Midgenemo eased into his sleeping place. He covered himself.

Item turned and wrapped her arm around him.

"What took you so long?" she asked.

"I spent time with Wisdom. Wisdom healed me."

She tightened her arm as if it were a half hug. She remained silent. She was filled with joy. She believed for the first time since the sea crossing that Midgenemo had come back to her.

Chapter Seven

Tuksook sat with Gumui on the rock overlooking the meadow. Plants were new green and the meadow seemed to pulse with life.

"Do you remember when we realized that volcanic ash fed some of the growing things? At first, we considered it an irritant because it burned our skin, and now we know it makes plants grow healthy. Look how green our meadow is. It's life—our life," Tuksook said leaning on Gumui. She loved sharing the rock with him briefly when either of them had a free moment.

"Yes, I do remember. I remember also the first of the sun tracking rocks we moved here. That was such a challenge. Look at them! When the elders suggested we move the other rocks here for better sighting, we already knew how to move them. What a wonder our meadow is."

"I just wish my father had lived to see what we see now. He would have been so pleased."

"He was a good man. He loved the People."

"You're right, Gumui. He did. It still bothers me a little when I think how I misjudged him, but he taught me to turn loose of things that Wisdom and the People had forgiven. He taught me to turn loose of it without ever knowing that the thing I needed to turn loose of had everything to do with him. He was considerate that way. Gumui, do you think we'll ever have a child?"

"You know I don't speculate. You have some eighteen cold times now. There is plenty of time. As often as you talk to Wisdom, I'd have thought you'd have asked him. Wisdom knows."

"And that's probably why I don't ask. Wisdom does know. If the answer is that I'll never have any, I don't think I'm ready to know that yet."

Tuksook stretched and braced back, resting on her forearms as she looked into the sunny sky.

Gumui put his hand on her shoulder. "Tuksook, you have been successful at living life knowing what is—is. We just have to know that all things will be as they should be in our lives. Don't wish away the present for something that's unknown."

"I know, and I don't ever forget the shower of roses. Sometimes life seems so short. Below us in the ground with my father lies Hapunta, just a child when the illness took her, and then Ottu. He was so old! And Lupo. Poor Lupo. That cat killed her while she was berry picking. It was awful."

They gazed out at the white topped mountains across the river. It was a clear day when everything was in sharp detail. An eagle flew by, chased by a raven.

There was a noise on the path that led to the rock where they sat. They both turned their heads to see what the commotion would bring.

"Wise One, will you come? Something terrible has happened." It was Twim, Moki and Heek's twelve-year-old son. He was breathless.

"What's happened, Twim?" Tuksook asked already on her feet.

"My grandmother is having trouble. She can't walk or talk. She looks scared." He was twisting his hands.

"Is anyone with her?" Tuksook asked, feeling as if she'd been hit in the belly. Twim's great-great-grandmother, Bruilimi, was so special to Tuksook.

"No, she was walking beside the house on the southeast side when she fell. I saw her fall. I asked Remui where you were and he told me."

"Gumui, please ask Mother to meet us there," she said as she carefully walked down the path to the meadow level. "Twim, lead me to the place where she fell," she asked.

Twim walked quickly to the place where he'd left his great-great-grandmother. She was not there.

"I don't know where she went," he said obviously confused and deeply concerned. "I didn't think she could walk at all."

"Let's go inside. Maybe someone brought her inside," Tuksook suggested.

They went inside through the east entryway. Sure enough, Remui stood beside Bruilimi's bench/sleeping place, talking to Item. Bruilimi lay on her bench/sleeping place, her face oddly contorted as she tried desperately to talk. Item sat beside her and put her hand gently on Bruilimi's head.

"Aunt," Item said, "Rest. Don't try to speak. You had a spell. It will take much time to heal. You must lie here and rest. We know what happened, and we will look out for you. Are you frightened?"

Bruilimi made the hand signal with her right hand to indicate "yes."

Item reached out and took Bruilimi's hand in both of hers. It was cold. She looked into Bruilimi's eyes and said, "I understand. You know, though, that this happens to some people. It takes time. You've cared for so many people over the years. It's time now that we take care of you. Just rest your body and know we are here. We love you Aunt." Item stood up to cover Bruilimi lightly with a skin.

Bruilimi lay there. Slowly tears came from her eyes. Yes, she'd seen this. She remembered. Her mother had experienced the same thing not long before she died. Bruilimi rested. Soon, she thought, she'd be together with Ottu again. She missed him so much. She tried to smile but felt it didn't quite work.

"There you are, Tuksook," Item said.

"It seems I arrived with all things well done," Tuksook replied. "Twim came to call me as fast as he could."

Remui touched Twim's shoulder. "You did a good thing to bring the Wise One. As soon as you told me about Bruilimi, I hunted for her and found her. I brought her and found Item. She's had a spell that some old people have. It makes it so they cannot talk or walk well. Time will tell how well she'll recover. But you acted fast. That is a good thing for one of the People."

Twim tried to feel better, but his great-great-grandmother's face had him frightened. He didn't want to see her hurt, and he didn't want her not able to talk or walk.

Suddenly, a little child ran past the people standing by Bruilimi's sleeping place. Bruilimi had gone to sleep. Very quickly Hustep followed behind.

"I'm sorry," Hustep made her habitual apology for the little one and herself. Her son, Toagrurt, was an unruly child. He wanted his way always. He was too old to be behaving so badly. Fortunately, his younger brother and sister were well behaved as most of the children of the People were. Tuksook made a decision to talk to Hustep later. She and others had talked to her about this child, but there had been no positive change in his behavior. What the parents were doing didn't seem to bring about the desired result. Hustep chased after the boy.

Hustep slowed quickly. Loraz had grabbed Toagrurt by the arm. He dragged him to the east entryway and literally threw him by the arm from the house.

The boy was hurt and he cried, but his cries were cries of outrage more than from pain.

Loraz shouted to him, "Don't come back in here unless you are ready to act like a good child of the People. I'm tired of your willful disrespect and disobedience. Stay out there."

The boy decided to push back into the house, rebelling at the words of his great-uncle.

Loraz grabbed the boy by his leg and arm and threw him more forcefully from the house.

The boy tried yet again to run past Loraz.

Loraz grabbed the boy to Hustep's horror and threw him over his head out of the house.

This time the boy cried from real pain, not rebellion. He had broken his leg. Hustep was aching to go to the boy to ease his pain. She knew better than to counter Loraz. She had no idea what to do. She went back to Item.

Item and all the others had listened to all that they could hear from Bruilimi's bench/sleeping place.

"Hustep, this has gone on too long with Toagrurt. Loraz is teaching him the hard way, because he has refused to learn the easy way. Leave him to Loraz," Item said. "With Loraz he is safe."

"Item, you can tell Toagrurt's leg is broken." Hustep believed Loraz was too violent.

"Sometimes, it takes something like that to deal with an evil-spirited child," Item replied.

"You see Toagrurt as an evil-spirited child?" Hustep was dumb-founded at the term.

"I have for a long time. He wants what he wants when he wants it. Everyone may want the same thing, but everyone except Toagrurt knows that is out of the question and they are peaceable. Toagrurt has to learn this or he'll become another Rimut. We have Wisdom's way and we have the People's way. Wisdom's way is perfection. None of us can reach it, but it's something to strive toward. The People's way knows that in each of us there is a tendency to evil and to good. We balance. When that balance is thrown off into the evil area, there is a problem. That's what happened with Toagrurt. He is way off balance. Rarely do we find someone whose balance is toward perfection. Usually that person doesn't fit well among the People. It is the evil-spirited ones that we have to guard against, because they can destroy the good functioning of the People. Rimut was evil-spirited and nobody stopped him, until he became adult. We learned from that."

Hustep was horribly upset to discover that not only did the People have a bad view of Toagrurt but also they compared his future to Rimut's, if he failed to change.

Hustep sat on the edge of Bruilimi's sleeping place while her son howled outside.

"I've been a terrible parent," she said.

"Not exactly so. This is not your problem any longer. You didn't stop him earlier, but now, the problem is Toagrurt's. He has no choice but to change. He cannot be permitted to live here among us as he is. Loraz has made that very clear by his action. Broken leg or no broken leg, Loraz is finished with the boy's evil-spiritedness. Toagrurt will be forced to stay outside the house until his spirit changes. Don't go to him to offer sympathy, unless you want Loraz to throw you out there with him," Item said calmly.

"Surely, you're exaggerating about his throwing me out there also."

Item said, "If you interfere, no, I'm not exaggerating. Many have waited patiently for Toagrurt to change, but he becomes worse. This is a lesson he'll remember for the remainder of his days. It is not a bad thing, Hustep—if it can change his evil-spirited ways."

"But Item, Loraz doesn't seem to care what his actions do to Toagrurt."

Item looked at Toagrurt. "He doesn't care? You think Loraz doesn't care? He's seen this evil-spirited, spoiled brat do things that other children would be severely beaten for doing. He has concluded that the end of it is here. You do realize that the time has come? It's because he does care that Loraz has decided to act. He cares about Toagrurt and the People."

"I realize that Loraz has decided the time has come. What about the rest of us?"

"Oh, Hustep. You are so kind-hearted, forgiving. Your strength is your weakness! If you were to go to each of the People and ask, how many would recommend you go to your son and coddle him now? I can tell you—not one. Most would tell you, it's past time for this to occur. They're sick of him. So am I. He is totally disrespectful of you and Orad. If Loraz hadn't stepped in, someone else would have sooner or later. Loraz will try not to kill him. Some others might not be so careful."

"I understand. I also understand that Toagrurt is only five years old and he keeps being injured more and more severely."

"That's his making. As long as he fights to have his own way, as he seems determined to rebel against authority, he will be hurt worse. He has to learn right now to change. He has to learn that when an adult tells him to do something, he will do it right away. He will do it well. He will respect the person who tells him to do it. Or, he can learn though pain. Or, he can die. He is making the choices. It's just not time for you to step in. This cannot go on any longer. You've had a chance to change it. Now, it's out of your hands." Item felt for Hustep, but she knew her words carried truth and that Hustep knew it.

Loraz came into the house while Toagrurt screamed in pain outside. He walked straight to Hustep. He cupped her face in his hands.

"It had to stop, Hustep. Stay away from him. Tend to your other children. Go about your daily routine. I will stay with this until the boy changes or dies. Occasionally a child starts behaving in an evil-spirited manner. I don't mean a spirit lives in him that doesn't belong there. What I mean is that the boy has decided that he can coerce others to let him do as he chooses. He manipulates, acts in ways that are unacceptable, is disrespectful. You cannot like what he does."

"No," she admitted, "I don't like what he does."

"Well, it is better for him to break a leg or an arm or lose teeth than to end up like Rimut, taken to a far off place and left there alone."

"I understand," she admitted.

"Now, girl, it will do you no good to remain here watching this. You have other children and other things to do. By now Remui will have already explained to Orad what's happening and why. Ask Wisdom to lead the boy to see the truth, if you want to help."

Hustep left and returned to what she was doing before Toagrurt decided to run away. She was torn in her belly but it was the way of the People. She had to accept that.

Item, Renwen, Tuksook, and Ghopi tended to Bruilimi. She was not doing well. In her mind web she was far from the trouble that was taking place near her sleeping place, so it didn't affect her. She was experiencing a number of different internal changes and she wondered at them, but she could make no sense of them. Bruilimi began to shake and shake. Something was very wrong. She foamed at the mouth, had trouble breathing, and finally sighed. Her last breath left her body with ease. Bruilimi would be with Ottu and Wisdom. She no longer lived among the People.

Tuksook ran her hand over her leg to dry it off from wiping her tears. She remembered it was Bruilimi who had made the lovely tunic for her from the cat skin. It fit her perfectly now. Some of the fur was wearing thin, but the tunic was wonderful. Tuksook treasured it. Bruilimi gone? Tuksook loved her. Emotions flowed through Tuksook like a river made of many contributing streams.

Gumui came to her after high sun. "It seems this morning sparked a day filled with many conflicting emotions, Tuksook."

"Yes," she replied taking a moment to listen to the area east of the house. "It sounds as if Toagrurt has become quiet."

"Leave it to Loraz," Gumui said, noticing where she was looking. "Now, Tuksook, if we would have children like that, I'm glad we don't have any."

Tuksook looked at him as if his remarks made no sense and she was far away. She really wanted to have children, but she certainly didn't want one like Toagrurt. Admitting that to herself opened up a place in her mind web and belly that had never been explored. Tuksook ached for the child outside in some ways, knowing that as a child, she'd had to change with no desire to make that change or understanding that she needed to make it. She wondered whether all children went through this same self-centeredness or whether it was limited to just a few.

Gumui touched her. "Tuksook, are you in your mind web?"

She looked at him and clearly saw him. "Of course. I'm sorry. There has been so much to think about. This day feels like ten."

"Ten days?"

"Yes."

"I can understand that, Tuksook. Why don't you grab your spears and you and I will take a short walk."

"Gumui, that would be helpful." She turned and went to pull out her spears from the spear storing place.

Gumui and Tuksook left by the west entryway. Gumui steered her to the south. They followed the trail that led to the place where they'd taken the rocks to track the sun's travel. The two went to a hilltop in the mountains to the east. Gumui, followed by Tuksook, climbed rapidly until Tuksook had to call for a rest. The muscles in her lower legs were burning. They snacked briefly looking up into the mountain tops. It was a day of sunshine with a temperature perfect for taking long walks. There was a cool edge to the air, but it wasn't cold.

"Look, Gumui, what's that?" Tuksook asked. High on the mountain, there were tiny white dots that were moving.

Gumui studied the white dots for a short time. "I believe they're sheep. When I hunted our first year here, I saw them. That must be the place where they have their young," he said. "They are animals that have horns that grow wide and curl to the front, and they may be good to eat, but I don't want to hunt females who have just given birth to young."

"Sometime, let's climb to a place where we can see them better." she suggested curious about the animals.

"We'd have to leave early in the day. Sheep are hard to find. It might take you from your duties for too long, but we should be able to make a trek just to see them where they are giving birth. That hill might be a good viewpoint and it's not far from here." He pointed to the hill and watched to be sure that Tuksook knew which one he meant. "Right now, we need to start our return home, so we arrive there before time to lay Bruilimi in the ground." He gave her a hand to help her stand.

"Thanks, my Gumui."

They began their walk back to the meadow.

The way back seemed so much faster than the walk to the hilltop. Gumui observed that the heavy weight of emotion that Tuksook had been carrying seemed to have lifted during the walk. He hoped that the walk would make it easier for her to continue through the remainder of the day. She still had Bruilimi's burial to face and council to lead.

"I wonder how Toagrurt is doing," Tuksook said as they entered the meadow from where they'd taken the rocks.

"I hope he's come to his senses," Gumui said flatly.

"I wonder whether Item has set his leg yet."

"We'll know soon."

They entered the meadow and went to the house to put their spears away. People in the meadow were going about their routine lives quietly. Unmo, Momeh, Togomoo, and Wave were digging the space for the body of Bruilimi. Children had gathered branches of the little gray fuzzy budding willows that they called puppy paws. No colorful flowers had bloomed yet, but there would be covering from the puppy paws to show respect.

Seeing that Tuksook had returned, Item hit the rocks together to call for the People to attend Bruilimi's burial. People came from all over the meadow. They circled the grave where Bruilimi had been carefully placed. Her body was wrapped in a skin, but the People could see that her body had been covered in red ochre. Around the circle at the grave each person told their special connection with Bruilimi and why they'd miss her. It was as if with words they tried a final embrace. Then, Tuksook told the creation story.

People dispersed quietly talking to each other as they left. The men who had earlier dug the grave filled it back in.

After there had been a time to adjust, Item hit the rocks together again, calling for the evening meal. When the People arrived at the outside food preparation place, Item announced that there would be no council that evening. Tuksook asked her to make that announcement because after the day they'd had, there really wasn't anything left to discuss.

At the grave side, Tuksook had searched for Toagrurt. She had seen his parents and Loraz, but no Toagrurt. She wondered what happened to the boy.

Now after the evening meal, she continued to wonder. She walked over to Item after she ate. "What of Toagrurt?" she asked.

"He remains evil-spirited. He lies where he came to rest when Loraz threw him. He continues to seethe with anger. He may have to remain outside and unfed for us to reach the part of him that will consider change. At least with the weather we're having, he won't freeze to death. I've never known one so hard to reach. I will tell you, Loraz is not straying for any reason. He came to the grave side, but his ears were probably with the boy. This hurts Loraz, but his concern is the boy and the People. He won't let the boy know he's watching over him this night, but I assure you, Loraz will not leave him outside without watching."

"I understand, Mother. I know I was hard, but this boy is beyond anything I can imagine."

Item put her hand lightly on Tuksook's shoulder.

Tuksook looked into Item's eyes. For a moment they shared a bond.

Toagrurt had spent the night frightened from every night noise. During the night he cried quietly not wanting anyone to know that he was frightened and lonely. He never saw Loraz who crept up from around the house, not the east entryway. No one used the east entryway that night. Toagrurt hadn't taken any hunter sessions for young children, because the leaders would not accept him into the group. He had no idea how to protect himself, and with the leg in such pain, he couldn't move. He envisioned animals finding him and feasting on him.

When the sun lit the sky once more, Toagrurt was hungry and thirsty. He saw Item. He told her to bring him some water. She walked by as if she hadn't seen or heard him. He grew louder. Then he realized she'd heard and seen him but chose to ignore him. That angered him greatly. It took until late after high sun for him to realize the disaster of his continuing to do what he'd been doing. He called to people who walked by, but all ignored him. Finally, feeling as if he'd been discarded on the trash heap, he began to weep. This sound is what Loraz had waited to hear. He had been sitting inside the east entryway behind the skins where he could not be seen. He waited for a long time. Then, he went outside to look at Toagrurt.

He told the boy that his behavior was despicable and that it would no longer be tolerated by any of the People. He had to have respect for every one of the People. He had to stop demanding things and doing things the way he wanted. He had to find out what was the People's way and do that. Deviation, he had to understand, would put him back where he now lay. Loraz wanted him to understand that his life was not certain. There were

People who thought his behavior so bad, they would have set things up to kill him. That frightened the boy badly.

In the late afternoon, Loraz came to Hustep. He sat on the ground across from her where she was cutting greens for the evening meal.

"I come from talking to Orad. I know it has been tough to see someone else step in to try to reach Toagrurt. The break in the boy finally occurred. Item is setting the bone now and some other women are cleaning him up. I don't know whether he has changed or just given up for the moment. For a while he will be dependent totally, because he will not be able to walk about. What I want from you is assurance that you will in no way give in to a single demand he may make. Not one. If he tells you he wants water, tell him you'll provide it when it's convenient and make him wait. If he tells you he needs to go to the privy, tell him you'll help him when it's convenient. Do you understand what I'm telling you?"

"Yes, Loraz. Orad and I have spent much time talking about Toagrurt. He was our first child and we let him do things we knew we shouldn't have. We were just so happy to have him."

"And he learned how to manipulate you and Orad to continue to have whatever he wanted even if it wasn't convenient or something he should not be granted. That is the evil that cannot be permitted. I hope it dies now, but if not, there will be more of what has occurred. If he even seems to question what would happen if he returned to his old ways, let him know that I and many others are waiting for that to happen, because we have stronger ways of dealing with evil-spirited children."

"That would frighten him," Hustep replied.

"Then, let him be frightened. I speak the truth. It doesn't matter whether he is frightened. He has to know the truth, and he has to learn to live by it. He wants no one in authority over him. That is not real. He has to learn the reality of the life of the People and the way of Wisdom. There is authority from many places among our People. I warn you, if you give in to him at any point, you are contributing to any future discipline that comes his way. You are a parent. You must be a parent. You must have authority over him and show it. You've let him display authority over you. That is all wrong. Children have no authority over parents. Do you remember the monkeys near where we lived?"

"Yes."

"What did they do with their young when they misbehaved?"

"They grabbed them immediately and shoved their little faces to the ground," Hustep replied remembering.

"Was that effective?" Loraz asked.

"Well, they held them there until they stopped the irritating behavior."

"I'll ask you again. Was that effective?"

"Yes." Hustep was beginning to see the point Loraz was making.

"They did it immediately," Loraz emphasized. "The little ones learned immediately who had the authority and to obey. With Toagrurt, you have to make up for a long time of giving in to every whim he had. It won't be easy, but you have no alternative but to toughen up. He's not like a little monkey who wants to steal his mother's food. He's like a larger monkey who is breaking the monkey way of doing things. At that time numbers of monkeys would discipline him—hard. You've seen that?"

"Yes, I've seen numbers of monkeys attack a single monkey. Sometimes they lame the one they're after or cause it to lose a finger or an ear. I've seen them kill one."

"That's what I'm trying to have you to see. We are not a lot different from the monkeys. Toagrurt has come to see himself as a chief, who can order things to happen. He's come to see himself as having authority over you and Orad. You have to cause him to eliminate that notion now and forever. I charge you with doing that. We don't have chiefs here. If we did, it wouldn't be a child!"

"I understand, Loraz. Toagrurt is not the only one who has to change. I have to change."

"Yes," Loraz said, tired, "And Orad."

"Thank you for your help. I'm glad it was you and not someone who wouldn't care at the beginning whether he lived or died."

"You're welcome. I believe it is Wisdom's way to provide every chance possible, but not to deviate from what's required along the way. I don't want another Rimut among the People. I want to see Toagrurt grow into a responsible adult. We need every person we have."

Loraz stood up, cursing his stiff knees in his mind web. He left, heading towards Item and the boy.

"Did the leg set well?" Loraz asked Item.

"I think so. It wasn't a bad break. I took him to the food preparation area where he's leaning against a log. He's hungry and tired, I hope he learned."

"I hope he learned also. At least the process to turn him around has begun. The child was becoming a total irritant to me."

Renwen hit the rocks together calling all the People to the evening meal.

Orad and Hustep walked hand-in-hand with their two other children. Toagrurt saw them coming and looked at Hustep.

"Mother, I need food," he called out.

"You'll have food when it's convenient," she said coolly.

Toagrurt was shocked at the reply but remained silent. He was trying to find what was the People's way, but he had no understanding.

Orad and Hustep chatted briefly with some of the other People and slowly began to fill the bowls of the two youngest children. Orad carried the bowls to the children and told them where to sit. They were well outside the reach of Toagrurt. They sat and began to eat.

Hustep filled her bowl and Toagrurt's. Orad came over to fill his. He carried the bowl to Toagrurt and he and Hustep sat on the far side of the other children, not near Toagrurt. When they finished eating, Orad collected the bowls from all three children. He merged the remains to one bowl and took the filled bowl to the trash heap to empty out the contents.

There was no council planned for the evening. Orad suggested the family take a brief walk. He told Toagrurt that he was too heavy to carry any distance, so they'd stop for him when they returned from their walk. They all left and walked down the path to the lower level and followed a path that led to the boats and beyond. The little children loved to look in the watery spots where occasionally they'd see minnows. The evening sun was lengthening and they enjoyed their walk. The little ones were happy not to have to put up with the mean things Toagrurt would do. They didn't realize life could be so pleasant on a walk.

By the time Orad, Hustep, and the children returned to the meadow, Toagrurt was becoming anxious. They did not forget him. Orad carried him to the privy and then to the house. He was frightened by what Loraz had told him. He was frightened because his parents were acting very differently toward him. All he seemed to remember is that Loraz had told him to learn the People's way and Wisdom's way. He didn't know what Wisdom's way or the People's way were. He watched the People around him.

"Mother, bring me water," he said later in the evening.

"You need to ask this way, 'Mother, please, bring me some water.' Now, I'll bring it when it's convenient," she replied and continued doing what she was doing.

"I thirst." His tone was demanding.

"Son," Orad said, "Your mother told you she'd bring it when it was convenient. It's not convenient yet. The People's way is this: if you have a need, take care of it yourself. If you cannot do it yourself, ask politely for help from someone else at their convenience. You cannot get water for yourself because you were disrespectful and disobedient. Your rebellion was rewarded with a broken leg. So now you have to learn for a long time what it is to have to wait for things at the convenience of others. Just be glad that her answer was wait. She could have refused."

Toagrurt thought on that for a while. Life had changed. He knew he had to learn to live this new way, but he didn't like it. The rebelliousness he had exhibited was significantly reduced as he struggled to learn how to be.

The sounds of the bent tree house quieted immediately. Oneg had begun to play her flute. She had come to love the flute and the People loved to hear it. Oneg didn't play it every night—only when she felt drawn to play it. Sometimes she played alone; other times she played with others she could neither see nor talk with, but their music merged. Oneg would play for quite a while. Sometimes she would play long enough that some of the People would ready themselves for sleep and drift off to sleep listening to the clear notes of her tunes.

Her mother, Bit-n would play with her for brief times. Bit-n played well, but she did not have the talent Oneg had for picking up new tunes and winding them into ways of communicating through feeling.

This evening Oneg realized that she found Nal very attractive. Nal was Item's fourth child. The two had been down on the river level after the evening meal. They had talked back and forth as People did about routine matters, but Nal found himself looking at her, as if he'd never seen her. Something about her at that moment drew him in a way that he'd never experienced. The sun behind her made her red curly hair glow around her head in a way that reminded Nal of the glow of fire embers. Nal had stopped her, though he felt clumsy, and told her she looked beautiful. Oneg hadn't known how to respond, so she thanked him and said he was a good looking man. She had believed that for a long time. Nal asked Oneg to walk with him. They walked along the path by the water's edge. When they were out of the People's view, they stopped and looked at each other, and Nal bent down to kiss her. She stood on her toes to return the kiss. For them it was their first kiss and quite startling. They returned to the meadow silent, hand-in-hand.

Oneg found comfort in the music. She could express her feelings that she couldn't verbalize through the tunes and the moods of the music. It was as if the ancient musicians could understand her feelings and give her the sense that she was part of feelings that had begun at the beginning of time. As Oneg flowed with the music, she should feel freedom to flow with the feelings she'd just experienced, things she wished she could have said to Nal, but knew no way to express.

Nal heard the music and listened intently. It spoke to him in a language of feeling—a language he'd never heard until this evening. It spoke to him as if she played for him, saying things she couldn't form in words—things he couldn't form in words.

Oneg felt a comfort from the music she could find nowhere else. Finally, she realized it was very late and past time to put the flute away. She packaged it in its protective skin and put it safely away in the box under her bench/sleeping place. She snuggled down in the skins and soon went to sleep.

Many days passed. Toagrurt had learned some of the ways of the People. He was developing a polite approach to asking for things he needed. He found that the People responded much better when he was polite. He was trying, but the behaviors were not natural. Toagrurt felt awkward.

After high sun, Oneg, who never had said anything to him, walked over and sat on the edge of his bench. He was surprised. She was, he knew, the woman who played the flute.

"How are you doing, Toagrurt?" she asked.

"Better. The pain is mostly gone."

"That's good. I had a broken leg once. I wore a splint for a long time."

"And you're walking like your leg never broke?" he asked.

"I was fortunate. I only am reminded that I broke my leg when the weather turns cold or rainy. Then, the bones that broke ache."

"I hope my leg heals well."

"Be sure to do what they tell you to do. It makes a difference," Oneg said.

Toagrurt looked at her. He wondered why she stopped by.

"What do you do, while you sit here all day?"

"Nothing. It's boring."

"Do you know how to make tools or anything like that?"

"No, nobody taught me to do anything like that yet."

"Is there anything you think you'd like to be able to do?"

"I can't think of anything."

"Well, spend some time thinking about what might interest you. Having something to do can make your stay in one place worthwhile. That's how I learned to play the flute. It was a good use of my time."

Toagrurt remembered what he'd been taught, "Thank you, Oneg. I will think on it."

Oneg went to help the women at the food preparation place.

Oneg walked over to Item who was looking at the food servers. "Item, I just came from Toagrurt. I wondered what he might do while he cannot move about. I learned to play the flute. Is there something he could work to learn? I asked about his interests and he seems to have none. It would give him good use of the time."

Item stood up. Her back was not comfortable from all the leaning over she'd been doing. Item placed her hand on her forehead to shield her eyes from the sun. "That's a very good thought. It would occupy his mind web with things that would contribute well to his growing a good spirit. Let me see what I can do to find something. Good help, Oneg."

"Thank you, Item. Is there anything I can do here?"

"You can relieve my back. I'm trying to go through the bowls to see whether any are cracked or needing to be replaced. Would you check them?"

"I'd be glad to help." Oneg began by placing the bowls on the log where food was served. Then, she'd examine each one in full sun.

Item went to each of the men who taught young hunters things that didn't involve moving from a single place. She asked each one to make the attempt to teach Toagrurt a little of what they taught. Each agreed to try, but they would not put up with the evil spirit in the child. If he displayed that, they would stop.

The first to respond was Taman. He brought Ren with him to Toagrurt. "Toagrurt, today you're going to begin hunter training. You'll work on the slingshot. Ren has hung a leather sphere from a tree in the south meadow. She will show you how to use the slingshot. Already she has gathered many pebbles so that you can do much practice. These are practice pebbles, smaller than what a hunter uses. You must pay attention and practice. You must use your best effort. You must show a good spirit the whole time. You must show respect to Ren and to me. Nobody is perfect right away. It takes time to learn and much time to perfect your shots. You will work with her for days to learn this. This is one of the first things a hunter learns. Do you want to do this?"

"Yes, please, Taman. I want to learn it very much." Toagrurt did want to learn. He'd been barred from hunter training in the past. He had a chance to catch up with the skill of others his age.

"Good. Then, I'll carry you to the place in the meadow where we have a practice area set up. Remember, People keep going even when they tire. Push to learn all you can while you are practicing."

"Thank you for this opportunity. I will learn to make the best of this."

"Good," Taman said and lifted the boy. He carried him to the log he had positioned for the boy to lean against. It was off angle to the hanging sphere, and it was designed for a left-handed slinger. Taman had observed Toagrurt long enough to know that Toagrurt favored his left hand. Ren welcomed him and immediately introduced him to the hanging sphere, which would be his target, and the round pebbles. Then she began to introduce the slingshot. While she talked to Toagrurt, Taman left. Ren was great with children.

"Now, Toagrurt, watch what I do and how I do it. I'll throw five pebbles, and then you'll begin."

Ren showed him how she put on the sling. It was a single strip of leather. The far thin end had a hole into which she inserted her middle finger. The other thin end had a tiny knot tied in the end. Ren showed him she held the knot between her index finger and her thumb, pinching it to hold it. She explained that letting go of the pinch was how the pebble was released. Ren put the round pebble in the wider center part of the sling. "You hold the pouch out from your head and as you release you swing the pouch up and back to the front in a great circle. I stand off to the side, so I'm not face-to-face with the target. Then when the time is right, I let go of the pinched strip and the pebble flies out stronger than I can throw it. Watch."

Ren demonstrated twice, hitting the target with a thud each time. "Any questions?" she asked.

"Not yet," he replied.

Ren showed him three more times, hitting the target each time again. "Any questions?" she asked.

"I see you step forward when you throw. I don't think I can do that."

"That forward step just adds more power to the throw. You don't need to do what you can't do. You can learn well how to use the slingshot without that step. Later, when your bone heals, you can add that for more power."

"Now, you try it. Remember, at first you'll be all over the place with your pebbles until you learn when to release them. Don't worry about how well you do, learn from where your pebbles go. Keep your eyes on the target until after you release the strip between your fingers."

Toagrurt tried several times and, just as Ren warned, his pebbles were all over the ground in different places.

"I am not very good at this, Ren," he confessed.

"You're as good as anybody I've ever seen," she replied. "It takes sometimes a whole moon for young hunters to hit the target for the first time. That's considered normal."

"That long!"

"Yes. This looks so simple, but you have to train your arm and your whole body along with your mind web to learn it right."

"I've watched women take slings to the lake. They would hide in the grass. Quickly, they'll rise and release a stone from the sling to kill a goose. It looks so simple."

"Well, it's not simple until you've been doing it for years, and then it feels as if it's part of you. You can kill a deer with one of these things."

"Like a giant deer?" he asked.

"I don't know whether anyone ever killed a giant deer with one, but back in the old land, People killed smaller deer with these all the time. They could throw from a distance farther than they could spear the deer. It let them kill more deer at one time than spearing would."

"I understand. Ren, you are making it sound like every hunter can do this."

"It is a basic hunter skill. It teaches you to use your body as a unit with a purpose. That is what hunting is."

Toagrurt began to practice earnestly. He paid close attention to the timing and place in the arc when he let a pebble go and where the pebble landed. He cleared all things from his mind web but that, maintaining a focus that few children were able to hold. Just before the evening meal was called, Toagrurt hit the sphere once. He was thrilled. It was a feeling of achievement from hard work that he'd never experienced. He hoped all days would be sunny, so he could practice every day. He wanted desperately to learn this skill and to learn it well.

When Item struck the rocks together calling for the evening meal, Ren congratulated Toagrurt on a good practice, and she went to join her family. After some time, Orad came to carry Toagrurt from the log to their place to eat. Orad said very little. Toagrurt wanted desperately to blurt out how well he'd done, but he had learned enough about the way of the People to know that would be seen as outrageous pride, so he remained silent. He was trying to learn what he needed to know. It was hard, but he had a stark terror of having to endure any more ill will from his People.

After the evening meal there was a brief council. Tuksook told the story and there was nothing put forth by the hunters.

Tuksook asked, "Is there anything to add?"

Ren said, "I have something."

Tuksook nodded to Ren.

"Today I spent time teaching Toagrurt to use the slingshot. He worked very hard to learn it and he was successful in hitting the target one time before the end of the day. I have never seen anyone work so hard nor have as much success in one day as he did. I look forward to continuing to work with him."

Older adults looked at each other silently but with surprise. Even Orad and Hustep exchanged glances, surprised that anyone would say those words about their first son. For the first time they had a spark of hope for the boy.

Tuksook asked, "Is there anything to add?"

"Yes," Togomoo said.

Tuksook nodded to him.

"Hamaklob and I want to fish for sturgeon tomorrow after the morning meal. We could use two more to make the boat."

"I'd like to go," Wave said.

"Me too," Anvel said.

"Thank you," Togomoo said without waiting for a nod from Tuksook. "Don't forget to bring your fishing gloves. We've had too many People develop deep cuts in their hands from holding onto fishing lines when the fish wants to fight hard."

Tuksook smiled, "Is there anything else to add."

There was silence.

"The council ends," she said.

Nal found Oneg as the meeting closed. He walked with her back to the bent tree house. Just outside the bent tree house, Nal asked, "Oneg, will you join with me?"

"Yes, Nal. I would like to do that very much."

He smiled a smile she didn't know he had. His joy was great.

"When shall we do this?" Oneg asked.

"Let us have Tuksook announce it tomorrow night and we can prepare the north part of the house so we're ready to leave after the announcement.

They kissed and went into the house, Oneg to the east part and Nal to the west part.

Nal noticed that Tuksook had just entered the house. He went to her.

"Wise One," he addressed her.

Tuksook realized he had something official in mind. Usually, he addressed her as "my sister."

"What is it, Nal?" she asked.

"At council tomorrow, Oneg and I would like to join."

Tuksook grinned. "I am so happy. The two of you go well together. I'm happy to plan that for tomorrow night."

"Thank you, Wise One," he said formally.

"You're welcome."

Gumui came in and was ready to end the busy day. Tuksook noticed and took his spears and placed them in the little space where he kept them. Gumui went to the inside food preparation place, not often used in the warm part of the year unless it rained. He took the dipper and drank some water, not enough to cause him to rise early but enough to quench his thirst.

He hung up his tunic, rolled into the sleeping place, and covered himself with a light skin.

Tuksook sat on the edge of their sleeping place. "Are you well, my husband?" she asked.

"Yes. Just tired from a day of hard work. I've been attending to roof work all day."

Tuksook smoothed the wet hair on his head. He took a shower before coming to the house, she realized. She felt his head to assure herself his body heat was normal.

Oneg played her flute briefly, this time the tunes spoke of triumph, as if great things had happened and People were trekking around the center stone to celebrate. Not that the People had ever celebrated by trekking around the center stone. No one had ever heard her play such tunes.

Her father, Pago, walked to her sleeping place and said, "Daughter, the music is not restful. It makes me want to stand up and trek. Please, if you play when People are going to sleep, make the tunes ones that are restful."

Oneg looked up with dismay. "I'm sorry, Father. I'll put it away for this night." She did, though her mind web was filled with the new tunes of joy.

Toagrurt lay on his sleeping place. Never in his life had he experienced the feeling he had this night. He had worked hard with his body and his mind web to learn to throw stones with a slingshot. Never in his brief life had Toagrurt worked so hard. He had been delighted when he hit the sphere and thought he could repeat that the next day. Toagrurt had never experienced the joy of hard work. He'd also never experienced having to prevent his words from praising himself. When Ren spoke of his effort and success at the council, Toagrurt's joy almost burst forth. So, that was the way of the People, he thought. Toagrurt had to admit that the way of the People was a good way.

Loraz lay there in his sleeping place with Kouchu. She had fallen asleep. He thought back to Ren's comments at the council. How he hoped that the boy would continue to grow in the way of the People. He didn't like disciplining someone else's child, but in this case there seemed no alternative. It exhausted him. But he saw the look on Toagrurt's face while Ren talked. The boy was experiencing joy. Loraz wondered whether it was the first time he'd ever had that feeling. He guessed it was. He would keep a close watch on this child. For him to have hit the sphere the first day of learning was amazing. It meant the boy was giving it everything he could, no slacking, no lack of attention. Maybe this little child would develop into a seriously contributing member of the People.

In the night there was another earthquake. It hit hard and made a horrible noise. It shook the bent tree house for a long time. Everyone stayed where they were, not knowing whether it was best to run outside or remain inside. After a brief time, which felt like forever, the shaking ceased. Much later there was a slight tremor, but nothing like the first. Pieces of the ceiling had fallen in little chunks throughout the bent tree house. Some ties were obviously broken. But the main structure still served as a solid shelter.

Although Gumui awakened still not fully rested, he would spend the day repairing the damage from the quake. He was surprised that the damage wasn't greater than it was. Nal, Nipe, Velur, and Guw offered to help. He had been trying to encourage younger People to help with this task. It was not easy for the older People to climb, tie, mud upside down, while hanging from the roof. For the young, it was a great challenge. If they fell, few would be hurt. If older people fell, the damage could be extensive.

During the day little earthquakes occurred as was usual. The People fully expected that in a day or two the earthquakes would cease to be felt. This had been the largest quake they'd felt since moving to the meadow.

Item was at the food preparation place when Tern came running to her. "Please, come. Enzuvel is in labor and is asking for you."

Item laid down the tools she had in her hands and followed the young man to the house. At the far end of the south part of the house, Enzuvel was still in labor. It had begun the night before. It was her first. Item wasn't terribly concerned at this point. She watched the girl.

"Enzuvel," she called her to direct her attention, "Stop pacing and trying to push so hard right now. It's not time for that. You're working too hard."

"I just want it out of here," she said breathless.

"Tern, I want you to take her for a little walk outside," Item said.

That was the last thing Tern expected to hear. "What if the baby comes outside?"

"Well, it won't be the first that did. Enzuvel needs to move her mind web to something else. She's pacing around like a trapped wolverine! Make her walk with a slow walk. Talk to her about other things."

"Very well, Item," Tern said. He reminded himself he'd asked for help. That was the help.

He took Enzuvel by the arm and led her from the house. Enzuvel didn't want to go, but she'd heard Item, and she was obedient. The two went outside and began to walk. Tern planned on a walk around the perimeter of the meadow. He tried to stay on the walked down grass and avoid the tall grass of the perimeter's edge. He wanted to be certain to avoid the mother of red rash plant.

The day was warm and the sun was out in a cloudless sky. Enzuvel found that the walk was relaxing her, though she'd been appalled to think that walking was a good idea when Item mentioned it. She moved through the grasses. Her favorite feeling from grass was when the damp grass dragged across her ankles. It reminded her of walking in the eel grass at the ocean's edge. It was a comforting feeling to her. Occasionally, a contraction would cause her to stop. Then, she'd go on as if it hadn't happened.

She and Tern saw Ren teaching Toagrurt to use the slingshot. They could see that he was becoming proficient. He was still in the splint, but he was hitting the sphere with regularity, even when Ren put a spin on it.

"He's going to think he's learned it until she starts swinging the sphere," Tern laughed. "Then, he starts all over again in learning."

"That's true," Enzuvel smiled and then grimaced.

"Another one?"

"Yes. They seem to be coming faster now. Not fast enough, though."

"I think you're doing fine," Tern said, unable to think of anything else but wanting to be supportive.

A fishing boat returned from the day's travel. The meadow became busy with different groups of People preparing to tend to the function they had for returning fishing boats. Hawk walked to the area where he could see the arriving boats from the meadow. He could tell that they had a large sturgeon and numbers of smaller fish that lay in the bottom of the boat. The men started cleaning and beheading fish at the river's edge. They sent the fish by young boys to the meadow where others opened the fish and decided whether the fish went to the drying poles or the smoker. Women would come from the food preparation place to see whether any of the fish were likely products for that night's evening meal.

Tuksook walked to the southwestern part of the meadow. From there she could watch Ren teaching Toagrurt. Tuksook was delighted to see how her little sister, Ren, was growing. The girl was a natural teacher. Children loved her. She encouraged them realistically, and Ren never missed a chance for a positive comment. She took care not to make her praise gratuitous, though. Each word of praise was earned, most of the time with difficulty.

Item hit the rocks together calling for the evening meal. All hurried to the food preparation place. Orad came sooner to pick up Toagrurt to take him to the place where they'd eat. Toagrurt noticed that the closer his behavior came to the People's way, the sooner his parents responded to him. In fact, the change was noticeable among the People.

It was Loraz who noticed that Toagrurt was learning that the more his behavior fit the way of the People the faster People responded. Loraz had been waiting for that, for he knew that such understanding could be another way to manipulate the People. Loraz hated above all things manipulative behavior. He hated it because it was so far from Wisdom's way and it could appear good, when it was deeply buried evil. He wanted to stop any chance that Toagrurt's behavior was just the opposite side of the evil manipulation he'd done before—being overly polite could be evil disguised.

Loraz went to Orad and Hustep and talked to them about the change in Toagrurt. Both parents were thrilled with Toagrurt's changes, but Loraz warned them of his concern. Hustep tried to minimize the need for concern, but Orad spoke up, "I see what you mean. Toagrurt has an excellent mind web. It's just the kind of thing he'd figure out. What do you want us to do?"

"I've seen both of you respond quicker to his requests, and I do see they're requests instead of demands. Your responding quicker is the reason I'm concerned. You need to return to doing things at your convenience, even if you need to draw out your convenience longer than necessary. He must learn that he cannot use good to manipulate you or anyone else."

"Oh, I understand what you mean, now," Hustep said, finally realizing what manipulation by good was.

"Will you return to your caring for him at your convenience?" Loraz asked.

Both replied, "Yes."

"This is something you need to do for the rest of time with him. You don't race to tend to the other children. He should be treated no differently at all, except now maybe take a little longer to respond. To cure him will take years, maybe from now until he's an adult. He didn't become like this in a few days." Loraz was tired. He still had other People to talk with about how they treated Toagrurt, starting now with Ren.

Enzuvel hadn't made it to the evening meal. She finally delivered a baby girl. By the time council ended and People began to come into the house for the evening, Enzuvel was cleaned up and the baby had nursed. All was well with the newborn.

Vole, Wave, Momeh, Unmo, and Anvel decided to hunt a giant deer. They would leave early, before the morning meal. They were eager to hunt again. It was so easy to depend on the sturgeon, smaller fish, and sea aurochs. Each yearned for some roasted giant deer or some other four-legged animal that walked the land. They left before sunrise and headed north on the narrow ledge that skirted the rock face across the arroyo. They passed through the first meadow where a couple of horses grazed and headed for the larger lake filled land where few trees grew.

Ren continued training Toagrurt after the morning meal, but now she began to swing the sphere. Toagrurt was horrified that he was unable to hit the target.

"You have to anticipate when it will reach a certain point and aim for that point. You know how to hit a still target now, but you need to learn how to hit a moving one. It just takes more learning."

Toagrurt worked for a while and then seemed to lose all interest. Ren tried to encourge him without success.

"Well, if you plan to learn the skills of a hunter only for still targets, then you're living in the wrong world, Toagrurt," she said with some irritation. "I'm going to go to do some things that are a better use of time than this," she stated and left him.

Suddenly, Toagrurt found himself in the meadow alone. He had learned that when he put himself in a position like this, it would be much time before anyone came to him. Toagrurt picked up the sling and reached for a pebble. Ren had always handed them to him, because they were piled on the ground. In reaching for a pebble, he fell over on his side. He had to twist and turn, holding onto the log to put himself back into position. It took him a long time. By the time Toagrurt was back, he realized he'd left the pebble on the ground. It took him a long time to try to reach a pebble again. This time he was successful, but he could only hold a few at a time. Toagrurt lined them up on the log.

Hidden in the vegetation Loraz tossed a rock and set the sphere to swinging. Toagrurt was shocked. He knew someone had to have done that, but he didn't see anyone anywhere nearby. He could see Ren at a distance, so he knew it wasn't Ren. Toagrurt took the slingshot, loaded a pebble, and tried to hit the sphere. He missed. He tried five times and missed each time. Toagrurt had to gather more pebbles. The fun he'd been having each day had turned to frustration. He admitted to himself that Ren left, because he had become irritating and showed no interest in working hard to learn the next skill. He didn't know that when a student became irritated and refused to try, the student was dismissed immediately. Toagrurt learned. He gathered more pebbles, and he shot at the target. The target was as still as stone. To make matters worse, his father was late in picking him up for the evening meal.

Renwen was not feeling well. She had burning pain in her chest and arm. She wondered whether she was having a spell like Bruilimi had. She made a little sound and fell over. Kew lifted her up and knew instantly his wife was gone. He had the awkward thought that she hadn't eaten any of the sturgeon, her favorite meat. They were both seventy-five. He wasn't terribly surprised, but somehow he had been convinced that he'd die before she did. Kew's belly ripped apart. They'd been joined for sixty years. Somehow, he couldn't imagine life without Renwen. He wasn't sure he could even remember life without her.

Item, Tuksook, Ghopi, and Brill immediately began to take care of the body of Renwen. Gumui and Bit-n brought cloths and containers of water to clean her. Men left their food unfinished and went to the house for tools and then to the place for burials to begin to dig a grave. Others went to comfort Kew. Young People sat quietly, a little fearful, having minimal experience with death.

Finally, Ren realized the children were a bit daunted. She called them together and suggested they tour the meadow's edge looking for flowers. There were many flowers blooming. She warned them to stay away from the mother of red rash, but any of the others were fine. With some goal in mind, the children became very busy. Ren paid no attention to Toagrurt at all. Instead, she watched over the very little children with Pilly, Meha, Lamo, and Pica.

Toagrurt called to her.

She looked at him disinterestedly.

"Ren, I apologize for earlier today. I was wrong. If the weather's good tomorrow, will you teach me to aim for the moving target?"

"I'll consider it, but you had better not disappoint me again."

"I'll be very serious about it, Ren. I really want to know."

"Then hope the weather's good," she said and turned to other things with the smaller children, including his brother and sister.

The girls encouraged the young ones to continue their evening meal. Most did very well without help from their parents. Some were just too small, so Pilly, Lamo, and Pica helped them. Meha took care of the infants.

Although it was becoming late, the men who'd been hunting returned with the giant deer they sought. They were surprised that there were none to meet them, but, looking towards the south part of the meadow, they realized soon someone had died. The young boys and new hunters eagerly helped the men with their burdens. The men took care of storing the meat in the catch pond, put weapons away, and washed up. They were very hungry, so they stopped to eat.

Item returned to the food preparation place and hit the rocks together to let everyone know to assemble at the grave. All the People went there except Toagrurt. It was half way through the circle before Orad realized he'd left

Toagrurt. He had already made his comments, so he ran back to Toagrurt and picked him up. He carried him to the grave side. Tuksook had just begun the creation story.

Toagrurt remained silent about having been left. He realized the finality of being one who could order others about, and now, being just like everyone else, only maybe a little lower when it came to the concern of others. He knew he'd brought this on himself. It hurt Toagrurt to have been forgotten at Renwen's grave. He thought the flowers were wonderful. There were so many that you couldn't see the body of Renwen. She was completely covered in a deep layer of flowers. Toagrurt thought that when the People one day put his body in the ground, he'd like it, if People cared enough for him to pile flowers on his body, as they did for Renwen.

That night, Oneg brought out her flute. She played music that was gentle, as if one floated on a slow moving stream. It wasn't sad, just peaceful. Oneg played tunes no one had ever heard—tunes even she had never heard. They came from down deep inside. Oneg did not play too long. After a brief time of playing four tunes, she put her flute back in its wrapping and stowed it beneath the sleeping place she shared with Nal.

Tuksook snuggled against Gumui. He had recovered from his fatigue. He put his arm around her and pulled her close. Tonight Gumui was taken by Oneg's music. It wrapped him in feelings that were deep and abiding. Timeless feelings. He thought of Kew and Renwen. Gumui hoped that he'd die before Tuksook and then realized that was not a very thoughtful wish. He pulled Tuksook to him hoping deep down inside that both would live long, healthful lives. Tuksook lifted his hand and kissed it before replacing it on her belly.

Chapter Eight

"I lost it," Tuksook said to Gumui, her face filled with grief. "It's the fourth one I've lost. I feel a total failure. Four lives, and I couldn't hold onto even one of them."

She looked so small lying there. So hurt. Surely, Wisdom would not prevent Tuksook from being a mother, he thought.

"Tuksook, I love you. If you never have a living baby, I'll love you no less. I know you wish to be a mother. I'm so sorry this one didn't make it. In no way are you a failure." He held her in his arms while she allowed water to flow freely from her eyes and his joined hers.

Item walked by. She saw the grief of Tuksook and Gumui. She stopped. "I'm so sorry. We tried the best we knew. It's that so much of the original People continues on in us. Those of us who have the beautiful sloping heads also have trouble giving birth. That's just how it is. It doesn't make it any easier on you at times like this."

Tuksook looked at her mother. She knew that People with her head shape had difficult births, but somehow she hadn't applied that to herself. So that was the curse. There was an old saying that the beautiful were cursed. The saying was from the women of very long ago, she thought, not Wisdom. Tuksook never considered herself beautiful, but the People prized the head shape she had as the greatest sign of beauty. Gumui's head had a little slope, and his family had the trait. Still, Tuksook thought, she might have had an easier time had she chosen someone with a straight forehead, but that would be impossible—she loved Gumui. She could think of being with no one else.

"Gumui, will you bury the baby?"

He nodded. It was not usual to bury the body of a baby that didn't live, but there was no rule against it. He would do it. Gumui laid her back on their sleeping place and touched her shoulder. Their eyes met in silent understanding. He picked up the little leather wrapped bundle.

He went to the tool container for digging tools.

"Want some help?" Togomoo asked.

"I'd appreciate that a lot."

Togomoo gathered tools and headed toward the burial place with Gumui. Together they dug the grave, gathered some flowers, and laid the little body in the ground, covered it with the flowers, and replaced the dirt.

"If there is life in you, little one," Gumui said, "go to Wisdom."

"Do you think they go to Wisdom when they've never breathed?" Togomoo asked.

"I have no idea. I just know that it's very important to Tuksook to bury these babies with the People who have gone before. When I look at that tiny little perfect body, I cannot see why it is not one of us, even though it failed to breathe. Its looks are what I reason as being People. The little body looked exactly like People."

"Brill lost two. It's terrible for the women to have carried a baby they could feel and then it comes dead."

"If you can say the babies came dead, that means that once they had life, doesn't it? Tuksook could feel this one kick from time to time. Even though it never breathed, I think it still had life. So, burial may be appropriate," Gumui said.

"I guess it's just how the parents feel whether it's buried or goes to the trash heap." Togomoo picked up the tools he'd brought.

"I think so. I don't know that anyone has ever known what Wisdom's way is regarding burying these little ones. Thanks for the help. It was good to have someone else here," Gumui said as he picked up the tools he'd brought.

In another part of the meadow, Oneg and Ren were teaching children to sing and dance. Because there was little space in the house in the cold time, they taught the children to dance in place, moving no more than two steps at any given time all in the same direction. They danced using their whole bodies. They made dances about fishing for the sea aurochs, hunting the giant deer, and bringing down a goose with a slingshot. They made dances about the sun dying and coming back to life, about the sky lights, about the big earthquake. The favorite was the dance about fishing for sea aurochs, because they had some People act like a boat with other People rowing, two People crawling out of the boat and looping the tail of the sea aurochs, and People rowing with great effort back to the meadow. One person played the sea aurochs. That person's feet represented the sea aurochs' tail. On the way back, the person playing the sea aurochs would roll from side to side, while People rowed twice as hard in imagined travel to go against the current of the river and carry the heavy load.

Oneg's flute and Bitro's drum were wonderful accompaniment for the song and dance. Taman had made the drum for Bitro. Oneg taught him how to count. The drum and the flute together were a wonder to People just introduced to music. The dance would entertain People during the cold time when they rarely went outside. Oneg wanted the children to respond to the music by making their moves correspond to the beat of the music. It was difficult, but they were learning it. Oneg thought that not only would the dancers provide cold time entertainment, but also they'd give the children exercise when they were limited in time outside. Dance encouraged them to move without running about inside. Running about inside the house was not permitted.

Tuksook could hear the happy sounds in the meadow. She found herself resenting the happiness of children learning something that made them laugh. She felt her sense of humor left when her child arrived lifeless. Tuksook reasoned in her mind web that this was part of life, but at the moment she felt wrapped in death. She knew that it was good that the music and laughter went on, but she wished she could avoid hearing it. Tired from the labor, Tuksook fell into a deep sleep.

In her sleep she drifted into a long tunnel. The tunnel was the green color of the sky lights. It seemed to go forever pulling her along quickly. Then, she could see white light. She wondered whether the tunnel was ending. Tuksook slid out of the tunnel into a room of white light. She stood, a little shaky on her feet after the strange pull through the green tunnel. Wisdom walked into the room.

Tuksook immediately lowered herself to her knees. "Wisdom," she murmured.

"Your body does not hold children well," Wisdom said without emotion. "Stand."

"That is true," Tuksook said chagrined while rising to stand.

"Tuksook, even in Ki'ti's time they learned that the original People had difficulty in birth. Now, the People are beginning the final change for life in the future. Some things are more helpful to life in the future. One of the ways success in the future is assured is through births. Those who would survive better in the future will have more children than those who would have difficulty in the future. It is my way. The original People will seemingly die off, leaving only traces of themselves in those who follow. You will not disappear altogether—your original People will live in others. The others will not remain unchanged. They will carry the original People and others while part of them vanishes. Do you understand?"

"That is why my baby died?"

"Yes. It lacked what is needed for the future."

"There's no way to eat certain things to put back what is lacking?"

"No, Tuksook. It isn't a function of eating right things. The People all eat the same things. If eating would do it, all would have the same health, but such is not the case."

"I understand. It's sad, Wisdom."

"It's just change, Tuksook."

"It seems unfair somehow," she said.

"Tuksook, life is not fair. You of all People know that. I will explain differently. Individuals have life lines. So do peoples. Those with Mol, Big Lake, and original People heritage have far, far longer life line experience than the people with Minguat heritage. Your lines are drawing short, but theirs are just reaching their fullness. They will carry you and those others with long life lines into the future. You don't disappear, but you lose the prominence you've had. The Minguat take on that prominence. Future People will look more like the Minguat."

Tuksook stood looking at the floor. In front of her were Wisdom's feet. One foot was longer than she was tall.

"Come with me, I will show you things to come."

Tuksook followed.

"Tuksook, what are you thinking?"

"I'm sorry, Wisdom. I was thinking that my expectation is that when you walk, the earth should rumble, but I feel nothing."

"Ah, Tuksook, after all this time do you still not know that I am spirit? I do not weigh as you weigh. I made this representation of me to be with you. What you see is not real. You knew that as a young child. It is a way you can be with me and see me to communicate seemingly face-to-face. If you were to look on my face as it really is, you would die. Yet, when you die, you'll see my face, because you'll be fully spirit. When a spirit does not make the earth rumble when walking, don't expect a representation of a spirit to do it."

"I understand."

"Now, look here. What do you see?"

"It is Eagle's Grasp and the land around it."

"Yes. Now, watch this."

The picture that Wisdom had created, looking down at the land where Tuksook and the People lived, began by small degrees to change. The river carried much more water from rains, and then there was snow. Lots of snow. The snow became ice. The ice grew. In time the whole land was under the ice—very, very thick ice.

"When I flew over Eagle's Grasp the first time, that's what I felt put pressure on the land, but I didn't see it then?"

"Yes, Tuksook. The land, like People, changes. This ice will come and remain for a long time. When it goes, well, watch."

Tuksook watched the ice melting. She saw that the ice had carved out the valley very, very wide. She was amazed. Hills where the sheep had their young were gone, and the dirt from that land meandered down the valley and was cast into the sea. Tuksook was overwhelmed with the enormity of the thing.

"Wisdom, is this inevitable? It looks to me that our meadow will be under water."

"Yes. It is certain. Yes. Your meadow land will be gone and the place where it is will be under water. You have a special time to live in Eagle's Grasp. It is a time of plenty, a place of peace, a good time in a good land. All living things have life lines. All living things are temporary."

"Thank you, Wisdom, for leading us here now."

"Reach out to the picture of Eagle's Grasp and touch the water by the location of where your meadow was. Then taste the water."

Tuksook did.

"Wisdom, the water is salty." She shook it from her fingers.

Wisdom smiled. "There will be huge change after the ice sits above the land. The ice weighs much, lowering the land and when the ice leaves the valley, the sea will replace your river, and the People who remain will have to survive all this change. They'll survive by changing. The land makes a significant change and so too do the people and all life. This occurs normally, but People rarely see it because in your time things change slowly. Most People are born and die without ever knowing of anything like the volcano of Ki'ti's time or the massive ice that is about to come—the significant winds of change. They see little things as the winds of change, but it is the enormous earth changes that are the real winds of change. The small ones merely hint at the big ones. Small ones make a change in lives of individuals or groups of individuals; large ones affect the inhabitants of earth."

"Wisdom?"

"Yes."

"I'm blessed in the shower of roses to be alive now. I would not like to be there when the ice comes."

"You are blessed by living in the time in which you live—more than you can know."

"Will the sky lights remain?"

"Yes, Tuksook, they will remain."

"Why are you showing me this?"

"Sometimes, Tuksook, you'll find that, if you can see far ahead, it makes it much easier for you to turn loose of things that hurt you."

"The baby?"

"Yes. Here is something else I'll share. Watch."

Tuksook looked at the vision Wisdom created for her. In it she saw, first, a man in his prime. The man did not have a sloping forehead. He was tall and stood straight and strong. Second, she saw the man fighting with his People against another group. His group was outnumbered. Yet with odd weapons, the function of which she failed to understand, the man's group of People fought off the others, killing every one of them.

"That is a descendant of Toagrurt's. He lives far, far into the future. He becomes a leader of the People in the fight of their lives. Through his responsibility, diligence, and discipline, he saves the People."

"Toagrurt's descendant! How wonderful! What happens after the fight?"

"They move from the north by the sea far inland to avoid the people who will come by boat and have easy access to the land where they fought. They become a quiet hidden People, but People who don't have to continue to make war to keep their land. Even so, the knowledge of living to have to fight is part of what is new to these People as they change. Hunters become hunter/warriors, and hunting tools also become tools of war along with new tools developed for war."

"Oh, so despite the change, some of how we live is still part of them? If I understand, they'd prefer not to fight but know they have to be prepared in case it's necessary."

"Yes, Tuksook. You have lived in the time of peace. It has lasted a long time. It began with the volcano during Ki'ti's life. Many people died from that eruption. The time of peace followed that eruption. The time of war comes. When the great ice sheets melt, the world of peace melts and changes to a world of war. There have always been some wars and some warriors. Now, the balance shifts. The rule will be war, not peace as is the case now. The life line of the time of war will be long. If permitted, people in the world of war would destroy the earth, but I will not permit that theft of my power."

"That makes me understand better."

"How's that?" Wisdom asked knowing the answer.

"Well, first, I'm glad I live now. It means that what we do today will continue to matter in the future, and despite the balance shift there will be some peace. The balance shift will still require new learning and new ways of living. It looks as if People will have to be prepared for war, even if they're at peace. It seems we help maintain the balance with the desire for peace, so they don't destroy themselves."

"Of course, what you do today will matter, just as the things done at the time of Ki'ti and Manak-na matter to you today. Gumui knew about building a bent tree house, something he learned from the stories. You knew to seek refuge in the bent tree house when the ash from the volcano fell. The People learned that from the ancient stories. Yes, the way of peace you know leaves with the coming of the ice. The mind webs and bellies of men will change as the earth changes. They will come to seek war, not avoid it. They will seek for bloated gain, not only for what they need. They will seek an empty dominance over others, as if they were gods. Yes, the descendants of the People will carry the torch of peace in the mind webs of those to come, so they don't forget. Sometimes, they will find it hard to hear your reminders, but your presence will help keep the balance."

"It makes me sad that all I walk on today will be gone one day. It frightens me that People will change to such extent."

"It shouldn't sadden or frighten you. All things change always. The certainty of life is that life will experience change. What you walk on matters not; what you live in matters not; what you eat matters not; what you are—that matters today and forever. Ease yourself with the memory that what you are will touch memories of peace in the time of war."

"I begin to understand, Wisdom."

"Yes, you do."

"It's overwhelming to realize that the cold I felt flying over Eagle's Grasp the first time is a very thick piece of ice."

"Look at this."

Wisdom made the vision change so Tuksook could see the world of the sea the People traveled and much of the land north of the middle of the earth. She could see the ice on the land at the north extending from sea to sea. It covered so much area it took her breath.

"Wisdom, it's huge. Where will my People seek refuge?"

"Do you see how the ice doesn't completely cover the area? North of where you live there is space where the ice is missing. They must go far to the north. It is there your People will find refuge. Life will be very tough, but they are tough and will survive. It is best they go very far north, as far as to the sea. A smaller number of the People will go far to the south."

"Wisdom, I am overwhelmed."

"All's well, Tuksook. When you awaken you will remember all I have showed you. You may share with Gumui, but he must not repeat anything he hears from you. I know that he will not. Remember that all you can share with the People is this: tell them that when the heavy snow comes, go far north or take a boat far south. Go immediately. Do not share the knowledge of the heavy ice with them. Only the heavy snow."

Before she had time to ask a question, Tuksook found herself back in the green tunnel on her return to her sleeping place. Returned to her place, Tuksook continued to sleep for most of the rest of the day.

When she awakened, she saw Gumui there.

"The evening meal is about to begin. I cancelled the council for tonight."

"Thank you, Gumui."

"Come, let's eat."

Tuksook did not want to stand up, dress, or eat, but Gumui's face was so encouraging, that she could not fail to do as he asked. He brought her a comb, so she could make her hair presentable. She walked with him to the food preparation place, feeling odd, as if this world were one where she visited and the other was where she lived. Tuksook had a strange smile when she thought of a world that Wisdom created for her—a world that definitely wasn't real—a world that in many ways somehow felt more real than the real world. She did not speak of those feelings to anyone. She looked at the meadow, one of the most special places of her life, and thought of it mashed under so much ice, the dirt washed out to sea, and then the place where the meadow used to be buried under salt water. It was an awesome thought.

Tuksook and Gumui walked to the trash heap together to empty the remains from their bowls. Tuksook said, "Walk with me somewhere we will be alone, for I need to share."

"Let's go to the rock, then. Can you make the climb?"

"Yes, I can."

They climbed up to the rock and sat on its still warm surface.

"What do you have to share, Tuksook?"

"When I slept, I dreamed. Wisdom filled the dream."

"Oh, did you ask about your pregnancies?" Gumui asked as he took her hand in his.

"Wisdom said the old People will seem to die off because they are not as able to survive the future as those who are of the Minguat heritage. He says that time comes closer now. Birth problems have been going on back to the time of Ki'ti and Manak-na. We are at the end of it. But Wisdom did not mention me specifically. He told of a change the earth is taking. In some ways the earth's changing is like the People's changing. It's not soon, but it is certain. Remember I told you of the cold I experienced over the land when I flew over Eagle's Grasp the first time?'

"I remember," he said wondering why she mentioned that.

"Wisdom showed it to me. I saw way into the future, Gumui. I can share with you, but you are not allowed to talk with anyone about what you hear from me."

"You have my promise and I vow to Wisdom I will listen only. Wisdom knows I don't repeat things from others. I speak only of what I know directly."

"I love you, Gumui."

"Well, what did you see?"

"This land on which we live. I saw the changes that will come to it." Her eyes were large and her face was focused seriousness.

Tuksook continued. "A heavy snow will fall. It will grow worse and worse. The snow will turn to ice. Where we live will be covered with ice. The ice will be thicker than the meadow is long. More than five times as high as the meadow is long."

"Are you serious?" Gumui had difficulty imagining what she described.

"Yes."

"That will destroy everything we know." Gumui was shocked. Tuksook had just lost a baby and here she was talking about Wisdom's sharing what would happen in the future with another loss.

"Shhhhh. That's what I'm trying to explain."

"Were you ripped apart when you saw this?"

"It wasn't a time for feeling but for learning," Tuksook said, as if she were back there. "Wisdom showed me what he did, so I can understand that all living things change—even the earth. All is temporary. Knowing what will come helped me turn loose of some of the grief I feel over the loss of our little one." She paused. "I guess that sounds strange. I simply have a greater understanding now, knowing that all is temporary even to the earth, all except, I think, Wisdom. All living things are temporary. Wisdom gives life. Wisdom is life and created life—that must be different from being a living, created thing. Wisdom exists outside of time. I am convinced that Wisdom is eternity, without life line. As for us, People with my ancestry will cease to bear.

Our line will not continue except as it is carried in the bodies of the others who are part of our descendants. The others will be changed because they carry us and others. We will not be lost; we will become, how can I put this? We will become secondary," she paused, "Yes, secondary is a good word for it. We will be secondary in a temporary world. We will still have an effect, but our effect will be secondary."

"The earth will experience great change. The great ice will move the land. It will take enormous parts of this land, including our meadow, push it, and deposit it out at sea. It will be so heavy that it will press down the river and sea water will back fill the river as the ice melts. The river that we think of as wide will become much, much, much wider, filled with salt water. As the earth changes so does all life—from a world of peace to a world of war."

"Tuksook, are you well?"

"What do you mean?"

"I know the loss of the baby was rough. This sounds so much worse. Are you handling it well?"

"Remember, Gumui, what is—is. I will say that Wisdom explained that this is in the far future. We have been blessed to live in the time we're in. This is a time of plenty and peace. What I've seen is in the far future. What I must do is to make it so that the People hear that when snows become deeper and deeper, it is time to move far north or go by boat far south. Our stories have to prepare the People like the stories of Maknu-na and Rimlad prepared the People for volcanoes."

"Oh, I see. Wisdom wants you to provide stories to warn the People of an event in the future?"

"Yes."

"It's sad to think of the old People ceasing to be." Gumui felt the effect of the change of the land on the rock were he sat. The effect was shattering to him, but he reasoned it would come to be, and he had no power to stop it. Gumui was amazed that Tuksook was taking the knowledge in some ways better than he was. He wondered whether it had anything to do with her being together with Wisdom.

"We should have seen it coming, Gumui, but we don't actually cease to be. In the stories that Ki'ti told of her time, women of the People were struggling with childbirth then. Think of the uncountable numbers of years it's been since their time. It had to come. Already, there has been great merger with all of us from different ancestry. I don't see what about us would not successfully survive into the future, but then I'm not Wisdom. And Wisdom told me that groups of people have life lines just like the individual people do. Groups like ours and those of Mol and Big Lake heritage have life lines that are running short. The Minguat's life lines are just barely reaching fullness. The happy part is that we are not lost but are carried as part of those who do survive. What survives carries all of us. The People will look more like Minguat, but they are a mixture. There is the certainty that we somehow continue, even if our shape changes. We help to maintain the balance so people do not destroy themselves with war. Where the new People focus on war in their mind webs, we lie inside their mind webs calling for peace—keeping a balance."

Tuksook lay on the rock, her head resting on Gumui's leg. They both looked at the stars above them. The stars were countless. Brilliant in the almost night sky. They had been on the rock a long time talking. They could hear music and singing from the bent tree house.

"Wisdom said that sometimes when you look far ahead, it makes it easier to accept a sad time. I believe him, Gumui."

"I can see a change in you from your time with Wisdom today. It must be true."

"All the stars in our not quite dark sky and Wisdom—I feel so small. Oh, I almost forgot. After the ice melts, some people come to fight the People. A strong warrior leads our People and even though they're outnumbered, they manage to slay all the others with strange tools we don't have now. The leading warrior is a descendant of Toagrurt. He is a great warrior. He is known for his responsibility, diligence, and discipline."

"Interesting. If Loraz were alive, he'd be so cheered by that information. Tuksook, I think we should go in."

"Not yet, Gumui. Look!"

Over across the river above the white topped mountains, the sky lights began to dance. The sky lights were multi-colored, dancing an active dance. They watched, fascinated as always.

"They're rarely similar. The various patterns are amazing."

"I love it that you can see the stars through them," Tuksook said.

"It seems to be so powerful. I wish I could understand what's happening. It's as if one power comes in contact with another power and they burst into moving lights."

"Oh, Gumui, if you knew all the little details, don't you think it would spoil the effect?"

"No," he replied. How it works fascinated him since his arrival.

They remained on the rock watching the sky lights until they faded. Occasionally, they could hear others below who had gone out. They called to

People in the house to watch the display. It was spectacular that night—and it wasn't the cold time.

Item realized something had happened to Tuksook to raise her spirits after the loss of the baby. She waited until after the morning meal the next day and asked.

"You're right. Mother, I was terribly saddened. When I slept, I was able to meet with Wisdom. It cheered me. Then, the sky lights came out last night and that cheered me even more. I cannot change what was before, what is, or what will be. I have to remember that all of life is temporary, and in that temporary world, I can only try to live a day at a time. I had to remember that. It was so hard to know the baby was born lifeless. Last night I waked up and cried for a while. It still hurts. It will take a long time for me to turn loose of it completely. Grief sticks like the hoof glue that holds spear tips in place. Mother, could you tell whether the baby was a girl or boy?"

"You really want to know?"

"Well, I asked. Of course, I want to know."

"It was a boy. He looked perfect, but he had not been inside the womb nearly long enough. He was way too tiny. He was beautiful."

"I have to hope, Mother, but each year my chances dim. Mine all seem to come too soon, as if they cannot wait to be born."

"I ache for you, my daughter. You'd be a good mother."

"Thank you," Tuksook said, looking Item in the eyes. She'd never known her mother thought she'd be a good mother. "Life is changing so fast. It wasn't that long ago when we arrived in this land. Only fourteen years, yet look at the change. If I cannot have children then I will be a good aunt and love them all. So many People have gone to Wisdom, so many have been born. We found a wonderful place to live. We're blessed with plenty and peace. It is a good life here."

"It truly is, Tuksook. So much better than in the old land. You must have gained some of what you say from Wisdom. I don't understand your time with Wisdom, but it always seems to have a wonderful effect on you."

"Ever since I began to talk with Wisdom, my life has been blessed. I didn't always see it that way, but the truth is that I love Wisdom and need Wisdom as much as I need air or food or sleep."

"Your father used to say that, too. Never having had that experience, I cannot understand of what you speak, except it compares well with what he said, and he also talked to Wisdom. Oh, Tuksook, I watched a little of the children's performance of the song and dance, and they are becoming so good at it. It's a joy to see them."

"I want to stop by when they begin again to practice. I could hear them yesterday, but I didn't see them. Mother, you're not aware of any of the children beginning to learn the stories?"

"No. Not yet. Usually, Tuksook, you'll be older before a new Wise One appears. Don't worry about it. Wisdom always provides."

"I just thought I'd ask."

"Believe me, if anyone spots one, they'll tell you right away. You hid yourself too well, Tuksook."

A few days later Tuksook left the house and looked around the meadow. She had been struggling to decide how to put together a story to share the information Wisdom wanted her to make known. She'd never created a story. Certainly, she knew stories, countless stories, but repeating and explaining a story was not the same as making one. The responsibility weighed heavily on her.

Tuksook went to the rock and sat. There were plenty of People about, so she was in no danger from predators. Lurch was working to repair the water diversion to the shower; Sutorlo, Pod, and Nipe were diverting a new water channel that aimed for the house when it reached the meadow level. They had to divert more to the east before it turned south. Numbers of the men were repairing the roof.

Tuksook felt the warmth from the rock and it was soothing. She looked at all about her. The stories were about life. She looked out upon the meadow below her. She envisioned the meadow becoming deeper and deeper in snow. The People could not travel during the time of snow. They would have to see a cold time of unprecedented snow and leave as soon as travel became possible. That would mean many things. Preparedness would be critical. Tuksook wondered whether she needed to include preparedness. She wondered whether the People would stay together or whether some would go north and some south. Tuksook tried to dream up a story but nothing happened. Her mind web was not a creative one but rather an amazing place where stories lived that others had already put together. She leaned back resting on her forearms. Wise Ones before her had faced the same need. How, she wondered, did they form the stories. Tuksook had to tell a story about something to happen instead of something that had already happened. She had no way to know which of the stories she told had been formed that way—if any.

She thought of the change in the earth she'd seen. She realized that it was as if the earth were being born anew. People were also being born to a world of war and unrest as a result of the coldest of cold times. Tuksook decided that idea held the story together. Tuksook rose up and descended to the meadow.

She walked the meadow deep in thought. Others avoided her, because she seemed separate.

The sound of music broke through her deep thought. Tuksook stopped and leaned against the center stone in the meadow. She watched the children dance and sing. They were becoming very good at this newly learned singing and dancing. She listened. How Tuksook wished the world of peace would continue forever. She knew better. After pausing to enjoy the children, Tuksook continued her pacing and thought.

Later that evening, she shared the evening meal with Gumui. He teased her for being in a world to herself during that day.

"I was," she admitted. "I had to develop the story or whatever you call it for the People. I'll share it tonight at the council.

"I'll be interested to hear."

"Well, it's almost time."

The people gathered for council that night out under the stars on the rocks and skins they used from the beginning for their council. The sky was clear and partly dark, typical of the sky at night in that part of the world. It was warm and no bugs were biting.

"The council is now open," Tuksook said. "Is there anyone who would speak?"

Stencellomak looked directly at Tuksook.

She nodded.

"Three of us plan to boat down to salt water tomorrow to take at least one sea aurochs. We need a fourth rower. Is there one more who'd like to go with us?"

Dipcaco spoke out, "I would like to learn sea aurochs fishing." At fifteen he was definitely of an age to participate.

"Good! Thank you Dipcaco," Stencellomak accepted. "You'll join with Vel, Vole, and me."

Dipcaco lowered his head to Stencellomak.

"Anyone who would speak?" Tuksook said again.

Item looked directly into Tuksook's eyes.

Tuksook nodded to Item.

"We are low on beaver and giant deer skins."

Hunters made little sounds and looked at each other.

Wave looked at Tuksook, who nodded at him.

"We will talk with you further, Item, to see if there are other skins needed. Then, we'll take the treks to bring back exactly what you need."

Item lowered her head to Wave.

"Anyone else?" Tuksook asked.

Silence.

Tuksook said, "I have some information that I have tried to turn into a story. It doesn't work as a story, but it will become part of our stories. It involves the future. I will tell it tonight. It came from a dream Wisdom gave me." She paused.

"This is a message about the future, not a story of the past. It is a message for the People. Wisdom made the earth, and Wisdom made People. All things balance for the right working of the earth. All things balance for the right working of the People. The People go about their lives for countless years in Eagle's Grasp. But all is temporary. People begin to feel things changing. There are more earthquakes. There is more rain for years and then little rain, then years of more rain. The People can feel the earth shifting out of balance. Little bit by little bit, the imbalance shift increases. People who do well with others suddenly find difficulties occurring. They argue in anger instead of taking time to reason. The time is coming but is not yet. Watch the balance. When the balance is destroyed so that the snows deepen more and more, and fighting breaks out among the People, the time is right. Do not wait until the cold time storms bring snows above the top of the bent tree house. Go when it becomes difficult to do well with each other and to walk the meadows even when you've made the paths through the snow. Go when the temperature becomes biting even with the protective clothing you have. The earth moves to a loss of balance and upheaval like nothing the People have ever seen."

"The People must go either far north to the sea or take boats to travel east and then south far away from here, far away enough so that the cold times are warm. The People will survive in either of those places. The People must survive. Prepare as always to have much more food than needed to make it through a cold time."

"When the need to move is clear, begin as soon as travel is possible. Take what food you can carry. The trek north is very, very long. It may take more than a full cycle of seasons. For those going to the north, keep going until you reach the sea. For those going south, keep going until the cold times are warm."

"The earth will be out of balance for many, many years, as if part of it were dead. People will be against one another. The time is changing from a world we live in, a world of peace, to a world of war. Much will change. When balance is restored there will be war—the world of peace will be gone. It will go on longer than you can imagine. The People must be prepared to live in a time of war. New tools will be necessary. The People must become good at

211

war to survive. It is how it will be. We cannot change it. What we must do is to be prepared."

"Failure to leave in time will cause the People to cease to be. That is not acceptable. Failure to learn to war well would also cause the People to cease to be. That is not acceptable. Learn what you must to survive. Learn it well. Keep in your mind webs the importance of not fighting among one another, for doing so weakens the People, increasing the likelihood they will not survive. Keep in your mind webs the importance of learning skills of cunning behavior to avoid fighting, if at all possible. In that you keep your People alive. Keep in your mind webs that, if fighting is inevitable, you must fight as if your very survival depends on success—for it does. Know the best tools of war and learn to use them perfectly."

Tuksook looked up to see startled faces staring back at her.

"This does not happen in the life line of anyone alive here now. It will happen, though, very, very far into the future."

"Why are we learning about it now?" Pago asked.

"Remember the stories of Ki'ti's time when the People were told to flee from a volcano. When they did need to flee a volcano, they had the information when they needed it because of the story of Maknu-na and Rimlad. It wasn't new to them. It wasn't known to only a few. In this case we are being prepared in advance. Winds of change can affect a single person, a group of People, or the whole world. Fleeing the volcano was a big change, but it did not involve an earth out of balance or People out of balance. The weather remained cold for years after the volcano. When the time of war arrives, it will seem to last forever. People will remember no other way. Our People have always lived in a world of peace. This change will be huge. Wisdom has given us the information to begin to understand ahead of time, so the People will have the information when needed, and it will be part of them."

"Thank you. I understand. It's just such a shock" Pago said.

"It is a shock," Tuksook concurred. "Anyone else?"

Silence.

"The council ends," Tuksook said.

Tuksook felt emptied. She had finally put together a message, not a story, but it had the same effect. The People would be warned. She had the story firmly locked in her mind web. Tuksook would repeat it with the other stories.

People left the council, some muttering and some silent. They had much to reason.

The next day when the morning meal was finished, Stencellomak, Vel, Moki, and Dipcaco headed to the boats. They checked to be sure that everything they needed was in the boat. All was there. They pushed the boat to the river's current and climbed in. The day was crisp and clear with the occasional puffy white cloud. The many shades of green on the mountains between which the river ran were deepening. On the west shore Stencellomak pointed out a bear at the water's edge. An eagle flew overhead. Vel wondered where the raven was. Often, when you saw an eagle fly, it was chased by a raven.

The river, so clear the last time Stencellomak had been on it, had muddied up. He wondered about it until he realized they'd had a time of rain recently that had probably contributed dirt to the water. Stencellomak fingered the two large cat teeth that hung around his neck on a strip of leather. He did it automatically, not really aware he did it.

Six ducks flew from west to east. It was a good day to be on the water. Vole thought about the water and the People. Some loved to be on the water and others did not want to be in a boat on the river. The reasons interested him. Most of those who didn't want to be on a boat gave reasons he could not understand: "I don't like the feel of it," "It makes me feel nauseated," "I want my feet where they belong—on the land."

Something rammed the boat hard.

The men in the boat turned to look. The trunk of a dead tree was in the water and it had somehow managed to travel faster than they were traveling. Dipcaco climbed to the back of the boat to unhook the root that had become tangled in the bamboo. He tried to shove the boat to the side of the tree trunk, but had no success. Suddenly part of the tree hung up on something under the water and the boat broke free, almost causing Dipcaco to fall overboard.

The very young hunter changed the direction of his seating. He faced the rear of the boat and rowed backward. The other hunters were glad that the young hunter knew what to do. He would alert them, they reasoned, if the tree trunk freed and once again headed for the boat.

Evening arrived and the men neared their habitual stopping place for the night. It was a small cove with a sandy beach. They landed the boat and tied it to the same tree where they'd tied up for years. Suddenly a great noise trumpeted. It was a mammoth trumpeting. The men were alert, but not frightened. The animal was near but not visible. Dipcaco climbed the rock wall on the south side of the cove. He looked hard but could not see the animal through the trees.

Stencellomak had chosen to start to set up the campsite, despite the mammoth noise. His lean-to was constructed and his backpack stowed inside. He set the fire in the hearth. He had brought some meat for roasting in smaller pieces, and he proceeded to cut it up and skewer it. Vole had set up his lean-to. He'd taken the birch bucket to the river to fill it with water. When he reached the camp, he put the drinking dipper in the bucket. Vel had made his lean-to and gone way down the beach to dig out a v-shaped privy line, since he had great need. Dipcaco returned and began to set up his lean-to. The trumpeting of the mammoth now came from a greater distance, so they were comforted it was leaving the area.

Dipcaco dragged up some logs for seating and the men held their skewers over the fire, eating when the meat was ready. It was giant deer and camel. Both very good. There was no talking while they ate.

When they finished eating, Dipcaco asked, "Do trees float down the river often?"

Vel replied, "That's the first time I've seen one."

The others replied that they had seen none until this day.

"You did the right thing, Dipcaco," Stencellomak told him.

"Thank you," the young one said.

Stencellomak went to his lean-to first. He lay flat on his back, resting the muscles that were tight. Soon the others also decided it was time for sleep. There were no more sounds of mammoth.

Back at the meadow people were busy preparing for sleep. Mongo did not feel well. He stumbled to his sleeping place and slumped over, grabbing the side of it. He twisted himself so that he managed to sit on the edge. He held his chest. The pain was awful. Cadpo, Wave's wife, ran to his side.

"Father, are you well?" Wave asked Mongo.

The man couldn't speak, because of the pain. Cadpo helped him lie down.

"I'll be right back. I'll find Item."

Cadpo went as quickly as possible from the south part of the house to the west part where Item's place was.

Item looked up when Cadpo arrived.

"It's Mongo?" she asked.

"Yes," Cadpo said, frightened.

Item slipped on her tunic and followed Cadpo. When she arrived, she was surprised. Mongo no longer breathed. Wave was at the side of the old man's body, holding it, weeping silently. Both Stencellomak and Vole were gone sea aurochs fishing.

Cadpo and Za, Stencellomak's wife, washed the body and covered it to wait for morning for the burial. Za and Mela, Vole's wife, comforted each other while Cadpo and Wave held each other in grief. Some of the children were already sleeping. The older ones, like Elfa and Ubassu, who had joined and were in a different part of the house, would learn of the death in the morning. Others like Tak and Ulu, Tern, Solong, Velur, Pica, and Abet gathered in little groups to weep and share their grief, all done silently in the bent tree house.

Item returned to her sleeping place. Instead of lying down, she went to Tuksook. She touched Tuksook's shoulder.

"Tuksook," she whispered, "We have lost Mongo."

Tuksook sat up. She looked at Item and tears fell from her eyes. Gumui sat up. He had heard Item tell about Mongo. He also allowed tears to fall from his eyes. Loss of Mongo was a great loss. He had taught them much. He was special.

"I'll be ready after the morning meal. It will take some time to dig the grave."

"Yes," Item agreed. She returned to her sleeping place. The people were losing their elders, those people at the last of their generations. Only Kew and Taman remained. Kew wasn't in good health. He was eighty-one. Taman seemed well. He was sixty-nine.

At sunrise, which was early, the men heading to fish for sea aurochs waked up, put their gear in the boat, ate a few sticks of jerky, drank water, and headed to the boat. They were eager to reach the salt water to find a sea aurochs.

Back in the meadow, people arose a bit later, since the light from the rising sun dimmed in the interior of the bent tree house. They were called to the morning meal, where those People who didn't know about Mongo heard the announcement. Quiet followed. People ate and then Wave, Vole, Gumui, and Momeh went to gather tools to dig the grave. Children who were old enough ran about the meadow gathering flowers to add to the grave. When it was time, the People gathered in a circle around the grave. Mongo's body was placed on its side as if he slept. Mela and Za had covered his skin with red ochre. The children placed flowers on Mongo's body, as it lay atop his sleeping skin. His body was almost covered. It was very quiet. They began the ritual speaking about the deceased. No one had any difficulty speaking about Mongo. From the time they were all very young, Mongo taught them, both male and female children, about how to survive in the world in which they lived. They considered they had three basic teachers: Mongo, Taman, and their Wise One. Tuksook recited the creation story, and the grave side tradition ended. The People dispersed. Tuksook wondered who would replace Mongo as teacher.

The fishers reached the salt water. They looked to the west to see whether they could spot any heaps of kelp lying on shore. There were none to the west or east. They paddled to the west. By mid-morning, they found a kelp heap on shore and paddled out to the usual depth looking down into the clear water. Finally, Vole spotted the dark baggy shape of the sea aurochs.

"Vole and I will go down," Stencellomak said. "Vel will handle the tie down as soon as he sees that we've secured the tail. Dipcaco, it is your assignment to watch all that happens. The water is freezing cold. We will do this quickly. We have to put the slip looped rope around the beast's tail and tighten it. It's not hard if you know what you're doing. You must watch. Look down to see for yourself what we do. It's very important to place the loop on there at the first try. When we come to the surface of the water and shout to row, begin to row with all your strength. We'll swim with all our effort to reach the boat quickly, but the boat needs to start moving. That, along with its tail tied seems to keep the sea aurochs in submission. Any questions?"

Dipcaco said, "No. I understand."

Vel handed the rope to Stencellomak as soon as he was in the water. Vole followed him down. They had a little difficulty encircling the tail because the sea aurochs kept moving. Fortunately, when it moved it didn't go far.

From above the two on boat observed carefully.

"Time to tie down," Vel said with some excitement, having seen them tighten the rope at the tail. Just as he had the tie down completed, first Vole popped up and then Stencellomak, both shouting, "Row!" They swam to the boat quickly, arriving shivering hard from the very cold water.

Like all the People, Dipcaco had been taught to observe, not talk. As the evening arrived, he was ravenously hungry and his arms felt as if they would freeze into position and never move again. No one had spoken from the time of the capture until the present. Stencellomak said, "We don't overnight at the camp on the return, Dipcaco. We push for home as hard as possible. That's why from time to time you'll see hunters return from sea aurochs fishing and leave the butchering to the People while they go to their sleeping places to sleep. Can you hold up?"

"I will do what is necessary," Dipcaco said.

"Good. Inside my backpack are many sticks of jerky. Give each of us one and keep replacing as long as someone extends a hand to you. Then, we'll have you fill the dipper and hand it to us so we can drink. You participate in eating and drinking too."

"Yes, I will," Dipcaco said. Despite the fact that his arms were killing him, Dipcaco found he reveled in his inclusion on the sea aurochs fishing travel. He'd do whatever was called for to be included.

Stencellomak glanced at Vole. The parceling out of jerky and water would give Dipcaco a chance to rest his arm muscles briefly. The older men knew only too well how Dipcaco must be feeling. Rowing was not easy and when going against the current with a heavy load, it required great fortitude both of mind and body. It pushed the men to their limits, but they loved it. The challenge to return with a sea aurochs was one thing, but to start homeward with no stops for food or sleep was another thing. The second was the greater challenge by far. Dipcaco was just developing the feel of it. He had not felt the elation of success at meeting the challenge, now that he knew what it was. The challenge seemed overwhelming. He just wondered how they stayed awake all night. He was determined to do what the others did, giving all the effort he had. After all, he considered, he was young and they were old.

They reached the place where the tree had become stuck. "It's gone," Stencellomak shouted.

Dipcaco wondered what was gone.

"Sure surprised me when that thing rammed us," Vel said.

"Yeah, me too," Vole added.

"How'd you know where the tree was stuck?" Dipcaco asked.

"You learn the river and its sides as you travel it. When you're familiar with it, then, you can locate things easier. You just make references in your mind web to things that stand out on the land, like that outcropping mid-way up that hill." Stencellomak pointed.

"Oh," Dipcaco replied.

Night wore on and the sky finally became dark. They continued on. This time of year there was always enough light to see, even after the sun had fully reached its lowest depth.

The river at night fascinated Dipcaco. He wondered whether the men still saw their references on the land. They could see the river. Occasionally, the sea aurochs would snort. The animal breathed using lungs instead of gills. When it exhaled, it could snort with some force.

Morning came and the dogs began to growl their quiet alarm. People left their bowls to see what the dogs were seeing. The fishers were returning with their catch. The People finished eating. It would take time for the boat to arrive at their shore.

As soon as the boat turned to the tie up place, Dipcaco felt the exhilaration of meeting the second challenge. He had rowed the whole way stopping only to feed and water the others and himself. He didn't know he could demand that much from himself. He was delighted. He was exhausted.

Za, Mela, and Item met the boat, when it arrived. Men of the People quietly took over the boat, while Item called the men to her. She explained the loss of Mongo. She suggested they come to the meadow, stop at grave side

217

a moment to be respectful, and then have some food and go inside the house to rest and grieve. The men did so. Loss of Mongo diminished their happiness in the results of their fishing, but their fatigue blunted a little of their feeling of grief. All of them were at the point of exhaustion.

Stencellomak saw Tuksook. He put his hand on her shoulder.

"Tuksook, I wish that Wisdom made temporary last a little longer."

She touched his arm gently as he walked to the house.

Item waved to Tuksook. Tuksook walked over to her mother.

"I have a surprise for you. Kouchu has been doing something for you. Come inside."

Tuksook followed Item into the bent tree house. She wondered what Kouchu did for her. It was mysterious to Tuksook.

At sixty, Kouchu was having great difficulty walking. The death of Loraz struck her hard emotionally, and the arthritic condition of her hands and legs severely limited her mobility.

"Thank you for coming to me, Tuksook," Kouchu said. "It's just becoming harder and harder for me to move around. I loved my mother and miss her daily. Loraz too. But my mother made the tunic you wear, and I love her enough even though she's not here, that I couldn't bear to look at the tunic much longer. It's split on the side and the fur is rubbed off in several spots. When it was new it was the most astonishing tunic I ever saw. Now, it's just sad. I've made you another, my Dear. Please accept it and wear it in good health." Kouchu pulled the new tunic from behind her.

Tuksook looked at the new tunic. It was made in much the same way as the tunic Bruilimi had made for her. The differences were that the bottom was parallel to the ground between her ankles and knees, not higher in front and lower in back, and there was a yoke that was rectangular instead of the partial sleeves formed by the upper part of cat legs that graced the tunic Bruilimi had made.

When Bruilimi first arrived in Eagle's Grasp, she and Loraz would go to a creek to find gold pieces. They kept them. Kouchu had found that she could work the gold so that she could turn the end into a circular form. She took a very thin, soft, narrow leather strip and halved it. Kouchu put the loop at the half point through the gold nugget. Then she threaded the ends of the leather strip back through the loop in the leather. She cut two slits into the yoke. She threaded one of the ends of the leather through the first slit and the second end of the leather strip through the second slit. Then Kouchu pulled the strips forward through the slit that they had not been threaded into. She took the two strips of soft leather and tied a double knot, without gathering the leather. Kouchu trimmed the ends of the long leather strip so that the ends extended just a bit beyond the double knot. It gave a striking effect to the tunic. On the yoke of the new clothing near the neckline, a gold nugget from the stream hung, suspended on a strip of leather tied with a double knot. It was special.

Item helped Tuksook into the new tunic. The fit was perfect. Tuksook felt the lovely soft leather bend with her every move. She bent over and hugged Kouchu maybe a little longer than normal. She kissed the cheek of the old woman.

"I thank you so much, Kouchu. This is lovely and I really needed it. You are so very kind."

"You're welcome. Now, when I look at you I can smile for two reasons. The first is that I love you and the second is that you look lovely."

Tuksook chuckled quietly.

"Thank you again," she said. "Now, is there anything I can do for you?"

"Not a thing, my Dear. Thank you for asking."

Tuksook touched her shoulder and left to find Gumui. She wondered what he'd think of her new tunic.

When she went outside, whoever saw her made approving comments. Apparently, her need for a new tunic was far greater than she guessed. Gumui saw her first. He came running.

"That looks so nice. Who did it?"

"Kouchu," she replied.

"It is wonderful and this little addition," he said fingering the nugget which was about the size of his thumb, "is so unique. What a wonderful sur-prise—or did you know she was doing it?"

"I had no idea she was doing it. I wish I could do something for her in return."

"You cannot bring Loraz back from the dead," he said wondering whether he should have thought, let alone said, what he said.

"Gumui!"

"I know. I don't often speak without reasoning. This was an error."

"Well, maybe not. Of all the things she might want, that's probably at the top of her choices."

"I'd guess so."

Topo, one of Nipe's three-year-old twins, came running up to Tuksook and Gumui.

"What is it, Little One?" Gumui asked.

"White birds! White birds! Over here!" He began to run in the direction of the path to the river level.

Gumui and Tuksook looked out. Swans in large number were resting in the still water between the land and river. Gumui whistled the hunter—come call that did not require immediate response. Numbers of hunters came at a run anyway. When they saw the swans, they ran for slingshots. Some of the men started down the path without tools. The hunters with no tools slipped into the water and went under water to a swan, grabbing them by the legs and pulling them down. There, they'd twist the necks, killing the bird, and put the bird somewhere safe until they had captured another. When they had two, they'd take them to the food preparation place to the women. After the hunters finished they had sixteen swans. They would feast that night.

Tuksook found Topo and said to him, "You did a good thing this morning by letting us know about the white birds. Topo, someday you'll be fine hunter!"

"Thank you, Wise One," he said.

The evening meal was a little late that night so they could enjoy the roasted swans. Tuksook had asked the women to save six of the roasted livers for her from the swans. She knew that Kouchu loved liver. When they were ready, Tuksook took a bowl of roasted swan livers to Kouchu.

"What do you have there?" Kouchu asked her.

"I wanted to do something special for you for your kindness to me. Topo, Nipe's boy, called to Gumui and me and kept saying white bird. The watery land below was full of swans on their way to somewhere. Hunters hurried and took many. I asked the women who are cooking to roast six of them for me. These are for you." She handed the bowl to Kouchu.

Kouchu lost a few tears. "How kind of you! I didn't know you knew of my love of liver."

"I've known for a while now. So many of the People don't care for it. When I found you did, it interested me."

Tuksook stayed and chatted with Kouchu. She realized that often Kouchu sat inside because moving was too difficult, but in doing so she was lonely. Tuksook would think on how to help. She decided that there might be a quicker answer. She went to find her mother.

Item was busy in the place where the sea aurochs strips were being sun dried. The girls had been putting the strips too close together. Once she took care of the meat strips, Item walked over to where Tuksook sat.

"Are you tired?" she asked.

"A little," Tuksook replied. "I have no reason to be tired, but I just am. There's something I'd like to do, but I'm not sure how to do it. Kouchu is lonely. I'd like to find a way to relieve her loneliness, but I have no thoughts. I reasoned you might know of a way."

"Let me think, oh, I know," Item said.

Tuksook was amazed at how fast her mother responded.

"Tuksook, there are numbers of girls who are over ten years of age, who don't know how to sew. Why don't you ask Kouchu if she'd be willing to teach the girls to sew? If she's willing, we can set it up so they come to her to learn."

"That's a great idea, Mother. It's just what we need. It would introduce her to some of the People she doesn't know very well, and they'd come to know her. She has great sewing skill. Passing it down is a wonderful idea."

Tuksook was delighted. She went back to Kouchu and asked whether she'd be willing to teach some of the girls to sew.

"I will teach them if they will approach it seriously and be willing to do what I ask them to do."

"Great," Tuksook replied. "I'll let you know when I have the girls together."

"I know why you're doing this, Tuksook," the old woman said smiling.

"Does it matter?"

"No, I guess not."

"They need to learn, and you're the best at sewing of all of us."

"If you look at it that way, it makes even more sense," she said and laughed an old lady laugh.

Tuksook left with a wry smile. She spent the remainder of the afternoon looking for girls of the right age to learn to sew. She talked to numbers of girls and then selected five to start. She went to the mothers of each to obtain permission. Once the sewing lessons began, there could be other classes with other girls. Tuksook set up the classes for the next morning after the morning meal. The girls who were chosen were delighted. Tuksook knew because of that, they'd put forth extra effort. She wanted this to go well for Kouchu first. She also wanted to assure that the People had plenty of individuals who could sew well.

After the evening meal and the council were over, Tuksook took a walk around the meadow with Gumui.

"How are you doing now?" he asked.

"It improves, Gumui. My belly still aches for the little boy, but I'm reminding myself this time what is—is. I am happy that between mother and me, we found a way to relieve the loneliness of Kouchu and teach a new generation of girls to sew."

"I think that idea is wonderful. Kouchu is someone who doesn't stand out, but she's so kind and thoughtful, so sweet, and she loved her husband."

"She did!" Tuksook replied. "She also is expert at sewing."

"You only need look at your new tunic to know how true that is," he said. "Let's go back. You look tired and I am tired. We can crawl into our sleeping place and be comfortable."

"Great idea," she concurred.

Chapter Nine

Tuksook and the male elders: Moki, Togomoo, Hamaklob, Stencellomak, Unmo, Anvel, Hawk, and Wave stood near the center stone. They had marked a series of horizontal lines about a finger long, one under the other, to show the numbers of years the People had lived in the meadow. They were planning to mark the twenty-fifth line. Unmo, the oldest at sixty-eight, held a piece of sandstone. While the others watched, he made a dun colored line on the stone. Later, they'd have Sutorlo cut the line in the stone.

The stone carried an image of Eagle's Grasp. A few years back, Kew had asked Tuksook to mark Eagle's Grasp on the flat part of the rock. She had done it exactly as she had when she drew it on sand in the boat. Toward the top of the rock was the south part of the land and to the bottom was the north. That showed the Eagle's Grasp as one might easier see the leg of the bird. The size was precise. On the rock it measured two man forearms (elbow to middle finger tip) tall. It was a very special thing to the People. Once the image was drawn, Kew asked Sutorlo to make it permanent on the flat face of the rock. Sutorlo had learned to make marks on rocks that had good depth and would last a long time. He made sharp cut straight lines and curves. When he worked on the chipping of Eagle's Grasp into the center stone, a sliver of rock lodged in his left eye. Item removed it, but Sutorlo lost his vision in that eye. Sutorlo did his work with his own tools, tools he made for this specific purpose. He was teaching Dipcaco to chip out designs in rocks. If the People could be said to have had a treasure, their center stone would qualify.

Often when People talked with one another about locations, they'd walk to the rock and point out the specific place or places, so there was no confusion. They could precisely point to special hunting areas for bison, where to have the best opportunity to fish for sturgeon, areas the last kelp heaps from sea aurochs had been washed ashore, where to find good stone for spear tips, places shelters could be found quickly—the uses seemed endless. At the very first, it took some of the People a long time to understand how to see the drawing. Once they understood, it was a great help. All of those old enough to use the drawing could see it.

"I'll let Sutorlo know it's time to mark the line," Unmo said.

The elders began to disperse walking off, a few stopping to chat.

"Is she doing better?" Stencellomak asked Tuksook.

"Kouchu has been in severe pain for so long," she replied. "She claims she's becoming a stone," she added. "I am so awed by her continuing to teach the girls to sew, day after day, and she never complains. They learn well from Kouchu."

"Hunters could learn something from her ability to withstand pain while keeping her attention on the duty she has," Stencellomak said.

"We all could," Tuksook said quietly. "It hurt so badly to hear of her fall back by the privy. To see her cry ripped my belly apart. She didn't want any of the girls to see her like that."

"I think we should make a privy for Kouchu that she can use privately in her part of the bent tree house, one that we could take to empty. She has a need for help there. Kouchu could break a bone going off and falling like she did."

"Stencellomak, that's a wonderful idea. Will you do it?"

"I'll do my best."

"We must remember that she's seventy-one. Because she's so tough, it's very easy to take her abilities for granted."

"I agree. I'll talk with others and we'll find something as fast as possible."

Elfa walked across the meadow quickly. She stopped at Tuksook and Stencellomak and waited to be recognized.

"Yes, Elfa?" Tuksook asked.

"Ren, is having her baby now. Can you come?"

"I'll be there very soon. Thank you, Elfa."

"I'd better go," Tuksook said to Stencellomak.

"Me, too. May your day be good."

"And yours," she replied.

"Wise One!" Awk, Abet's six-year-old, shouted out.

Tuksook looked up and saw Awk running toward her followed by Mi, his sister, who was two years younger. Tuksook waited for them to arrive.

The two children remembered to wait for recognition.

"Slow your mind webs," Tuksook said, and the children lowered their heads. "Now, Awk, with deliberation, tell me what you have to say."

"I, I, my sister won't stop following me."

Tuksook almost laughed.

"I just want . . . ."

"Wait, Mi. It isn't your time to speak yet," Tuksook admonished.

Mi hung her head as low as possible.

"I just want to have some time with the boys," Awk said. "She interrupts us; it's more to annoy me than to be with me!"

"Sit," Tuksook said. All sat, including Tuksook.

"Mi, what do you have to say?" Tuksook asked.

"I don't want to be by myself. It hurts my belly that Awk doesn't like me. He's my brother, and he is supposed to like me. I think nobody likes me." Mi shed tears quietly, wiping them on her arm.

"Awk, what are you and the boys going to do?"

"Practice slingshot."

"Mi, you're too young for slingshot."

"I could watch," Mi defended.

"What do you do while you watch?" Tuksook asked.

"Well, sometimes I talk to the boys or Awk." Mi looked pleading at Tuksook.

"Mi, there's a problem right there. When they practice slingshot, they have to concentrate. It isn't a time for talking."

"They talk," she countered.

"And what do they say when they talk?" Tuksook asked.

"They say things like, 'I guess I missed that by a day's walk' or 'Just a bison's hair and I'd have had it,' things like that," Mi replied.

"Well, you paid attention, but you neglected to reason with your mind web, Mi," Tuksook said. "When you talk at slingshot practice, you're not talking with them about what they're doing, because you lack understanding of what they're doing. You're distracting them, not helping. That's why they don't want you there."

Mi lowered her head.

"That's why I don't want her there," Awk interjected.

"Hold, Awk. We'll return to you," Tuksook said. "Mi, where do you think you're going?"

"There isn't anywhere for me. I'm going back to my sleeping place," Mi replied.

"Sit down," Tuksook ordered her firmly. "All right, Awk, do you like your sister?"

"I love her, but sometimes I don't like her."

"What could you have done to persuade her to do something other than follow you?"

"I don't know." Awk was confused as to why Tuksook questioned him as she did.

"Do you realize you hurt Mi?" she asked.

"I could see her cry, but Mi does that to have what she wants. I've learned to ignore it."

"And what makes you think you know what's in her mind web that causes her to do things?"

"Wise One, I was only guessing. I may be wrong."

"Guessing is like a tree that is supposed to bear fruit—only it bears none or it bears fruit unfit to eat. It is a poor use of your time. When you're wrong, you can hurt someone badly. Your guessing fits here. Some of those wounds never heal. If you could have found something to occupy Mi, you might have solved the problem and kept her from being hurt. Isn't that what you'd want, if you were younger and she were older?"

"I, I'm sure you're right."

"Awk, think on what I just asked you. **Think** how it is to be younger and want to participate and be rejected. **Reason,** if you love your sister, what you could do to help her feel included somewhere. You're free to go."

Awk stood. "I will do as you say," he promised. "You have made me see what happened a little differently."

"Good," Tuksook said dismissing him.

"Now, Mi, most of a boy's life involves learning to be a good hunter. To be a good hunter, Awk has to put his mind to what he learns. He doesn't have time for chatting. Awk must focus on what he's learning so he takes in the information with his mind web and body. You'll learn some of that when you're older. Right now you're between that part of your life and confinement in the little children's area."

"Are you going to put me back there?" Mi asked crestfallen.

"Do you think I should?" Tuksook asked.

"Probably, but I don't want to go back there."

"For today I have something different in mind for you. You are going to follow me—not Awk—everywhere I go. You will remember to be polite and keep quiet. You will observe. If I need anything carried, you'll carry it. If I need anything brought to me, you'll bring it. Mi, you'll be to me like my shadow this day. Watch everything I do. I may ask you what you've learned later. Do you understand?"

"Yes," Mi replied totally intimidated.

Tuksook stood up. "Come," she said to Mi.

Tuksook headed to the east part of the bent tree house. Mi followed her. When they reached the west entryway, they entered and passed the central area heading towards Ren. Tuksook's hopes were that Ren would have a better time of it than she did. Ren had joined Noriwhet, because they loved each other, but with his lack of visible signs relating to the old People, Tuksook hoped her childbirth would go well. Just as they arrived, Ren ejected the infant and it cried out. Mi peeked around Tuksook to see the baby.

Tuksook waited. Women hovered around her sister cleaning up and preparing her. Item cleaned the baby. Tuksook sighed with relief when she realized the baby was a boy. He would not have to experience childbirth with ancestry which was partly original old People.

Item looked at Mi. "Go to the grass basket and bring me moss," she told Mi.

Mi looked at Tuksook. Tuksook nodded to her. Mi walked quickly to the basket and brought moss. Item absently lowered her head in gratitude.

Mi went to stand near Tuksook. She watched as Tuksook bent over her sister and took her hands. "He's beautiful," she whispered.

Ren smiled. She was exhausted. Item brought the infant and laid him on Ren's chest. Ren let tears of joy fall from her eyes. The baby lived. Noriwhet came in and saw them lying there. He was very excited. He'd withheld hope that their baby would live based on the experiences Tuksook continued to have. Noriwhet was so excited that to kiss his wife, he leaned on the side of the sleeping place too hard and broke the side. He managed to catch Ren, and she held tight to the baby. He helped her climb out of the sleeping place, which now was in serious need of repair. Everyone was laughing except Mi, and she was frightened, hiding behind Tuksook.

"There's another sleeping place in the north part of the house," Togomoo pointed out. Noriwhet gathered the skins and moved them to the sleeping place on the north side of the bent tree house. He laid the caribou skins on the sleeping place and put the other skins on top. Ren sat on the side and he helped her slide over so she could lie down. Noriwhet covered her with the sleeping skins. People were still chuckling.

Tuksook looked for Mi. She saw her standing way off from all the others. "Come, Mi," she said. "It's time to say stories." Mi ran to her, stopped abruptly, and walked the rest of the way.

"Do you know where the big rock is up there?" Tuksook pointed.

"Yes, Wise One."

"Go take some jerky, and meet me there," Tuksook told her.

"What kind?" Mi asked.

"I prefer sea aurochs," Tuksook replied, surprised that she'd ask. "Take for you what you want."

Mi went running, while Tuksook climbed to sit on the warm rock. Moments later, Mi returned with her hands filled. It was clear that Mi preferred salmon, a jerky most thought of as dog food. Tuksook smiled to herself.

"You will sit here, while I say the stories for practice. All of us who learn have to continue to practice what we learn while we live. Without practice, we lose skill."

Tuksook began to recite the stories. Mi had listened when Tuksook talked earlier. She knew when people are practicing they're focused. It was a bad thing to interrupt. Mi sat there listening to story after story. In practice, Mi noted, Tuksook said the stories faster and without much feeling. Nevertheless, Mi also noted, she didn't skip anything. Tuksook sat with her back against the rock on the hill behind the rock where she sat. Mi did the same. Tuksook had her right leg resting over her left leg. Mi did the same. Tuksook's hands were in her lap, and Mi put her own hands in her lap.

As evening wore on, Tuksook sent Mi to bring water. The little girl returned with a water container. Tuksook realized she hadn't chosen the smallest one.

Tuksook started to begin when Mi asked, "You want me to say the stories with you?"

Tuksook was dumbstruck. "You know the stories?" she asked.

"Some of them. I don't think I know them all," she said frankly.

"Yes, of course," Tuksook said, "Say them with me."

Until the evening meal, Mi sat beside Tuksook—in every aspect of the way she placed herself, the mimicry of Tuksook was perfect. In addition, Mi told the stories without error. Tuksook knew that she had her replacement. She chuckled at the manner in which the discovery came to her. Mi was so young. Tuksook wondered whether she should have Mi work on the things she needed to know only for part of a day, until Tuksook realized that had never been the People's way. Once one with the memory was discovered, that immediately put the newly discovered storyteller in a shadow position. In that position it was required that they follow the Wise One and practice the stories daily. With that position came protection by the People and lack of privacy.

"Mi, it's almost time for the evening meal. I want you to take the water holders back down to the food preparation area. I'll be down soon."

Tuksook looked for Abet and Lamo, Mi's parents. She saw Lamo near the house. She hurried to catch up with her.

"Lamo, may I speak with you?" Tuksook said a little louder than she normally spoke.

Lamo stopped and turned around. "Of course, Wise One. What is it?"

"Lamo, I've been wondering for quite some time who would replace me. I have found my replacement." She paused. "It's Mi."

"Mi? You're actually serious?" Lamo was astonished.

"I am. She knows the stories."

"That is so hard to believe, Wise One. She always seemed to me to be scattered."

"I think that was because she wanted to follow Awk, and he didn't want her to do that. Mi felt he didn't like her. She's had some childhood misunderstandings all mixed together. We talked—the three of us. Then, I had her follow me around. I went to practice the stories. Imagine how I felt, when Mi asked me if I wanted her to say the stories with me." Tuksook laughed a delighted free laugh. "I need permission from you and Abet to train her."

"Of course, you have mine. I'm sure you'll have Abet's too. It's just so unexpected."

"If I haven't caught him by the evening meal, please let him know I'm looking for his permission."

"I will," Lamo promised. "Oh, congratulations on the new nephew."

"Thanks. He's a beautiful little one," Tuksook said with feelings of wistfulness that she tried to conceal.

Stencellomak and Gumui met at the tool storage area. Each was on a different mission.

"I'm repairing a broken sleeping place," Gumui said. "What are you planning?"

"I have to come up with a privy for Kouchu. She's too disabled to make the walk to the usual privy."

"I heard about her fall," Gumui admitted. "Your thought is a good one. Want to work together or separately?"

"We work well together, Gumui. Together we'll probably finish much quicker."

"Then let's start. Which work would you like to do first."

"Let's take care of the inside privy first," Stencellomak suggested.

"Good."

The men carried some poles to the east part of the house. There was a good space between two of the bench/sleeping places. Kouchu's bench/sleeping place adjoined the space.

"What are you men doing?" Kouchu asked.

"We are just doing a little construction. Tell us if we are bothering you," Gumui said.

Kouchu snorted and returned her attention to the girls and their sewing projects.

Stencellomak drew in the sand of the floor what he had envisioned. "It'll make a little square room. We can hang skins along the sides. Then, put a bench here with a basket underneath that can be filled with lots of moss."

Instantly, Gumui understood.

"What a well reasoned application, Stencellomak. That should definitely make things easier for her."

"I think it will. Glad you like the idea."

"Let's do it," Gumui encouraged.

The two men began to work diligently. Once they shared the vision, there was no need to talk much, they worked together as the flute and drum.

Stencellomak and Gumui finished the work on the inside privy quickly. One wall was the side of the house. The other three were formed by braced posts that had skin drapes tied to the top of all three cross pieces. It was fully private from the house. Inside was a bench with an opening in the seat over a moss-filled pull-out basket under the bench. One of them would explain it to Kouchu when the girls left.

They moved further down the east side of the house to the broken sleeping place. Stencellomak and Gumui took the prepared poles they had stored for repairs and pulled the broken ones from Ren and Noriwhet's sleeping place. Gumui wished he'd been there to see the collapse of the sleeping place. It made him smile to think of it, since no one was injured. Noriwhet was one to do the unexpected, Gumui reasoned. Gumui let his thoughts wander. Noriwhet was known for being a little clumsy. His awkwardness was the subject of humor from time to time, and that didn't bother Noriwhet. He would even laugh at himself. When he had an awkward experience, Unmo would sometimes refer to him face-to-face as Grace, a name for a way of moving, not a People name. Although Unmo hadn't been at the place when Noriwhet broke the sleeping place, Gumui could imagine Unmo saying, "Ah, Grace, be careful." Gumui snorted thinking of it.

"What causes you to snort, Gumui?" Stencellomak asked.

"I was imagining hearing Unmo, had he been there, saying, 'Ah, Grace, be careful.'"

Stencellomak exhaled a gentle laugh. "Only Unmo could do that."

"Everyone knows him well enough to know he might tease gently, but he'd never hurt anyone intentionally."

"That, and he's old," Stencellomak added.

In little time the sleeping place was in good repair. The two men gathered their tools and returned them to their place. They stopped to let Ren and Noriwhet know that whenever Ren was ready, she could return to her place.

Amuin was hitting rocks together calling for the evening meal. The girls quickly put their sewing materials in their bags, and thanked Kouchu for the lesson. They thanked her with a hug. They loved the woman elder.

Stencellomak and Gumui went straight to Kouchu.

"Today we decided that it was good to make something to ease you as much as we can," Stencellomak said, beaming.

"That's what all that noise was about?" she pretended to sound annoyed.

"Yes. What we have done is to make an inside privy for you, so you don't have so far to walk."

"You did what?" she asked, not believing what she was hearing.

"Let us help you up," Gumui offered.

Kouchu lifted her arms and they helped her up. She looked at the outside of the structure behind her. She stood and they walked with her to the inside privy. Gumui pulled the skin aside. Kouchu didn't need any explanation.

She looked at each man, eye-to-eye. "I can use this right now, you two kind men. Hand me my stick so I have help when I'm finished." Kouchu grinned and cackled a laugh that was a delight for the men to hear. They knew she was very pleased.

Item came in just after the men left. She carried Kouchu's bowl. Kouchu wasn't on her bench/sleeping place.

"Kouchu?" Item called wondering where the woman could possibly be.

"I'm in here. Look in here!"

Item put the bowl down, pulled a skin from its draping position, and looked into the newly built structure. She laughed with Kouchu. "Now, doesn't that just do it?" Kouchu asked.

"That is wonderful. Who made it?"

"Stencellomak and Gumui."

"That was so thoughtful."

"It was and it'll save me from the walk and the weather."

"I'm so happy for you. Do you want help returning to your bench?"

"No, thanks. They thought of everything. See the rail around these sides. That is a great place to rest my walking stick."

"I will go to eat now," Item said. "I'll return soon."

"Don't you worry about me. I'm just as happy this moment as a flea on a dog's back."

Item walked away from Kouchu feeling better about leaving her than she had in a long time. The wiry little old woman was someone to remember. Someone special. She had been given greater independence in her disabled condition. It would be safer for her. It was good. It was good indeed, she thought.

Tuksook walked past the central stone to obtain her bowl. She noticed that sometime during the day Sutorlo had made the new line in the stone. Twenty-five years. That was a long time. She looked at the incised Eagle's Grasp. She touched it. How she would like time with Wisdom.

After the evening meal, the People had council. Tuksook asked whether anyone had anything to say. Unmo looked right at her. She nodded to him.

"If anyone isn't already aware, Sutorlo has made our twenty-fifth line today. We have lived in Eagle's Grasp for a long time. It is a good place, even if our Wise One would have us think sometime it will cease to be a place where People can live." Unmo looked at her with a smile and a twinkle in his eyes.

Tuksook asked for other sharing.

Hawk looked at her. She nodded to him.

"Two of us are ready to fish for sea aurochs. Are there two more who would like to go in the morning? The weather looks good."

Gel and Vole indicated they wanted to go.

"Very well, Gel, Vole, Olog, and I will leave after the morning meal."

"Wait!" Unmo said with a bit of a shaky voice.

Everyone turned to look at him. Unmo was sixty-eight.

"I want to go. I realize I can't row like a young person and I cannot dive, but I want to return to the sea again. I also want to know whether you could let me off in the shallow water to search for limpets and shell fish while you fish for sea aurochs." Unmo was old but his eyes were sharp and so was his mind web.

Hawk thought about it fast and said, "I would be honored to have you come with us, Elder. Yes, we can stop for you to gather the food you want. There is enough room for six People in the new boat. Do you want someone to help you gather the things you want?"

Kiramuat, Hawk and Meg's son, showed an interest in helping the elder.

"Very well," Hawk said, "Gel, Vole, Olog, our Elder Unmo, and Kiramuat will leave for the sea after the morning meal tomorrow."

From far away in the distance came the trumpet of a mammoth. And another. Then, all was quiet.

Tuksook asked, "Is there anyone who wishes to add anything to this council?"

Silence.

Tuksook said, "I have something to add. Today, I found the next Wise One. She is very young, but she knows the stories that I have asked her to tell. The next Wise One is Mi."

Mi was sitting behind her mother, Lamo. She lowered her head as far as it would go.

"Mi, stand up," Tuksook said.

"Take a good look at her, so you know who she is. I ask that all of you guard her, as you guard me. Keep her safe so that the stories remain intact."

Awk was shocked. The little seemingly scattered sister of his would be the new Wise One?

"Does anyone wish to speak?"

The People looked at each other showing a happiness that a new Wise One was identified, but among them was silence.

Tuksook began, "The story I have to tell tonight is a very old one." Tuksook began the story taking them back in time to a long ago that they could only imagine, but a story, which applied to their lives as if it occurred where and when they lived. After the story, the People dispersed to their sleeping places.

After the morning meal the next day, Hawk gathered Vole, Gel, Olog, and Kiramuat together. Unmo came at a slower pace. The younger men rapidly transported their few needs to the boat. They took the hunter sleeping rolls from the storage in the bent tree house, water skins the women had filled, and the jerky to the boat. Vole checked on the ropes and camping materials they'd need. When they all gathered at the boat, Hawk did a final check. He noticed the little sail had acquired a small hole. That would not present a problem for the sailing, but it was something to watch. He was proud of Pica and Meha who had listened to the stories, talked to those who remembered the sea crossing, and taught themselves to weave the sail to hold air. The sail was very helpful to the rowers, especially on the way back, when rowing against the river's current with a heavy drag from sea aurochs challenged the strongest man.

Unmo climbed into the boat and sat where Hawk had told him was his place, the very far forward position. The others pushed the boat out as far as they could go without losing their footing. Then they entered the boat and paddled out to the current. They were off. Each fishing occasion was an adventure to Hawk. He loved to see the wider aspect of Eagle's Grasp whether he was hunting or fishing.

The men made good time, stopping overnight to sleep in lean-tos and cook over the fire the meat the women had cut up for them. They no longer carried sleeping skins from their bench/sleeping places, but rather used rolled sets of sleeping skins, all the same, that were specifically designed for hunter travels. Hunter sleeping rolls were stored in the south part of the building when not in use. It was easier that way, and hunters who were joined didn't have to search to find skins they could use. They found it gratifying that each time they stopped at their camping place, the same logs were available for the lean-tos. It made camping so much easier than it had been years ago.

Gel and Olog began to set up the lean-tos. Unmo took the birch water carrier to the river to fill it. Hawk started the hearth. Vole and Kiramuat began to accumulate wood for the fire. Very quickly the little camp was set up. The men ate and then entered the lean-tos to sleep. There was very little talk.

In the morning, the men packed their things in the boat, stacked the logs where they would stand to await their next stay, and they pushed the boat out to go to sea. Already there was a scent of the tangy sea. It was refreshing, invigorating to Hawk and Vole, who loved the sea.

Once they cleared the river's entry into the sea, they headed west. Already they could see mounds of kelp on shore. They beached the boat briefly to let Unmo and Kiramuat out with their grass bags for carrying sea creatures.

Just as Hawk, Vole, Gel, Olog, Kiramuat, and Unmo were about to push the boat back to the sea, Unmo said, "Wait! What's that?" He pointed west.

Off in the distance a boat was sailing. Unmo squinted. "I believe that's one of ours!" he shouted.

Hawk and Vole looked at each other. How could an elder like Unmo have better far off vision than they had? Or, was he guessing? They wondered.

Hawk decided not to push off until they knew the significance of the boat. He didn't want the men separated.

"Should we remain here or hide ourselves? There are likely more men on the boat than the six of us." Vole voiced the concern of several of them.

"I tell you they are our People. You know they travel the sea circle each year. They make stops to check on the People and sometimes to trade things. Who else would be out here?" Unmo was adamant.

Wave looked at the man. "Who else, indeed? Have you forgotten that Wikroak came up our river?"

"No, but Wikroak didn't have a boat like ours. Look at that. It's exactly like the one that brought us here." Unmo was very excited.

They sat on the beach while the boat came closer and closer. It was clear that the men on the boat had spotted them. The boatmen brought the boat as near the shore as they dared and dropped anchors. Unmo recognized one of the boatmen.

"Huaga!" he shouted as loud as he could.

A swarthy man with white hair that shielded his eyes from the sun looked at the men on shore.

"Unmo?" he asked.

"I am Unmo," he replied. "Come to shore for a little time before you're on your way."

Huaga turned to talk to some of the People on the boat. Four People entered a small boat used for boat-to-land travel, usually to obtain fresh water. Huaga was one of them. Unmo was very excited. Hawk and Vole were prepared for whatever would take place. They were both aware that the times were changing and that the time of peace would one day change to the time of war. They would be vigilant despite the old man's enthusiasm.

The little boat beached. The two old men walked toward each other. They stood face-to-face and then hugged.

"It has been so long," Unmo said.

"It has," Huaga agreed.

"How are the People?" Unmo asked.

"If you can imagine, the drought worsens. We have lost many People."

"We have lost the usual number from age and injury or sickness. But we have a good life here. There is plenty for all of us. The rest of the People should migrate."

"You know they will not leave the old land. This talk is stale."

"I know, but I wish they'd reconsider. Ileg?" Unmo asked.

"He died long ago, Unmo. I'm sorry to bring such knowledge. Midgenemo and Ottu?"

"Both in the ground. Sorry."

"If I were young and not a boatman, I would migrate here. The green speaks of life and warms my heart. As it is, we who take the boats are the fortunate ones. We do not face the drought all the time."

"Huaga, when's the last time you had aurochs?"

"More years than I can remember."

"Before you leave you can fish for sea aurochs. It doesn't take long. The meat tastes better than aurochs and they are easy to catch if you have a couple of men who can withstand cold water. They are very hard to skin. Do you have sharp knives? The skin is tough!"

"You suggest to me that there would be boatmen who couldn't withstand cold water or have sharp knives?"

"I'm sorry, Huaga. We become soft here," Unmo said to Huaga with resignation. Then he turned to Hawk. "Hawk, would you permit a couple of the boatmen to go with you while you fish for the sea aurochs? These People have had little good meat for a long time. They could take a couple of these fish with them to eat as they travel."

"Yes, but you'll have to be ready to leave when we return."

"I'll forgo my collecting, if that's necessary," Unmo assured him. "I'll be ready."

"While they watch your men fish, I'll help you collect," Huaga volunteered.

"Good. There will be three of us."

Hawk pushed off with the two boatmen as observers. Unmo, Huaga, and Kiramuat quickly began to scan the rocks for limpets. With their sharp knives, they were able to secure just the leverage needed to separate the tightly stuck limpets from the rocks. Limpets were everywhere. The limpets were surprisingly large ones. A single shell came close to filling the palm of the men who separated them from the rocks where they busily ate algae.

On the little boat Hawk pointed out the connection between the kelp on shore and the dark body down in the water. He told the strangers to watch what they did to capture the sea aurochs. He explained that they had to tie the rope around the tail of the sea aurochs, tighten it, and then start to row while the fishers swam fast to the boat. The men watched. When Hawk entered the water, so did the men. They wanted a better view of the fishing.

Hawk was alarmed that the strangers had entered the water, but he was relieved that they had climbed in the boat quickly, ready to row. The men weren't even shivering. They seemed completely comfortable. Hawk headed back to pick up Unmo.

By the time the boat returned, the men had collected three grass bags full of limpets and sea snails. Unmo and Huaga hugged, both realizing it would probably be the last time they saw each other. Unmo and Kiramuat walked to their boat, and they began to row to the river.

On the recommendation of Unmo, Huaga had his People fish for two sea aurochs. They would have tasty meat on their travel.

Hawk and Vole began to warm as they rowed. All had the meeting prominent in their mind webs. Hawk found it hard to understand why People would remain in a terrible drought when they could migrate to lands like theirs. It made him sad for People he didn't really know. He smiled to think of their eating sea aurochs. As good as that meat was, Hawk was certain that even that wouldn't cause those who chose to stay in the old land to move.

Unmo's belly ached for those who clung to the old land. He couldn't just dismiss them. They were People, some of whom he knew. They had the same heritage he had. It was just so unnecessary in his opinion. He took the bags of limpets and put them into a bag of seawater. They should be fine, he thought, until they returned to the meadow.

There was a little off shore breeze and the sail caught. They rowed, but it was a lot easier when the wind pushed the sail. They had a good catch and brought it to the People with information all would want to hear. They arrived very early, just in time for the morning meal.

Back in the meadow, the People had been hearing distant mammoth trumpeting all morning. Togomoo and Hamaklob had walked to the meadow where the People found the rocks they moved. After climbing a small hill, they could see numbers of mammoths walking around, appearing disturbed for some reason that they could not determine. Although they listened carefully, they could hear no noise from a predator that might be planning a kill.

It was well past high sun and suddenly to the surprise of all, there was thrashing noise coming from the south meadow. Everyone headed quickly for the bent tree house. Hunters stood guard at the entrances of the bent tree house, watching from the outermost leather strips that served as entryways. At the entryway, there were three leather hangings all parallel, offset so that the wind could not blow cold air into the house. They hung from the top of the opening to the ground. People wanting to go outside from the west entryway had to walk between the inner leather strip and the middle one heading north. Then they had to turn to walk south between the inner leather and the outside one. Then they'd turn east to leave the structure.

The mammoths trumpeted as they entered the meadow. People scattered to the bent tree house. Those butchering the sea aurochs, young men who transported the meat, girls who were making strips to hang, ran in disorganized paths unsure whether to leave their work or race to the bent tree house. Hunters watched the mammoths, spears ready, hoping they didn't have to use them. They were outsized if not outnumbered. The animals seemed unsure what to do in the meadow. There were mammoths of all sizes and ages mingling in the meadow. The dogs were hackled up and growling low. Mammoths would look at them with eyes big enough to show white. Then they'd turn on a back foot and head away from them. After a very long time, the mammoths headed down the path to the river level. Those cutting up the sea aurochs on that level hid behind trees to avoid the creatures. The hunters watched for a long time. They expected a predator was following the mammoths, but they had no idea what predator it might be.

The women decided to prepare the evening meal for inside cooking and consumption. The savor of freshly caught salmon baking under the ground filled the home. Early on girls had gathered greens and some berries. This would be a special meal.

Men who were not watching spent time with an ear to the entryway, spears close at hand, and some work in their hands, generally work that did not require significant concentration.

Top, Kiramuat and Pica's youngest son, pulled on Unmo's tunic. Unmo turned to look at the boy.

"What's that noise?" Top asked.

"Mammoths," Unmo answered abruptly.

"I mean the other noise," Top persisted.

Unmo stared at the boy. He didn't hear a different noise. Because of the boy's intensity, Unmo didn't dismiss the question again. He looked at Top. "Bring Awk here," he told the little one.

Top turned and walked quickly to the south part of the house where he found Awk.

"Unmo wants you to come," Top told Awk.

Awk gave the People who heard a quizzical look, but he followed the little one to Unmo.

Unmo turned to Awk, "You are known for having good hearing. Top wants to know what the other noise is—a noise that is not the mammoths. I can hear none other."

Awk went to the part of the entryway that led outside. He stood in the open and his expression, had anyone seen it, would have been of surprise. He returned to Unmo.

"I hear the noise of People, People singing. It makes no sense to me. The mammoths seem to have moved to the north. Otherwise, I hear the dogs growling in low voices and bird tunes."

Unmo turned to his mind web. He found four options: Wikroak, the boatmen, some people they didn't know, and nobody. His desperate hope was that the sound came from the boatmen.

"Thank you Awk," Unmo said. "Please ask Stencellomak to come here."

Awk lowered his head, turned, and went to find Stencellomak.

Unmo turned to Top. "You have very good hearing little one. Thank you for telling me what your ears heard."

Top lowered his head.

Stencellomak found Unmo at the west entryway.

"You asked me to come?"

"Yes, Stencellomak, Top alerted me that there is a strange noise outside. Awk verified it and said it sounded like People. Would you please go to the edge to assess what may be the cause of the noise that I cannot hear?

"Of course. I need my spears." Stencellomak picked up his spears and asked Wave to accompany him. Wave took his spears and joined Stencellomak.

"We are going outside to see what the source of the noise is. In case I cannot hear it, I want your ears. They're better than mine."

"Probably nothing," Wave replied.

"You could be right."

The two men reached the west entryway and went straight outside. They looked carefully to see whether a stray mammoth might still be in the area, but saw and smelled nothing out of the ordinary. They walked quickly across the meadow to the edge.

"Could that be? Surely, it isn't? I'm certain now." Wave said. His jaw muscles reflected his tension.

"What would the boatmen be doing in our river? And where are the mammoths?" Stencellomak asked.

"The mammoths must have gone north and rounded the curve to our right. I can still hear them, but they are a good distance away. We should be free to come out from the house."

"Would you alert the women at the food preparation area that we may be in need of more food this evening and let those at the entryways know we have a boat arriving? We need to show them where we are. I'll watch."

"I'll return when I have done as you asked," Wave replied. With that he ran across the meadow.

"Unmo, it seems the boatmen are coming up the river. The house should be free now to return outside," Stencellomak said, turning to walk to the food preparation area.

Stencellomak walked over to the women where he let them know that there might be a need for more food for the evening meal, and that he'd let them know as soon as he knew. Unmo whistled the hunter—come alert. Hunters came, spears in hand.

"It seems that the boatmen are coming up the river," he informed them. We need to free those hiding in the house since the mammoths are gone, and we need to let the boatmen know where we are." Unmo whistled the all clear sound that told the People in the house that they could return outside.

Wave, returned back from the women, said, "I'll take a small boat out to meet them."

"I'll join you," Unmo said.

Wave and Unmo wasted no time. They went quickly to the small boat and pushed out into the deeper water.

People poured from the house. Girls went off to gather more greens. Elfa, who had turned over the care of the dogs to younger girls, went to the dogs to quiet them. They knew her as their leader though others fed them.

Tuksook went outside with Gumui. They walked together to the meadow's edge where they could see between the trees. They saw the large boat turning at the curve in the river some distance from them. She wondered what would bring a boat up the river. The boatmen had already met with the hunters who just recently fished for sea aurochs. It was a long distance to row to their meadow. Tuksook thought the boatmen must have a significant reason for their deviation.

Gumui watched the boat, remembering the tough sailing of the past. He marveled at the boat but had no desire ever to return to the sea. He realized that there must be something significant that the boatmen had to share, but as was typical of Gumui, he chose not to speculate as to what the boatmen's reasons might be.

The big boat took much time but finally arrived and Wave and Unmo led them to a safe turnoff from the river where they could anchor. Once anchored, the two men rowed over to the big boat. They tied up and met briefly with Huaga.

"I would like to see the place where you live," Huaga said. "I will come bringing Yumo. The rest will remain on the boat."

"Yumo," Huaga said, I want you to meet Unmo and Wave. I have told them you'll go with me to the home of these People. We should see with our own eyes what this place is where the People have moved." Huaga had chosen him because Yumo was very vocal that the People should not even consider migrating to this land. If it was as it appeared, he wanted this man to see it, so he could describe it.

"Very well. It's near the evening meal. Will you want food sent to the boat?" Unmo asked.

"That's not necessary. We have sea aurochs to eat on the boat. The men are delighted, as you said, with the meat," Huaga assured him.

"Come with us, then," Unmo said. "We will show you our home here."

Huaga and Yumo followed Unmo to the boat.

"How did you learn to make boats?" Huaga asked.

"It was difficult," Unmo said. "Our People had to try to remember what they could of the boat on which we traveled and then make it smaller. It may not be made as you'd make it, but it works."

240

"I saw its use both here and on the edge of the sea. I would compliment you and your People for the success they've had."

"Thank you, Huaga. Coming from you, that means a lot," Unmo said.

Yumo was overcome with the green. Green was rare where the People lived in the old land. They were in starving times. Here, he'd eaten aurochs and found it wonderful. He was interested to see how these People lived in this north land.

They beached and the men climbed out, tied up the boat, and went to the meadow. At the meadow there was a line of People.

Unmo went down the line introducing the two men to the elders, Togomoo, Hamaklob, Moki, Anvel, Stencellomak, Hawk, and the Wise One. He explained that they were interested to know how they lived in this north land.

Unmo took them to the bent tree house and had Gumui describe how it was constructed. He showed them the storage areas as well as the bench/sleeping places. They were surprised to see the bent tree house, something described in a very old story. Yumo went to a wall and examined it. They were interested in the mudded ceiling and the flaps to keep out volcanic ash. The winding flaps of the entryway amazed them, for the People assured them it kept it much warmer inside when the snow fell.

Outside, they looked at how blocks of turf insulated the house and the skins of aurochs kept it waterproof and helped to hold the roof in place when the winds were blustery. The design of the two interlocking long rectangles amazed them.

Amuin hit stones together signaling the evening meal. The boatmen accompanied Unmo to the food preparation area where they filled their bowls with sturgeon, greens, and berries. They hadn't tasted sturgeon and liked it very much. The greens were wonderful, something their bodies craved. Huaga and Yumo walked with Unmo to the place where they removed the food from their bowls. They emptied them, carried them back to the food preparation area, and left for the outside council place.

"We will all want to know why you stopped, Huaga," Unmo said.

"I will be glad to share when we meet," Huaga said quietly.

Yumo remained silent.

People arrived at the council meeting as they were able. It took quite a while before all were gathered.

Tuksook said, "We have People from our old land with us tonight. This is Huaga," she gestured to Huaga, "and this is Yumo." She pointed out Yumo.

"We are delighted to have them here among us, and we are interested to know the purpose of their visit. Huaga, would you care to speak?"

Huaga looked around at all the People. They were in good health. Their home was amazing to the boatman. They were a happy People.

Huaga began, "I see about me healthy and happy People, living in a land of green that the People who remain in the old land can hardly imagine. The old land is a land of dust as some of you may remember, only it is worse since you saw it. Where your People are healthy and thriving, the People in the old land languish. Water runs low. The People often despair."

"I say this not for sympathy, but for understanding. As they cannot imagine this place, you probably would have difficulty imagining that a low wind stirs dust in the old land. People have to cover their faces to avoid breathing in the dust. We used to have water nearby. It dried up. We have to walk long distances to obtain water. Many People have died from lack of food. Where your People have increased largely, ours have dwindled. I will return to our People to let them know they must move. I ask whether you have enough food sources for us to move here, or whether we must look elsewhere?"

Tuksook looked at the hunters.

Stencellomak asked, "How many People remain in the old country?"

Huaga looked at Yumo. "How many do you think?" he asked.

Yumo reflected in his mind web. "I think at best we have thirty."

"Tuksook," Stencellomak addressed her directly, "We should be able to add thirty People here with no difficulty. Prey in this land is abundant.

Tuksook asked them, "When could we expect additions to arrive?"

Huaga said, "We go now on our sea circle. We still stop over the cold time with the People. We try to bring foods to them, but many will have perished while we are sailing home. We would start as you did with your migration in the time of the year when the vegetation begins again to grow. Unfortunately, we have little of that anymore. They would arrive here about the same time of the year that you did."

Tuksook was still stuck on the maximum number of People as thirty. The drought must be awful, she thought.

Stencellomak was staring at Tuksook. Suddenly, she was aware and nodded.

"Your timing is perfect, Huaga. That would leave us much time to add to the bent tree house to take in the addition."

Tuksook shook herself out of her sympathetic shadow and said, "We would be glad to receive as many People as are willing to migrate. It would probably save lives, if they'd agree to do it. This is a land of abundance and peace. How I wish I could just say, 'Appear,' and they'd all just be here. The boat crossing is daunting, but worth it."

"May I speak?" Huaga asked.

"Of course," Tuksook invited.

"If I cannot convince them, I will bring my family here. Knowing what I know now, I cannot leave them in the old land when they could spend the rest of their lives here."

"We welcome any and all who are willing to come, Huaga," Tuksook said it firmly so there was no question."

He lowered his head and so did Yumo.

"Are there any others who wish to speak?" Tuksook asked.

Silence.

Tuksook waited briefly and then said, "Since there are no other speakers, the council ends for this night."

Some of the People were surprised that she had no story that night until they realized the boatmen might want to leave, since they sailed regardless of the time.

Huaga went to Tuksook. "The offer of the People is most generous."

Tuksook replied, "We have a land of plenty here. It is only right that we share it with those we left behind. If we can help them grow healthy and strong in this place, it is our pleasure, and, Huaga, our duty."

Huaga lifted an eyebrow. He said, "We must depart. I thank you for the wonderful evening meal, another meat we never ate."

"I too thank you for your wonderful hospitality," Yumo said.

"I will share your words with the People," Tuksook replied. "You must wait for a moment before you go to your boat. We will provide you with jerky made from giant deer and sea aurochs. Men will bring it to the little boat." At her words Jum, Velur, and Kig raced to the bent tree house and filled large skin bags with giant deer and sea aurochs jerky. They ran with them to the little boat on the river level.

The men talked briefly with the other men. Unmo and Wave walked with them down to the little boat. They pushed the little boat out into the deeper water, climbed in, and paddled out to the big boat.

"There are no bamboo trees here," Unmo said.

"I noticed," Huaga replied, "I will tell those People where we usually stop that this may be the last visit from us. I do not intend to go to sea again. When we return, the other boatmen can decide whether to continue the visits. They aren't really needed any longer. Any help they could have had from us earlier was lost in the drought. None of the places we visit have asked for anything for as long as I can remember. It's time for change in many ways."

"May Wisdom protect you on your sailing and help you convince the People to come."

"Thank you, Unmo. You are most kind."

They reached the boat and Huaga and Yumo went from the little boat to the larger one with much greater ease than Unmo and Wave had experienced earlier.

They waved as they worked to turn the boat around to head out to sea.

Unmo and Wave watched for a long time instead of returning quickly to shore. The grasses held the little boat in place. Finally, Wave put his oar in the water. It was the special oar that Wikroak made. He wondered whether Huaga noticed the oar.

"Unmo, do you think Huaga noticed the oars?"

"There is not one part of this boat that Huaga didn't see and consider. He's a boatman. We are not boat builders. They may see boats before they see us."

"I'm sure you're right. He doesn't share much of what he thinks. He never said a word about the place we have here."

"Oh, Wave, of course he did!"

"What do you mean?" Wave was confused.

Unmo turned to look at Wave. "Huaga plans to ask the remaining People to migrate. If they don't, he will bring his family here. Of course, he shared his thoughts. Huaga wants to live here. What greater statement could he have made?"

"Oh, I see what you mean. Just because Huaga didn't tell us at council what he thought of our life here specifically, he shouted it when he let us know he wants the rest of the People to migrate here. If they won't come, Huaga will arrive here at the time the green comes to the trees that shed their leaves. Yes, I see what you mean."

"It used to be the way of the People long ago not to speak too highly of anything lest somehow it come to ruin. It is no longer the way of the People, just like we know what a hand strike is, but we don't do that anymore."

They rowed on silently and beached the little boat. Wave tied it up while Unmo for the second time that day made his way up the path that very much pained him to ascend.

Tuksook and Gumui had taken a walk after the council ended. They circled the meadow and then went up to the rock to sit. The warmth remained and it was a pleasant thing to stretch out on their backs, looking into the sky, letting the warmth of the rock warm their bodies.

"Gumui, will it be terribly difficult to add on to the bent tree house to accommodate thirty more People?"

"I've been thinking about that this evening," he replied. We cannot go to the east or west because in either place there are no more trees. But to the north and south, the house can be expanded without difficulty. I think we'll need to expand the north for more food storage and the south for People to have their own place to sit or sleep."

"When would you do the expansion?"

"I think we can do it now when we're not involved in something else. I can take time to mark it off right away. We could finish it before it becomes too cold. Then, if they don't come, we have more space for food, tools, spears, and other things like sleeping rolls for hunters, and we will eventually grow into It despite the fewer babies born. If they do come, we will be prepared for them instead of wandering around wondering how to do it fast. The People sound as if their health is awful. I'd rather they didn't have to spend time in a lean-to."

"Gumui, I love the way your mind web works. You are so thoughtful."

He reached for her hand.

"Do we have any dried salmon?" Tuksook asked.

"Dried salmon?" he asked. "You only want dried salmon when you're pregnant. Are you pregnant?"

"I think so."

"Are you frightened about losing another baby?"

"Of course, aren't you?" Tuksook asked.

"Yes, I am," Gumui replied.

"I will be careful, but if I must end up childless, there are other things that could happen that would be far worse. Today, I see the blessings far more than I scrutinize the things that are tough. I will accept whichever way it goes. I won't become greatly hopeful or concerned that I'll lose it. I'll simply take each day as it comes. That is the best way for me to remain in balance."

"I am so glad to hear you say that. I will follow your lead in this."

"Don't talk about it just yet, Gumui. Sometimes I lose them very early.

"I won't."

"Are you ready to go inside?" Tuksook asked

"Yes, it's been a long day."

"Much change is in the air," she said.

The two of them sat up. Gumui extended a hand to Tuksook to help her up. They walked down the path to the meadow, his arm around her.

Chapter Ten

"Land ahead!" Yumo called out in his deep resonant voice. All the boatmen prepared to ease the boat into its space that had been cut out of the beach. The workers on land were digging furiously to open the barrier to the water so the boat could enter. The sail home had been a tough one with multiple storms and rough seas. Huaga was happy this would be his last crossing of the huge sea. They edged the boat into the prepared space, dropped anchors, and tied up. Some family members had noticed their arrival and come down to meet the boat to reunite with their boatman relative, husband, or friend.

Yumo could see his wife waving frantically to attract his attention. He gathered his things and climbed down off the boat. The boatmen were leaving the boat rapidly. Huaga waited until all had left. He met with the land workers and told them where the traded items of food were. He wanted to store them in a certain place he had in mind, until he chose to transport them to the cave up the hill, where most of the People lived. Then, he gathered his things and left the boat to meet his wife and children, who had been waiting patiently for him to leave the boat. They understood that after the other boatmen left, he had things to do with the land boat workers.

Huaga's oldest son, Toti, walked up to his father; they touched shoulders; and he took the bag of his father's things to carry. Huaga hugged his wife, Jowlichi, for a long time. Then he hugged his second son, Paq, and his daughter, Loafete. He was as happy to be reunited as they were to have him home.

With Yumo's family, things were a little different. His wife, Limilow, hated his sailing. She felt deserted each time he left. There had been talk about her and a hunter named Phantic acting as husband and wife, though he was joined to another woman. At least she had come to meet him and brought the children with her.

It was late in the day when they arrived home. The path was dusty and the wind made the climb uphill to the cave unpleasant. It was a long distance, since they wanted to be far from any threat of high waters that sometimes crashed on their shores and sped uphill to the lower cave levels. At those times it seemed to them that the sea wanted to eat some of the People.

Food was ready, because the People had held off eating until the boatmen arrived.

"I'm so happy to be home," Huaga told his wife, "I'd rather sleep than eat, but I will eat first."

"You'll be the better for it," she replied.

He noticed how much weight Jowlichi lost since he last saw her. Her face was shrunken in at the cheeks and her sunken eyes did not look like her. The children also reflected that they had eaten poorly in his absence. It pained him.

The evening meal consisted of a soup with very little water. It contained a little fish and some greens. There was barely enough for all to eat something, certainly not an adequate amount of food. It wasn't seasoned, as if the women who made it either no longer cared, or there were no seasoning plants left.

"You look good," Jowlichi said, smiling at Huaga.

"I wish I could say the same about you, my wife. You look starved. So, too, the children."

"We do the best we can," she said defensively.

"I know you do. I intend to change things."

"What can you do?"

"I will explain to the People tonight that we are leaving for the meadow of the migrant People who left here twenty-five years ago and have found a land of peace and plenty."

Jowlichi looked at him as if she couldn't comprehend his meaning. He did not try to clarify his intent but would wait for the council. His head spun with fatigue.

Yumo ate with his family as if there were nothing wrong. He was too tired to argue or accuse or ask for explanations. His wife was doing everything to make him feel welcomed at home, as were his chidlren.

Finally the council was called by one of the elder hunters. All gathered at the hearth in the largest cave.

"Who wishes to speak?" Exit asked.

"I would speak," Huaga said strongly.

Exit nodded to him.

"We have met the ones who migrated to the cold place. They call their valley Eagle's Grasp. They have a huge valley where fish swim in the rivers, big ones that taste wonderful. They have animals in the sea called sea aurochs that taste better than aurochs. Sea aurochs are easy to catch. Our People there have a wide selection of plants to eat and animals we've never seen to hunt. The People are healthy. They are happy. They live well. I had thought that we might wait until the leaves on the trees that lose leaves begin to sprout again, but the starvation I see says we cannot wait. In three days the boat leaves again. I would like to see every person here on that boat to migrate to the new land. The People there are willing to take us into their home. We will have a wonderful life, but we must go there to do it. I cannot let my family die of starvation, when there's an alternative. I encourage all to come with us. When we completed the sea circle, we talked to those we've visited in the warmer places since time began. They know we will not return. Our days of sailing are over. Even the boatmen plan to come with us to Eagle's Grasp."

Huaga's wife was beginning to understand that in three days she'd be traveling on the boat that she feared deeply. Her husband had said it would be, so it would be, but she was frightened.

Exit asked whether anyone else wished to speak.

Yumo said, "Yes."

Exit nodded to him.

"I have spent cycles arguing against moving. When Huaga asked me to go with him to see how the People lived in their land, I dismissed the idea. Then, as the leader of us boatmen, he simply told me I would accompany him. I could not refuse the order, so I went. I now admit I was terribly wrong. The People are healthy as was the case with us before the drought. They have children who live and grow fat on their bodies. The place abounds with happiness and health. When I saw them there, I wanted to fall on my face and weep for those of you who were here. What is possible there is a wonderful life, now. I will take my family three days from now and travel with Huaga to this land. I urge all of you to come with us. We have lost our Wise One; they have one. If only you could see what I've seen, you'd be joyfully preparing now, filled with hope."

Exit looked up.

"Does anyone else have anything to say?"

One man said, "In the stories, sometimes a boat is lost."

There was silence.

"It sounds as if you're making some kind of ultimatum, Huaga," Exit said.

"I'm trying to save your lives! If you hadn't gradually become used to seeing yourselves starve, you would be where I am. In fact, I was planning to wait, but it's impossible to wait. Too many of you will be dead by then. As I see it, you have only one chance, and this is it."

"We could die at sea!" Exit argued.

"Here you will definitely die. At sea you have a chance," Huaga argued. He was blindingly tired and had to talk to the boat workers about the things he'd had them unload from the boat. "I'm not willing to remain here to watch my family die before my eyes, when I know I can change their lives for better. What manner of man would I be if I chose to do that?"

"I will go," one of the hunters stated, "I will take my family."

"I will also take my family," another hunter said.

"Well, this is my home and my family—we will stay here!" another said.

"Yes, me and my family, too," said yet another. "This is home!"

Huaga looked at those who blindly chose to remain. "All I ask is that until we leave, think about it. Realize that your bellies could be full daily, your hunter skills brought back, your happiness return. It can happen—but not here. The boat has room for every person who wants to come with us. You will eat on the boat. We catch fish while we travel. We stop at islands for other food and water."

Exit realized that silence once again struck through the extraordinary message Huaga was delivering.

"Does anyone have anything to say?"

Silence.

"Then, council is ended for this night."

Huaga found Slantmin and asked him to reserve the foods he'd brought. He wanted them to go back on the boat.

"I'm coming with you," Slantmin said.

"Good, Slantmin, I'd hate to leave you here. Protect that food. None but the boatmen and you and I know it's here and where it is. We'll need it for the sailing."

"Have no fear, it's safe."

"Thank you, Slantmin."

"I'm eager for this change, Huaga."

"So am I. I fear for my family whether they will survive until we reach them, but I must try. I must go now to sleep. I am very tired."

"Sleep well, Huaga," the boat worker said.

"Thank you, Slantmin."

Huaga stumbled back to the cave where his wife had prepared their sleeping skins. He knelt down and stretched himself out on the skins. His last thought before he slept was of the bench/sleeping places in the bent tree house.

There was unrest in the cave. The People were frightened. Huaga had been at sea for what seemed to be always to most of the People. He would no longer go to sea? That was extraordinary. And the way he described the land where the migrating People settled, could any land be so filled with food? Why should they believe this man? Maybe he was so tired then, he just didn't see correctly, except Yumo was verifying what Huaga said. It was all so confusing.

The morning meal was more of the same soup and not enough of it. Huaga went outside. The wind blew moderately and the sand and dust flew about sometimes making spirals of sand run across the dirt. They looked like tiny tornadoes. Huaga wondered where the People found the food they ate.

About high sun, Yumo found Huaga and told him they needed to talk where they'd not be overheard. They walked a distance from the cave.

"I hear that Slantmin is planning to remain here. He plans to take the food from the place where you told him to store it, to hide it for the use of few."

"Very well, how ready are you to go back on the boat?"

"Any time you're ready, I'm ready. There is something desperately wrong here, and I want to escape from it."

"Will you call a special council?"

"Right away!" Yumo stood and called, "Special council meeting, right now. Special council meeting, right now."

The People were curious and they gathered quickly, sitting in their usual places, looking like gray ghosts.

Huaga and a few boatmen entered the cave later than others. He looked around himself and noticed that Slantmin was among those who were attending.

Yumo asked, "Does anyone have anything to say?"

"I do," Huaga said. "We leave as soon as the boat is packed. Those who will go with us, stand, please."

Huaga's statement threw the entire People into confusion. They had not made up their minds. His family and Yumo's family stood. All the boatmen stood. Slantmin stood with his family.

"While I continue here, boatmen, load the boat."

Slantmin was shocked. It was boat workers, who loaded the boat, not boatmen. He wondered at Huaga's change. He had a faint fear that his plot to steal the food might have been uncovered.

The boatmen were quick to follow through on the order. They left before the council ended. They would load the food first, knowing where it was, for Huaga had told them before the meeting.

"My People," Huaga pleaded, "Please suspend your fears and think of the future. Bring your families to the boat so you return to health in the new land. Come with us. Those of you who plan to come, gather up your things and move down to the boat. Do it now!"

Huaga's wife and children immediately set to gathering their things. In little time they went to the boat to wait to be told to climb on. Yumo's wife was hesitant, but she did start gathering their things and he helped her carry them to the boat. Her children also helped.

Two other households came with their children. Then nothing more. Huaga counted the People. There were twelve boatmen not counting Yumo and Huaga. The boatmen had only two family members still living, both boys almost grown. There were five in his family counting himself; there were four in Yumo's family counting him; and counting the two other families, there were a total of nine. Huaga counted thirty-two People. Yumo's guess regarding the number of People who might migrate had neglected to count the boatmen when telling the People the number. Huaga had overestimated the number he could convince to migrate. There were no infants on the boat. People had been barren since the time of starvation.

The boat was loaded and the People left. They asked no help to push off; the boatmen did that themselves. The People who remained watched them go from a great distance. They did not regret their choice.

After they had taken off and had gone some distance, two young children, Paw and Lumu, both aged eight, came to Huaga.

He noticed them and said, "What have you to say?"

"We sneaked on the boat. Our parents are not here," Paw said quietly.

"You what?" he asked unsure that he was comprehending.

"Please don't take us back," Lumu said. "We don't want to die. We want to live."

"You're safe here, girls," he said. "I wish your families understood as well as you do. Find Yumo and ask him to give you sleeping skins. Tell him I said I agree that you should stay with us."

The girls went to find Yumo while Huaga returned to the task of controlling the boat. It was late in the year, he knew. After a while, Yumo went to stand near Huaga.

"Those girls were brave," Yumo said.

"They were reasoning," Huaga replied, "something many People there no longer seem able to do."

"Did you notice the vacant stares of some of the People? They seem to have lost their mind webs."

"Yes. That with your information about Slantmin is why I decided to leave early. I think the starvation has ruined their ability to reason. That, and they've had no Wise One for a very long time. With no guidance, they strayed too far away. Within a year, not one will be left alive, I think." Huaga's belly ached for them.

"I noticed that Slantmin, who said he was coming, didn't even come near the boat."

"Maybe he realized we left when we did partly because of him," Huaga said.

"That may be so." Yumo looked to the western horizon. "We seem to be having good weather at least for now."

Huaga wanted to weep for the People left behind. He couldn't lose his memory of the way the People who stayed behind looked at them as they left. The vision would remain with him for life. The People who stayed behind didn't show a wish that they had changed their minds. What Huaga saw looked like hate. He could not know what they thought, he reminded himself. They just didn't know what he knew, and he had not been able to convince them all. It hurt him deeply. Huaga would grieve for days, but the boat would require his attention, and the grief would fade for the living dead as life replaced it.

When it was time for the evening meal, the People on the boat ate. They had many fish caught that day and fruit stored from their tropical travels. Huaga cautioned the People to eat slowly small amounts at a time, because of the starvation. Eating too much too fast could make them sick.

Back in Eagle's Grasp, the People had set about preparing for those who might come. They did it immediately, instead of doing it in their spare time. Hunters had sought animals that would be good for food and skins for clothing during cold times. They knew if the People had the right protection, the cold would not be a problem for them. The expansion on the north side of the bent tree house provided plenty of additional space to keep extra skins so they'd be ready when needed for those who might come. Some of the women had already begun to make cold times protection that was standard. They made beaver hats and mittens in various sizes, keeping a conservative count until they actually knew how many to expect and the size. For jackets they used a variety of skins. They made some standard sized jackets. The boots would have to wait for the individual wearer.

Men worked diligently on the north side of the bent tree house and the south side. They had the knowledge now of how to build it. Children brought sand from the river level for flooring once the men had smoothed the ground as much as possible. Children put the sand inside the extension close to the standing structure. The men would spread the sand. The sea aurochs fishers went to sea to fish for the food that tasted so good wrapped in skin that was excellent material to cover the bent tree house. The People spent time tying the sea aurochs' skin down. They lashed it with ropes that kept the wind from pulling it loose, and the skin proved strong, sturdy, and waterproof. The pace was much faster than they had ever experienced since their move.

As she'd known it would be, Tuksook had found little time for solitude, so she enjoyed it fully by walking the meadow. Mi sat on the rock reciting the stories within sight of people working on the water diversion. Tuksook looked at the bent tree house. It seemed enormous to her. The extensions were longer than the structure already built. A noise above caused her to look up and she saw a large number of cranes flying overhead making their noise that reminded her of laughter and too many talking at one time. She wondered whether the People from the old land would come. Somehow, based on what she'd heard from Unmo and the older People, it did not sound promising to her.

"Oh, there you are," Dipcaco called out.

"You are looking for me?" Tuksook replied.

"Yes. Sutorlo has fallen. Item is going to him. Will you come?"

"Of course," she replied and turned to the house.

"Oh, he's not there," Dipcaco explained, "He's down on the lower level."

She followed him. "How did he fall down there?"

"He and I were standing at the edge of the meadow on the river side. Sutorlo started to sneeze and he kept sneezing. He was too close to the edge, Wise One, and he fell backwards when he sneezed."

"Why did he choose to stand so close to the edge?"

"We were looking at a set of stones in the ground. They are covered with designs. We were curious about their purpose, and who might have put them there. You could see the carvings in the rock better from where he stood."

"Hunter safety is so important; it's just hard to imagine his not keeping that in mind."

"Looking back, I can see that, but we were both fascinated with the stones. Also, Sutorlo couldn't see with his left eye," Dipcaco said as if that might explain the fall.

They reached the bottom of the path and there was Sutorlo lying on the ground. His head had struck a big rock at the bottom on the path. Tuksook hurried toward him.

"How does it look, Mother?" Tuksook asked Item.

Item did not speak but instead shook her head negatively.

Meha came screaming down the path. Sutorlo's eyes turned towards her, though he saw nothing. He was also unable to move. Blood oozed from his mouth.

Meha threw herself on Sutorlo's body. He tried to smile. He let out a great sigh, and all knew they had lost Sutorlo. Meha was thrown into deep grief. Item closed Sutorlo's eyes.

Sutorlo's sons, Echa, Knom, and Snum, and Vole went to the tool storage and gathered digging tools. Children who heard spread the word to other children. They began to pick flowers. Mi left the rock to gather flowers with them. Bitro and Lolrin brought the stretcher down the path. The men helped slide the body onto the stretcher and Bitro and Lolrin carried it up to the place where the grave was being dug. They put it gently on the ground, showing respect for the man even in his death. Amuin and Meg brought skins for washing, a pouch of ground red ochre, and a bowl of water. They washed the blood from his mouth and head wound. They washed the rest of Sutorlo's body and began to apply red ochre to it. The grave depth was reached and Knom and Echa inside the grave took the body from Bitro and Lolrin. They placed Sutorlo's body on his side in the grave, using the man's hands to keep his jaw placement looking normal. Children circled the grave, tossing flowers in it to cover the red stained body of Sutorlo. All the while Meha was near the grave, weeping quietly, belly ripped apart.

Tuksook grieved the loss of Sutorlo but also the fact that the People had become complaisant. Each person was cherished. There was no need whatever for someone to fall over the edge. She found Dipcaco.

"Will you show me the rocks?" she asked Dipcaco.

"Certainly, follow me," he replied.

"They are right here. Please, stay away from where you stand," he asked.

"Is this where he stood?" she asked.

"Yes," he said. "Then, he sneezed, and it threw him backwards."

Tuksook never doubted Dipcaco, but she found it unbelievable that Sutorlo had sneezed to his death. She wondered whether the sneeze was a sign of some other part of the body struggling and what that might be.

"These are the rocks," Dipcaco said, diverting her attention back to the stones.

"I expected them to be small, Dipcaco. These are big enough I couldn't lift one. I doubt you could alone."

"Look at this curious work on the stones. You could see them better, if I put some water on them."

Tuksook shook her head. She had no difficulty seeing the designs. The designs included circles around circles, spirals, odd shaped things that looked like People with heads too large; there were wavy lines and many dots; there were what appeared to be fish on another rock. There seemed to be many rocks under the grasses buried or partly buried.

"I can see why this drew your attention," Tuksook told him.

"He was my teacher and friend. I miss him already," Dipcaco was on the verge of tears.

Tuksook put her hand on his shoulder. "When the length of your life line ends, Dipcaco, it ends. We ache for our loss, but it is not a bad thing, simply a part of the temporary nature of our lives here."

Dipcaco nodded. Tuksook realized he was choked up enough that he couldn't speak. She began to move to the grave side. Dipcaco followed, staying on the periphery of the assembled People. He didn't want to talk to anyone.

Slowly the People gathered from all over the meadow. Tuksook said, "Let us speak our bellies about Sutorlo. Start here, please, Stencellomak."

Mi slipped into the circle next to Tuksook.

The circle took a long time. There was much to say about this very talented, quiet, humble man. Everyone loved him. He encouraged others when he saw the need, and his judgment was right. When the circle was complete, Tuksook told the creation story, and the People slowly drifted away from the site. They resumed the work they had been doing.

Item stood by Meha and put her arm around her. "Come with me Meha, I will make you some chamomile and fireweed tea."

Meha went with her, her mind web switching from disbelief to grief and back. In the house, Item left Meha at her bench and went to make the tea. Women came to comfort her and deliver their sympathy. Meha wanted to crawl into a small cave to be alone. That was not the way of the People.

Item brought the tea. Meha drank it, while Item watched.

"Do you want to lie down to rest for a while, Meha?" Item asked.

Meha nodded. She stretched out on her sleeping place, and Item covered her. Item hoped the rest or sleep would help her through this initial stage of her grief.

Meha covered her head and in the dark continued to weep until she slept."

Later, Item waked Meha when the evening meal was called.

"Item, I don't want anything to eat. I just want to sleep."

Item gently took the skin and pulled it over Meha's head. She watched for a while, stopping the few who came to awaken Meha. Then, she went to the food preparation place to find her bowl, fill it, and eat.

When the council began, Tuksook took the time to speak.

"We had a terrible accident occur today. It seemed needless, but we have to remember that each of us has a life line. His ended. I do not want to see anyone else fall from the edge. We are a group of People whose lives revolve around hunting. Safety is the first rule for hunters. We teach this to children as soon as they can speak. We have become complaisant in this land of peace and plenty. We must wake up! Stay alert! Life depends on it!"

Her emphatic ending startled the People who were accustomed to her quiet way of speaking. She wanted them to remember. Their responses encouraged her to think the People would take more care for safety. Tuksook noticed that Echa, Sutorlo's oldest son was looking at her, communicating his desire to speak.

"Echa," she said rather than nodded.

"As some People know, my father was looking at the stones most of which are buried under the dirt. They are fascinating stones, but my brothers, Knom and Snum, have found a safety use for them. We want to dig them up, level the ground beneath them, face the designs so we can see them, and lay them end to end as a barrier beyond which People should not stand or walk. We ask permission to make this barrier."

"From whom do you ask?" Tuksook asked, amazed at a possible speedily addressed safety answer to a specific problem from the sons of Sutorlo.

"From the People."

"Is there any dissent from the request of Echa?" Tuksook asked.

Silence.

"You have your permission, Echa."

Kiramuat looked at Tuksook.

Tuksook nodded.

"I would like to help. Would others, who wish to help, stand?"

Five more people stood.

"That is all I have to contribute," Kiramuat said.

Tuksook said, "That is good. I suggest all of you meet after the morning meal."

"Is there anyone else who wishes to speak?" she asked.

Silence.

"The council ends for this night."

After the council met, Tuksook found Mi.

"Mi, I want to speak to you."

Mi looked worried, thinking she might have done something wrong.

"I want you in the future to sit next to me at council. You need to see how it works from where I sit, not among the People. All we do goes to prepare you to become the next Wise One."

Lamo heard the exchange. She and Abet had been wondering whether Mi should go to be with Tuksook. They had no knowledge of how to teach a Wise One. Mi ran off to talk to Awk.

"Wise One," Lamo said, "may I speak with you?"

"Certainly," Tuksook replied.

"Abet and I have wondered whether it would be best for Mi to stay with you. The People adopt. Abet and I have no understanding of raising a future Wise One. You and Gumui could be her parents and she would call you Mother and him Father. We don't want to be rid of her; we want to do what's best for her and the People. You would no longer need to find her for reciting or ask our permission. Please, don't answer now. Talk to Gumui and see what he thinks. I will seek you out tomorrow. Abet and I both think it best." Lamo gave Tuksook no time to reply. She turned to find Abet.

Tuksook stood there with her mouth open. Off to the side she could see little Mi. She had brown wispy hair that flew in the breeze. In her round face she had brown eyes, a tiny nose, and a tiny mouth. She had no look of the old People, but she did have the memory. For Tuksook the idea of having a child, even if she couldn't give birth to one was a startling concept to her. She would discuss it with Gumui.

Tuksook found Gumui talking to some of the elders about Sutorlo's fall. He saw her and excused himself.

"Walk with me, Gumui," she said.

"I will," he replied putting his arm around her.

"Gumui, Lamo said she and Abet have been talking, and they think it best that we adopt Mi. I was so startled I couldn't really respond and she didn't give me the opportunity. She said she'd find me tomorrow for our answer."

"And I thought all this time, I'd have you to myself," Gumui teased, squeezing her.

Tuksook pulled away, distressed.

"Wife, I am only teasing you. Of course, I think it would be wonderful. She is so adorable and you'd be a great mother as well as teacher for her. With both together, it should be ideal, and you won't have to keep asking their permission for things you want to do. I fully approve. What are your thoughts?"

"I don't think Ki'ti had to be adopted. I cannot think of another future Wise One's being adopted."

"Tuksook, you have the memories. How is it that I know Ki'ti was adopted and you don't remember."

"What are you talking about?"

"Your father would be undone, if he knew you missed this. Do you remember the story about the death of Wamumur and Emaea? Say it in your mind web."

Tuksook and he continued to walk while she went through the story. She stopped and looked at him. Ki'ti was adopted in the same manner as Abet and Lamo proposed with Mi.

"I've said that story more times than I can count and I missed the point of adoption. Abet and Lamo must have remembered it and used that to do what they've proposed. You're right, of course. How could I have missed that?"

"Tuksook, you aren't perfect. No one is. Remember how Wisdom taught you that?"

"Oh what a confusion I made of things, misunderstanding a story I tell. I wonder how many others there are."

"Stop being so hard on yourself. I insist! Slow your mind web. Reason."

Tuksook sat down on the trampled grass. "I think it would be my dream come true, Gumui."

"Then, tell her tomorrow that you and I approve wholeheartedly, for it would be good for all of us. Decide when the move will occur. Be prepared for Mi to be confused and disoriented for a while."

"I will, Gumui. You're really happy about this?"

"Oh, yes. To have a daughter! I can teach her to hunt."

"Gumui, you can teach the skills but she cannot go on a hunt."

"I know," he said, smiling his special smile.

Tuksook stood up and gave Gumui a hand to help him up. They walked to the bent tree house.

At high sun the next day, Lamo found Tuksook, and they made the agreement. Since Mi was with Tuksook, Lamo explained what would happen. It would happen now.

"But will Awk still be my brother?" she asked.

"Yes, Mi," Lamo told her, "but Gumui will be your father and Tuksook will be your mother."

The little girl stood there looking confused.

"Mi, come with me. We have my old bed that is not used at all. It will be perfect for you. It has a nice soft caribou to sleep on and soft skins for covering.

"If I want to talk to my old mother and father, is it permitted?" Mi was trying hard to capture the details.

"As long as I haven't given you a task to complete at the same time, of course."

Lamo stood there watching Tuksook interact with Mi. She knew they loved each other. What she also knew is that Tuksook yearned desperately to be a mother. Lamo saw this as the right thing to do for many reasons.

"I have some things I must do," Lamo said smiling. "I'll see you both later." Lamo went to the edge of the meadow to help remove flesh from small beaver skins.

Tuksook reached for Mi's hand. The little girl gave her the hand. They walked together to the bent tree house where Mi would have a new place of her own.

"This surprised me," Mi told her.

"It surprised me, too, little one," her new mother replied.

On the way to the bent tree house, Gumui came running over, picked up Mi, swung her around in circles high in the air, and said, "I understand, Mi, that you've made me a father."

"I have?" she said, laughing at the swing through the air.

"Well, if you're my daughter, I'm your father."

"Please, do it again."

Gumui turned her about up high in the air. She giggled. He put her down, and watched over her as she staggered off balance briefly. Then, the three of them went to the bent tree house.

"This is my bench/sleeping place with Gumui," Tuksook told her once inside. "And this one is the one I had when I was young. This is yours now."

"I don't have anybody else to sleep with?"

"No, it's all yours," Gumui assured her.

"I like it," she said convincingly.

The entryway flap to the west part of the house opened enough for Abet to walk through.

"I thought you might want this change," he said smiling at Mi. Looking at Gumui, he said, "I think this is for the best. It will be a little empty for us for a while, but it's not like we're far away."

"You have made two people very happy. I hope Mi finds this good for her, too," Gumui replied.

Mi was snuggling in the soft caribou skin that formed the base of her bench/sleeping place. She was trying to hold the longer caribou hairs in her toes. The bed she shared with her sister did not have skins as soft. She missed the presence of her sister, but not her sister. The two didn't do well together. She missed the nearness of Awk. All the newness had her slightly off balance. She determined to make the best of it.

The bent tree house became silent as one after another families settled for the night.

Out at sea days later the sun rose following a horrible storm. People were severely frightened. After all the boat had tilted to such an extent several times they thought it would overturn. Yumo called all the People together.

Huaga stood before them. "The storm you experienced was a big one for you. That's why we tied everyone to the boat. For those of us who are boatmen, it was an average storm. You lived! We knew you'd live. This is as safe a boat as you can find. We are on the way to a better life. No life comes without dangers whether you're on land or sea. You learn to live with what you must. Look how long you lived without enough to eat. That was more likely to kill you than a storm. The earth does some things that can be frightening. You must learn to expect the things the earth can do in order to keep on going, whatever the earth brings. Continuing to keep going when times are tough is the difference between those who fail and die and those who live and thrive. Do you understand what I'm saying?

The People nodded. Even some of the boatmen nodded.

"We are going to a place where the People are examples of those who continued to keep going. They are welcoming us. I don't wish to transport a group of People who flinch at every hard time. I want to show them that even though you've survived starvation, you are still People, still ones who continue on when times are hard, People who don't fear what naturally occurs on the earth, but rather accept what is and keep living well. Is this clear?"

The People and some of the boatmen nodded seriously.

"Now, each of you has things to do to make this sailing a good one. I want to see you disperse and continue on."

The People dispersed. Huaga had no certainty that his words would affect anyone, but it did cause People to turn loose of their death grips on bamboo and begin to do what they were asked to do.

Paw and Lumu had not been terribly frightened by the storm. They rolled their sleeping skins and stowed them at the edge of the wall in the covered sleeping place. The night boatmen were preparing to unroll theirs so they could sleep after the morning meal. The women helped the boat's cook prepare the food. They had some grains the women couldn't identify, which they boiled. There were the remains of the fruit: melons, coconut, and two kinds of fruit they didn't recognize but had eaten on the boat. They had jerky, a gift from the migrant People. Each meal was a feast to the People who had been starving. They had learned to eat in a way their bodies made good use of the food. On the boat, the People from the old land still looked like skeletons. It would take longer than a sea crossing to change that.

Huaga noticed the People were dirty. He suspected lice filled their hair, except no one was scratching. For so long water had been in short supply. Bathing was limited to the sea. They had dirt on their skins when they arrived at the boat. The salt water spray had streaked but not removed the dirt. A few had matted hair. Their clothing made them look ghostly. Clearly they had worn the same things for decades. No new skins had been available. Animals, they had refused to follow, had fled north. Huaga planned to have them wash when they reached the river.

Huaga walked over to Jowlichi. "Wife, is lice a problem among the People?"

She was a little surprised at the question but replied, "I think some of the People we left behind still had some. There was an outbreak a long time ago, but then they seemed to go. Some of us bathed frequently in the salt water, staying under as long as possible to dislodge them. Most of us on this boat never had them. I can check with the few who had them."

"Please do that. We are going to live in a shared house, not a cave. I don't want to introduce lice."

"I'll let you know what I find out."

"Thank you, Jowlichi. You are a good woman."

She held his gaze. "You, my husband, are a good man."

He left for his duties aboard the boat.

"Yumo," Huaga called out, "it looks like we have good weather for this day,"

"I agree. It is good!"

The People on the boat were fascinated by the boatmen. Except in a storm, they ran all over the boat as if they were on land. They walked on bamboo poles, yet there was no hesitation to gain a foothold. Often the men didn't even look where they placed their feet. Huaga and Yumo's children were awed by their fathers. They were more attentive to what the men did than other migrating People.

As the day wore on, the boat moved along with a multitude of salmon returning to their home waters. They swam close together as if intent on their purpose. The boatmen took long poled nets and netted numbers of them. They would have them for the evening meal. They knew how good they would taste.

"Land ahead! Land ahead!" Yumo shouted.

The People looked and saw no land. They wondered what Yumo saw, but they already realized that the boatmen knew what they were doing.

Huaga walked over and Yumo pointed out the island.

"I'm not certain which one it is. With that storm we probably came further north than usual."

"We'll be near it soon enough," Huaga said.

Wind was blowing strong enough to move the boat at a good speed. The island became larger and larger. "It's Island Nineteen!" Yumo boomed.

"Are you sure?" Huaga asked.

"Sure as the feet of Wisdom," Yumo said laughing.

"Feet of Wisdom?" Huaga laughed back.

"Well, there are People who aren't boatmen on the boat."

"I see," Huaga said, still laughing. It was Island Nineteen. He could now see for himself.

"Special council," Yumo called out.

All gathered.

"My People," Huaga began, "The island we see before us is Island Nineteen. The way we move the boat through these waters, it is the last island before the mouth to the river we will sail up. We are close to the place where we meet with the People of the new land called Eagle's Grasp."

There was a sense of relaxation among the People. They were delighted to know that the sailing was reaching its end.

"We're not going to stop," Huaga told Yumo. We have no need as close as we are to the river.

"I agree," Yumo said.

Using the wind they avoided the island and headed off to the river. By the time they reached the river, they still had a stiff wind and swells were moderate. The men continued on sailing in the mixing of water from the sea with water from the river mouth's rushing out into the sea. Increasing wind did not make the river entry easier. The boat pitched and rolled. People became alarmed again, but they kept very quiet about their fears. They were supposed to continue on unafraid of what the earth offered.

Finally, the boat entered the river. The moon was out and almost full. There was no difficulty seeing. The further up river they traveled, the less pitching and rolling. The boatmen pushed onward to a place they knew they could anchor briefly. They set the boat in this cove and the night crew watched to be sure the boat didn't drift.

After the morning meal, Huaga told the People they would bathe and clean their tunics so that they were presentable to the People in the new land.

It was hard to pay attention. The People gawked at the green landscape surrounding them. It was truly wonderful and totally different from their old land. It wasn't long before people were letting themselves into the water to wash. Many had never learned to swim. Water was over their heads, so they clung to the boat while washing. The water was very cold to them. They came out shivering. It had been a long while since they had been able to bathe. Rivers and creeks were dry with only little pools here and there. The fatigue from starving also made them less aware of their need to bathe. To the People on the boat, this chance to wash was a luxury, cold or not.

Back in the meadow, the People noticed the leaves beginning to turn yellow. They had completed the addition to the bent tree house. They had harvested green plants and tubers that would keep through the cold times and gathered herbs to dry for teas. They had more than enough food for dogs for the cold times. The People were as ready for the cold times as they could be. With thought to the People from the old land arriving earlier than planned, they had hunted prodigiously, and they had dried meat and hung legs that had soaked in sea water for half a moon. They had enough food for two full years in their storage room. Women continued to make clothing from skins without becoming overstocked until they found how many People would actually migrate. They had stacks of skins ready to use. They had done what they felt was their duty by telling Huaga that some thirty People were welcome to come to live with them. The People understood ants. They tried to be as prepared as the ants. The way of the People included the belief that animals had lessons from Wisdom for them to learn. They learned much from ants. Though apparently ready, the People still pushed to add to the items they gathered and to check and recheck that all was in order.

Tuksook felt a sudden need for solitude, but she realized this was not a good time. There was too much final checking required on the house and its contents to take time for solitude, and Mi needed to continue to practice the stories. She was learning the stories she didn't know. But the need for solitude pressed on her with a heavy weight. At the evening meal, she picked at her food.

"What is it?" Gumui asked.

"Same need as always," she replied.

"You can take the time," he said.

"Gumui, there remain too many things to check. I must wait."

"Then eat, Tuksook. Do not play with your food."

Mi sat with them watching. Her brown eyes didn't miss anything.

"Hi, little feather," Gumui said to Mi.

The little girl laughed. "Feather? Why'd you call me a feather?"

"Today I was down on the river level. I looked up to see an eagle feather floating down from the sky. It made a spiral motion as it came down. It was a sight to see. It's a little thing from a big bird. You're a little thing, too. I don't know why I said that, but you're special like the descending eagle feather."

Mi was fascinated. "You really saw an eagle feather fall from the sky?"

"Yes."

"What'd you do with it?" she asked.

"I let it lie where it fell."

"Will you show it to me?" Mi asked.

"Tuksook, do you have her reciting stories tomorrow?"

"If you will take her there, go after the morning meal. Then, she can recite."

Gumui reached over and squeezed her leg. He smiled.

She smiled back. There was more delight than she imagined in having a child, she thought. Little things became special. To see with Mi through her eyes was a treasure she had never considered.

Council was brief. The People were tired. They headed back to their sleeping places ready for rest.

Tuksook dreamed. Her dream took her back to the vision Wisdom provided long ago. It was where she saw herself playing while her People were dying. Gumui waked her because she was mumbling.

She looked at him.

"You had a bad dream," Gumui explained.

"Yes," she replied, as if he had questioned her.

He held her to him comforting. They drifted back to sleep.

In the morning, Tuksook tried without success to shake the awful vision from the dream. Why she wondered did that vision occur at this time? Gumui took Mi to the river level, a place she was not allowed to go unless accompanied by a hunter. He went to the place where the eagle feather still lay, where he had seen it reach land. He picked it up, holding it for her to see. Mi took it, twirling it in her finger tips.

"Can you make it spiral?" she asked.

"We'll see. Come up to the meadow with me."

They found Tuksook, and Gumui said, "I plan to climb out on the leaning tree. I would like you to take Mi and a hunter to the lower level so you can see the eagle feather spiral."

"You know you're not supposed to go out there."

"I know, but this is for learning something otherwise too difficult to show. If it works, we can show the People and let them know the tree remains a place where People cannot go."

"Sometimes you're exasperating."

"You'll do it?"

"Yes," Tuksook replied.

"Oh, Mi, I need the feather," Gumui said.

Mi handed it to him. She took Tuksook's hand to find a hunter. Hai was nearby. She asked him, explaining what Gumui planned to do.

Perplexed, Tuksook reminded him for the second time, "You know nobody's supposed to go out on that tree, but I'd like to see an eagle feather spiral."

The three of them walked to the lower level and turned to the right to stand near the large overhanging tree. Gumui had moved out onto the tree with great care. He had no place in his life for an accident. He had a wife and now a child.

"Are you ready?" he called to the three below.

They nodded. He let the feather go. It did spiral just enough that they understood the way it moved. Tuksook understood why Gumui was so fascinated with it. They were awed.

When they gathered together after the feather drop, Gumui hit rocks together. All the People except Kouchu gathered in the meadow.

"I have called you here to see something I saw yesterday. To me it was special to be able to see this and I'd like to share it with all of you, so you have the same opportunity that I did. I saw an eagle feather fall from the sky. It does not float as some feathers do, but instead it spirals earthward as the adult eagles do together when they are in their mating time. It's as if the feather retains eagle ways. In order to do this, I have to crawl out on the forbidden tree. I do this only to share with you. After that the forbidden tree is still forbidden. Any of you who want to see this will need to go to the river level and stand near the tree."

The People were astonished, but all of them wanted to see the spiraling eagle feather. Not one, even Unmo wanted to be left out.

Gumui waited until Unmo reached the place to see the feather fall, before he dropped it.

"All of you are ready?" he asked.

The People nodded, eyes fixed on the feather in Gumui's hand.

Gumui let loose of the feather. It spiraled. The People were fascinated. They'd seen small feathers fall, and they didn't fall like that. Surely, Gumui reasoned, the feather retained the way of the eagle at mating time.

Gumui carefully returned to the meadow and the People came up the path.

Unmo walked over to Gumui. "Then, you think a part of an animal retains the way of the animal?"

"I cannot prove that, Unmo."

"It is an interesting thought. I wonder whether, when we are dead, our bodies retain the way of us?"

"Wouldn't it be amazing if someday someone dug up my leg bone, spine, or tooth and could learn something about me from that part of me?"

"There is so much we don't know," Gumui admitted. "We have learned so much, but there is still infinitely more to learn."

"I agree with you, young man."

"Oh, Unmo, I lost young long ago."

"Not from what I've seen of you and Mi," Unmo said, eyes twinkling.

Mi was with Tuksook when Tuksook fell to her knees.

"Mother, are you well?" Mi asked.

Tuksook could not answer. The old vison repeated in her mind web. She could not clear it. Mi ran for Gumui. The unique voice of Wisdom spoke, "Tuksook, reason. If you had not played, what would you have done? Don't ignore this. Reason."

"Father," she called, "Mother is not well."

Gumui came running.

He found Tuksook on her knees.

"Tuksook, what is it?"

"The vision keeps returning. Wisdom told me to reason what I'd have done if I hadn't played. Gumui, I tremble inside that some catastrophe is coming where I will be required to hold the People together. It is an enormous responsibility. I don't know whether I'm up to it."

"Tuksook, where's your faith in Wisdom? Call on Wisdom for guidance."

"I understand that, but, Gumui, Wisdom told me to reason what I'd do."

"Then, take the time to do it. Wisdom has given you a duty. Do it. There is a purpose."

Mi went to him and he caught her in his arms. "Let Mi come with me today and you take the rock. No one will bother you. Stand up, Tuksook. You have to do this."

Tuksook stood feeling as if she weighed far more than she did. She walked across the meadow silently and climbed to the rock. She sat there, staring at the meadow below. It was a different perspective but the vision kept repeating. She intentionally slowed her mind web. Tuksook breathed deeply. She began to reason.

Gumui took Mi into the bent tree house. He put the eagle feather on the rock in the central part of the house. Then, they went to the storage area. He found a small leather sphere used as a target for slingshot practice for those proficient in the skill. They went back to the meadow.

"Mi, I am going to throw the sphere to you and you are supposed to reach your arms out and grab it with your hands. Don't let it fall to the ground."

He threw the sphere and Mi missed it. He moved closer and tried again. Mi missed it. He moved even closer. This time Mi caught the sphere. Her face danced with surprise and delight.

"Now, you throw the sphere to me."

Mi tried, but it didn't go more than an arm's length from her feet.

"Mi, watch. I will turn sideways. You watch what I do with my hands, arms, and body."

He threw the sphere several times. Then, he handed it to Mi.

"Now, do what you've seen," he encouraged.

Mi tried to put it all together. She reviewed in her mind web what she'd seen. This time it almost reached Gumui.

"Don't lose desire to succeed. Try again. This is practice."

Mi tried repeatedly. Then, she began to learn how much force she needed to supply to make the sphere reach Gumui, and he was finally able to grasp the sphere when it was thrown.

"That's good," Gumui told her. "Now, we are going to throw it back and forth from you to me."

For quite some time they tossed the sphere back and forth. Mi improved to beome better and better.

Gumui said to her, "Now, I'm going to move back a little, and you'll have to use more force to make the sphere reach me."

Mi tried and failed.

Gumui threw her the sphere and she caught it, grinning widely.

"Now, throw it to me this time," he said.

Mi added force and tried again. This time, Gumui caught it.

They threw the sphere back and forth for quite some time, until Mi developed some basic skill. Then, Gumui held the sphere and said, "It's time to put this back."

They emerged from the bent tree house and Gumui said, "Let's walk."

After a short time, Gumui said, "Now, Mi do you understand how you have to concentrate when you learn a new skill?"

"You're teaching me about when I bothered Awk, aren't you?"

"I want you to know what's required to develop a body skill. Can you imagine if someone were trying to chat with you while you learned to throw the sphere?"

"It would make me angry, Father. I need to use my mind web to learn this body skill. Talking would interrupt my reasoning."

"Mi, you learned the stories because Wisdom gave them to you. When you learn a skill it takes much effort and many repetitions. Each effort requires reasoning to know why you succeeded or didn't. That's how you correct to become better. You reasoned well."

"It's very hard to learn a body skill, but it's fun," Mi admitted.

"From time to time we'll do more of this. You'll learn to use the slingshot when you've trained your hands to work with your eyes. Then you'll learn to use a spear. You'll learn all that hunters learn, but you will not be allowed on a hunt. You will be Wise one. You have to be protected. But you will learn, and you'll be well skilled."

"Are you sure?"

"Yes, I'm sure."

Amuin hit the rocks together for the evening meal. Tuksook left the rock and met Gumui and Mi on the meadow.

"Success?" he asked.

"Success," she said without elaborating.

They headed toward the food preparation area. The People greatly preferred the outside food preparation area. They had a giant deer stew for the evening meal. The savor of it was wonderful. Gumui went back for more.

There was no council that night, so after cleaning the bowls, the People headed for the bent tree house or for a walk after the evening meal.

Tuksook and Gumui sat side-by-side on their bench. Mi walked over and gave both of them a hug.

She stood there, her face beaming, and she said, "I learned much today. When I first came here, I wondered why I had to be adopted. I'm starting to reason it. Living here is so different."

Mi turned and went to her sleeping place. She hung her tunic on the peg and climbed into the softness of her sleeping place. Tuksook covered her.

Tuksook and Gumui prepared for sleeping, and that night, there were no bad dreams.

Chapter Eleven

"There's the last of the right-sided land points," Yumo announced as they followed a bend in the river.

"Won't be long now," Huaga replied.

"This has been a surprisingly easy sailing. Makes me wonder what happened." Yumo scratched his arm. "I never thought I'd turn from the sea to land."

"Yeah, me either. I'm having stiff joints and my back is sometimes sore. For me it's definitely good to do it." Huaga stared out at the river ahead. His hair, cut just above shoulder length and bound with a leather tie, had turned white along with his trimmed beard, and his skin was bronze from the constant sun exposure during much of his travels. He was a tall man with a very straight build. His muscles stood out from constant use. His headband had loosened in the salt spray, so he took it off, retied it, pushed his hair from his face, and put the band back on.

Yumo stared at Huaga, and Huaga felt the stare and turned to look into Yumo's dark blue eyes. his hair and beard were not as fully white as Huaga's. He wore his hair in the same manner held by a leather band and his beard was trimmed in the same way. Yumo was shorter than Huaga, and his arm and leg bones, though a little bowed, were very strong. He was a stocky man.

"What do you imagine our People will think when they reach the meadow?" Yumo asked.

Huaga laughed a deep laugh. "They're going to be so happy to have their feet on land—they'll hug and kiss the ground!"

"I don't doubt it. I've never seen so many People at one time cling to bamboo with such a death grip! Ever since you talked to them about eliminating fear, they've tried to hide it, but it's still there."

"It's been hard for them. Think what it would have been, if we'd had some of our wild sailings."

"We might have lost some of them from fright." Yumo kept scratching his arm.

"Very possibly. They do look improved since the bath, but they still look awful."

"They'll fatten up here, I'm sure. Wait until they taste sea aurochs roasted or sturgeon. Jerky's one thing; fresh cooked meat is quite another."

"What in Wisdom's feet are you scratching for?"

"So you like my words?" Yumo said smiling at Huaga, who used his terminology. "Oh, a bug bit me and it's on fire."

"Normally, those bites just itch. Are you making too much of it?"

"No, not at all. Look how this swells. We've both been bitten by mosquitoes, but this is different."

Huaga looked at the exceptionally large swelling.

"That doesn't look good," he said with a frown, wondering what bit his friend. "I think if you scratch it, you'll make it worse. Maybe to the development of pus."

"I'll try leaving it alone, but it won't let me forget it," Yumo replied.

Yumo hand signaled the boatmen to turn the boat more to the left side.

Huaga watched as they rounded the point. His brown eyes were sharp and his memory precise.

"They'll notice us now," Huaga said.

"Look, already children stare at us through the trees at the meadow's edge."

On the meadow, dogs had alerted the People to the boat's arrival before the boat rounded the point. More and more of them came to the trees to see the arrival of the People from the old land. People were not permitted to go any closer to the edge of the meadow than a man height. On the south side of the path that led down to the water, the stones dug up by Sutorlo's sons and others provided a barrier that was clearly marked. Most of the People remained on the meadow, having listened to the hunters who primarily used the boats. At council they explained that too many of them on the lower level would interfere with the arriving People.

The men who used the boats went running down the path to prepare for the arrival of the big boat. They had cleared an area of extensive vegetation as well as they could to provide a good place for the boat to anchor. Hawk and Vole rowed out almost to the freely running river to guide the boat to its anchorage. They were relieved that they had prepared in advance. Their Wise One guided them well, suggesting an early arrival was possible. Hawk stood in the little boat, waving. Huaga and Yumo waved back. Others on the boat began to wave somewhat timidly, communicating much to the two men in the little boat and the ones who could see from the meadow. Boatmen were lowering the sail.

Hawk put his hands to his face to increase the volume of his voice. "We'll guide you in," he shouted.

"Very good," Yumo shouted back.

The big boat turned with practiced ease into the channel the men had made and maintained. Yumo called directions to those who rowed. Those who rowed had the skill to row at different paces or directions on either side of the boat to make turns smoothly. Little by little and slowly the big boat eased into the anchorage the People of Eagle's Grasp had provided.

"Oars up! Drop anchors! Give each rope a two man length of slack." Yumo shouted.

Huaga walked to the edge of the boat. "Most can't swim, so we need to bring them to shore in the little boats. We have one."

"We have two more. Counting this one, there will be four small boats. That should be good." Hawk hand signaled to the People who used the boats that all of the small boats were needed. Those on shore went quickly to the small boats and rowed toward the big one, while Huaga's boatmen prepared their small one.

Four People transferred from the big boat to the small one occupied by Hawk and Vole. The other boats of Eagle's Grasp could take no more than two at a time. The small boat from the big boat could take four in addition to the boatmen who rowed.

Huaga said, "People, leave your things here. The boatmen will bring your things and put them in the meadow, where you can find them, when you know where they should be placed. All we want now is People."

There seemed no specified order of transfer of People from the big boat to the smaller ones. Whoever was nearest the small boat transferred over. Boatmen stood by to help. One small boy fell into the water. A dive from a boatman brought him to the small boat, while the child sputtered and cried from fear.

All of the People from the boat including the boatmen gathered at the bottom of the path that led to the meadow. The People from Eagle's Grasp led the way. Huaga and Yumo led the People from the boat. Instead of noisy bustling activity, there was little sound from the People as they climbed the path to the meadow. They went to the center of the meadow where Tuksook and the elders waited to meet the new People. Huaga introduced the name of each one of his People while Hawk, also an elder, introduced the elders, Stencellomak, Unmo, Moki, Togomoo, Anvel, and Hamaklob. Hawk introduced them to their Wise One. Those with exceptional memory remembered all the names. Those without that memory knew they'd know them as time passed.

During the introductions, Item touched Yumo's arm where the bite had caused significant swelling.

"I see you've been bitten by a black-and-white legs," Item said.

"What's that?" Yumo asked.

"It's a bug with shapes on the legs like this." She put her thumbs and forefingers together forming a squarish shape standing on a point. "The shapes like this on their legs are black and white all fitted together. They give a mean bite."

"That they do!" Yumo replied.

"We have expanded our bent tree house to accommodate all of you. We'll show you where the space is, and Huaga and Yumo can lead you there to select your bench/sleeping place."

The People from the old land had no knowledge of a bench/sleeping place, but they understood sleeping place. They were dumbstruck at the health that seemed almost to vibrate from the People of Eagle's Grasp. They were also amazed by the size of the structure in the trees. It was nearly as long as the meadow, and it was covered by grass squares. They had never imagined anything like that.

People from Eagle's Grasp had been warned to give the newcomers a chance to find their place and settle their things before becoming acquainted. The People of Eagle's Grasp were horrified at the condition of those who weren't boatmen. They certainly knew of the drought. That's why they had migrated, but these People looked as if they might die. The single reaction to the People from the old land was intense sympathy.

"Follow me to your new places," Hawk said and started walking to the south entryway. Huaga led, and the People followed.

Yumo went to the boatmen and told them to start unloading. He told them they had a place in the structure, and they would locate their individual places after the boat was unloaded. The men from Eagle's Grasp who had helped in the transfer of people went to their boats to help transfer the unloaded things. With four boats the transfer shouldn't take long.

When the People wound themselves through the entryway skins, they saw an amazing sight. The structure was not unlike a cave, except it was straight and provided space along the walls for the bench/sleeping places. There were holes at the top along the length of the structure, holes with poles attached to flaps. The holes let light in. Under the holes were hearths. The People didn't see the wood piled all along the east side of the house or the bone pile near the dogs where the People would gather wood and bone to burn.

People of Eagle's Grasp had prepared thirty-six bench/sleeping places. They had no idea how many of them should be double. As it turned out, they had made far more double bench/sleeping places than were needed. Hawk explained to Huaga that he should organize his People to determine where they'd sleep. All the bench/sleeping places had a furred skin covering for comfort.

Jowlichi burst into tears. Huaga walked over to her and put his arms around her. "What's causing the tears?" he asked.

"I weep for those we left behind. You were right. For those of us who can fatten, this is the likeliest place for it to happen. All those we left will die. They might have lived."

"I understand," Huaga said and loosened his arms. "Some people will cling to a false hope like limpets on a rock, instead of risking change. They had a choice." He had to assign his People to the bench/sleeping places.

Huaga set about the task with the help of Yumo. "I think with all these doubles, we should put the two girls without parents on one. They can share and comfort each other," Huaga said. He called Paw and Lumu, and they came to find a soft fur cover on a large bed he told them they'd share.

"Girls, you may go to the meadow to find the bundles that Yumo gave you from the boat's supply. Bring those for your covering skins and put them on your sleeping place. You'll remember which one is yours?"

"Yes," Paw said, "This one has a tree that has the face of a cat. See?" She traced the face and Yumo actually saw what she saw. "This is for us? I've never slept off the ground. It is so special. I don't feel deserving."

Yumo laughed. "That's what they provided for you and all of us. Just be grateful." He'd been looking at the place Paw showed him. "I see the face of the cat! You will find your place again easily."

Paw and Lumu went to see whether they could identify the skins that they'd used on the boat.

Huaga had decided to put the families nearest the People from Eagle's Grasp and the boatmen at the end nearest the entryway. Everyone was delighted to have a place to sleep already provided. The quality of the new place was beyond their comprehension. Almost all of the People had to take a moment to try the sleeping place. The comfort of it was unexpected. They marveled that they had left a desolate place and come to a place of comfort.

Little by little the People returned to the meadow to gather their sleeping skins or anything else they'd brought. They carried them to the bent tree house and put them on their bench/sleeping places. They went shyly to the meadow to observe the place where they had come to live. The boys and girls and men and women of Eagle's Grasp went to meet those of their age. The newcomers were shy but warmed up quickly to the People who welcomed them so generously. The People of Eagle's Grasp were careful that no one was left out.

Meanwhile the women of Eagle's Grasp had to plan to feed all the People at the evening meal. They brought the women from the boat with them to show them the food preparation area and how they functioned to put together the evening meal. Women scurried about selecting the meat and sending girls to gather whatever greens they could find. The Eagle's Grasp children warned the others of the mother of red rash. They showed them plants that were food. Boys were sent to gather wood and smaller bones to build up the hearth fire for the evening meal. The boys also brought wood for the hearths inside the bent tree house to provide warmth through the night. Hunters instructed them to lay the materials beside the hearth, not add to the fire. Some of the boys wanted to practice slingshot after they finished gathering materials for the hearths.

Gumui stood by Tuksook. Mi was at her side. They looked at the far greater peopled meadow and the way the People were coming together. They did not see any of the newcomers alone, instead they were mixing well.

"You did well to foresee the possibility of their early arrival. Had we not hurried to complete the bent tree house and gather meat and skins for the cold times, we could have had a disaster. The cold times are near."

"I am not responsible, Gumui; Wisdom is."

After the evening meal of sturgeon, all the People attended the council meeting outside where there was much to discuss. Tuksook had just nodded to Yumo.

"We wish to thank you for welcoming us. We arrived here from the terrible drought in the old land. It is hard for many to imagine the luxury you have made in this new land. Never had any dreamed of such bench/sleeping places. It's almost too much to believe. We're very grateful. All of this means life to us."

Tuksook replied, "Know that all of you are completely welcome. We are one People. The luxury you describe, Yumo, is our rendering of the stories of Ki'ti and their bent tree house."

Huaga laughed.

Tuksook was surprised but she nodded to him.

"That's what made me feel that there was something familiar about this place the first time I saw it. Just now, I felt as if I'd been here long ago, but I knew that wasn't true. It's from the old stories?" Huaga shook his head and continued, "I've heard the stories many times but never thought of the structure as having meaning to us. This structure probes my mind web. It's as if you created a cave from trees. I never could imagine how the place looked that Wamumur had the People build."

In the clear sky, a full moon began to crest the hill. Paw wondered whether her family back home could see the same moon, and she wanted to cry when she thought of her family. She doubted Lumu was happy to remember her family well. Her father had assured her that when they ran out of food, she'd be the first eaten. Where once he had cherished her, she could tell that his feelings toward her had hardened. In the conditions under which they lived, Lumu knew that was not an idle threat or a tease; it was a certainty. Yet she had no place to run—until the boat arrived. Lumu escaped murder, and Paw came for two reasons: to live and to keep her friend from being alone. They leaned against each other for reassurance.

Tuksook looked up. "Hawk, would you introduce the People to what they need to know in this land?

Hawk hadn't prepared to speak so he remained silent briefly while he reasoned. It was a common practice. Then, he began.

"This land becomes very cold. Colder than you've ever felt. Protected with the clothing the women have been making and will continue to make, until all are prepared, you won't feel the cold. This land has very little sun in the cold times. We spend time in the bent tree house doing what is hard to do in the warm times, such as making or repairing spear tips and other stone tools, making spears, grinding ochre, sewing. We have tunes and dance. We have a food preparation area in the house and a council area. To sit outside when it is very cold is unwise. In the cold times that are coming you'll go out quickly and return quickly. This is much like life in the old land, but colder."

"In the warm times, this place transforms! You can see the green, though it now turns yellow. You have tasted sturgeon. It is a huge, strange looking fish that lives in the river." Many of the newcomers smiled at their memory of the evening meal they'd just consumed. Hawk continued, "Sea aurochs live in the sea. We take boats out to sea to fish for them. We have to enter the cold water to swim down to encircle their tails with rope. Then we haul them back. They are wonderful. They have much fat; their skins make a protective barrier against rain, snow, and wind over the bent tree house structure; and their meat is very tasty. You've had jerky from sea aurochs, but that's not as good as the roasted fresh meat. We eat other animals, such as camel, giant deer, beaver, and an occasional bear. You've noticed we keep the dogs. They eat horse and dried salmon. Salmon come upriver in masses. Dogs bring our packs in pouches we attach to them when we hunt, so we can carry home the meat. Animals that lived here before we came are different from the ones we had in the old land."

"Besides temperature and food, we call this river valley Eagle's Grasp. We have a large stone over there that marks the rising and setting sun and high sun. High sun isn't overhead in this land. It is that general area." He pointed. "Sun arcs the sky near the horizon here in the warm times with little dark. Carved on the stone is our valley. It looks like the leg of an eagle. We use it to communicate places to each other. The carver, a man named Sutorlo, recently died when he fell from the edge of the meadow down to the river level. We have few rules, but one rule is that no one puts himself closer to the edge than a man height. Another is that no one climbs out on the tree that leans over the lower level. It grows near the area where the dogs are confined. Another rule is that no one goes anywhere alone. There are large cats in this land that can sneak up from any side and from above in the trees. Finally, we do not bend the rules of Wisdom. If you see wrongdoing, report it at council or speak to the Wise One. Do not remain silent about it."

"At dark in the cold times, we often see colored lights dance in the sky. We call them sky lights. They are white, green, blue, and red. One night we were greatly awed, because the entire sky turned red. Imagine looking at the sky and seeing it in red. It was frightening until we learned that the colored sky is part of the sky lights. Sky lights can move straight or wave through the sky, or they can cover it. Rarely do they cover it. We also have earthquakes. Some of them are powerful, but they have not done damage here that wasn't repairable. Occasionally, in the cold times, we have very strong winds. That's why you see the black cover over the bent tree house tied and then lashed to the trees at their base. The sea aurochs skins protect us from wind and water. When it's very cold, when the wind blows fiercely, or when mammoths walk through the meadow, you must come inside."

"That is all I have to say."

Tuksook looked out over the People. She waited for eye contact. There was none. She said, "Is there anything else that we should share tonight?"

Silence.

"I feel certain that all who traveled here are tired. Best for that is rest. There is much more to share. We will share it. Right now, council ends, and I encourage you to go to your sleeping places for some sleep."

People dispersed for the bent tree house quickly. Fatigue was great.

Lumu and Paw unrolled their sleeping skins, hung their tunics on pegs, and crawled into their sleeping place. Each covered in her own sleeping skins. They lay there looking around. The bent tree house was warm from the hearth fires and the numbers of People. There were many People, but the noise was muted. They felt surrounded by caring People, where starvation certainly was unknown.

"The children are snuggled in their sleeping places, my husband," Jowlichi told Huaga. "I still cannot believe the difference in what was and what is."

He sat with her on the bench they shared. "This is a good place. Can you see why I caused the boat to leave early?"

"Knowing what you knew, it must have pained you to see us gathered together weak and hungry."

"It ripped my belly apart. I changed the timing when I learned that a boat worker named Slantmin planned to steal the food we brought with us. I couldn't let that happen. I suppose we might have convinced some more, if we'd had three days, but it wasn't worth the risk of losing the food we needed to bring us here."

"What is this skin on our bench/sleeping place? It's a beautiful brown color and it's soft," Jowlichi asked.

"I think they call it beaver," Huaga replied.

"What's beaver?"

"I have no knowledge. That's something we'll learn. All I can know is that they are very large."

"And soft," Jowlichi agreed.

Down the south part of the house from them, Yumo and his wife, Limilow, sat beside each other on the bench that would soon become their sleeping place.

"Husband, I must speak," Limilow said anxiously, her head lowered.

"Speak," Yumo said.

"I have wronged you. I ask your forgiveness. I was lonely. I found comfort in Phantic. I knew he was joined, but we would sneak off together. It

279

ended before your return, but I feel unclean next to you. Do you wish me to find a different sleeping place?

"Do you still wish to remain my wife?"

"More than anything," she admitted truthfully.

Yumo took a soft skin and said, "Come with me."

He walked with her to the place where water fell for bathing, where he sat on a stone.

"Bathe, Limilow. Wash all the uncleanness you feel away," he said, putting the soft leather across his leg.

Limilow looked at him in disbelief, but she removed her tunic and walked under the water. She scrubbed her scalp and ran her fingers through her long scraggly hair. She took some sand from the place where the water went when it left the bathing area, and she rubbed it vigorously on her skin. It felt wonderful. Limilow asked Yumo to rub her back with the sand. He did. She was shivering cold, but she felt that once again her skin could breathe. Limilow felt clean. Yumo handed her the soft skin so she could dry the water from herself. Yumo remained horrified at her emaciated body and thinning hair.

"Wife, I forgive you. You have just washed away the uncleanness. Do not stray again with another."

"I will do as you say," she said, wringing the water from her hair by twisting it tightly. She pulled her tunic over her head.

She and Yumo returned to their bench/sleeping place. She hung her tunic. He removed his leather strip. Despite her emaciated condition, he wanted her.

The boatmen spent no time preparing for sleep. The south part of the bent tree house was quiet. Some were asleep and the rest were on their way.

Suddenly there was from a far place in the bent tree house a tune played on a flute. It was gentle and soothing. When the tune ended, there were no more tunes, just quiet. Hamaklob had the first watch on the south entryway, later to be relieved by Vole. Hawk quietly walked the length of the south part of the bent tree house content that they had offered safety to these People.

Days later as the newcomers became adjusted and the yellow leaves began to fall, Gumui and Tuksook walked the meadow hand-in-hand. Mi was with them.

"Now, tell me what happened last night. You slept fitfully, moaning and twisting and turning. I'd wake you up; you'd go back to sleep; and it would begin again."

Tuksook took time to respond. Mi looked at her mother's face wondering what she would say.

"It was the same dream. I played and the People perished. There is something wrong, something about to happen. I can feel it, Gumui, but I cannot discover what it is." Like a flash of lightning, she threw her arms out to stop Gumui and Mi.

"Tuksook, think what you would do if this happened."

"Wisdom?" Tuksook asked looking around herself. "Is this going to happen here?"

"You will see what you will see," the unique, special voice replied, "Think what you should do, if it happens." And, then, he was gone.

Tuksook had spent a day reasoning through this disaster. She thought she had prepared herself well. Clearly, Wisdom implied, she was missing something.

That night, Kouchu died peacefully in her sleep. She had been such an inspiration to so many. Girls and boys spent the time during the grave digging to collect the few flowers that remained and the seed puffs that grew where flowers had been. They made a huge collection beside the grave while they searched for more.

At the grave side, Tuksook told the newcomers, "You didn't know Kouchu, but the cold time protection you will have was likely made by girls she taught, when she could barely move. She never complained, she had a smile and encouragement for all. Today we bury a treasure to the People."

They began the circle of remembrances for Kouchu. When the circle returned to Tuksook, she said, "Mi, you will tell the creation story."

Mi looked at her in disbelief. "Me?" she whispered as if she'd not heard what she thought she'd heard.

Tuksook nodded.

Mi began in her childhood voice, "In the beginning, Wisdom made the world. He made it by speaking. His words created. He spoke the water and the land into existence, the night and day, the plants that grow in the dirt, and the animals that live on the dirt, and those that live in the water and in the air. Then he went to the navel of the earth. There he found good red soil and started to form it into a shape with his hands. He made it to look a little like himself. Then he inhaled the good air and breathed it into the mouth of the man he created. The man came to life. Then he took some clay left from the man and he made woman. He inhaled and breathed life into her. Wisdom created a feast. He killed an aurochs, skinned it, made clothing for the man and woman from the aurochs, and then roasted the aurochs for the feast. The man and the woman watched carefully and quietly to see how he killed the aurochs, how he skinned it, how he made clothing from its skin, and how he roasted it. They paid good attention and they were able to survive by doing what they had seen done."

"The People were special and Wisdom announced that the man was to treat the land and the water and the animals and the woman the way he wanted to be treated—good. And the same was true of the woman. And it went well for a long time. But Wisdom hadn't made the People of stone. He had made them of dirt, knowing that they shouldn't have lives that would go on too long, for they might become prideful and forget Wisdom. That is good, because People should not be without Wisdom. They would die."

"That is why the People return to Wisdom when they die. They are placed in the earth and Wisdom knows. When Wisdom hears of a death of the People, Wisdom waits until the grave is filled back. He waits until it is dark. Then he causes the earth to pull on the spirit of the dead to draw that person's spirit back through the dirt of the earth. Wisdom draws that spirit to the navel from which all People came, the navel of the earth where the red clay for making the first man was. The spirits of the dead depart for the navel of Wisdom. That is where they reside for all time. All People's bodies return to the dirt. But their spirit, that essence of the person made by the One Who Made Us, is pulled back to Wisdom in the place where first man was made, and Wisdom keeps all those he chooses with him there. Safe and loved. There is a cycle Wisdom made, a cycle from the navel to the navel. He keeps the spirits of those whom he chooses and he destroys those whom he hates. Wisdom hates those who hate him, those who ignore him, those who would be hurtful to him or the land or water or to those living things Wisdom made including People."

When she finished, Mi looked at Tuksook, silently asking whether she was successful. Tuksook smiled back with assurance. People talked quietly among themselves as they dispersed. Tuksook hadn't moved, still struggling with what she was forgetting. She had to be prepared to act in an emergency. She wondered what emergency? She knew she was giving her mind web a staunch exercise but still couldn't find what she was missing. Tuksook was mildly alarmed that whatever this warning was, it preceded some event that would occur soon, and she must be prepared.

"I will go to the carved rocks by the edge," Tuksook said. "Will you listen to Mi tell her stories?"

Gumui looked at Tuksook with many things occupying his mind web. "But I . . . ."

"You know the stories," she said with her mouth, but talked beseechingly with her eyes.

Gumui understood. "Come on, Mi, let's have you practice your stories until after high sun, and then we will throw the sphere."

Mi clasped her hands in delight and ran to Gumui, who caught her and lifted her to his arms. "You're not very big, little feather," he laughed. He looked at Tuksook, "Take the time you need, but remember not to go to the edge side of the rocks.

"I'll remember," she promised with lowered head.

Tuksook walked to the rocks. It was a little chilly and she felt it. She walked briskly back to the bent tree house and picked up one of the sleeping skins. Tuksook pulled it around her shoulders and returned to the rocks. She sat there and suddenly she felt wrapped in another world. There were voices she couldn't understand, and she pushed them away. Tuksook heard the voices, but they were in the distance. She ran her fingers over the tracings in the rocks. She went from one rock to another. Whoever made the carvings all spoke the same language, she realized. It was a single people, maybe many carvers, who made the carvings. Sometimes when she traced a carving, she could feel her fingers tingle. Sometimes she knew things that reasoning told her she could not know. Yet, she felt more certain of this strange knowledge than some of the things she knew in her world—things provable with reason of the mind web. She became closer and closer to the spirit from the rocks.

Suddenly, the spirit from the rocks said, "We made these so people like you would know we were here. It's a building to honor ourselves and to show our greatness to all who see it."

"Why would you make a building to honor yourselves?" she asked. "Only Wisdom is great and worthy of honor."

"We are a smart, strong people. We have conquered the beasts, the land, and the sea. The world should know of us. There is no god. From your imaginings and fear, you have made a god to lean on because you are weak; we are strong in ourselves. Our superior building attests to that."

"You fool yourself. You are dead," Tuksook said.

"We lived here before you. We lived here long. You built of vegetation; we built of stone. Great stone structures. You have not seen them."

"No, we have not seen them."

"You would have to trek further south," the spirit from the rocks replied.

"We will not look for your buildings. We believe it is evil to set one's self up for praise from others. If you do well, who needs anyone else to say that it is so?"

"You miss much," the spirit told her. "Adoration from others is a wonderful feeling."

"No, we have all that anyone could ask for right here. We have what you lack—Wisdom. We are stronger with Wisdom than you were in yourselves." She challenged the spirit, angered at the disrespect it showed for Wisdom.

The spirit laughed an ugly laugh. "You fool yourself, you disillusioned wretch."

Tuksook was irritated but remembered what to do. She'd call on Wisdom.

"Wisdom, you are power. Please, show this spirit that he speaks nonsense. Show him your power by removing him and his people's spirits as far from this site as possible. Wisdom, please show your power."

Immediately the spirit from the rocks began to sputter and then, all was silent. Tuksook sat there dumbfounded at the conversation she'd had. People built structures to themselves? What manner of men were these? She wondered at the foreign ideas. Whoever they were, they were rude, and she didn't like them.

Tuksook sat on the grass leaning on a rock. We don't have to be strong in ourselves, she thought, we have faith that Wisdom who made us will provide for us when we have a need. We can even ask for his help.

Tuksook sat up straight. That's what she'd been missing all this time. The first thing in the event of a calamity was to call on Wisdom. She chastised herself. She'd been thinking like the spirit she asked Wisdom to ban. In the event of what she saw in nightmares, Tuksook imagined she had to do all she could. Her emphasis was on herself. It had not crossed her mind that she was supposed to call first on Wisdom for guidance in what she did and said. Tuksook had nightmares because she had not worked her knowledge into her practice of the first basic rule for Wise Ones—call on Wisdom first—just like her father had forgotten the same rule. She severely cramped in her belly. The old arrogance of her childhood reared up its ugly head and bit her again and again. She wondered whether she'd ever learn.

She traced the carvings on the rock absentmindedly, while she watched Gumui and Mi playing with the sphere. Tuksook watched a little boy from the newcomers go to Gumui and Mi. Obviously, he was greeted warmly and the three of them played with the sphere. A few other children went to their sphere toss and also participated, all near the same age. Tuksook was delighted to see this. What a change it must be for the newcomers, she thought.

Tuksook pressed upon the rock with her hands. Then, she felt as if she'd fallen into a downward spiral. She turned around and around as she plummeted downward. What, she wondered, what caused this?

Tuksook landed on her feet in a white room, and she understood. "Wisdom?" she called quietly.

"Tuksook, you learned something," Wisdom said, suddenly transforming the room to the cave-like place she'd known for these meetings as a child. Wisdom sat on the white stone seat.

Tuksook automatically climbed the two steps, throwing her arms around the knee of Wisdom, resting her head so she could see the familiar face Wisdom presented to her. Despite her love of Gumui, Tuksook often felt alone. In this presence Wisdom presented to her, she felt wholly complete, not alone.

Wisdom looked very serious, not stern, but more concerned. "This is, first of all, what the spirit told you about."

Where Wisdom had shown her visualizations in the past, in that same place in the artificial room there appeared a vision of a hillside where a building of huge blocks of stone covered much land and rose high into the sky. It appeared that some of the top of the structure had been removed or knocked down. Pieces of stone were scattered about on the ground. The size of it was overwhelming. Tuksook wondered how people could have made anything like that.

"Shut your eyes, Tuksook," Wisdom said.

She could feel herself rising up and, then, there was Eagle's Grasp in her dream-like mind web. She flew to the south and located the large building. Tuksook was impressed.

"The carved rocks you saw that edge the meadow are carved by different people from those who built with stone. The carvings were their attempt to communicate with others who would follow, not to puff themselves up, but to provide knowledge from their experience. It is too old to benefit you now. Things were different then. Those who built the stone structure—they are different. Do not be impressed by structures people make to honor themselves, Tuksook. It is not the right order of things. If people feel a need to do that, it's due to their own insecurity as people, not because it's something deserved. It causes the person honored and those close to him to think more of themselves than they should. After the age of the ice I showed you, there will be much more of this, and memorials to self will become common, feeding great pride, when none is deserving. The idea will grow and spread across the world—not just from land to land. It will spring to life in each place as if uniquely born there. It comes from the massive change in the earth. The two things are tied together."

"The builders of this place were so prideful that they do not reside with me in the navel of the earth. They spoke of conquering so much. They conquered nothing—not even themselves. Puffed with pride, they built wanting anyone who passed the mouth of the river to know that exceptional people lived there. Trees grow there now so that from the river and the sea, it's hidden. They also built to the south a structure that made the one you overflew seem small and insignificant. The truth is that they were all killed when an enormous wave, higher than any you've ever seen or could imagine, rose from the sea and washed every one of them to the sea. Pride makes it impossible for people to see factually. They overlooked the enormous waves, just as those filled with pride overlook truth." Wisdom paused. "Tuksook, you listened to a spirit. The spirit who spoke to you was a spirit of evil, not the voice of one who lived. That spirit will tell you enough truth to have you to believe them and then lie to you to pervert you. They always have harm in their bellies. I have warned you twice. Talk to them no more. I have removed them from the valley, but you must conquer yourself."

"Tuksook," Wisdom said in a gentler voice, "I choose People who are weak, not the strong and boastful. What need do the boastful have? Their vision stops at their own skin. It is impossible to lead when your vision stops at your skin. The weak with me can overcome the strong and boastful. They can see. Remember that. In truth the strong and boastful are actually the weak, and the weak ones with me are actually the strong ones. However, you must consider what that means. You saw the stone building and were impressed. That's not how I want you to see. That's not how I want you to be. To be impressed is not wise. You need to know what's important. What I want you to see is that your integrity is what's important. Tuksook, you have a special house in keeping with my way and the way of the People. None who built the bent tree house were ever puffed up to want or find themselves deserving of praise from others at this time—certainly not far into the future. Do not guide the People to the stone buildings for they may become impressed and their bellies hunger for what they see."

Tuksook raised herself up and looked at Wisdom. She saw how big the gap was between the spirit of the rocks who spoke and Wisdom's People. It was too wide for either to cross.

"I will obey," Tuksook said.

Wisdom continued, "My People have within them integrity which I will liken to a crystal. Pride and seeking to be adored destroys the crystal that is their integrity. First, it fractures, and, then, it crumbles. When the crystal of integrity becomes fractured, there is the option to repair it. It would never be totally clear as a crystal, but it would still hold integrity. When there are so many factures that the crystal can no longer be repaired, it crumbles into pieces that cannot be reassembled, and integrity is lost forever, as was the case with Rimut."

There was a long silence. Wisdom knew Tuksook had to store the words she'd heard in her mind web.

"Now, look at this," Wisdom said.

Tuksook watched the place in front of Wisdom's feet where Wisdom caused her to see things. A sparkling swirl turned into the earth.

"That's the earth?" Tuksook gasped. The slowly rotating blue sphere was breathtakingly beautiful. She'd never imagined it. Had she tried, she couldn't have thought it so beautiful, and she knew it.

"Yes. This is Eagle's Grasp." Wisdom pointed to the image and showed her their place on the earth.

Red lines appeared on the earth as it circled slowly. There were four of them. One arced in the water below Eagle's Grasp.

"The earth lives, but it lives with a life different from yours. Land moves. Sometimes there are barriers that block that progress. Stress builds up. Consider how it would be if you cleared the land to the dirt. You then pushed the dirt with your hands to smooth it. Eventually, if you kept pushing the dirt, it would pile up, and it would become too difficult to push the dirt any farther. The dirt makes a barrier at a certain point. You'd have to break through that barrier to continue to move it. You don't move the land, but for the earth moving land must occur. When the barrier is overcome, there is a jolt while the barrier is broken. You call it an earthquake. Then the earth settles down with the stress relieved. Remember, it's absolutely necessary to break that barrier. Do you understand?"

"Yes." Tuksook gulped.

"I think she's waking up," Mi said after Gumui had tried unsuccessfully to awaken Tuksook.

Tuksook was answering Wisdom, but Mi and Gumui took it for a question as to why they waked her. Tuksook shook her head. She'd never gone from Wisdom to the People that fast, and she felt cloudy in her mind web as she tried to assess what she'd seen.

"The evening meal has been called, Tuksook. Take my hand."

She took his hand and stood. They walked to the food preparation area, Tuksook still holding the skin around her.

"I'm glad you had some sleep," Gumui chatted.

"It wasn't sleep," she muttered.

"Did you find what you sought?"

"Yes," she replied, "and more."

Gumui understood that she wasn't going to discuss anything with Mi there.

Mi saw Awk and left to talk to him. She smiled to herself. He was not practicing slingshot.

"Gumui, after the evening meal, please cancel tonight's council, unless there is something important to discuss."

"I will. After we eat, I'll ask the elders of both groups whether there is anything. Then, we'll know."

"Good. I am very tired."

"Tuksook, will you talk to me tonight about what burden you carry now?"

Tuksook had seen Mi walk over to talk to Awk, so she said, "After Mi sleeps, we will walk outside."

The evening meal would be special. The women had used a new combination of plants to put on the sea aurochs meat for seasoning. They had boys dig them a pit of an arm's depth. Then, the women filled the bottom of the pit with coals from the fire in the hearth about a hand in depth, and added alder wood. Women rubbed the seasonings on the roasts, and they placed the roasts atop the alder wood. They had many people, so there were many roasts. After carefully removing the stems, women, who could touch the plant, laid mother of red rash leaves atop the meat and placed alder wood atop the leaves. They covered the pit with dirt. Others hunted for the few greens remaining.

Later, Amuin hit rocks together and the People came to the food preparation area. The women had placed the roasts on slabs of wood atop the big log. The aroma was a foreshadowing of the taste. People could hardly wait to eat. Women had cut the roasts into meal-sized pieces, and eagerly People filled their bowls.

Two of the boatmen leaning against a particularly large tree enjoyed the meat. One went back for more. He reseated himself and ate.

"It almost makes me reconsider," Go, the one who had seconds, said.

"It's wonderful, but nothing would make me reconsider."

In another place, Gumui was watching Tuksook. She thought the meat tasted very good, but she was definitely far away in her mind web. He wondered what she was reasoning. Mi, always curious, watched Tuksook, but she asked no questions. She also took the time to pull strings of meat from the hunk meat she had in her bowl. Mi liked to eat the meat tiny piece by tiny piece. It made the taste available longer.

Shortly after the People ate a short council began in spite of Tuksook's fatigue.

"Is there anyone who wishes to speak?" Tuksook asked, already knowing that only the boatmen had something to discuss.

Go looked at Tuksook, and she nodded at him.

"We boatmen have a desire to take the boat further south, where the days are equal and it's warm. There are numbers of people there, far more than here. There are not nearly enough women here for wives. We don't know whether you had plans for the big boat, but if not, we would like to use it to travel south."

Quiet fell on those at council. They could appreciate the desire of the boatmen.

"Is there any reason not to approve this request?" Tuksook asked.

Silence.

"Are you certain?" she asked.

Silence.

"Your request is granted, boatmen. Will all of you leave?"

"Yes. We have been together for so long and shared so much of life, it would be hard to separate," Go said.

"When will you sail?" she asked.

"We have little but our sleeping skins to put on the boat. We're ready to sail after the morning meal."

"Before you leave check with Item. Be certain you are well provisioned for the sailing," Tuksook said.

"Thank you Wise One and all People. What you have is wonderful, but there is no hope of wives here," Go replied.

Tuksook said quietly, "Go, I ask one thing of you and the boatmen."

He looked at her expectantly.

"I ask that you not disclose where we are."

"I will promise you that I won't talk about it. Boatmen, if one of you cannot now vow to Wisdom that you will keep silent on this, speak now."

Silence.

"Then say these words one at a time: I vow to Wisdom that I will never discuss the location of the People who migrated to Eagle's Grasp."

One by one those who would leave on the boat stood and repeated the vow, until every one of them had said it, including the two older boys, sons of the boatmen.

None of the People expected Go to have each person individually vow. It made them realize that they were leaving for personal reasons and would protect the People.

"Do any others have anything to discuss?" Tuksook asked.

Item looked at Tuksook, who nodded.

"How many days of provisions will you need?" Item asked.

"Do you have enough for as many as a hundred days?" Go asked, instead of answering.

"We have enough to fully feed every person here, including you, for far more than cold times to cold times—not fresh roasts like tonight, but jerky. Of course we have adequate supplies for you for a hundred days. We will have that amount put in baskets that you can transport to your bins after the morning meal. Please, return the baskets," Item requested.

Most People had no idea how well prepared they were, and they were truly amazed.

"Does anyone have anything else to add?" Tuksook asked.

Silence.

Then, council ends for this evening.

Slowly People stood up and began to walk to the house.

Ubassu and Eilie walked together. "I wonder how many jackets we made that we won't need," Eilie said.

"Probably not too many. Some of the adult men's jackets we made can go to our own People whose jackets are wearing thin. We can use pelts from their old jackets for other things," Ubassu replied.

Tuksook and Gumui prepared Mi for sleep and they sat quietly on their bench watching the child. They spoke little.

As time passed it seemed clear that Mi slept. Gumui stood up and offered Tuksook a hand. He took her cloak that was ready for the used skin basket, and he put it around her shoulders. They went outside by the west entryway.

"What happened?" Gumui asked.

Tuksook began, voice flat, "Gumui, before we lived here, others lived here. They honored themselves by building a huge stone building south of us where the river enters the sea. It stood above all so that anyone sailing could see it. They were a boastful people. The sea brought a huge wave that was bigger than any we've ever seen. It tore some of the building away. It washed all the people there out to sea. Today, none of them reside with Wisdom. The structure they built still stands, but it's hidden by trees."

"I was in the meadow by the rocks and a spirit from the rocks spoke to me. It was an evil spirit not a spirit of the dead. I failed to ignore it, and instead I talked to it."

"Tuksook, you're not supposed to talk to them." Gumui was horrified.

"I know." She hung her head.

"Please, continue," he asked.

"I sat by the carved rocks. Suddenly I was with Wisdom. Wisdom showed me the structure the men made. It was huge, and it's still there. Wisdom does not want us to go there. Wisdom also showed me how the earth looks from far away like from the moon—I don't know from where, I just know I saw the earth turn so slowly. I saw it about this size." Tuksook used her hands to form the best circle she could. It exceeded the size of her head. "The earth is incredibly beautiful. There appeared on the earth four red lines. Wisdom showed me where Eagle's Grasp is on the earth. One of the red lines arced just below Eagle's Grasp." Tuksook inhaled deeply and slowly let the air escape.

"Wisdom told me that the earth lives and moves land around. The land has to move or the stress could become too great. Wisdom compared it to our clearing vegetation to the dirt, pushing the dirt until it stops, and then pushing it very hard to break through the barrier. We have to face a jolt, probably soon. I have reasoned it will be a very large earthquake."

"Finally, Wisdom let me know that I'd learned what I needed to learn. Oddly, I learned it though disobedience. Wisdom had told me never to speak with other spirits or the dead. I found the evil spirit troublesome, and I remembered to call to Wisdom. Wisdom rescued me by removing the evil spirit far from Eagle's Grasp. It took me a while to realize that in the event that something catastrophic happened, my first act should be to call upon Wisdom for guidance. I had thought about all the things I should do, but I neglected to think to call upon Wisdom first. I was just like my father and the people who built the stone structure to honor themselves and show forth their pride to impress others."

"Wisdom told me that by living in Wisdom's way and the way of the People we have in us something like a crystal—a crystal of integrity. When we go outside Wisdom's way and the way of the People, the crystal fractures. With effort, a fracture can be repaired. Once the crystal crumbles into pieces that can no longer be repaired, there is no hope, as it was with Rimut."

"Tuksook," Gumui said comfortingly, wrapping her in his arms, "go ahead; cry if you want. I'm here and no one is nearby. You had a significant time with Wisdom. You learned much. How I'd love to have seen the vision of the earth."

Tuksook wept, leaning against Gumui's chest. Losing the tears helped somewhat to ease the tension in her.

"I fear the vision I've been having. I begin to understand that we're about to have a huge earthquake. I know if there is damage to the structure, the People will—like ants—repair it quickly, unless the earthquake rips it apart. We have just repaired for the cold times and now this. I have a leadership role to play and I just cannot quite see ahead far enough to know what to expect. I know that the earth has to let something break a movement barrier. I understand that much."

"Tuksook, what did you learn from Wisdom today?" he asked holding her at arm's length by the shoulders.

She looked at him. "Oh, Gumui, what would I do without you? I'm falling right back into the way of pride instead of the way of Wisdom for a Wise One. My crystal of integrity is in danger of cracking. I shall call for Wisdom for guidance, before I make decisions, and I will receive the guidance I need. I will not panic regardless how monstrous the earthquake is. And, Gumui, until the earthquake or anything of significance occurs, I will change the vision of myself skipping stones and practice calling on Wisdom first for guidance to show me what the problems are and how to remedy them. Then, when necessary, I will be equipped to lead with good guidance available." Tuksook felt a wave of relief wash over her. "Now, I think I might sleep."

Gumui walked with her back to the bent tree house.

When they reached their bench/sleeping place, Gumui and Tuksook saw Mi sitting on her sleeping place, legs crossed, covered by a skin around her shoulders, waiting for them.

"You were going to wait until I was asleep to sneak out of here, so I wouldn't hear you. Any time you want to do that, you need only tell me to stay in a certain place, and I will do it and not move," Mi said positively in a loud whisper.

Tuksook and Gumui stared at her and then at each other.

"You were awake when we left?" Tuksook whispered back.

"Yes. You were acting very strange, Mother, ever since you were by the rocks. I knew you had learned something from Wisdom you wanted to talk to Father about. It was clear you wanted to do that where I couldn't hear you. I wish you'd just let me know that. I'd make it easier for you, like when I went to talk to Awk today. That gave you time to talk."

Gumui went to her, picked her up and squeezed her. Tuksook pulled his arm, and he bent over so that Tuksook could kiss Mi.

"Let us sleep now, for the morning comes. Mi, we have heard you. No longer will we sneak away. We'll tell you and have you stay in a certain place," Gumui promised.

"Thank you Father," she said, snuggling back into her sleeping place. "Then, I won't worry about you."

Tuksook laughed barely audibly. This child was filled with Wisdom at such an early age, she thought. "What a one you are," she whispered, tousling Mi's hair.

Gumui and Tuksook crawled into their sleeping place. Tuksook gave a look at Mi, who was peeking at them. She laughed again.

"What makes you laugh?" Gumui asked very quietly, glad that her mood had changed.

"Mi is peeking at us," she replied.

Finally, there was no more noise from the west part of the bent tree house. Sleep came to the bent tree house.

The noise of rocks being beaten together waked Gumui and Tuksook. They looked for Mi and saw her sitting cross-legged on her bench. Her sleeping skins were rolled neatly at the wall edge of the bench. She had put on her tunic and combed her hair, a little oddly, but it was combed.

"I've been waiting for you," Mi said.

"I finally had a very good night's sleep," Tuksook said. "I feel refreshed again."

"Wonderful, we'd better run a comb through our hair and dress very quickly," Gumui said reaching for Mi's shoulder to squeeze it.

The three left the west part of the bent tree house and headed for the morning meal. While they ate, Item, Za, and Brill helped the boatmen with the baskets of jerky they'd need for those who sailed. Baskets of jerky for all of them for a hundred days was the plan. Item knew how to calculate it, and she made it for one hundred and twenty days to be safe.

Boatmen carried basket after basket of food to the bins on the boat and brought the baskets back. Everyone was careful not to step in their way. The boatmen didn't run, but they lengthened their strides and moved as fast as possible. They had help from two of the Eagle's Grasp boats to transport the food to the boat.

Once the boat was loaded and Go had counted all on the boat, they were ready to leave.

"Anchors up!" Go shouted. He gave orders how to row to move from the anchorage to the river.

Yumo and Huaga watched from the meadow. Go was doing wonderfully at maneuvering the boat to the river. He had learned well to lead the boatmen. They both wished the boatmen well. They had been like family for more years than they could remember. They knew it was the right thing for them to do. It was sad to leave part of the People in the drought in the old land and now to lose another part of the People to the south. All along the edge of the meadow the People watched. Huaga and Yumo watched until the boat disappeared around the point of land on their side of the river. When they turned back to the meadow, the reduction in their population was visually obvious. Twelve boatmen left with the two boys who were almost grown. Fourteen People missing from the meadow made a distinct difference.

Men, women, and children returned right away to the tasks they had planned. Tuksook took Mi to the rock and began her recitations. Gumui went to the house and began to walk through it, considering what would happen inside if a great earthquake occurred. He looked at how they had stacked tools and spears. He considered the storage of meat, plants, and curing plants. He looked at hearths, considering fire. Gumui walked through each part of the house looking at the arrangement of the bench/sleeping places. He could find nothing but the addition of water containers to change.

Out on the south meadow, hunters had taken a skin and laid it over a stack of turf they'd dug up from the river level. The turf had dried. They took charcoal and marked a large dot on the skin. They lined up the boys for tipped spear throwing practice. Along the way out from the target, they marked stakes in the ground to show distance. For all the remainder of the day boys age ten and up practiced very seriously. For the practice, they used repaired tips, knowing they'd need to repair the tips again after several days of practice.

Item gathered the women together and looked at what had been made but not distributed, what the need was now, and what remained to be made before the cold times set in. They found they had more than enough adult jackets, but were lacking for the children. Some still would need boots, hats, and mittens. A few could not fit the jackets that had been made, so they needed alteration or to have a new one cut and sewed.

"How many of you know of men who need a replacement jacket? Some of these would satisfy that need," Item asked.

Za spoke up, "Stencellomak's jacket is worn badly on the arm. I've tried to patch it, but he feels the cold there."

Meg said, "Hawk's jacket has a split in the back. If you can replace it that would be good."

"Unmo needs one that fits him better," Brill observed. "His jacket is not overly worn enough to return it to the basket for new application, but it's so large that cold air rushes in at the bottom.

"Tuksook isn't here to say, but I know that Gumui's is terribly worn," Eilie said.

Then there was silence.

"We have fourteen adult jackets for men and seven for women completed. The only difference in the men's and women's jackets is the width and arm length. Do you think one of the women's jackets would fit Unmo better?" Item asked.

Amiz looked up. "If you give me a woman's jacket, I'll carry it to my husband and try it on him. Then, I can answer.

Item carried the new jacket to her. Amiz took it and left the house by the west entryway. She found Unmo by the food preparation area, eating a slice of roasted swan. She was concerned because Unmo had been eating a lot recently, but he continued to lose weight.

"Wife, what brings you here?" Unmo asked.

"Put the food down. I want to try this on you," she replied.

"That's a beautiful jacket," he admitted.

Amiz helped him put it on. It fit with a little room to spare.

"Is this for me?" he asked.

"Yes it is."

"It'll keep the cold air from coming up the bottom of the jacket. I like it."

"Let me have it back. I'll take your old one and hang this on your peg."

"Sounds like a good idea to me," he said with a smile and wink.

Amiz went back to the bent tree house, walked to the women, and told them the fit was good.

"I'll bring you his old one, which is like new, and hang this on his peg," she told them.

Women busily prepared the evening meal. The meat was swan, caught after the boat left, camel, and some aurochs that remained from the last meal. Those who could touch the plant without effect had taken some mother of red rash and peeled off the leaves and outer stem. They had washed them at the falling water for bathing. They cut them into cylinders about a finger long, and called them mother fingers. There would be greens for the evening meal. It was late for these still to be green. Most stalks were brown to black, but the women would make use of any vegetation they could find still fresh.

The sound of rocks being hit together called the People to the evening meal.

Tuksook took some of everything except the mother fingers. The smell was inviting, but knowing what the plant did to her skin made her avoid having anything to do with them. Mi loved their crunchiness, though this late in the year, they were losing some of that crunch. When Mi and Gumui ate the mother fingers, they would wash their hands well afterward to keep from transferring any of the plant to Tuksook's skin.

The People gathered for council as soon as all finished their evening meals. They decided to have council outside, but they soon realized they'd have to move inside because it was becoming colder, especially at night.

Tuksook said, "Our boatmen guests have left for the south. I ask Wisdom to protect them in their sailing and keep them. Let them arrive at their destination safely," she paused. Then she continued, "Does anyone have anything to say this evening?"

Yumo said, "I heard that this is the last of the fresh sea aurochs. Would taking a sail to the sea to fish for sea aurochs be something you'd do at this time of year?" he asked.

Hawk said, "I'm ready to fish for sea aurochs any time I can have People go with me, except when it becomes too cold, and that coldness is near but not here yet. I am willing to accompany you. We need two others."

Orad said, "I've increased my muscles this year and rowing would be good for me. I'll go to row, but I'm not interested in going in the water."

Vole, always ready for a sail said, "I'll make the fourth man."

Yumo said, "After the morning meal, then?"

The other three planning the trip nodded.

Tuksook asked, "Are there others who would speak?"

Item made eye contact, and Tuksook nodded.

"I need to have each one of you check jackets, boots, mittens, hats for cold time protection. If something is worn or torn or just doesn't fit right, if boots are outgrown for children, let me know. We are trying to assure that all are ready for the cold times. For those of you who just arrived, you have to be certain that the things given you fit well and are not torn. You cannot permit your skin to have much exposure to the very cold. If something isn't right, speak up. We already replaced Unmo's jacket, which was too large. We know that Stencellomak, Gumui, and Hawk need replacements."

"Does anyone else have anything to say?" Tuksook asked.

Gumui stared into her eyes. She nodded.

"I went through the bent tree house, looking for anything that needed attention before the cold times. I realized that we should have a bladder of water across from each hearth. If a fire occurred, the means of stopping it would be available. We need to have the bladders added and someone to assure that they are always filled and ready."

It was surprising when Paw made eye contact with Tuksook. Tuksook nodded.

"Lumu and I would be glad to contribute to the People by assuring the bladders are filled," Paw said.

"Does anyone else have anything to say?" Tuksook asked.

Kiramuat made eye contact with Tuksook. She nodded.

Kiramuat said, "I will take the bladders needed tomorrow and fill them. I'll peg the inside of a nearby tree to hang each one."

"Does anyone have anything to say?"

Silence.

As the People dispersed after the meeting, Huaga walked over to Tuksook.

"Tuksook, I want to thank you for talking to Wisdom about our boatmen. We were so close for so long. I worried about them on this sailing. After you talked to Wisdom about them, I am no longer fearful for them."

"I enjoyed meeting those I had a chance to meet. They are good People, Huaga. I'm sorry they had to leave, but it's true that we have few females available."

"Well, thanks again," Huaga said and turned to walk with his wife.

The People walked a little faster in the chill of the air. Once inside, the bent tree house was warm and cozy. Some People checked their jackets, boots, mittens, and hats. Others would wait until they awakened. Quickly, rest fell on the bent tree house. A flute played a short two tunes and stopped. All was well.

Chapter Twelve

Five years passed. Tuksook had been confused, expecting an imminent earthquake. Then, she had become irritated, because it hadn't come. Ultimately, she lost full trust in Wisdom. She still talked with Wisdom, and Wisdom knew her thoughts on the earthquake and that she'd lost trust in the long wait. Tuksook lacked patience and understanding. Wisdom did not interfere with her learning; it was as it was. To speed Tuksook's learning would throw her out of balance in the way of the People. Wisdom would not disclose the time of the earthquake, only that she needed to practice calling on him when anything significant occurred to be sure to obtain the guidance Wisdom might want her to have. To that she was obedient.

Tuksook walked over to the stones and sat on one, while Mi sat on a skin on the grass and recited the stories. Tuksook looked at Mi as the girl recited. What a different child Mi was from the other children—or from herself for that matter. She was single minded when it came to the stories; she had perception way beyond her years; she was good natured. Tuksook wondered whether Mi had any childish behaviors such as the expected rebellion, greed, pride, or any of a number of others that would need correction. Tuksook had never found any. She wondered whether Mi's integrity crystal was as shiny and perfect as the day she was born. Tuksook knew that if called on to name a single problem with Mi, she would be unable to name one. Tuksook would not count the times that Mi followed Awk when he didn't want her to be with him, because she was too young to understand without guidance what she did. Once she understood, she never repeated that behavior, but, then, she was occupied reciting stories.

Gumui walked over. "Let's walk down on the lower level path today to see what the pooling waters have to show us," he said.

Tuksook looked surprised that he'd interrupt the recitation, but she realized it was a lovely day and she agreed. Mi couldn't believe it.

They walked down the path. As they walked to the south, Gumui and Mi examined each pool for minnows or worms or water bugs, whatever they could find. Tuksook's intake of breath caused Gumui and Mi to turn around. She had pulled a leg bone from the hillside. Beside it was a jaw-less skull. She pulled both bones from the dirt and wiped them off.

"What are you going to do with the bones?" Mi asked.

"I plan to ask Gumui to bury them," Tuksook replied. She smiled at Gumui.

"Where our People are buried?" Mi asked.

"Does that matter to you?" Tuksook asked her, wondering what her reasoning was to question it.

"The bones are not from our People. I cannot reason that they should be buried in another place, but it seems odd to have the bones of strangers in our meadow."

"Mi, according to the stories, what becomes of one of the People when they die?"

"Wisdom draws them to the navel of the earth. Oh, I see what you're having me see. The bones are laid there from respect for the person, but the person isn't there. I can also see that these bones were once buried in our meadow."

"Yes," Tuksook replied.

"So my question wasn't really one I should have asked. But I tried to reason and didn't find the right pathway in my mind web."

"It happens to everyone, Mi. Don't worry over it."

"Now, I am comfortable with the stranger's bones in our meadow. The spirit of that person is not here."

"True," Tuksook said, realizing how well she knew it was true.

They went up to the meadow with the bones. Gumui carried the bones over to the place where the graves were.

"Before we do this," he said, "do you think it wise for us to poke around in the dirt where these were to be sure there are no other bones that should be added?"

"Why don't you ask a few men to help," Tuksook said.

"Good idea," he replied. "I'll see who I can find."

Tuksook looked at the graves just beyond her feet. Unmo and Amiz were buried there. A rock covered with red ochre was buried representing

Togomoo. What appeared to be a huge black and white fish with a large fin on top along with others with proportionate fins of smaller size had eaten him, while he was fishing for sea aurochs. Hawk called the beast a whale, but others were certain it was a fish. His body was at sea. She thought how the People had refused to fish for sea aurochs for a while. By this time they had returned to it assuring themselves they'd avoid or leave the water, if fins appeared on the surface. They carried rocks to hit together underwater to warn the fishers to surface. So far, no one else had encounters with the large black and white fish.

The season had just changed. Trees were just leafing out. Soon green would color the land that in the cold times lost color, resorting to black and white on land, leaving color to the sky. Flowers would bloom to bring color to the ground; hardwoods would green up. Tuksook's favorites were the lovely wild roses and the pink plant that grew where fires from lightning had burned up forests.

The dogs made low growls, so Tuksook and Mi looked to see whether there was a boat on the river. They looked at the dogs. The dogs walked about stiff-legged, their hackles up. Hunters who noticed ran to the various places where they looked from the near to the distance to see what they could see. Nobody saw anything.

"I wonder what's making them restless and set them to guarding," Tuksook mumbled to Mi.

Hunters gathered together in the meadow by the center stone. No one had seen anything. The dogs had calmed. The People returned to what they'd been doing.

A little later, the dogs became restless again, pacing and uttering low growls. Then they calmed again.

Amuin hit rocks together calling all to the evening meal. People gathered from all over the meadow and nearby places. That night they had fresh sea aurochs. That was always viewed as a treat. As they finished eating, there was a loud noise and a large crash. People looked at each other in horror as the ground began to move beneath them. They could see the rise and fall of the land in the meadow. Dogs were cowering in their house. People who had been in the bent tree house ran outside. Some little children in one part of the meadow would be on their feet and then in an eyeblink they were lying on their backs. Then, they'd stand again, not of their own doing. The ground shook so that Tuksook, Gumui, and Mi were thrown to the ground. Trees were leaning one way and then they would sway to lean the other way.

Tuksook remembered the guidance of Wisdom that she had practiced for five years. "Wisdom!" she shouted looking at the sky and trying to rise to her feet on the violently shaking ground.

She looked at Gumui with her eyes and her ears heard that special voice, "Check the fires."

"Gumui," she said with her voice shaking from the shaking of the ground, "It's going to be very important to check for fire in the bent tree house."

Gumui managed to rise to his feet, and he began to run on the still shaking ground. He headed to the bent tree house. A large limb that hung over Tuksook and Mi broke off, and it landed on Tuksook's right leg and foot, up to the knee.

"Want me to find Father?" Mi asked when she saw the huge limb on her mother's leg.

"No," Tuksook told her, looking up to see whether any more branches could fall on them. She didn't see any. Her leg began as horribly painful when the limb hit, but the feeling had decreased to one of pressure, not searing pain. She sat up as the rolling subsided.

"Mother, your leg has to be a mess," distraught Mi said.

Tuksook touched Mi and said, calmly, "Mi, stop worrying. I'm in Wisdom's hands. Be quiet. I have things I must do."

Elders gathered around her. She was their Wise One, even if pinned to the ground. Tuksook had listened to the guidance from Wisdom.

She told them, "Do not worry over me right now. Search through all the People. Bring any who are terribly injured to the meadow away from trees. Use stretchers, don't carry them in your arms. If they have broken bones, you don't want to make matters worse by carrying them bent. Gather the injured together. Do you know if Item is doing well?"

"Item is fine," Anvel assured her, "a little shaken, but she is unhurt."

"Good, ask her to gather people who can treat injuries. Have those who can treat injuries go to the meadow to wait for the most critical cases that are likely to survive. Bring the critically injured first. I understand we had some die?"

Hawk said, "Yes, Guw and Kiramuat both died. Gilo is probably going to die later. He has a terrible head injury, but he breathes."

Tuksook nodded.

"Be sure that you know where every one of the People is. Have the ones who are well check the meadow and the nearby places People commonly go. We must find any who are injured."

At the far north end of the meadow, Limilow was shouting at Yumo. "We could've stayed in the old land. You brought us here. It was supposed to be a wonderful land. Well, it becomes horribly cold in the cold times, and now this. I'm scared and my mind web is screaming. I hate this. I hate it. This land is cursed."

Yumo was trying desperately to calm her, but she would not be calmed. Some of the People had circled around them and were agreeing with some of what she said. Yumo was frustrated but realized her words could make things a lot worse. He slapped her.

When she looked at him, he said, "Wife, control yourself. From fear, you say many things about which you know nothing. You need to find the children to be sure they are well, not make a laughing bird out of yourself. Fear has you in its grips. Break out of it now. You are unhurt, so you are needed to help those who are hurt. The rest of you," he said looking at those who had gathered, "go to the aid of those who are injured. Now!"

The People scattered, each looking for others who might have been hurt.

Tuksook said, "Elders, we already know we need two graves, maybe more. Some of those who are in fear, have them start digging. Please, someone, check to be sure Gumui is well. He went to see whether fire was a problem in the bent tree house, and he has not returned."

Hamaklob went running.

Tuksook continued. "If you find anyone who is unhurt and is not busy in the way of the People, tell them to do something that you can think of to make them busy with purpose. Being busy should remove the fear from their mind webs. Finally, some People need to check the river level."

The elders went to carry out the things she told them.

Hawk sat in front of Tuksook, so it was easier for her to see him.

Without waiting for a nod, Hawk said, "Wise One, you are injured badly. You know that. Should I call Gumui and Item now?"

"No, Hawk, my dear friend. Not yet. As long as the log doesn't move I'm fine for the present. Listen to what I'm about to say, so you can tell my mother. Don't move the log off my leg until someone is ready to take care of my leg. My leg must be removed below the knee. If necessary it may be that you have to shorten the bone in the upper leg, because there must be skin left to cover the end of the remaining leg. Someone must thoroughly wash the opened part of my leg with salt water. Any vessels that bleed from the leg must be burned with a hot coal quickly. The skin that remains must be sewed together. If any of the students of Kouchu have the belly for it, they would do good work. Then someone will have to cover it with honey and whatever the preservative herbs are available and wrap it."

"Tuksook, I'm so sorry this happened to you."

"Hawk, I could be dead. I'm grateful to be alive. Once I heal, I can still do what I am supposed to do. That is good. Any sign of Gumui?"

"Yes, he comes here now. I will go to number the People to be sure we have them all."

Tuksook nodded.

Gumui arrived and sat cross-legged facing Tuksook. "Tuksook, I'm so glad you mentioned checking the hearths. There were two hearths that had caught some skins on fire when they fell off bench/sleeping places. If you hadn't said what you did when you did, we could have lost the bent tree house."

"How is damage to the bent tree house other than fire?" she asked.

Gumui had difficulty looking at her leg under the limb, but he replied, "Many tree branches that were tied together to make the top broke the ties. We will have to use the handholds to climb up to retie them and then re-mud. We need to replace some blocks of grass squares. Many things scattered all over the ground where the jerky, tools, weapons, and other things are stored. We must clean that up and replace some split sea aurochs skins that cover the house. Some of the openings that are covered by the poled squares above must be repaired. A few trees seemed to have been pulled to lean when the land rippled, but the ties and the connections of bamboo we attached to the trees, they held well. Some bench/sleeping places may need to be repaired. Now, Wise One and wife, it is very important to take care of you."

"Not yet. The tree keeps me from bleeding. Just don't move the tree. I will have my mother take care of the removal of the leg with the help of hunters, if necessary. I just gave the information to Hawk. I want to wait until those who need help from healers have it. I can wait. When my mother has finished there, she can take care of me here. We will need salt water, honey, and whatever plants are used for wounds. We also need needles and probably horse hair, since it's strong, to sew up the flaps of skin over the bone."

"The pain will be unbearable," Gumui said.

"Can you hit my head so I sleep the sleep from which one cannot be awakened, so I can bear this? Can you do it without interfering with the way my mind web works?"

Gumui, sitting in front of her, put his hands on his head and bent way down. Her request was one he could readily understand, but he could not guarantee that a blow to the head was ever a safe thing to do. Gumui told Tuksook.

Tuksook looked far out over the river level that she could see from where she sat. She wondered if she would shame herself. She could not ask Gumui to do what she knew frightened him.

Gumui sat up straight. He looked all around himself for someone speaking. "Gumui," the voice said, "When she is unaware hit her where you see the light on her head. I will guard her mind web."

Gumui looked at Tuksook. "I heard Wisdom's voice."

"I remembered to call on Wisdom when the quake began. Gumui, listen to the words of Wisdom. Don't be afraid." Tuksook looked at him with love. Mi had walked over to him and sat on his leg.

Gumui lifted Mi to her feet. She stood as he rose up. Item was approaching.

"Oh, no!" Item exclaimed.

"Hawk has talked to you, Mother?"

"Yes, Tuksook."

"Have all the injured been treated?" Tuksook asked.

"Yes," Item replied while she was already thinking of how best to take care of Tuksook, while silently groaning from her belly at the sight.

"Then, I am ready as soon as you are."

Some women were arriving from the meadow carrying armfuls of things. Hawk brought salt water bags and a skin of honey.

Item told Gumui to run for some sleeping skins, at least two of them. He ran. Mi stood there fretting over Tuksook.

When Gumui returned he looked at Mi. "Remember telling me that if I wanted to do something without you, just to tell you to go somewhere and stay there?"

"Yes, Father."

"Go now to the bent tree house. Sit on your bench until I come for you. If you hear Tuksook cry out, cover your ears, but remain where you are. I will come for you. Don't argue with me. Go now." He kissed her forehead.

She went.

Gumui knelt behind Tuksook. He'd told no one about Wisdom's words to him. He waited for his opportunity to strike. He saw Tuksook rigidly trying to be brave. He struck. Tuksook was in the sleep from which no one can awaken another.

"Thank you, Gumui," Item said. "That makes it so much easier on her and the rest of us."

"Gumui, put a skin under her. Remove her tunic, and put the second skin over her," Item instructed.

"Where are the coals?" Item asked a little louder than she intended. "Do you have the sticks to hold them?

Gumui said, "They are here and so is the holding stick."

"Thank you, Gumui," Item said. "I need you and Hawk to take the log off her leg. If you must vomit, do it far from here. The leg will be a mess. I don't want to complicate things by having something like vomit around." As she talked she tied a leather band around the upper part of Tuksook's leg.

The two men tried to move the tree limb, but it was old, big, and very heavy.

"Roll it off," Item snapped at them. "It won't matter."

They pushed it as hard as they could, and it finally moved. Gumui was revolted by the sight of the damage. He'd never seen something so awful, and it was part of his wife. His belly seized. He wanted to vomit, but he toughened himself to recognize what Tuksook always said, "What is—is." Gumui wanted to be there in case of a need he could fill.

"Gumui," Item said, "Go to the house and ask Heek to supply a poultice of mother of red rash root. That part of the plant will help her, not hurt her."

"Hawk," Item said sharply, "come here and take the coals. Be ready to put a coal against the bleeding vessels and hold it there while you count to three. You have to stop the bleeding fast."

Hawk picked up the coal holders and lifted a coal from the stone bowl. He began to stop the bleeding of one vessel at a time. When he finished, Item removed the band she'd tied around the remains of the leg. There was no significant bleeding. Hawk seared the few vessels that threatened to bleed. Item was trimming the skin to make it possible to sew together as neatly as possible.

All of the People working on Tuksook were deadly silent. They separated the leg and there was adequate skin to pull over the rounded part of the leg bone, so it didn't have to be cut off to bring the skin together. That pleased Item.

As she worked she asked, "Of those of you brought here to sew, tell me which of you does the best."

Everyone pointed to Mo, Rimut and Pito's daughter, who had been raised by Hamaklob and Amuin.

"Mo, start thinking. You have to sew this skin to cover the end of Tuksook's leg. Forget that it's the Wise One and just start thinking how to best sew it together.

"Before you sew, run your horse hair through the honey in this bowl," Item told her.

"I will," she acknowledged. She'd have done anything not to have the task, but she took it on and thought seriously about the best way to sew it together. She was doing this for the People's Wise One. She needed to do her very best.

Mo dropped her head low. Wisdom, she prayed silently, I need you to help me. Mo did not know that people all around Tuksook were also sending their wishes to Wisdom. Tuksook slept through it all.

"It is time to pour salt water over the end of the leg to clean out anything that might be in there," Item said quietly.

Gumui picked up the first skin of salt water and emptied it in a shower over the end of Tuksook's leg. Then, he emptied the second one, stopping midway to pick off a piece of what looked like dirt. Then, he emptied the second bag being sure to wash it over the place where he'd found the little piece of dirt.

"Mo," Item said, "It's ready for you to sew."

Mo sat with the end of the leg propped on her upper leg. She dragged the hair through the honey and began to pull the skin together. She spent more time than some of the others would have, but she wanted to make it as pucker free as possible. Item first sat and then stretched out on her back while Mo worked. She was very tired, and she worried for her daughter. As she lay there, Za came with both a piece of leather and a band of leather.

"Item," Za said, "I remembered a piece of new leather that was clean and very soft. I hunted until I found it. I think this might help."

"Thank you, Za. It was kind of you to search for it. I appreciate that." She took the leather from Za.

Just in time, Heek arrived with the mashed mother of red rash root. She laid it near Item.

"Thank you, Heek," Item said.

"I was happy to do it, Item," Heek replied and left for the bent tree house.

"I'm going to return to help with the little children," she said. Za had no desire to be near the place where People were working on Tuksook's leg.

Mo finished with the sewing. She laid Tuksook's leg on the skin where Tuksook lay. Item took some honey and rubbed it into the leg where it had been sewed. Then, she took the boiled and mashed mother of red rash root and applied it to Tuksook's leg at the place where the honey was applied and around it. She took the soft leather, using it to cover the end of the leg and tied it with the band of leather, careful not to tie it too tight.

Item looked at Gumui and said, "Take her to your sleeping place now. I will tend to her wound for as many days as it takes."

Gumui scooped her up without the bottom skin and carried her to the bent tree house. When he arrived, Mi was sitting there anxiously waiting.

Gumui laid Tuksook carefully on the sleeping place. Part of the bench/sleeping place gave slightly, probably loosened during the earthquake.

"Mi, do you mind if I put Tuksook on your sleeping place with you, until I can repair this one?"

"I'd like that a lot," she assured him, "I'll look out for her."

Mi looked at her mother lying there with half a leg. She was glad she hadn't seen the leg where the log fell on it. She was glad she didn't see her mother's leg cut off. Mi wanted her to wake up, but she did nothing to try to encourage her to awaken. She simply sat there watching over her, ready to run for her father, if Tuksook stirred.

Gumui returned to begin to repair their bench/sleeping place.

Cadpo walked over to Gumui and said, "We need Mi to tell the creation story for Guw and Kiramuat."

Gumui looked up and told Mi, "Go with her, Mi. Do your best telling the creation story. Return here when you've finished. To Cadpo he said, "Please, ask the grave diggers to bury the eight bones we found in the ground at this time and the remains of Tuksook's leg."

"I will," she said and went hand-in-hand with Cadpo. "I will also," Cadpo echoed.

Finding himself alone, he said, "Wisdom, I'm sure you're here. Will Tuksook wake up today?"

That unique, quiet voice said, "No, Gumui. She will sleep for three more full days, awakening on the morning of the fourth day."

"Wisdom, may I ask you? Is the earthquake over?"

"There will be tiny jolts for a brief time. None will do further damage."

"Thank you, Wisdom," Gumui whispered.

Gumui felt as if Wisdom touched his shoulder, but he dismissed the idea. Wisdom was spirit.

Gumui found another place on their bench/sleeping place that needed to be repaired. He took time to repair it well. When he finished, he laid aside the tools and leather strips, and moved Tuksook to lie on her habitual sleeping place. He sat near her head and stroked her head gently. His belly was torn because she had suffered so much. Why, he wondered, did this happen to her?

Mi returned carrying Tuksook's tunic. Gumui hung it on the peg.

"Is she sick?" Mi asked.

"No, she's injured," Gumui replied absently.

Sounding far away, a flute played several tunes, quiet ones that were calming.

"Mi," Gumui asked, "will you watch her?"

"Of course, Father," she replied.

Gumui went quickly to put the tools away and then he went outside to find some of the elders. He told them he'd conduct the council after the evening meal.

They said they'd tell the People, because Gumui at that moment wanted to return to Tuksook.

A little later, Amuin hit the rocks together. People went to the food preparation area, took their bowls, and sat to eat some distance from the reach of any trees.

Not knowing Gumui intended to have a council that evening, Item had gone to his bench/sleeping place to tell him to go to eat and attend the council. She would watch over Tuksook with Mi there to run errands, if necessary. She carried two bowls of food. One for herself and one for Mi.

Gumui thanked her and left to eat and prepare his mind web for the council. He wanted to do what he thought Tuksook would have done.

He ate camel, but hardly noticed what it was. He ate because he was expected to eat.

The People expressed their sympathy for Tuksook and wishes for a quick recovery. It was polite, but the words didn't penetrate the sea aurochs-like skin he'd imaginatively put around himself. He was hard to reach and his feelings were blunted.

When the council began, Gumui said, "I am a substitute for Tuksook until she can return. She still sleeps the sleep from which others cannot waken her. I want to know how Gilo is doing."

Anvel said, "He is awake but seems disoriented. Shut is with him."

"Are there any other injuries?"

Silence.

Gumui said, "I'm sorry to hear that Gilo is disoriented. I have some words to say. Wisdom, please, hear my cry. We have had a tough day today and two of our People are in serious condition. Please, watch over them and restore them their function as participating members of the People."

All the People at council lowered their heads.

Gumui continued, "Tuksook knew part of what happened today would happen some day. She knew that the land moves. You can't feel it, but it moves. Sometimes it hits a barrier. Imagine removing the grass from the ground until you reach the dirt. Imagine pushing the dirt for a little way, and then it hits a barrier. To keep moving, it's necessary to break that barrier. Today the earth broke a barrier that had kept it from moving. There may be some very small earthquakes that follow, but they probably won't do any damage."

Gumui said, "There are things that need to be done to repair the bent tree house. Tomorrow, after the morning meal, those who will work on the bent tree house, find me in the meadow. Then, those who don't wish to repair the house will need to explore outside to see whether any trees are weakened and might fall. You'll need to cut down trees that are weakened. We can use the wood for our hearths."

Gumui paused and then said, "Has anyone checked the boats and oars?"

Stencellomak reported that the boats were all unharmed and the oars were safely tied inside the boats.

"How are the dogs?" Gumui asked.

Elfa replied, "The dogs are doing well, without injury, some a little anxious yet."

"Is there anyone who would like to speak?" he asked.

There was silence. All People had their heads lowered.

"Then, let's end the council and return to the bent tree house. This has been a troubling day."

They returned quietly.

"Item, thank you for watching Tuksook while I ate and took Tuksook's place at council."

"You're welcome. Remember, she's my daughter. I will be here often to care for her. I have placed plenty of sphagnum moss under her, because she cannot run to the privy. While I sat here, I reasoned that you might construct another inside privy like you did for Kouchu. That will be a lot better for her than trying to use the outside privy with one leg."

"Thank you, Item. That's a very good idea. I'll do it."

"Do you have a hug for your grandmother, Mi?"

"I do!" Mi said, throwing her arms around Item who sat next to her.

"If you stir this night, touch her. Tell me if she becomes hot," Item told Gumui.

"I will do that also, Item."

"Gumui, before you sleep, take a damp cloth and wipe the inside of her mouth. Any time you see her mouth becoming too dry looking, do it."

"I will do that Item. Thank you again."

Item left and Mi went to Gumui for comfort.

"She's not going to die, is she?" the young girl asked.

"I don't think so, Mi. She is tough and she is a good Wise One. You're not ready to be Wise One yet, and Wisdom rarely leaves People without one."

"You'd be a good Wise One, Father."

"No, Little Feather, I don't have the memory for the stories."

"You haven't called me Little Feather for a long time."

"I know. I just feel very close to you this evening. You'd better go to your sleeping place now. Tomorrow will be a busy day. I expect, while I make repairs around the bent tree house, that you will watch over your mother while you recite stories."

"I will do that. I'll do my stories as if Mother were actually listening." Mi hung up her tunic and climbed into her sleeping place and pulled the covers over herself.

The flute played in the distance for a short while.

In the south part of the bent tree house, Limilow and Yumo sat on the edge of their bench.

"Why did you slap me today?" Limilow asked.

"Wife, you let your fear overtake your mind web. You babbled nonsense and others who also were wrapped in fear began to listen to you. Fear brings more fear. We had enough of it without adding more. To keep things calm I had to stop you, for you refused to calm yourself."

"I'm sorry. I was terrified. I felt as if what is inside me might explode outwards, waiting for another earthquake that lasts forever. I panicked. I will keep my mouth closed, if we have another earthquake, to avoid increasing the fright of others. I see now that all is well."

He put his arm around her. They sat side-by-side for a short time, then each undressed and crawled into their sleeping place to cover up with soft skins.

On the morning of the fourth day, Tuksook stirred. Mi ran through the house, a forbidden act, to find Item. She found her in the far south part of the bent tree house.

"Grandmother, she's waking up!" Mi shouted.

Item, too, came at a run.

Tuksook lay there confused at first and then the memory of the day of the earthquake blindsided her. She felt pain in her leg, and realized that part of her leg was gone. Tears fell from her eyes.

"Gumui?" she murmured.

Item said, "Tuksook, easy. Mi will find Gumui," Item nodded at Mi to find her father.

"Mother, I lost part of my leg?"

"Yes, but you seem to be doing well, even better now that you're awake."

"I did not dream. Where I was did not seem like sleep, it was as if dead— all black, all silent."

"I know, Daughter. Before we began work on your leg, Gumui hit your head and caused you to sleep that sleep from which others cannot awaken you."

"I asked him to do it," Tuksook said, still partially asleep. "He didn't want to do it. He feared it would affect my mind web."

Item put her hand on Tuksook's shoulder. "You'll do well. You must learn to walk using sticks to hold you up. Right now, I need to check the healing of your wound and put a new cover on it."

Item lifted the sleeping skin off Tuksook's leg. She sent Mi for the moss she'd boiled earlier. Item removed the covering that protected the leg. Instead of untying the part that held the skin to her, Item slipped it off the leg as if removing a boot, and examined the wound. She had never seen a wound of this size heal so well. It still drained somewhat, but that was normal. She thought back. The second night Tuksook had burned with raging heat to the touch and shivered with chills. Item feared for her life, knowing that sometimes, sickness from the wound turned bad and could take a life. Despite the excessive heat she had felt on Tuksook's skin, by the next afternoon, Tuksook's body heat returned to what was normal for healthy People.

Gumui arrived. He hugged Tuksook, slightly colliding with Item.

"Item, forgive me. I'm sorry," he said.

"You're forgiven, Gumui," she said with a knowing smile. Gumui, she saw, was relieved as much as she was.

Tuksook was still somewhat foggy, but she hugged Gumui with all the strength she could. "You hit me so I would sleep. Thank you, Gumui. Thank you so much," she murmured and let her arms fall to the sleeping place, for they seemed too heavy.

Mi arrived with the moss and a skin that she'd seen Item use when cleaning the wound. Item took the skin and placed it under Tuksook's short leg. She took the very warm moss and pressed it against the wound. She held it there, warming Tuksook's wound. Then, she replaced that moss with an additional application that still was warm. She wiped the wound.

"Mi, I need the honey and poultice."

By the time Item said half the words, Mi was gone. She knew exactly what Item needed. She returned with both things, walking as quickly as possible without running.

"That warmth feels comforting," Tuksook mumbled, slipping back to sleep—this time a real sleep.

"Mi," Item said, "you are a good help."

"Thank you, Grandmother," she replied, leaning against Item with her arm around Item's back. "I think she looks better."

"She is healing very well. This is not what I'd normally expect. I expect Wisdom has a hand in this."

Mi looked at her grandmother. She said, "He has answered many requests for good healing."

Item put her arm around Mi. "Yes, he has."

As the days passed, Tuksook began to make herself mobile. Single-mindedly she focused on the task. She asked for some sticks with a forked top to make the sticks People sometimes used when they had a sprained ankle or broken foot bone. She lined the top of the sticks with soft beaver fur. Gumui observed, but he didn't mention, the patience she was showing. That was something Tuksook had never shown to this extent. She used the inside privy he had constructed with Stencellomak's help. She had limited mobility by hopping. It was enough to have her there and back to her bench/sleeping place.

In time the covering was removed from the end of Tuksook's short leg. She was able to go outside to the meadow to walk. Daily her proficiency with the walking sticks grew. Her only sadness was that she could no longer walk to the rock where she and Gumui at times, and she and Mi at other times, had spent so many days. She would look at it realizing that there were some things she could no longer do. Because of her conviction that feelings should align with the concept of what is—is, she did not show self pity or anger. They were not part of her. Tuksook accepted what came and tried her utmost to make the best of it. She had not forgotten the shower of roses as blessings. She and Mi recited stories while sitting on the rocks at the edge of the meadow.

"Mother," Mi said after finishing reciting a story, "People are amazed by you."

"What do you mean, Mi?"

"I hear them sometimes say things like, 'She's a solid example to us.'"

"I don't want People to have the wrong idea, Mi. If I have done anything here, it's to make it so I can walk with my walking sticks. I want to be able to move about. That's how I can do it. It's not a big thing."

"Well, some of the People think it is. Jowlichi is really impressed."

"I'll have to think how to change that. I don't want People impressed with me."

"Mother, there are, as you well know, some things you have to live with."

"Wisdom cautions against it."

"I know. Even so, Mother, I am impressed. Could I do what you've done without self pity? I doubt it."

"I don't wish you to have that feeling."

"Mother, it's something you have to live with. You don't seem to know how you appear to other People."

Amuin hit the rocks together, calling out the evening meal. For the first time, Tuksook was very hungry. It surprised her that she was hungry. She hadn't thought about food since the accident.

She and Mi walked to the food preparation area. Gumui filled Tuksook's bowl.

"Gumui, that's too much!" Tuksook protested.

"You need to fatten yourself a little, Tuksook. Eat all of it."

Mi always found it amusing when Tuksook and Gumui differed on something. They didn't ever argue as many of the People did. They each were so nice about it. She had seen Tuksook make a face at Gumui, but her eyes were soft and loving, not squinty in the way that the People who argued used their faces. She watched People, but most of all she watched her parents.

The leaves had fully burst forth and the land was predominantly green. It was Tuksook's favorite time of the year. It was a time of hope, she felt, a time of rebirth. In her mind web, she thought of the seasons on the earth as phases of life: the greening time was a time of hope and birth, which led to death and rebirth as a spirit with Wisdom. She knew that the people of Wikroak believed they returned to earth after death, not as spirits but as living creatures or another person. Tuksook did not believe that. Both views saw cycles, but Tuksook could not accept people transforming to other people or living creatures. When, she wondered, would it end, and then what? She viewed the cycle linearly as, first, a spiritual seed. Second, at some time Wisdom touched the seed in the woman giving it life. Third, the birth of the baby occurred which grew to a child. Fourth, the time of growing from child to full grown youth occurred with all its strength and promise and self-centeredness. Fifth, the time of maturity and understanding the way of Wisdom and the way of the People occurred with its knowledge and recognition of the importance of putting others before themselves. Sixth, decline and death occurred. Seventh, a rebirth as a spiritual body in which individuals would be recognizable to those who were in the navel of the earth and had known that person in life. Tuksook also saw life as one part of a three part cycle: spirit to physical body to spirit. To those who asked, that was how she explained it. She believed it.

Tuksook walked to the edge of the meadow to see a returning boat. She wondered if they had caught more than one sea aurochs. Her long leg was not comfortable standing too long, so she sat on one of the carved rocks to watch.

Huaga walked over to her.

"Tuksook, it appears they have two sea aurochs," Huaga said.

"It's hard for me to see the ropes," she replied.

"It looks like two to me. I want you to know that some of the best years of my life have been spent living in this meadow."

"You don't miss the sea?" she asked.

"Sometimes I do. The sea can be like a wife."

"That's an interesting thought," Tuksook laughed.

"No, Tuksook, I'm serious. It has a call to it, an allure, lighting the fires of desire. It can present you the greatest heights and the deepest lows."

"I see," she commented.

"Tuksook, did you lose your leg, because you merited it by doing something wrong?"

Tuksook laughed a hearty laugh. Then, she said, "I'm not really laughing at you, Huaga, but that question is not a question one asks, when they live in Wisdom's way."

"Tuksook, I've been a boatman most of my life. I've called on Wisdom when the boat was in peril, or I thought it was. However, my knowledge of Wisdom is very shallow."

"Let me try to explain, Huaga. Would you like to sit on one of these stones?"

"Yes," he replied and sat.

"Huaga, each person is born with a purpose. All of us have different purposes, which is why we do well here at the meadow. There are many things that need doing. If we all had the same purpose, we might lack for shelter, food, warmth, and even knowledge of Wisdom. Our purpose begins with Wisdom. Each of us has at least one thing to accomplish. You have had more than one, and so has Gumui. I have one—Wise One. But as with others, sometimes there are other purposes that don't show immediately. I have lost a leg, not through Wisdom's retribution but for two reasons: the first is for me to learn patience, and the second is so that others can learn something from observing me. You, for example, wondered whether I'd done something wrong. You can learn today that such a thing is not Wisdom's way in my case, though in some other cases it could be."

"When my leg was pinned to the ground, I knew I had a small purpose within the larger one: to be sure all that needed to be done was done, and nothing was overlooked. I leaned on Wisdom for that. Elders and others would come to my presence and feel great pity for me. I had known for a long time I had to break through fear after the earthquake and have damage repaired whether to People or things like the bent tree house."

"But weren't you in terrible pain?"

"Have you ever had a serious injury, Huaga?"

"Yes."

"First, there was great pain. Then, do you remember a time when you didn't feel any pain for a short while?"

"Now that you put it that way, I think I do."

"It's a good thing that can save our lives sometimes when the body temporarily cuts off the pain so we can do what is immediately in our best interest."

"I think I understand."

"My best interest was first to find all the People to see where the injuries were and have them treated, and second, my interest was to be sure that things were taken care of. I needed that period of painlessness to do that. Once my contribution was made to the People, I could deal with my leg."

"I understand."

"When I awakened after being in that dark sleep from which I could not have been awakened, I didn't ask myself what I did wrong. I thanked Wisdom that my life continued."

"That's not how most People would see it," Huaga said.

"I wish I could change that. The key to the change is to know that every single thing that happens to a person is a blessing from Wisdom. People facing very tough times might have trouble seeing that, but if they could only focus on how the things they dislike are blessings, it changes their whole way of being. The focus becomes the time consuming effort to track the thoughts of Wisdom—not feeling sorry for self. I can only do that and be an example. Others can learn from it or not. That is how Wisdom works."

"You make me think thoughts I've never thought."

"What do you think of that?"

The boat had arrived at the shore and in fact there were two ropes hanging off the back of the boat. Huaga stood to take a better look.

"Do you need to go, Huaga?"

"No, I just wanted to see what they caught. It's two sea aurochs. What do I think of your words? It's hard for me to look at the People remaining in the drought and see blessing of any kind."

"Again you missed the point. The drought was fact, neither good nor bad—just something that happens in the earth from time to time and place to place. The blessing was that Wisdom told my father, Midgenemo, to leave the area, to travel by boat to a new place. Many heard Wisdom through my father's words, and some heard but set up a barricade to the full message. It is a blessing that some were saved. Those who stayed behind suffered starvation, not because their decision merited it, but rather that they chose to live a life that had a certain end in starvation. You returned there and gave them yet another opportunity to flee the drought. For whatever reason, they chose to stay. They may have feared boat travel more than starving, or they may have had a false hope that the drought would soon end. It's not that Wisdom is punishing them for something; it's that twice they had the opportunity to leave something they knew was awful, and they rejected it. The first time they rejected the leading of Wisdom. The second time they rejected your leading. They chose to remain where they'd surely die. They knew that. Wisdom didn't choose to slay them, they chose to die."

"You have relieved me of a heavy burden," Huaga said from somewhere deep within himself.

"How's that?" Tuksook asked.

"I have blamed myself for their starvation, as if I neglected to try hard enough, or because I took the food I planned to share over the cold times and used the food for the sea crossing."

"Had you left the food, you'd only have prolonged the inevitable."

"I understand, Tuksook. I feel as if you've taken my mind web and shaken it vigorously. Out of that I feel freed from guilt I carried since we left the old land the last time."

Tuksook laughed. "Stay free of it, my friend."

"Tuksook, is there anything I can do for you?"

"My needs are few and small, but there is one thing you can do for me, because you are big and very strong. I would like very much to spend the time from now until the evening meal on the rock up the hill where it's warm and I have loved the view. I'm too heavy for Gumui to carry and safely climb the hill. People work up there today. I would be safe."

"I can do it and would be more than happy to do it. Do you want to go now?"

"Yes, I'd love that," Tuksook replied, taking her walking sticks and standing. Together they walked to the path that led up to the stone.

Huaga's experience on the boat had made him very surefooted. He carried Tuksook up to the rock and put her down on it. He said, "I'll return in an eye blink, well maybe more than one."

Huaga came back with some jerky and a small bag of water. "I'll return when Amuin hits those rocks together."

"Thank you, Huaga," she replied. Comfort surrounded her that she usually felt on the rock.

Tuksook leaned against the rock behind the one on which she sat. She viewed the lowland river and the meadow, taking in each detail that she hadn't seen in years. She shut her eyes in rest. The rays of the sun were warming indeed. She felt wonderful.

Solitude at last! Tuksook reveled in it, and suddenly she slipped the bonds of the physical world to slide into the spiritual one.

"Wisdom!" Tuksook said, not realizing she walked on two long legs. She went up the steps in the special place Wisdom made to represent himself to her. She threw her arms around his knee and looked up into his face. The compassion she saw there overwhelmed her.

"Tuksook, I have something I can say to you now. You have grown strong and straight right to the sun."

Tuksook remembered the words and quickly she remembered asking Wisdom to let her grow to the sun, and Wisdom told her she had to experience troubled times and learn patience before she could grow to the sun. The person she'd seen grow to the sun was Oneg, a child immobilized by a broken leg. While spending day after day alone in the bent tree house, Oneg used her time to learn to play the flute. Her playing it had given joy and contentment to those who heard it year after year.

"But, Wisdom, I haven't learned patience, so how could I learn to grow to the sun?"

"Tuksook, while you labored to walk, you learned patience with the People and yourself. When you took time to explain things to others that would relieve their bad feelings, you learned patience. Before the earthquake, your impatience was sad to see. You lost faith. You turned again fully to the physical world, instead of remaining open to the spiritual world. You expected things told to you in the spiritual world to occur within the time constraints of the physical world. You were given a long time to learn patience, and you rejected it. Then, the earthquake struck, and you remembered what you'd learned in the spiritual world. After you waked up from the removal of your shattered leg, you had nothing but patience. Many others saw and marveled at your patience. You set a good example. In doing so you began to grow to the sun."

The beaming of Wisdom's face was something Tuksook had never seen. She gazed on it entranced. Suddenly it occurred to her that she had two long legs. "Wisdom what is this—I have two long legs?"

"When you live in the spirit you are whole, regardless of what happened in life. You are whole except for your physical body. While you live in the physical world, you have a long and short leg. When you come to live in the spiritual world, you'll have two long legs."

"Wisdom," Tuksook said after a long silence, "You gave me patience in the same way that you gave me the stories. I see it as your doing, not mine."

Wisdom smiled, saying nothing.

"Will you tell me whether we have to face yet another earthquake like the big one we just experienced?"

"Tuksook, you have no need to know, but I will tell you this, the land will experience many more of these jolts, some even larger. The size of the one you just experienced was a large one. In the lifetime of all the People who live in the meadow, none will ever experience another of this size. There will, however, be many of smaller size."

"Thank you, Wisdom. May I ask whether there are any of the People left in the old land."

"None of the ones your People knew. There are others at the edges of the drought, and yet others where the drought has had no effect."

"Will you explain to me how it is that we will be carried into the world by the People who were called Minguat?"

"Tuksook, I have told you that the People live in others. A part of your father lives in you. A part of Ki'ti lives in you. That does not mean a piece of that person, instead it is an unseen essence that is in every part of you and is passed to you through your parents, such as the color of your hair, eyes, and skin, and many other things. Other than that, you lack the ability to understand the actual way it occurs."

Tuksook changed the subject. "Wisdom, Mi is an extraordinary child."

"Some children seek and find me early in their lives. Living with you and Gumui has caused her to see the world differently. She will be a blessing to the People even as you are blessing her."

"Wisdom, I'm overwhelmed."

"Tuksook, I speak to you only fact."

"I love you Wisdom. Please be closer to me than we have been in the recent past."

"You have only to call on me. You know that."

"Sometimes I've felt your presence as if you walked right beside me."

"I am always there, Tuksook, it is your spiritual openness that makes you feel me there. But I am always there beside you."

"Then, the times I've felt spiritually alone, I was just closing off the spiritual world? It was my doing, not yours."

"Correct. Despite your closing me off, I was still there. You were just closed to me."

"Wisdom, I regret that I shortened the time I could have had with you."

"Remember that for the future."

"Oh, Wisdom, at times like now, when you tell me I have grown to the sun, I feel like the very young children who are kept confined to a small area until they show evidence that they can be given more ability to remain in the meadow. I don't mean that you've confined me. I mean that I am that spiritually deficient. Do I ever grow past this child-like level of spiritual development?"

"That depends. Most Wise Ones make it to the level of understanding that you have. Some who continue to push to know me better, go beyond. But that is rare, rare indeed. I know your thoughts, Tuksook. That is why you have pleased me. I will answer the question you will not ask. You and Gumui both have very long life lines. Now I will charge you with responsibility—lead the People well. Keep them strong, focused on right living in the way of the People and in my way. Continue as you have been doing. Know that when you come to the spirit world, you will grow fast. There is no hurry now."

Tuksook looked at Wisdom speechless.

"Tuksook, tell Gumui to stay awake until all in the house sleep but the entryway guards. Tell Gumui to climb to the rock. Tell him to hold his hands from him like this." Wisdom showed her his hands, fingertip to fingertip and heel of hand to heel of hand. "Tell him to open his arms a shoulder width apart. Tell him to wait."

"Tonight?" she asked.

"Yes, Tuksook."

"I will tell him."

Tuksook felt herself drifting back to the rock. She was overwhelmed.

"How did you come up here?" Gumui asked breathless from his climb.

"Huaga asked whether there was anything he could do for me. I asked him to do this. You cannot carry me and make it up the steps, but Huaga is very big and very surefooted. He walked up here with me as easy as if he walked the meadow. When Amuin hits the rocks together, he will carry me down."

"I see," he said. "I'm glad it was Huaga."

"I have a message from Wisdom to you."

"You have what?"

"Wisdom sent you your own message."

"And that is?"

"You are to come to this rock tonight. Sit here and do your hands like this." She showed him. "Once you've done that open your arms a shoulder width, and keep your hands like that—and wait."

Gumui laughed.

"It isn't meant to draw humor," Tuksook said.

"It's just such a strange thing to have me do."

"I'd suggest, my husband, that you do it to see what will happen. I assure you with Wisdom you will not be disappointed."

"I will do it. In fact, I wish it were late already."

"Where's Mi?"

"She's waiting at the bottom of this path for us."

"Please go to her. Huaga will return to me as soon as Amuin hits the rocks together. Then, I'll be down."

"Until then."

"Until then."

Gumui returned down the path to the meadow level. They went to the food preparation area.

"How much longer do we have until the call for the evening meal?" Gumui asked, snitching a string of meat from the sea aurochs roast.

"Almost there, Gumui. And, if you're going to snitch a piece of meat, the least you could do is to take one for Mi, too."

Mi lowered her head, put her hands over her mouth, and giggled.

"Thank you, Amuin," Gumui said, pulling another string of meat and handing it to Mi.

Mi looked up and said, "Thank you, Amuin."

Amuin bent down a little, held her arms open, and Mi went to her quickly for a hug.

Amuin picked up the two rocks and hit them together.

Huaga, who had been working to repair some of the ties on the dog house, finished up the last knot, and headed towards the rock to bring Tuksook down.

"Hi, Tuksook," he said after reaching the top of the path and the rock. "Did you enjoy your time on the rock."

"More than you could even guess," Tuksook said.

"If you'll hold the water skin and your walking sticks, I'll carry you down."

"I'll do it," Tuksook said, the joy of earlier still surrounding her both inside and outside.

"Sitting on that rock must do something special for you," Huaga said as he descended the path with her.

"Huaga, that's a place I often meet with Wisdom. I met with Wisdom today."

"You mean Wisdom was here today?"

Tuksook laughed as he slid her to her foot and held her shoulders until she had her walking sticks in hand. "Wisdom is here every day all day. It's just that we actually talked today."

"This isn't some kind of joke, Tuksook. You really talked like you and I are talking—but with Wisdom?"

"Yes, but Wisdom does not appear as one of the People. Wisdom is spirit. My spirit meets him in the spirit."

"Did you learn anything?"

"Always, Huaga, but today one of the things I learned I'll share at council tonight."

"I have to wait until then."

"Yes." Tuksook smiled her disarming smile.

"Enjoy your evening meal," Huaga said, rethinking what she'd told him. It may be, he thought, I should offer to take her there whenever she feels the desire.

Gumui and Mi were filling the bowls. Tuksook headed towards the place they usually sat to enjoy their evening meal.

"This look good to you?" he asked.

Tuksook looked at the too full bowl again. "It looks wonderful, Gumui. Thank you." She smiled her odd smile at him that told him with her lips he'd filled the bowl too full again.

"You are always welcome," he replied. "Eat it, Tuksook, you need some fat on your bones."

Mi looked at them. She wondered why Gumui kept pushing food at Tuksook. Her mother was terribly thin since the accident, but usually People let each other decide for themselves what they would eat. She did notice, however, that when her father overfilled her mother's bowl, she did eat what he put in it.

The council began shortly after the evening meal clean up.

All assembled and Tuksook asked, "Is there anyone who wishes to speak?"

Vole looked at her.

She nodded.

"There are five of us who plan to go back to the sea to fish. Is anyone willing to make it six People?"

"I would like to go," Velur said.

"Good," Vole replied.

"Anyone wish to speak?"

Item looked at Tuksook.

Tuksook nodded.

"Since you're going to the sea, will you bring me six skins of salt water?"

"We will," Vole promised.

"Anyone wish to speak?"

Silence.

"Well, I have something to share that you will be glad to hear," Tuksook said. "Thanks to the kindness of Huaga, I went to my rock today and sat in the sun. I talked with Wisdom. Wisdom says that during the lifetime of all alive now, there will be no more big earthquakes. Small ones, certainly, but no large ones that can damage the buildings."

"That is welcome information!" Huaga shouted.

"Thank you, Wisdom," Yumo said, thinking of his wife who still had nightmares.

Then, all the People said, "Thank you, Wisdom!" The shout resonated through the air for a long distance deep into the valley.

Then, there was silence.

"Anyone wish to speak?" Tuksook asked again.

Silence.

"The council ends," Tuksook said.

Gumui helped her stand up and handed her the walking sticks. The three of them walked back to the bent tree house.

"Wisdom told you there would be no more bad earthquakes?" Mi asked.

"Yes, Mi. There will come a time when you, too, will spend time talking to Wisdom."

"Me?"

"Yes, dear one, you."

They hugged. Then Gumui and Mi hugged. Mi pulled off her tunic and climbed into the soft sleeping place. Tuksook pulled off her tunic and crawled into her spot on their sleeping place. Gumui also crawled into their sleeping place, but he did not undress. For once Mi didn't notice.

Gumui waited and waited. Finally, after waiting for what he felt was an extremely long time, the bent tree house was filled with sleepers. Gumui cautiously stood up and went outside, careful not to awaken anyone. The entryway guard assumed he left for the privy.

Gumui ran to the path to the rock. He climbed it quickly. He sat on the rock. He did with his hands what Tuksook had told him to do. He waited. His arms began to tire, feeling very heavy. Still he held them out from him and kept them still. After what seemed an endless wait, he began to feel a tingling. He felt as if there were something between his hands. Light danced in the space between his hands.

He wondered whether this was what Wisdom planned to show him. He kept his hands still. What was between his hands continued to move but it changed shape.

That unique voice he'd heard once said, "Do not turn around, Gumui. I am with you."

At the sound of the voice, he almost dropped his hands, but he managed to keep them still. He looked at his hands. Between his hands, a sphere began to form and then it came into very clear focus.

"It's the earth?" he whispered, awestruck.

"Yes," Wisdom said quietly. "I decided to grant you your wish."

"There are no red lines," he remarked.

"The earthquake has reduced the stress, so the red lines are no longer there."

"Wisdom, this is amazing. It's beautiful."

Wisdom was silent.

"Are you still there, Wisdom?"

"Yes."

"What is the white on the top and bottom?"

"Ice."

"Is that the ice that will cover this land?"

"No, that ice is always there."

"Seeing all this—it's something I must keep to myself?"

"Yes, it is. When I permitted Tuksook to share the vision with you, I knew you would not tell anyone because of your strong desire not to speak of what you don't know directly. You don't gossip. But this requires that you not share something of which you have direct knowledge."

"I understand, Wisdom. I will treasure this moment for the rest of my life. To have seen such a beautiful image is precious."

"I leave now, Gumui. You may watch as long as you like. When you put your hands down, it will disappear. Raising them won't bring back the image."

"Wisdom, thank you. I know now why Tuksook yearns for time with you."

Gumui felt a touch on his shoulder.

"You are welcome, Gumui, and though spirit, I can cause you to feel my touch. I leave now."

Gumui watched the slowly turning earth. He tried to put it into memory so he could enjoy seeing it again, forgetting that his hands were tired. He had forgotten who he was or where he was. Gumui was seeing something only one other person he knew had ever seen. It was the most beautiful thing he'd ever known. It was precious. Wisdom had made it. He watched it, fixing details in his mind web, until he felt he contained the full image in memory. He lowered his hands and the strange lights reappeared and then vanished.

Gumui stood up. He thought, I must return to the bent tree house. I cannot wait to share this with Tuksook!

Bibliography

Achilli, A., Perego, U.A., Bravi, C. M., Coble, M. D., Kong, Q.-P., Woodward, S. R., Salas, A., Terroni, A., Bandelt, H.-J., "The Phylogeny of the Four Pan-American MtDNA Haplogroups: Implications for Evolutionary and disease Studies," *PLoS ONE,* 3(3) e1764.

Adovasio, J.M., Page, J., *The First Americans: In Pursuit of Archaeology's Greatest Mystery,* Modern Library, Imprint of Random House, 2003.

Alaska Northwest Books, *Cooking Alaskan by Alaskans,* Alaska Northwest Books, 1983.

Albino, A., Carlini, A., "First Record of *Boa Constrictor* (Serpentes, Boidae) in the Quaternary of South America," *Journal of Herpetology,* March 2008.

Alvarenga, H., Jones, W. Rinderknecht, "The youngest record of phorus-rhacid birds (Aves, Phorusrhacidae) from the late Pleistocene of Uruguay," *N. Jb. Geol. Palaontol. Ahh* 256/2, April 2010. (in English)

Ao, H., Deng, C, Dekkers, M. J., Sun, Y., Liu, Q., Zhu, R., "Pleistocene environmental evolution in the Nihewan Basin and implications for early human colonization of North China," *Quaternary International,* 2010.

Bae, C., "The late Middle Pleistocene hominin fossil record of eastern Asia: Synthesis and review," *American Journal of Physical Anthropology,* supplement yearbook, 143(51), 2010.

Bae, K., "Origin and patterns of the Upper Paleolithic industries in the Korean Peninsula and movement of modern humans in East Asia," *Quaternary International*, 211(1-2), 2010.

BBC Article Cites *Antiquity* on Oldest Evidence of Arrows Found (64,000 years ago), http://www.bbc.com/news/science-environment-11086110

Bailey, S., "A Closer Look at Neanderthal Postcanine Dental Morphology: The Mandibular Dentition," *The Anatomical Record*, 269, 2002.

Bailey, S. E., Wu, L., "A comparative dental metrical and morphological analysis of a Middle Pleistocene hominin maxilla from Chaoxian (Chaohu), China," *Quaternary International*, 211(1-2), 2010.

Bailliet, G., Rothhammer, F., Garnese, F. R., Bravi,C.M., and Bianchi, N. O., "Founder Mitochondrial Haplotypes in Amerindian Populations," *The Journal of Human Genetics*, 54, 1994.

Balter, M., "Child Burial Provides Rare Glimpse of Early Americans," *ScienceNOW,* Feb 2011.

Banks, W., D'Errico, F., Dibble, H., Krishtalka, L., West, D., Olszewski, D., Peterson, A., Anderson, D., Gillam, J., Montet-White, A., Crucifix, M., Marean, C., Sánchez-Goñi, M., Wohlfarth, B., Vanhaeran, M., "Eco-Cultural Niche Modeling: New Tools for Reconstructing the Geography and Ecology of Past Human Populations," *PaleoAnthropology,* 2006.

Bannai, M., Ohashi, J., Harihara, S., Takahashi, Y., Juji, T., Omoto, K., Tokunaga, K., "Analysis of HLA genes and haplotypes in Ainu (from Hokkaido, northern Japan) supports the premise that they descent from Upper Paleolithic populations of East Asia," *Tissue Antigens,* 55, 2000.

Bengston, John D., *In Hot Pursuit of Language in Prehistory,* John Benjamin Publishing Co., The Netherlands, 2008.

Benson, L., Lund, S., Smoot, J., Rhode, D., Spencer, R., Verosub, K., Louderback, L., Johnson, C., "The rise and fall of Lake Bonneville between 45 and 10.5 ka," *Quaternary International,* 235(1-2), 2009.

Boeskorov, G. G., "The North of Eastern Siberia: Refuge of Mammoth Fauna in the Holocene," *Gondwana Research,* 7(2) 2004, available in English in ScienceDirect, November 2005

Bogoras, W., *The Jesup North Pacific Expedition, Memoir of the American Museum of Natural History, Volume VII, The Chukchee,* Leiden, E. J. Brill, Ltd., Printers and Publishers, 1975 (reprint of the 1904-1909 edition). This publication is routinely referred to as *The Chukchee.*

Bolnick, D. A., Shook, B. A, Campbell, L, Goddard, I, "Problematic Use of Greenberg's Linguistic Classification of the Americas in Studies of Native American Genetic Variation," *American Journal of Human Genetics,* 75(3): 2004.

Bonnichsen, R. Lepper, B., Stanford, D., Waters, M., *Paleoamerican Origins: Beyond Clovis,* Center for the Study of the First Americans, Department of Anthropology, Texas A&M University, 2005.

Borrell, B., "Bon Voyage, Caveman," *Archaeology,* 63(3), May/June 2010. (possibility of seafaring by *Homo erectus* at 130,000 ya)

Bower, B., "Asian Trek," *Science News,* 171(14), 4/7/2007.

Bower, B., "Ancient hominids may have been seafarers," *Science News,* 177(3), 2010.

Brantingham, P., Gao, X., Madsen, D., Bettinger, R., Elston, r., " The initial Upper Paleolithic at Shuidonggou, Northwestern China," in *The Early Upper Paleolithic beyond Western Europe,* Ed. By Brantingham, P, Juhn, S., and Kerry, K., 2004.

Bryan, A. (ed.), *New Evidence for the Pleistocene Peopling of the Americas,* Center for the Study of Early Man, University of Maine at Orono, 1986.

Cannon, M. D., "Explaining variability in Early Paleoindian foraging," *Quaternary International,* 191(1), 2008.

Carmel, James H., "Homo sapiens and Neanderthals lived in peace, say researchers," The Times, United Kingdom, http://www.thetimes.co.uk/tto/news/world/middleeaste/article3552845.ece, 2013.

Carter, George F., *Earlier Than You Think: A Personal View of Man in America*, Texas A&M University Press, 1980.

Catto, N., "Quaternary floral and faunal asssemblages: Ecological and taphonomical investigations," *Quaternary International*, 233(2), 2011.

Catto, N., "Quaternary landscape evolution: Interplay of climate, tectonics, geomorphology, and natural hazards," *Quaternary International*, 233(1), 2011.

Chauhan, P. R., "Large mammal fossil occurrences and associated archaeological evidence in Pleistocene contexts of peninsular India and Sri Lanka," *Quaternary International*, 192(1), 2008.

Chen, C., An, J, Chen, H., "Analysis of the Xionanhai lithic assemblage, excavated in 1978," *Quaternary International*, 211(1-2), 2010.

Chen, X-Y., Cui, G-H., Yang, J-X., "Threatened fishes of the world: *Pseudobagrus medianalis* (Regan) 1904 (Bagridae), *Environmental Biology of Fishes*, 81(3), 2008.

Chlachula, J., Drozdov, N., Ovodov, N., "Last Interglacial peopling of Siberia: the Middle Palaeolithic site Ust'-Izhul', the upper Yenisei area," *Boreas*, 32, 2003.

Choi, C., "Denisovan Genome Sequenced, Reveals Brown-Eyed Girl of Extinct Human Species, Researchers say," *Huff Post*, August30, 2012.

Ciochon, R., Bettis III, A., "Asian *Homo erectus* converges in time," *Nature*, 458, March 2009

Cione, A., Tonni, E., Soibelzon, L., "The Broken Zig-Zag: Late Cenozoic large mammal and tortoise extinction in South America," *Rev. Mus. Argentino Cienc. Nat.*, n.s., 5(1), 2003.

Connor, Cathy, O'Haire, Daniel, *Roadside Geology of Alaska*, Mountain Press Publishing Company, 1988.

Coppens, Y., Tseveendorj, D., Demeter, F., Turbat, T., and Giscard, P., "Discovery of an archaic *Homo sapiens* skullcap in Northeast Mongolia," *Comptes Rendus Palevol*, 7(1), Feb 2008. Note: The findings are that the skullcap shows similarities with Neanderthals, Chinese Homo erectus, and West/Far East archaic Homo sapiens. Dating is possible late Pleistocene.

Corvinus, G., "*Homo erectus* in East and Southeast Asia, and the questions of the age of the species and its association with stone artifacts, with special attention to handaxe-like tools," *Quaternary International,* 117, 2004.

Coxe, W., *The Russian Discoveries Between Asia and America,* Readex Microprint Corp., 1966, copy of Coxe's document from 1780.

Cremo, M., Thompson, R., *Forbidden Archaeology: The Hidden History of the Human Race,* Unlimited Resources, 1996-2011.

Delluc, B., Delluc, G., "Art Paléolithique, saisons et climats," *Comtes Rendus Palevol,* 5, 2006.

Demske, D., Heumann, G., Granoszewski, W., Nita, M., Mamakowa, K., Tarasov, P., Oberhänsli, H., "Late glacial and Holocene vegetation and regional climate variability evidenced in high-resolution pollen records from Lake Baikal," *Global and Planetary Change,* 46, 2005.

Derbeneva, O. A., Sukernik, R. I., Volodko, N.V., Hosseini, s. H., Lott, M. T., and Wallace, D. C., "Analysis of Mitochondrial DNA Diversity in the Aleuts of the Commander Islands and Its Implications for the Genetic History of Beringia," *The American Journal of Human Genetics,* 71(2): 2002.

Derenko, M., Malyarchuk, B., Grzybowski, T., Denisove, G., Dambueva, I., Perkova, M., Dorzhu, C., Luzina, F., Lee, H. K., Vanecek, T., Villems, R., and Zakharov, I., "Phylogeographic analysis of Mitochondrial DNA in Northern Asian Populations," *The American Journal of Human Genetics,* 81, November 2007.

Dickinson, William R., "Geological perspectives on hte Monte Verde archaeological site in Chile and pre-Clovis coastal migration in the Americas.," *Quaternary Research,* 76, 201-210, 2011.

Dillehay, T. D., *The Settlement of the Americas: A New Prehistory,* Basic Books of the Perseus Books Group, 2000.

Dilley, Lorie M, Dilley, Thomas E., *Guidebook to Geology of Anchorage, Alaska*, Lorie M. Dilley and Thomas E. Dilley, 2,000.

Dixon, E. J. and G. S. Smith, "Broken canines from Alaskan cave deposits: re-evaluating evidence for domesticated dog and early humans in Alaska." *American Antiquity,* 51(2): 1986.

Doelman, T., "Flexibility and Creativity in Microblade Core Manufacture in Southern Primorye, Far East Russia," *Asian Perspectives,* 47(2), 2009.

Elliott, D.K., *Dynamics of Extinction,* John Wiley & Sons, New York, 1986.

Elston, Robert G., Brantingham, P. Jeffrey, "Microlithic Technology in Northern Asia: A Risk-Minimizing Strategy of the Late Paleolithic and Early Holocene," *Archaeological Papers of the American Anghropological Association,* 12 (1) 103-116, 2002.

Erlandson, J., Moss, M., Des Lauriers, M., "Life on the edge: early maritime cultures of the Pacific coast of North America, *Quaternary Science Reviews,* 27, 2008.

Etler, D., "The Fossil Evidence for Human Evolution in Asia," *Annual Review of Anthropology,* 25, 1996.

Etler, D., "*Homo erectus* in East Asia: Human Ancestor or Evolutionary Dead-End?" *Athena Review,* 4(1) [Cannot locate year. The author is from Department of Anthropology, Cabrillio college, Aptos, California.]

Etler, D., Crummett, T., Wolpoff, M., "Longgupo: Early Homo Colonizer or Late Pliocene Lufengpithecus Survivor in South China?" *Human Evolution,* 16(1-12), 2001.

Farina, R., Vizcaino, S. Iuliis, *Megafauna: Giant Beasts of Pleistocene South America,* Indiana University Press, 2013.

Fell, B., *America B.C.,* Artisan Publishers, 2010.

Fiedel, Stuart J., "Older Than We Thought: Implications of Corrected Dates for Paleoindians," *American Antiquity,* 64(1), 1999.

Finlayson, Clive, *The HUMANS WHO WENT EXTINCT, Why Neanderthals died out and we survived.* Oxford University Press, 2009.

Fitzhugh, W., "Stone Shamans and Flying Deer of Northern Mongolia: Deer Goddess of Siberia or Chimera of the Steppe?" *Arctic Anthropology,* 46(1-2) 2009.

Flam, F.: "Red hair a part of the Neanderthal genetic profile" *The Philadelphia Inquirer,* October 26, 2007.

Flannery, T., *The Eternal Frontier,* Atlantic Monthly Press, New York, 2001.

Forster, P., Harding, R., Torroni, A., and Bandelt, H. J., "Origin and Evolution of Native American mtDNA Variation: A Reappraisal," *The American Journal of Human Genetics,* 59(4): 1996.

Froehle, A., Churchill, S., "Energetic Competition Between Neandertals and Anatomically Modern Humans," *PaleoAnthropology,* 2009.

Froese, T., Woodward, A., Ikegami, T., "Turing instabilities in biology, culture, and consciousness? On the enactive origins of symbolic mateiral culture," *Adaptive Behavior,* 2 (3).

Gilbert, M. T. P., Jenkins, D. L., Götherstrom, A., Naveran, N. Sanchez, J. J., Hofreiter, M., Thomsen, P. F., Binladen, J., Higham, T. F. G., Yohe, R. M., II, Parr, R. Cummings, L. S. Willerslev, E., "DNA from Pre-Clovis Human Coprolites in Oregon, North America," *Science Express,* April 2008.

Gilligan, I., "The Prehistoric Development of clothing: Archaeological Implications of a thermal Model," *Journal of Archaeological Method Theory,* 17, 2010.

Gladyshev, S., Olsen, J., Tabarev, A., Kuzmin, Y., "Peleoenvironment. The Stone Age: Chronology and Periodization of Upper Paleolithic Sites in Mongolia." *Archaeology Ethnology & Anthropology of Eurasia,* 38(3), 2010.

Goebel, T., Waters, M., Dikova, M., "The Archaeology of Ushki Lake, Kamchatka, and the Pleistocene Peopling of the Americas," *Science,* 301(5632), 2003.

Goebel, T., et al, "The Late Pleistocene Dispersal of Modern Humans in the Americas, *Science*, 319, 1497, 2008.

Goldberg, E., Chebykin, E., Zhuchenko, N., Vorobyeva, S., Stepanova, O., Khlystov, O., Ivanov, E., Weinberg, E, Gvozdkov, A., "Uranium isotopes as proxies of the Lake Baikal watershed (East Siberia) during the past 150 ka," *Palaeogeography, Palaeoclimatology, Palaeoecology,* 294(1-2) August 2010.

Golubenko, M. V., Stepanov, V. A., Gubina, M. A., Zhadanov, S. I., Ossipova, L. Pl, Damba, L., Voevoda, M. I., Dipierri, J. E., Villems, R., Malhi, R. S., Beringian "Standstill and Spread of Native American Founders," *PLoS ONE* 2(9): eB29. doi;10.1371/journal.pone.0000829.

Goodyear, Albert C., "Evidence for Pre-Clovis Sites in the Eastern United States," unpublished and undated manuscript, [no longer has active link]

Grayson, D., Meltzer, D., "A requiem for North American overkill," *Journal of Archaeological Science,* 30(5), 2003.

Grove, C., "Ice-age child's remains discovered in Interior," *Anchorage Daily News,* 2/24/2011

Hall, R., "Cenozoic plate tectonic reconstruction of SE Asia," from Fraser, L., Matthews, S., Murphy, R., (Eds.), *Petroleum Geology of Southeast Asia,* Geological Society of London Special Publication 26, 1997.

Hapgood, C., *Maps of the Ancient Sea Kings,* Adventures Unlimited Press, 1966.

Hardaker, C., *The First American: the Suppressed Story of the People Who Discovered the New World,* New Page Books, 2007.

Haynes, C,. V., Jr., "Younger Dryas 'Black mats' and the Rancholabrean termination in North America," *National Academy of Sciences of the USA,* 2008. (See also: for photographs http://www.georgehoward.net/Vance%20 Haynes'%20Black%20Mat.htm)

Henry, A., Brooks, A., Piperno, D., "Microfossils in calculus demonstrate consumption of plants and cooked foods in Neanderthal diets," *Proceedings of the National Academy of Sciences,* 108(2), 2010.

Hoffecker, J. F., *A Prehistory of the North: Human Settlement of the Higher Latitudes,* Rutgers University Press, New Brunswick, New Jersey, 2005.

Honeychurch, W., Amartuvshin, C., "Hinterlands, Urban Centers, and Mobile Settings: The 'New' Old World Archaeology from the Eurasian Steppe," *Asian Perspectives,* 46(1) 2007.

Hopkins, D. M., Matthews, J. V, Jr., Schweger, C. E., Young, S. B., *Paleoecology of Beringia,* Academic Press, New York, 1982.

Huyghe, P., *Columbus Was Last: From 200,000 B.C. To 1492 A Heretical History of Who Was First,* Anomalist Books, 1992.

Igarashi, Y., Zharov, A., "Climate and vegetation change during the late Pleistocene and early Holocene in Sakhalin and Hokkaido, northeast Asia," *Quaternary International,* xxx (in process), 2011.

Inman, M.: "Neanderthals Had Same 'Language Gene' as Modern Humans," *National Geographic News,* October 18, 2007, http://news.nationalgeographic.com/news/2007/10/071018-neandertal-gene.html

Irwin-Williams, Cynthia, "Dilemma Posed by Uranium-Series Dates on Archaeologically Significant Bones from Valsequillo, Puebla, Mexico," *Earth and Planetary Science Letters* 6 (1969) 237-244, North Holland Publishing Comp., Amsterdam.

Jackinsky, M., "Evidence of woolly mammoths on Peninsula grows," *Alaska Daily News,* 3/13/2011.

Jackson, Jr., L. E., Wilson, M. C., "The Ice-Free Corridor Revisited," *Geotimes,* Feb. 2004.

Jiang, Y.-E., Chen, X-Y, Yang, J-X., "Threatened fishes of the world: Yunnanilus discoloris Zhou & He 1989 (Cobitidae)," *Environmental Biology of Fishes,* 86(1), 2009.

Jin, J. J. H., Shipman, P., "documenting natural wear on antlers: A first step in identifying use-wear on purported antler tools," *Quaternary International,* 211(1-2) 2010.

Johnson, John F. C., *Chugach Legends: Stories and Photographs of the Chugach Region,* Chugach Alaska Corporation, 1984.

Joling, D., "Warming brings unwelcome change to Alaska villages," *Anchorage Daily News,* 3/27/ 2011.

Joly, L. G., Guerra, S., Septimo, R., Solis, P. N., Correa, M. D., Gupta, M. P., Lrvy, S., Sandberg, F., Perera, P., "Ethnobotanical Inventory of Medicinal Plants Used by the Guaymi Indians in Western Panama, Part II." *Journal of Ethnopharmacology,* 28 (1990).

Jones, Anore, *Plants That We Eat: Nauriat Niginaqtuat,* University of Alaska Press, Fairbanks, 2010.

Joseph, F., *Discovering the Mysteries of Ancient America: Lost History and Legends, Unearthed and Explored,* New Page Books, 2006.

Khenzykhenova, F., "Paleoenvironments of Palaeolithic humans in the Baikal region," *Quaternary International,* 179(1), 2008.

Khenzykhenova, F., Sato, T., Lipnina, E., Medvedev, G., Kato, H., Kogai, S., Maximenko, K., Novosel'zeva, V., "Upper paleolithic mammal fauna of the Baikal region, east Siberia (new data)," *Quaternary International,* 231, 2011.

Kienast, F., Schirrmeister, L., Siegert, C., Tarasov, P., "Palaeobotanical evidence for warm summers in the East Siberian Arctic during the last cold stage," *Quaternary Research,* 63(3), 2005.

King, G., Bailey, G., "Tectonics and human evolution," *Antiquity,* 80, 2006.

Klein, H. S., Schiffner, D. C., "The Current Debate about the Origins of the Paleoindian of America," *Journal of Social History,* 37(2), Winter 2003.

Kolomiets, V. L., Gladyshev, S. A., Bezrukova, E. V., Rybin, E. P., Letunova, P. P., Abzaeva, A. A., "Paleoenvironment The Stone Age: Environment and human behavior in northern Mongolia during the Upper Pleistocene," *Archaeology, Ethnology, and Anthropology of Eurasia,* 37(1), 2009.

Komatsu, G., Olsen, J., Ormo, J., Di. Achille, G., Kring, D., Matsui T., "The Tsenkher structure in the Gobi-Altai, Mongolia: Geomorphological hints of an impact origin," *Geomorphology,* 74(1-4), March 2006.

Kornfeld, M., Larson, M. L., "Bonebeds and other myths: Paleoindian to Archaic transition on North American Great Plains and Rocky Mountains," *Quaternary International,* 191(1), 2008.

Krause, J., Orlando, L., Serre, D., Viola, B., Prüfer, K., Richards, M., Hublin, J., Hänni, C., Derevianko, A., Pääbo, S., "Neanderthals in central Asia and Siberia," *Nature LETTERS,* 449, 2007.

Kunz, Michael, M. Bever, C. Adkins, *The Mesa Site: Paleoindians above the Arctic Circle,* U. S. Department of the Interior, Bureau of Land Management, BLM-Alaska Open File Report 86, BLM/AK/ST-03/001+8100+020, April 2003.

Kurochkin, E., Kuzmin, Y., Antoshchenko-Olenev, I., Zabelin, V., Krivonogov, S., Nohrina, T., Lbova, L., Burr, G, and Cruz, R., "The timing of ostrich existence in Central Asia: AMS 14C age of eggshells from Mongolia and southern Siberia (a pilot study)," *Nuclear Instruments and Methods in Physics Research Section B: Beam Interactions with Materials and Atoms,* 268(7-8), April 2010

Kuzmin, Y., Orlova, L., "Radiocarbon chronology and environment of woolly mammoth (*Mammuthus primigenius* Blum.) in northern Asia: results and perspectives," *Earth-Science Reviews,* 68, 2004.

Kuzmin, Y., Richards, M., Yoneda, M., "Paleodietary Patterning and Radiocarbon Dating of Neolithic Populations in the Primorye Province, Russian Far East," *Ancient Biomolecules,* 4(2), 2002.

Lam, Y. M., Brunson, K, Meadow, R., Yuan, J., "Integrating taphonomy into the practice of zooarchaeology in China," *Quaternary International,* 211(1-2), 2010.

Langdon, Steve J., *Native People of Alaska: Traditional Living in a Northern Land,* Greatland Graphics, 2008.

Lee, H., "Paleoenvironment: The Stone Age. Projectile Points and Their Implications," *Archaeology Ethnology & Anthropology of Eurasia,* 38(3), 2010.

Lell, J. T., Sukernik, R. I., Starikovskaya, Y. B., Su, B., Jin, L., Schurr, T. G., Underhill, P. A., Wallace, D. C., "The Dual Origin and Siberian Affinities of Native American Y Chromosomes," *The American Journal of Human Genetics,* 70, 2002.

Lister, A., Bahn, P. G., *Mammoths: Giants of the Ice Age,* Richard Green Publisher, 1994.

Liu, W., Wu, X., Pei, S., Wu, Xiujie, Norton, C. J., "Huanglong Cave: A Late Pleistocene human fossil site in Hubei Province, China," *Quaternary International,* 211(1-2), 2010.

Lu, X., Xiong, D., Chen, C., "Threatened fishes of the world: *Sinocyclocheilus grahami* (Regan 1904) (Cyprinidae)," *Environmental Biology of Fishes,* 85(2), 2009.

Ma, S., Wang, Y., Xu, L., "Taxonomic and Phylogenetic Studies on the Genus Muntiacus," *Acta Theriologica Sinica* VI(3) 1986. (Translated by Will Downs, Dept of Geology, Bilby Research Center, Northern Arizona Univ., 1991)

Macé, F., "Human Rhythm and Divine Rhythm in Ainu Epics," *Diogenes,* 46(1), 1998.

Marwick, b., "Biogeography of Middle Pleistocene hominins in mainland Southeast Asia: A review of current evidence," *Quaternary International,* 202(1-2), 2009.

Mednikova, M., Dobrovolskaya, M., Buzhilova, A., Kandinov, M., "A Fossil Human Humerus from Khvalynsk: Morphology and Taxonomy," *Archaeology Ethnology & Anthropology of Eurasia,* 38(1), 2010.

Meltzer, D., *First Peoples in a New World: Colonizing Ice Age America,* University of California Press, 2009.

Merriwether, D. A., Hall, W. W., Vahine, A., and Ferrell, R. E., "mtDNA Variation Indicates Mongolia May Have Been the Source for the Founding Population for the New World," *The American Journal of Human Genetics,* 59, 1996.

Mol, D., de Vos, J., van der Plicht, J., "The presence and extinction of *Elephas antiquus* Falconer and Cautley, 1847, in Europe," *Quaternary International,* 169-170, 2007.

Moncel, M., "Oldest human expansions in Eurasia: Favouring and limiting factors," *Quaternary International,* 223-4, 2010.

Mueller, Tom, "Ice Baby: Secrets of a Frozen Mammoth," National Geographic, 215, 5, May 2009

Naske, C-M., Slotnick, H. E., *Alaska A History of the 49th State,* 2nd Ed., University of Oklahoma Press, Norman, 1979.

Neel, J. V., Biggar, R. J., Sukernik, R. I., "Virologic and genetic studies relate Amerind origins to the indigenous people of the Mongolia/Manchuria/southeastern Siberia region," *Proceedings of the National Academy of Sciences, USA,* 91, 1994.

Nikolskiy, P. A., Basilyan, A. E., Sulerzhitsky, L. D., and Pitulko, V. V., "Prelude to the extinction: Revision of the Achchagyl-Allaikha and Berelyokh mass accumulations of mammoth," *Quaternary International,* 219(1-2), 2010.

Norton, C. J., "The nature of megafaunal extinctions during the MIS 3-2 transition in Japan," *Quaternary International,* 211(1-2), 2010.

Norton, C. J., Jin, J. J. H., "Hominin morphological and behavioral variation in eastern Asia and Australasia: current perspectives," *Quaternary International,* 211(1-2), 2010.

O'Connell, L., "Sifting Through Garbage from the End of the Ice Age: It's a LIving for Frontier Scientists," *Anchorage Daily News,* June 1, 2011.

O'Neill, D., *The Last Giant of Beringia: The Mystery of the Bering Land Bridge,* Westview Press, Perseus Books Group, New York, 2004.

Oppenheimer, S., "The great arc of dispersal of modern humans: Africa to Australia," *Quaternary International,* 202(1-2), 2009.

Orlova, L. A., Kuzmin, Y. V., Stuart, A. J., Tikhonov, A. N., "Chronology and environment of woolly mammoth (Mammuthus primigenius Blumenbach) extinction in northern Asia," *The World of Elephants – International Congress,* Rome 2001.

Osipov, E., Khlystov, O., "Glaciers and meltwater flux to Lake Baikal during the Last Glacial Maximum," *Palaeogeography, Palaeoclimatology, Palaeoecology,* 294(1-2) 2010.

Palombo, M. R., "Quaternary mammal communities at a glance," *Quaternary International,* 212(2), 2010.

Park, S., "L'hominidé du Pléistocène supérieur en Corée, *L'anthropologie,* 110, 2006.

Pei, S., Gao, X., Feng, X., Chen, F., Dennell, R., "Lithic assemblage from the Jingshuiwan Paleolithic site of the early Late Pleistocene in the Three Gorges, China," *Quaternary International,* 211(1-2), January 2010.

Pietrusewsky, M., "A multivariate analysis of measurements recorded in early and more modern crania from East Asia and Southeast Asia," *Quaternary International,* 211(1-2), 2010.

Pimenoff, V., Comas, D., Palo, J., Vershubsky, G., Kozlov, A, Sajantila, A., "Northwest Siberian Khanty and Mansi in the junction of West and East Eurasian gene pools as revealed by uniparental markers," *European Journal of Human Genetics,* 16, 2008.

Pitulko, V., "The Berelekh Quest: A Review of Forty Years of Research in the Mammoth Graveyard in Northeast Siberia," *Geoarchaeology,* 26(1), 2011.

Ponce de León, M., Golovanova, L., Doronichev, V., Romanova, G., Akazaqa, T., Kondo, O., Ishida, H., Zollikofer, C., "Neanderthal brain size at birth provides insights into the evolution of human life history," *Proceedings of the National Academy of Sciences,* 105(37), Sept 2008.

Potter, B. A., Reuther, J. D., Bowers, P. M., and Relvin-Reymiller, C., "Little Delta Dune Site: A Late-Pleistocene Multicomponent Site in Central Alaska," *Archaeology: North America,* CRP 25, 2008.

Powell, E., "Mongolia," *Archaeology,* 59(1) Jan/Feb 2006.

Pratt, VErna E., *Field Guide to Alaskan WILDFLOWERS Commonly seen along the Highways and Byways,* 1989 Alaskakrafts, Inc.

Prokopenko, A., Kuzmin, M., Li, H., Woo, K., Catto, N., "Lake Hovsgol basin as a new study site for long continental paleoclimate records in continental interior Asia: General contest and current status," *Quaternary International,* 205, 2009.

Quade, J., Forester, R. M., Pratt, W. L., Carter, C., "Black Mats, Spring-Fed Streams, and Late-Glacial-Age Recharge in the Southern Great Basin," *Quaternary Research,* 49(2) 1998.

Ransom, J. E., "Derivation of the Word Alaska," *American Anthropologist,* 42, 1942.

Razjigaeva, N., Korotky, A., Grebennikova, T., Ganzey, L., Mokhova, L., Bazarova, V. Sulerzhitsky, L., Lutaenko, K., "Holocene climatic changes and environmental history of Iturup Island, Kurile Islands, northwestern Pacific," *The Holocene,* 12, 2002.

Reich, D., et al., "Genetic history of an archaic hominin group from Denisova Cave in Siberia," *Nature,* 468, 7327, 2010.

Rose, W. I., Chesner, C. A., "Dispersal of ash in the great Toba Eruption, 74 ka," *Geology,* 15, 1987.

Rudaya, N., Tarasov, P., Dorofeyuk, N., Solovieva, N., Kalugin, I., Andreev, Daryin, A., Diekmann, B., Riedel, F., Tserendash, N., Wagner, M., "Holocene environments and climate in the Mongolian Altai reconstructed from the Hoton-Nur pollen and diatom records: a step towards better understanding climate dynamics in Central Asia," *Quaternary Science Reviews,* 28(5-6) 2009.

Russell, Priscilla N., *Tanaina Plantlore Dena'ina K'et'una: An Ethnobotany of the Dena'ina Indians of Southcentral Alaska,* Alaska Geographic Association, 2012.

Ruvinsky, J., "The Great American Extinction," *Discover,* 28(8) 2007.

Saillard, J., Forster, P., Lynnerup, N., Bandelt, H.-J., Nørby, S., "mtDNA Variation among Greenland Eskimos: The Edge of the Beringian Expansion," *The Journal of Human Genetics,* 2000 September; 67(3): 718-726.

Saleeby, B. M., "Out of Place Bones: beyond the study of prehistoric subsistence," Arctic Research of the United States, *U. S. National Science Foundation,* 2002.

Sattler, H. R., *The Earliest Americans,* Clarion Books, New York, 1993.

Schepartz, L. A., Miller-Antonio, S., "Taphonomy, Life History, and Human Exploitation of Rhinoceros sinensis at the Middle Pleistocene site of Panxian Dadong, Guizhou, China," *International Journal of Osteoarchaeology,* 2008.

Schrenk, F., Muller, S. *The Neanderthals,* Routledge, 2005.

Seong, C., "Tanged points, microblades and Late Palaeolithic hunting in Korea," *Antiquity,* 82, 2008.

Shen, G., Fang, Y., Bischoff, J. L., Feng, Y., and Zhao, J., "Mass spectrometric U-series dating of the Chaoxian hominin site at Yinshan, eastern China," *Quaternary International,* 211(1-2), 2010.

Shepherd, Jill, "Winter Green," *Alaska,* February, 1999.

Sher, A., Weinstock, J., Baryshnikov, G., Davydov, S., Boeskorov, G., Zazhigin, V., Nikolskiy, P., "The first record of 'spelaeoid' bears in Arctic Siberia, *Quaternary Science Reviews,* 30, 2010.

Shichi, K., Takahara, H., Krivonogov, S., Bezrukova, E., Kashiwaya, K., Takehara, A., Nakamura, T., "Late Pleistocene and Holocene vegetation and climate records from Lake Kotokel, central Baikal region," *Quaternary International,* 205, 2009.

Smith, T., Toussaint, M., Reid, D., Olejniczak, A., Hublin, J., "Rapid dental development in a Middle Paleolithic Belgian Neanderthal," *Proceedings of the National Academy of Sciences,* 104(51), Dec. 2007.

Snodgrass, J., Leonard, W., "Neandertal Energetics Revisited: Insight Into Population Dynamics and Life History Evolution," *PaleoAnthropology,* 2009.

Starikovskaya, Y. B., Sukernik, R. I., Schurr, T. G., Kogelnik, A. M., and Wallace, D. C. "mtDNA diversity in Chukchi and Siberian Eskimos:

Implications for the Genetic History of Ancient Beringia and the Peopling of the New World," *The American Journal of Human Genetics,* 63, 1998.

Stephan, A. E., *The First Athabascans of Alaska: Strawberries,* Dorrance Publishing Co, Inc., Pittsburg, 1996.

Stone, R., "A Surprising Survival Story in the Siberian Arctic," *Science,* 303(5642): 2004.

Stringer, C., Finlayson, J., Barton, R., Fernández-Jalvo, Y., Cáceres, I., Sabin, R., Rhodes, E., Currant, A., Rodriguez-Vidal, J., Giles-Pacheco, F., Riquelme-Cantal, J., "Neanderthal exploitation of marine mammals in Gibraltar," *Proceedings of the National Academy of Sciences,* 105(38) Sept. 2008.

Stringer, C., *Lone Survivors: How We Came To Be the Only Humans on Earth.* Times Books, Henry Holt & Co., LLC, New York, 2012.

Strong, S., "The Most Revered of Foxes: Knowledge of Animals and Animal Power in an Ainu *Kamui Yukar,*" *Asian Ethnology,* 68(1), 2009.

Sunnyboy, Audrey, *Denyaavee: Medicinal Plants of Interior Alaska's People,* Audrey Sunnyboy, 2007.

Sykes, B., *The Seven Daughters of Eve,* W.W. Norton & Company, New York, 2001.

Szathmary, E. J. E., "mtDNA and the Peopling of the Americas," *The Journal of Human Genetics,* 53, 1993.

Tamm, E., Kivisild, T., Reidla, M., Metspalu, M., Smith, D. G., Mulligan, C. J., Bravi, C. M., Rickards, O., Martinez-Labarga, C., Khusnutdinova, E. K., Fedorova, S. A., Torroni, A., Neel, J. V., Barrantes, R., Schurr, T. G., "Mitochondrial DNA 'clock' for the Amerinds and its implications for timing their entry into North America," *Proceedings of the National Academy of Sciences, USA,* 91, 1994.

Tarasov, P., Williams, J., Andreev, A., Nakagawa, T., Bezrukova, E., Herzschuh, U., Igarashi, Y., Müller, S., Werner, K., Zheng, Z., "Satellite-and polllen-based quantitative woody cover reconstructions for northern Asia:

Verification and application to late-Quaternary pollen data," *Earth and Planetary Science Letters,* 264(1-2), 2007.

Tattersall, I., *Masters of the Planet, The Search for Our Human Origins,* Palgrace Macmillan, 2012

Than, K., "Neanderthals, Humans Interbred—First Solid DNA Evidence: Most of us have some Neanderthal genes, study finds," May 6, 2010 for *National Geographic News,* http://news.nationalgeographic.com/news/2010/05/100506-science-neanderthals-humans-mated-interbred-dna-gene/

Tianyuan, L., Etler, D., "New Middle Pleistocene hominid crania from Yunxian in China," *Nature,* 357, June 1992.

Tong, H., Moigne, A-M., "Quaternary Rhinoceros of China," in English, *Acta Anthropologica Sinica,* Supplement to Volume 19, 2000.

Torroni, A., Sukernik, R. I., Schurr, Tl G., Starikovskaya, Y. B., Cabell, M. F., Crawford, M. H., Comuzzie, A. G., Wallace, D. C., "mtDNA Variations of Aboriginal Siberians Reveals distinct Genetic Affinities with Native Americans," *The American Journal of Human Genetics,* 53, 1993.

Vasil'ev, S. A., Kuzmin, Y. V., Orlova, L. A., Dementiev, V. N., "Radiocarbon-Based Chronology of the Paleolithic in Siberia and Its Relevance to the Peopling of the New World," *Radiocarbon,* 44(2), 2002.

Vergano, D., "Modern humanity's ancient cousins, the Neanderthals, lived in small groups that were isolated from one another, suggests an investigation into their DNA. The analysis also finds that Neanderthals lacked some human genes that are linked to our behavior," *National Geographic,* April 22, 2014.

Vialet, A., Guipert, G., Jianing, H., Xiaobo, F., Zune, L., Youping, W., de Lumley, M.-A., de Lumley, H., "Homo erectus from the Yunxian and Nankin Chinese sites: Anthropological insights using 3D virtual imaging techniques," *Comptes Rendus Palevol* 9(6-7), 2010.

Viereck, Eleanor G., *Alaska's Wilderness Medicines: Healthful Plants of the Far North,* Alaska Northwest Books, 1987.

Volodko, N. V., Starikovskaya, E. B., Mazunin, I. O., Eltsov, N. P., Naidenko, P. V., Wallace, D. C., and Sukernik, R. I., "Mitochondrial Genome Diversity in Arctic Siberians, with Particular Reference to the Evolutionary History of Beringia and Pleistocenic Peopling of the Americas," *American Journal of Human Genetics*, 82(5), 2008.

Wagner, D. P., McAvoy, J. M., "Pedoarchaeology of Cactus Hill, a sandy Paleoindian site in southeastern Virginia, U. S. A." *Geoarchaeology*, 19(4), 2004.

Waguespack, N. M., Surovell, T. A., "Clovis Hunting Strategies, or How to Make Out on Plentiful Resources," *American Antiquity*, 68(2), 2003.

Wang, J., "Late Paleozoic macrofloral assemblages from Weibel coalfield, with reference to vegetational change through the Late Paleozoic Ice-age in the North China Block," *International Journal of Coal Geology*, 83(2-3), 2010.

Wang, S., Liu, H., Zhang, H., Sun, X., Yi, S., Chen, Y., Zhang, G., Xing, L., Sun, W., "Newly discovered Palaeolithic artefacts from loess deposits and their ages in Lantian, central China, *Chin. Sci. Bull.* (2014) 59(7):651-661.

Waters, Michael R. et al., "Redefining the Age of Clovis: Implications for the Peopling of hte Americas," *Science*, 315, 1122, 2007.

Waters-Rist, A., Bazaliiskii, V. I., Weber, A, Goriunova, O. I., Katzenberg, A., "Activity-induced dental modification in holocene Siberian hunter-fisher-gatherers," *American Journal of Physical Anthropology*, 143(2), 2010.

Wendorf, F., Hester, J., (eds.) *Late Pleistocene Environments of the Southern High Plains*, Ft. Burgwin Research Center, Inc. Southern Methodist University, 1973.

West, F. II., Ed., *AMERICAN BEGINNINGS: the Prehistory and Palaeoecology of Beringia*, The University of Chicago Press, Chicago, 1996.

Wiedmer, M., Montgomery, D., Gillespie, A., Greenberg, H., "Late Quaternary megafloods from Glaial Lake Atna, Southcentral Alaska, U.S.A., *Quaternary Research*, 73, 2010.

Woodman, N., Athfield, N., "Post-Clovis survival of American Mastodon in the southern Great Lakes Region of North America," *Quaternary Research,* 72(3), 20009.

Wu, X., "Fossil Humankind and Other Anthropoid Primates of China," *International Journal of Primatology,* 25(5) 2004.

Wu, X., "On the origins of modern humans in China," *Quaternary International,* 117(1), 2004.

Wu, X., Schepartz, L. A., Norton, C. J., "Morphological and morphometric analysis of variation in the Zhoukoudian Homo erectus brain endocasts," *Quaternary International,* 211(1-2) 2010.

Wu, Y-S., Chen, Y-S., Xiao, J-Y., "A preliminary study on vegetation and climate changes in Dianchi Lake area in the last 40,000 years," partial in English, *Acta Botanica Sinica,* 33(5), 1991.

Wynn, T., Coolidge, F. L., *How to Think like a Neanderthal,* Oxford University Press, 2012.

Xiao, J., Jin, C., Zhu, Y., "Age of the fossil Dali Man in north-central China deduced from chronostratigraphy of the loess-paleosol sequence," *Quaternary Science Reviews,* 21, 2002.

Xiangcan, J., "Lake Dianchi," *Experience and Lessons Learned Brief,* final version 2004.

Xu, J-X., Ferguson, D. K., Li, C-S., Wang, Y-F., "Late Miocene vegetation and the climate of the Lühe region in Yunnan, southwestern China," *Review of Palaeobotany and Palynology,* 148(1), 2008.

Yahner, R. H., "Barking in a primitive ungulate, *Muntiacus reevesi:* function and adaptiveness," *The American Naturalist,* 116(2), 1980.

Zang, W., Wang, Y., Zheng, S., Yang, X., Li, Y., Fu, X., Li, N., "Taxonomic investigations on permineralized conifer woods from the Late Paleozoic Angaran deposits of northeastern Inner Mongolia, China, and their palaeoclimatic significance," *Review of Palaeobotany and Palynology,* 144(3-4), May 2007.

Zhang, Y., Stiner, M, Dennell, R., Wang, C., Zhang, Sh, Gao, X., "Zooarchaeological perspectives on the Chinese Early and Late Paleolithic from the Ma'anshan site (Guizhou, South China)," *Journal of Archaeological Science,* 37(8), 2010.

Zhu, R., An, Z., Potts, R., Hoffman, K., "Magnetostratigraphic dating of early humans in China," *Earth-Science Reviews,* 61(3-4) June 2003.

Zorich, Z., "Did *Homo erectus* Coddle His Grandparents?" *Discover,* 27(1) Jan. 2006.

No author designated. "Bone fossil points to a mystery human species," *USA Today,* Mar 25, 2010. [Three types of humans lived within 60 miles of each other in southern Siberia.]

Websites

Alces latifrons http://books.google.com/books?id=BQtyg5m1zQkC&pg=PA58&lpg=PA58&dq=alces+latifrons&source=bl&ots=og5L12y8Tq&sig=jrDQlIfRaXGtU2bud_mlupblHww&hl=en&sa=X&ei=ZZe1U8OlKsagigKKhIDIAw&ved=0CEAQ6AEwAw#v=onepage&q=alces%20latifrons&f=false

America's Stone Age Explorers http://www.pbs.org/wgbh/nova/transcripts/3116_stoneage.html (8/23/2010)

Ancestral Human Skull Found in China (80,000 to 100,000 ya) http://news.nationalgeographic.com/news/2008/02/080220-china-fossil.html

Ancient bison bones supports theory about Ice Age seafarers being first in Americas http://www.thaindian.com/newsportal/world-news/ancient-bison-bones-supports-theory-abo... (9/5/2010)

Archaeobotany of the Central Aleutian Islands http://www.uaa.alaska.edu/honorscollege/achievements/Competitive_Grants/UnderGrad/upload/Holly-Thorssin-UGR-FA11-Proposal-for-Web.pdf

Archaeology of the Altai Republichttp://eng.altai-republic.ru/modules.php?op=modload&name=Sections&file=index&req=viewarticle&artid=20... (1/30/2011)

Archaic Human Culture http://anthro.palomar.edu/homo2/mod_homo_3.htm (9/9/2010)

As Old Clovis Sites, but Not Clovis, Paisley Caves, Oregon Yields Western Stemmed Points, More Human DNA http://www.sciencedaily.com/releases/2012/07/120712141916.htm

The aurochs is about to return to the mountains of central Europe http://www.eurowildlife.org/news/the-aurochs-is-about-to-return-to-the-mountains-of-central-europe/

Back Migration http://www.sci-news.com/othersciences/anthropology/science-back-migration-native-americans-01804.html

Bamboo http://earthnotes.tripod.com/bamboo.htm (9/13/2010)

Berelekh Map http://www.maplandia.com/russia/magadanskaya-oblast/susumanskiy-rayon/berelekh/ (8/31/2010)

China map http://en.wikipedia.org/wiki/File:China_100.78713E_35.63718N.jpg (8/20/2010)

Chukchee Society http://lucy.ukc.ac.uk/ethnoatlas/hmar/cult_dir/culture.7837 (4/5/2011)

Chukchi Directions of time and space http://www.cosmicelk.net/Chukchidirections.htm (4/5/2011)

Chukchi Language http://en.wikipedia.org/wiki/Chukchi_language (4/5/2011)

Cro-Magnon http://en.wikipedia.org/wiki/Cro-Magnon (8/12/2010)

Denisova Cave (Siberia) http://archaeology.about.com/od/dathroughdeterms/qt/denisova_cave.htm (8?31/2010)

Did Ancient Volcano Alter Human History http://www.livescience.com/1661-ancient-volcano-alter-human-history.html

Drum Talk Is the African's Wireless A. I. Good, Natural History Magazine, http://www.naturalhistorymag.com/htmlsite/master.html?http://www.naturalhistorymag.com/htmlsite/editors_pick/1942_09_pick.html

Dover Bronze Age Boat http://indigenousboats.blogspot.com/2008/01/dover-bronze-age-boat.html

Earliest Humanlike Footprints Found in Kenya http://donsmaps.com/erectus.html (9/11/2010)

Face of a Neanderthal woman http://www.femininebeauty.info/neanderthal-woman (8/23/2010)

First Americans http://www.nmhcpl.org/First_American.html (8/23/2010)

Four-horned Antelope http://en.wikipedia.org/wiki/Four-horned_Antelope (9/15/2010)

Geography of China http://en.wikipedia.org/wiki/Geography_of_China (9/3/2010)

Gold line fish is critically endangered http://www.thegef.org/gef/content/did-you-know-lake-dianchi-china-once-proudly-known-%E2%80%9Csparkling-pearl-embedded-highland%E2%80%9D-now-h

Historical earthquakes in China http://drgeorgepc.com/EarthquakesChina.html (9/24/2010)

Historical SuperVolcanoes and Archeology Indicate Nuclear Winter Climate Models Exaggerate Effects http://nextbigfuture.com/2010/04/historical-supervolcanoes-and.html (8/20/2010)

Hominid Tools http://www.handprint.com/LS/ANC/stones.html (8/23/2010)

Homo erectus http://humanorigins.si.edu/evidence/human-fossils/species/homo-erectus (8/12/2010)

Homo erectus http://en.wikipedia.org/wiki/Homo_erectus (8/12/2010)

Homo erectus http://www.archaeologyinfo.com/homoerectus.htm (9/5/2010)

Homo erectus Survival http://www.archaeology.org/9703/newsbriefs/h.erectus.html (9/5/2010)

Homo neanderthalensis http://humanorigins.si.edu/evidence/human-fossils/species/homo-neanderthalensis (8/12/2010)

How Two Retirees' Amateur Archaeology Helped Throw Our View of Human History into Turmoil http://blogs.smithsonianmag.com/smart-news/2013/05/how-two-retirees-amateur-archaeology-helped-throw-our-view-of-human-history-into-turmoil/#ixzz2VGdrPFOv

Humans wore shoes 40,000 years ago, fossil suggests http://www.stonepages.com/news/archives/002825.html (8/27/2010)

Hydropotes inermis (Chinese water deer)http://www.ultimateungulate.com/Artiodactyla/Hydropotes_inermis.html (9/8/2010)

Ice Age Climate Cycles http://earthguide.ucsd.edu/virtualmuseum/climatechange2/03_1.shtml (1/29/2011)

Ice-Free Corridor Revisited http://www.geotimes.org/feb04/feature_Revisited.html

Images of Neanderthals http://www.talkorigins.org/faqs/homs/savage.html (8/23/2010)

Ki'ti's Story, 75,000 BC The land where the giants played. http://www.youtube.com/watch?v=qgkPb_QfGtg

La Ferrassie Neanderthal Reconstruction http://s1.zetaboards.com/anthroscape/topic/2448167/1/ (8/23/2010)

Late Pleistocene, now-extinct fauna of the southwest http://www.saguaro-juniper.com/i_and_i/history/megafauna.html (8/22/2010)

Maars and Phreatic Eruptions http://geology.com/stories/13/maar/

Meet the Neanderthals http://news.bbc.co.uk/2/hi/science/nature/1469607.stm (8/23/2010)

Moose and Giant Moose http://www.tc.gov.yk.ca/publications/Moose_2007.pdf

Mousterian http://en.wikipedia.org/wiki/Mousterian

Muntjac (barking deer) http://www.itsnature.org/ground/mammals-land/muntjac/ (9/8/2010)

Neanderthal http://www.crystalinks.com/neanderthal.html

Neanderthal culture: Old masters http://www.nature.com/news/neanderthal-culture-old-masters-1.12974

Neanderthals more intelligent than thought http://www.msnbc.msn.com/id/39324819/ns/technology_and_science-science (9/24/2010)

Neanderthal reconstructions http://www.daynes.com/en/reconstructions/neanderthal-4.php (8/23/2010)

Neanderthal tools http://www.telegraph.co.uk/science/science-news/3345244/Neanderthal-tools-reveal-advanced-technology.html

Neanderthal tools http://www.paleodirect.com/mous1.htm (6/22/2013)

Neanderthal tools http://www.amnh.org/exhibitions/permanent-exhibitions/human-origins-and-cultural-halls/anne-and-bernard-spitzer-hall-of-human-origins/neanderthal-tools (6/22/2013)

New Evidence Puts Man in North America 50,000 Years Ago, http://www.sciencedaily.com/releases/2004/11/041118104010.htm

Origins of Paleoindians http://en.wikipedia.org/wiki/Origins_of_Paleoindians (8/22/2010)

Pedra Furada, Brazil: Paleoindiand, Paintings, and Paradoxes, http://www.athenapub.com/10pfurad.htm (2012)

Pompeii-Like Excavations Tell Us More About Toba Super-Eruption http://www.sciencedaily.com/releases/2010/02/100227170841.htm

Quaternary Period http://www3.hi.is/~oi/quaternary_geology.htm (8/31/2010)

Red hair a part of Neanderthal genetic profile http://seattletimes.nwsource.com/html/nationworld/2003975496_neanderthal26.html (8/26/2010)

Rethining Neanderthals, Joe Alper, Smithsonian.com, Science and Nature, June 2003 http://www.smithsonianmag.com/science-nature/neanderthals.html?c=y&page=1

Sacred Bones, Fields of Stones, Dr. Francis Allard Earthwatch Journal, October 2002, www.earthwatch.org

Savoonga artist to explore traditional native tattoos, Anchorage Daily News http://www.adn.com/2011/04/02/1788951/savoonga-artist-to-explore-traditional.html (4/5/2011)

Shamanism in Siberia http://www.sacred-texts.com/sha/sis/sis04.htm (4/5/2011)

Shiraoi Ainu Village http://members.virtualtourist.com/m/tt/52254/

Signs of Neanderthals Mating With Humans http://www.nytimes.com/2010/05/07/science/07neanderthal.html?_r=1 (8/26/2010)

Simple techniques for production of dried meat http://www.fao.org/docrep/003/x6932e/X6932E02.htm (9/27/2010)

Snout trout is critically endangered http://www.arkive.org/kunming-snout-trout/schizothorax-grahami/

Solutrean http://en.wikipedia.org/wiki/Solutrean (8/23/2010)

Stone Age Columbus http://www.bbc.co.uk/science/horizon/2002/columbusqa.shtml (8/23/2010)

Stone Age Site Yields Evidence of Advanced Culture http://history.cultural-china.com/en/51History9459.html (9/5/2010)

Stone Me! Spears show early human species was sharper than we thought http://www.guardian.co.uk/science/2012/nov/15/stone-spear-early-human-species

Stone Tools Point to Creative Work by Early Humans in Africa http://www.nytimes.com/2012/11/13/science/evidence-of-persistent-modern-human-behavior-in-africa.html?emc=eta1&_r=0

Stone-tipped spear may have much earlier origin http://articles.latimes.com/2012/nov/16/science/la-sci-hafting-spears-20121116

Straight-tusked elephant http://en.wikipedia.org/wiki/Straight-tusked_Elephant (10/3/2010)

Synoptic table of the principal old world prehistoric cultures http://en.wikipedia.org/wiki/Synoptic_table_of_the_principal_old_world_prehistoric_cultures (9/8/2010)

Toothpicks----*Homo erectus* used them http://phys.org/news/2014-05-tooth-picking-behavior-middle-pleistocene-hominins.html

Transmitting the Ainu wisdom http://www.town.shiraoi.hokkaido.jp/ainu-tradition/yamamaru/index.html

Umiaq skin boat http://en.wikipedia.org/wiki/File:Umiaq_skin_boat.jpg

Volcanic Ash http://geology.com/articles/volcanic-ash.shtml (8/20/2010)

When did humans come to the Americas? http://www.smithsonianmag.com/science-nature/When-Did-Humans-Come-to-the-Americas-187951111.html

Zhirendong puts the chin in china http://johnhawks.net/weblog/fossils/china/zhirendong-2010-liu-chin.html

Zhoukoudian Relics Museum hppt: www.china.org.cn/english/features/museums/129075.htm (9/5/2010)

www.ingramcontent.com/pod-product-compliance
Lightning Source LLC
Chambersburg PA
CBHW071159020726
47502CB00002B/466